Praise for *Mandalay's Child*

"*Mandalay's Child* is an extraordinary addition to the grand old tradition of epic literature. Covering historical themes as vast as World War II in the Far East and the traumatic birth of modern India, Prem Sharma brings history to life in the struggles of a family attempting to survive adversity and, even more, to defiantly pass on a legacy. …It is an essential read for all who enjoy epic works from the old school, works that both entertain and transform the reader. Prem Sharma has produced a literary experience that will touch your soul."

Arthur Flowers, Professor, Fiction, Syracuse University Creative
Writing MFA Program; Author of novels, *De Mojo Blues* and
Another Good Loving Blues

" …This life-affirming tale will truly touch your soul. His poetic narrative carries you forward in growing anticipation to the next page, and the next, and the next."

Jessie H. O'Neill, M.A., CET II,
Author of *The Golden Ghetto: The Psychology of Affluence*

"…Prem Sharma takes us on a journey through a labyrinth of cultures, values, beliefs and events, compelling the reader to reevaluate or even discover what is important in life. Take the journey…"

Alexander P. Durtka, Jr., ACSW, CFE
President, International Institute of Wisconsin
Editor, VILTIS Magazine

"A truly spellbinding saga which dramatically and accurately portrays historical events."

J.C. Sharma
Consul General of India, Chicago, IL

Selected reader comments from Amaz

"A riveting story told with captivating linguistic richness and creativity."

"Finest novel I have encountered in two decades."

"Once I started reading, I literally couldn't put it down."

"If I were a movie producer, I'd snap up the rights."

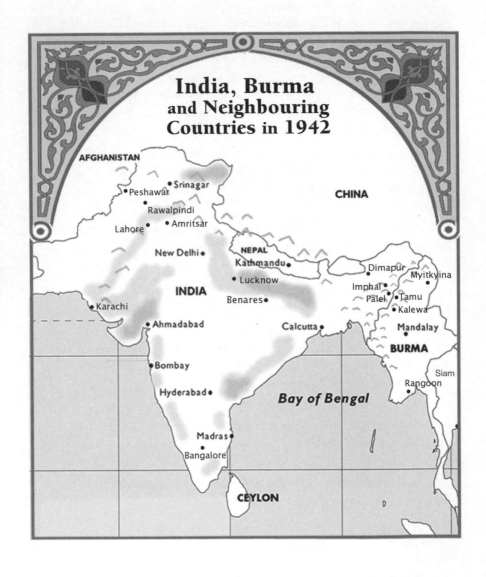

India, Burma
and Neighbouring
Countries in 1942

AFGHANISTAN

CHINA

• Srinagar
• Peshawar
Rawalpindi
Lahore • • Amritsar

New Delhi •

NEPAL
Kathmandu •

Dimapur •   • Myitkyina

INDIA

• Lucknow

Imphal •
Palel • • Tamu
• Kalewa

• Karachi

Benares •

• Ahmadabad

Calcutta •

Mandalay •

BURMA

• Bombay

Siam
Rangoon •

Hyderabad •

Bay of Bengal

Madras •
• Bangalore

CEYLON

MANDALAY'S CHILD

To Nancy
Best Wishes
Iren Marina

MANDALAY'S CHILD

Prem Sharma

BOOKWRIGHTS PRESS
Charlottesville, Virginia

Cover photo by Christophe Loviny/CORBIS
Cover and interior design by Mayapriya Long
Set in Adobe Garamond
Printed in the United States of America

Library of Congress
Cataloging-in-Publication Data
Sharma, Prem, 1932–
Mandalay's Child: a novel / Prem Sharma.
    p. cm.
ISBN 1-880404-20-6 (alk. paper)
1. Burma—History—Japanese occupation, 1942–1945—Fiction
2. India—History—Partition, 1947—Fiction. I. Title.
PS3569.H3429M36 1999
813' .54—dc21   98-50088
                CIP

Bookwrights Press
2255 Westover Drive, Suite 108
Charlottesville, Virginia 22901
804.823.8223   editor@bookwrights.com   www.bookwrights.com

10 9 8 7 6 5 4 3 2 1

Mandalay's Child is dedicated to the memory of my father, Dr. D.C. Sharma [Chibber], who was a man of infinite courage and compassion. Several episodes in this narrative are based upon real events from his life. This book is additionally dedicated to the memory of the countless innocent victims of the Holocaust in Europe and the blood bath of 1947 in India and Pakistan.

The poem *Mandalay* was written in fond remembrance of my mother, Laj Wanti, and her immense charm, grace and beauty. The poem *Heaven* was composed at the birth of my twin grandchildren, Rebecca and Benjamin.

Invaluable assistance in researching material for the story has been provided by my wife, Anita. The continued encouragement from my daughters, Leena and Madhu and son-in-law Solomon, kept me focused. Help from friends Carol and Doren Wehrley made writing this book a pleasure. My appreciation goes to all of them as well as to Mayapriya Long for her commitment in getting this novel published.

Mandalay

Mandalay the city of my dreams

Though I left you many moons ago

Your loving arms reach out to me

I see you each day if only in my imagination

When your gentle breezes caress my face

With the fragrance of roses and jasmine

I hear the sweet chimes of pagoda bells

And the laughter of your children

The music and gaiety of festivals

The rustle of brocade silks and satin

And the falling of the rain

You were scarred and ravaged by war

Waged by brutal men and machines

But I know you will shine once more

Enchanting and alluring as before

And though I may not see you again

I shall always love you dearly

As you will forever be

Dear Mandalay the city of my dreams

Prem Sharma

Friday, October 4, 1941

*A*n air raid warning siren began blaring. Its wailing sound gradually increased in volume and then became faint, only to grow loud and urgent again. The harried nurse in the crowded waiting room wiped the perspiration off her forehead and looked at her wrist watch.

"Ten o'clock already?" she moaned. "Come on, everyone," she called loudly, standing up and walking towards the front door. "Let's go out into the open. Hurry!"

"Oh, it's only a drill," a woman sitting on a bench along the wall complained. "The siren will stop in a few minutes. There won't be planes. Why can't we just sit here?"

"I know it's only a drill," the nurse answered, "but the British authorities require we take the drills seriously. Come on, everyone, out on the street!"

"Why don't these foreigners pack up and go home!" the woman complained again, picking up her child and following others toward the door.

"It's only for our safety," the nurse explained patiently. "We don't want to be caught inside a building should bombs start falling."

Doctor Devi Lal was about to examine a young boy. "Oh, there goes the siren," he said to the child's mother. "Come, we'll go and stand outside. I'll finish the examination when the drill is over."

A nurse took the mother and her child out. Devi Lal stood up and, taking a deep breath, stretched his arms above his head. He wore white cotton pants and shirt. His red silk necktie was held in place with a small gold clip. Almost six feet tall and sixty years of age, his rugged face, gray hair and neatly trimmed mustache gave him a distinguished appearance.

As he walked through the now empty waiting room, a young woman came out of a side door marked Business Office. "You look tired, Dad," she said, joining him. "Do you feel all right?"

"I'm fine, Khin May," he answered, putting an arm around her shoulders. "I didn't sleep well last night. Perhaps a brief nap this afternoon will refresh me."

Khin May, at age 32, was a strikingly attractive woman with a mixture of classical Burmese and Indian features. Her skin was smooth and fair, her face delicate. She had high cheek bones and a long dainty neck. Her eyes were large and brown. She wore a red silk *longyi*, an ankle length sarong, tightly wrapped around her slim waist. Her pink sleeveless blouse was made of silk. Long black hair, neatly tied in a knot behind her head, was adorned with a strand of white jasmine flowers. She was not a trained nurse, but helped her father in his clinic as an office manager with the large number of patients that came in each day.

The father and daughter joined the clinic staff and the patients milling around in the bright sunshine on the sidewalk. All traffic had stopped, and the people sitting in bullock carts, cars and buses talked to each other in lowered voices. In exactly five minutes, the siren went silent.

"There, it was a drill. I told you so," the same woman who had complained earlier muttered. "There's no raid." They waited for the "all clear" signal and a few minutes later the siren came on again — just a straight wail.

"Good," the nurse announced cheerfully. "Come on, we can go back in now."

The rest of the morning went by quickly. Devi Lal finished examining his last patient. "Your baby is better today," he informed the mother, removing the stethoscope from around his neck. "Her temperature is almost back to normal."

"Thank you, doctor," the grateful woman replied. "You saved my child's life. Thank you so much."

"You're welcome," he answered. "Now remember, improving your diet is crucial for your baby's health. Take the vitamins I gave you. Also, continue her medication and let me see her again in two days." A nurse ushered the woman and her infant out of the room.

Khin May poked her head in. "Ready to go home, Dad?" she asked, smiling. "Sophia and Neil are waiting in the car."

"Oh good, Khin May. Let's go. I hope the children haven't been waiting too long."

"No, it's only a few minutes past noon. They just arrived."

"Hello, *Naana*," Sophia greeted Devi Lal cheerfully as he came out of the clinic. "We've come to fetch you."

She called him *naana*, the Hindi word for maternal grandfather. Sophia was ten, a pretty young girl, slim, and tall for her age. She had large greenish-blue eyes and a fair complexion inherited from her Irish father, plus her mother's long neck and high cheek bones. She wore a white cotton dress and her golden brown hair cascaded down almost to her waist.

"Let me drive, Dad," Khin May offered. "You can sit back and relax."

"Yes, *Naana*. Please come and sit with me in the back," Sophia pleaded. "Neil can be in front with Mama."

"Why must you get to sit with *Naana?*" Neil complained. "I want to sit next to him too."

"Well, both of you can get in the back seat with your grandfather," Khin May said gently, getting behind the wheel.

Devi Lal adored his grandchildren. He was looking forward to spending more time with them over the next few days. Today was the first of a four-day school holiday for *Thadingyut*, the Burmese Festival of Lights.

The traffic on the road was heavy. Besides the usual buses, cars, rickshaws, horse carriages, bicycles and bullock carts, there were a large

number of military vehicles. For the past few months, intense preparations had been carried out by the British authorities to defend Burma
against an anticipated Japanese invasion. British, Indian and Burmese
soldiers were everywhere.

The war in Europe had been raging for two years. The Germans
had swept through France and were threatening Britain. This past June,
they attacked Russia.

In the East, the Japanese made rapid advances. The last of China's
seaports had fallen to the victorious Japanese armies. The only route
now available for war supplies from the United States to reach China
was through the port of Rangoon and over the Burma Road. Burma
thus became strategically critical to the Japanese, as well as to the Americans and the British. By July 1941, Japan had invaded and occupied all
of Indochina.

The Burmese were somewhat baffled by the sudden change of events
occurring in their part of the world. Usually a carefree people, they
preferred to celebrate their multitude of festivals rather than get em-
broiled in someone else's war. Their favourite pastime chronicled the
life of Lord Buddha as well as the deeds of their ancient kings through
elaborately staged musical plays that lasted all night long. Laughter,
music, dancing and lots of good food accompanied these festivities.

Descendants of three different waves of migration from Central Asia,
the Burmese for centuries enjoyed the fruits of their land of abundance. The last of their kings was deposed by the British in 1886 and
Burma was annexed as a province of Colonial India. The British, while
ruling the country, had left the Burmese alone to live their lives celebrating their culture and religion.

What lends richness and charm to the Burmese psyche is the mosaic
of their conflicting religious beliefs and practices. Although predominantly Buddhist, a religion which forbids animism, the Burmese continue to believe in the existence of spirits called *nats*. The supernatural
powers of the occult world influence their lives, and animistic practices continue to be an integral part of the fabric of their culture.

One of the Burmese kings, upon embracing Buddhism, wanted to
put a stop to spirit worship. But as a compromise, he declared that

there could be only thirty-seven *nats* instead of the hundreds worshiped by his subjects. Later, he even had the statues of these 37 *nats* tied in chains and locked away, but to no avail. Even modern-day Burmese believe that the *nats* must be kept appeased and seek their favor by worship and by placing food and gifts before their shrines.

Now their country was being threatened by an invasion. To the Burmese, this was not their war, yet they were drawn into it. In Mandalay, as elsewhere in Burma, daily morning air raid drills and nightly blackouts had frayed everyone's nerves. Khin May was especially worried about her husband, Tim O'Shea, whose British Army regiment was deployed around the eastern defensive perimeter of Rangoon.

"Please God, protect him. Keep him safe," she often prayed.

"Could we go to the cinema this afternoon, *Naana*?" Neil asked, grasping his grandfather's arm. "I want to see the newsreels about the war." At age 12, he was fascinated by planes, guns and tanks. He wore khaki shorts and a white cotton shirt. He had rolled the sleeves of the shirt almost up to his shoulders.

"What movie is playing?"

"It's new, Dad — called the Wizard of Oz," Khin May answered.

"I've read the book a thousand times, *Naana*. It's wonderful," Sophia added.

"Well, I think that's a fine idea," Devi Lal replied, thinking that a movie would be a good diversion for the children. "Why don't the three of you go to the matinee? I can drop you at the cinema and then pick you up when it's over."

Sophia was about to plead with her grandfather to accompany them when their conversation was abruptly interrupted by the sound of a siren.

"Oh no!" Khin May said, looking at her father in the rear view mirror. "Is that an air raid warning?"

The eerie wailing went on, waxing and waning in volume.

"It sounds like it," Devi Lal answered, with a worried look on his face.

"Are we going to be bombed by the Japanese, *Naana*?" Sophia asked nervously.

"I don't know, child," Devi Lal replied. "It can't be a drill, though. We had one this morning."

The siren now blared urgently. Several men in khaki uniforms and pith helmets started directing traffic and yelling out instructions.

"Get away from buildings! Get into trenches! Hurry! Move quickly!" they screamed. White arm bands with the word ARP in large red letters identified them as Air Raid Precaution wardens. A few soldiers and some policemen joined the wardens and started urging the people to take shelter.

Trenches had been dug around schools, hospitals and government buildings. Citizens had also been told to dig these crude shelters near their homes, with instructions to enter them whenever the air raid siren sounded. Most trenches were about five feet deep and three to four feet wide. Many were in an "L" shape so, if a bomb fell close by, people in the part of the trench running parallel to the direction of the blast would less likely be crushed to death.

"We don't have time to drive all the way home, Dad," Khin May spoke urgently, her hands gripping the steering wheel tightly. "But I don't see any trenches along the road."

"Let me think," Devi Lal answered. "The St. Joseph's Convent is just a block away. Sophia, there are trenches in your school compound, aren't there?"

"Yes, *Naana*."

"Good. Let's try there."

Khin May spun the car onto a side road and, racing to the school gate, drove into its compound. Most of the trenches there were already full of people from neighboring homes who had run into the convent grounds. Sister Rose Marie, Sophia's teacher, recognized them.

"Come, Doctor — come this way!" she called out. "There's room for all of you in this trench."

"Thank you, Sister. Thank you very much," Devi Lal answered, hurrying the children towards the nun.

The siren continued to blare and people sat in the trenches, nervously craning their necks towards the sky. Soon a faint drone could be heard over the sound of the siren.

"There they are," Neil pointed excitedly. "There are the planes."

Two small silvery dots became visible high in the clear blue sky. "Are they coming to drop bombs, Sister?" a young boy asked the nun.

"No, no, I don't think so," Sister Rose Marie answered, placing her arm reassuringly around the child's shoulders. "They could even be our own." Yet she made the sign of the cross and recited a silent prayer.

Sophia had seen an airplane on the ground only once. Several years ago, a small plane had flown to Mandalay and landed on the field where the British played polo. Her grandfather had taken them to see it. The drone of the planes was now louder and she wished they would go away. Oh God, what if they start shooting at us, she thought, remembering the news on the radio about thousands of people in China being machine-gunned by Japanese planes.

"Are we going to be killed?" she whispered, clinging to her mother.

"No, Sophia, we'll be fine. Don't worry," Khin May answered, feeling the dryness in her own throat.

"How dare they fly over our city?" Neil spoke angrily. "The British should shoot them down."

Devi Lal placed his arms around his grandchildren.

The two planes flew lazily in a big circle over Mandalay. There were no anti-aircraft guns to threaten them, nor were there any British planes to defend the city.

"Look, one of them is coming lower," Neil exclaimed. "I can see the pilot's head."

While one plane continued its slow circle high above, the other had descended very low and was flying at a high speed over the city.

"Look! It's dropping something," a man pointed excitedly.

"Oh, dear God," Sister Rose Marie exclaimed nervously.

The sky behind the low flying plane was now filled with tiny fluttering specks that glistened in the bright sun light.

"We're going to be killed!" a woman in the trench moaned. A young girl started crying.

"*Naana*, they look like sheets of paper," Neil said, standing up and pointing at the objects now some distance behind the plane.

Then another cluster of shimmering little specks appeared below the plane.

"You're right, Neil," Devi Lal said, relieved. "They are dropping leaflets of some kind."

The plane dropped more leaflets and gradually regained altitude. The two aircraft then turned to the southeast and disappeared from sight. Thousands of pieces of paper came showering down upon the city. The "all clear" siren had not as yet sounded, but people ran out to grab the leaflets. Some were falling on the road in front of the school. Neil suddenly scampered out of the trench and ran towards the gate of the Convent. He returned, triumphantly waving several pieces of paper.

"*Naana*, look at these. There's a message from the Japanese," he said breathlessly, handing his grandfather one of the leaflets.

The writing was in both English and Burmese: "Citizens of Mandalay: The brave Japanese Imperial Army will soon come to liberate you. You must welcome them and help them. Together we shall expel the British from our countries. Asia will be for Asians."

Slowly, everyone came out of the trenches and stood around, somewhat dazed. Devi Lal sighed deeply, trying to still his racing heart. No one had been harmed and he felt a flood of relief course through his veins.

"Come, children, we can go home now," he said, taking their hands.

"Thank you, Sister, thank you very much for letting us take shelter in your trench," he said to the nun.

"You're welcome, Doctor," Sister Rose Marie answered. "Thank God they didn't bomb us!"

Then, turning to Sophia and Neil, she cheerfully added, "Enjoy the holidays, children." They drove home through the once again crowded streets.

Later in the afternoon, Devi Lal dropped his daughter and grandchildren off at the cinema. Several British soldiers standing on the street leered at Khin May as she walked towards the ticket office. One of them whistled at her as she followed the children into the cinema hall. Within a few minutes an electric bell rang loudly.

"Oh good, the movie is starting," Sophia said, sitting back in her seat. The ushers at the doors drew the heavy curtains together, blocking out the bright glare of the sun, plunging the hall into complete darkness. Suddenly, the white screen lit up. It was a Fox Movietone newsreel on the Battle of Britain. The deep-voiced commentator dramatically described the relentless air raids by the German Luftwaffe. German Dornier and Heinkel bombers were shown flying over the English Channel in impressive formations, protected by swarms of Messerschmitt fighter planes.

"The Nazis believed they could conquer Britain with the same ease with which they swept through Europe," the commentator stated. "But they were surprised. The outnumbered pilots of the Royal Air Force in their Hurricanes and Spitfires are putting up a brave fight. The Germans are losing scores of their aircraft, blown out of the sky by the courageous defenders of the British Isles. The Stuka dive bombers, so successfully used by the Luftwaffe in their lightning strikes in Poland and France, are no match against the valiant RAF fighters. German dive-bombers and their Messerschmitt fighter escorts have been routed from the skies over England by Spitfires and Hurricanes streaking down at them from out of the sun."

The sound track filled the cinema hall with the eerie noise of an air raid warning siren. They watched pilots in the newsreel running toward their fighters. Other defenders manned anti-aircraft guns. Women and children were herded into air raid shelters by steel-helmeted air raid wardens. The footage then documented an actual raid. Bombs exploded and entire city blocks went up in flames. The sky was dotted with black puffs of smoke from anti-aircraft shells. Planes blew up and came spiraling down to earth. Sophia watched, horrified, but Neil was fascinated.

"Oh good, it's over," Sophia said when the newsreel ended. Much to her relief, they then showed two Looney Tunes cartoons. Then the main feature started and they all watched, fascinated, absorbed in the fantasy.

When they came out into the bright sunlight, Devi Lal was waiting for them in his car. "How was the movie?" he asked.

"It was all right," Neil answered. "But the newsreel was great, *Naana*! They showed dog fights and fighter planes bursting into flames and falling to the ground."

"No, it was terrible, *Naana*!" Sophia complained. "Everyone had to leave their homes and run into shelters. The bombs exploded loudly. All the buildings burned and many people died. The movie was great, though, *Naana*. It had lots of good songs."

"Well, your Uncle Hari is coming home tomorrow. Tell him to get you gramophone records of these songs from Rangoon. He can bring them the next time he comes."

After dinner that evening, as usual, they listened to the news on the radio. The broadcast from Rangoon mentioned the planes that had flown over Mandalay.

"Two unidentified aircraft, coming from the southeast, flew over Mandalay shortly after noon today," the commentator said. "No bombs were dropped and, after circling the city, the planes flew back in a southeasterly direction. All citizens are instructed to continue strictly observing air raid precautions during any future air incursions." The announcement made no reference to the propaganda leaflets dropped by one of the planes.

The children wanted to stay up late but Khin May herded them to their rooms as soon as the news broadcast was over. They'd all had enough excitement for one day and she was afraid that Sophia, especially, might have trouble falling asleep. But Sophia slept comfortably, and was awakened in the morning by the sound of birds chirping below her bedroom window. Sweet Pea, the cocker spaniel Uncle Hari had given her on her tenth birthday earlier that year, was barking excitedly. The dog was busily engaged in her daily morning ritual of chasing butterflies fluttering among the rose and jasmine bushes in the garden.

The summer's oppressive heat was now replaced by the milder weather of October. A gentle breeze from the window blew through the mosquito netting around Sophia's bed, pleasantly brushing her arms and face. The soft tinkling sounds of the gold leaves atop the neighbourhood pagoda floated into the room, almost lulling her back to sleep. Mandalay was peaceful and quiet this morning.

Sophia heard the grandfather clock in the entrance hallway two floors below strike six. On any other day, she would have gotten out of bed to get ready for school. But today was *Thadingyut*, her favourite Festival of

Lights, celebrated with great joy and merriment throughout Burma. According to Buddhist scriptures, this was the day Lord Buddha descended from heaven where he had gone to preach to his mother, who had been reincarnated into a higher plane of existence. The Lord's radiance illuminated the earth with a gentle glow as he returned.

To celebrate this very auspicious day, every home in the country — from mansions to peasants' huts — would be illuminated tonight. Thousands upon thousands of candles and little earthen oil lamps would be placed on every ledge, window sill and fence, as well as around gardens and pagodas. Even the glow of the full moon, when this festival is held, is unable to match the sheer brilliance of the shimmering lights that bedeck the villages and towns throughout Burma.

The blackouts, so diligently enforced by the city's ARP wardens, would not take place tonight. No threat of arrest — or even the unthinkable likelihood of an air raid — would keep the people from celebrating this festival.

Sophia knew there would be gifts for her from her mother and her grandfather. She wished her father could be home today. She had not seen him since August. She thought about the threat of war. The newsreel yesterday was horrible: it had made her feel terrified. Why do people have to kill each other, she wondered. Were they all going to die? She forced herself to think of pleasant things. Today was the Festival of Lights! Uncle Hari is coming home this afternoon, Sophia remembered, arriving on the four o'clock train!

Hari was five years younger than Khin May. Since completing his medical studies, he worked as a House Surgeon at the Rangoon Medical College and Hospital.

The thought of her uncle brought a smile on Sophia's face and she sat up in her bed. Parting the mosquito netting, she stepped out and walked to her desk. She opened her desk drawer and brought out a box containing a dozen brightly coloured glass marbles. She knew Neil would be very pleased with her gift. She had gladly paid the shopkeeper the one *rupee* he had asked without trying even once to bargain for a lower price — which the shopkeeper fully expected her to do. In fact he was a little disappointed that the young girl had not haggled.

He would have been quite willing to sell the marbles to her for 12 *annas*.

Sophia took the sheet of bright red paper the shopkeeper had given her and carefully wrapped the present. She took a white ribbon and tied a neat bow around it. Satisfied with the packaging, she placed it next to the box of handkerchiefs she had bought for her uncle.

Then she went to a large cardboard box in the corner of her bedroom and gently picked up her pet rabbit. "Good morning, Mr. Fluffy," she cooed. "How are you today?" Stroking its soft white fur, she walked over to the large window that overlooked the gardens towards the front of the house.

Her grandfather had built this spacious and comfortable home fourteen years earlier when he left Government Service and moved to Mandalay to set up his medical practice. The house stood on a small hill in the southwestern corner of the city in an attractive neighbourhood called *Sein Pun*, which in Burmese means "Diamond Flower." Devi Lal had spared no expense and built this three-story home with top grade Burmese teak. A white wooden gate opened to three attractively landscaped acres, with the house set halfway back.

A small teak board was fastened to the gatepost with the words *Shanti Gaeha* chiseled into it. Devi Lal had named his house taking the first word from Hindi, the language of the land of his birth and his ancestors. The second word was Burmese, the language of his adopted country and of the people he had come to love. *Shanti*, peace, and *Gaeha*, house, aptly described this serene dwelling.

Sophia loved this house where she had been raised. She found the talk about war very unsettling. "Mama, I hope we never leave *Shanti Gaeha*, ever," she would say. "I'll just die if anything should happen to it."

The driveway leading in from the white gate of *Shanti Gaeha* ran straight for forty feet, then curved into a large loop in front of the house to allow carriages and cars to enter and leave without having to turn around. The ground within the driveway was covered with a luxuriant, lush green lawn outlined with flower beds of snapdragons, daisies, sweet williams, marigolds and sweet peas.

On the outer side of the driveway, neat rows of rose plants with a profusion of red, orange and yellow flowers alternated with beds of jasmine bushes covered with fragrant white flowers. Some of the jasmine, named "Queen of the Night," were a variety which bloom only after dark and fill the night air with their rich sweet fragrance. Along the fence on each side of the white gate, rows of hibiscus plants were laden with large, delicate red flowers. On the right corner of the lot, a tree almost completely covered with bougainvillea vines was bathed in an explosion of fuchsia-coloured flowers.

Toward the right of the house, the ground had been leveled for a tennis court, and deep, comfortable cane chairs and a table were set on a narrow strip of lawn next to the court. Devi Lal played tennis twice a week with his friend and neighbor, U Ba Kyi, a leading Advocate of the Mandalay High Court. Despite his age, Devi Lal played a competitive game, moving around the court gracefully and surprisingly fast. To the left of the house was a swimming pool filled with fresh water from the deep well on the grounds.

There was a gentle knock on the door. "Who is it?" Sophia inquired.

"Are you awake, child? Would you like some milk?"

It was Daw Mu, the old Ayah who was hired as a nanny in 1909 when Khin May was born. She stayed on to look after Hari, then Neil and Sophia, and was treated like a member of the family. Now at age 72, she led a comfortable life, spending most of her time admonishing the servants for not working hard. She doted on Neil and Sophia, buying them sweets and gifts and covering up for Neil when he got into mischief.

"No thank you, Daw Mu," Sophia called back. "I'm not hungry yet. I'll wait until breakfast."

"All right, child, come down whenever you're ready," the old woman answered, walking towards Neil's room.

Devi Lal, like many well-to-do in Burma, could afford many servants. There were two full-time gardeners. An excellent cook, Ko Than, and his wife, Daw Tin, worked in the kitchen. The children called the old cook *U Gyi*. The Burmese use the words *U*, meaning Uncle, and *Gyi*, meaning elder, to courteously address an older person. The elderly couple had worked for Devi Lal for nearly sixteen years and prepared excellent

Burmese, Indian, Chinese or English meals. An Indian houseboy named Swami helped serve meals, clean the house and polish the silverware.

Bahadur, the night watchman, hailed from Nepal and belonged to the Gurkha race—known for their prowess in battle. Sher Khan, a Muslim from India, began working for Devi Lal 36 years ago. Initially he looked after the horses Devi Lal used for traveling to remote villages as a young District Medical Officer in Northern Burma. Now Sher Khan drove and maintained the family's two cars in tiptop condition.

Daw Mu occupied one of the bedrooms in the house. The servants lived in comfortable rooms provided for them in the servants' quarters, located towards the back, behind the tennis court. Devi Lal paid his servants well, and provided them with clothing and medical care. He also encouraged and paid for their children to attend school.

The large window in Sophia's third-story bedroom gave her a panoramic view of the city. Looking to the right, she could see the Burmese Royal Palace within Mandalay Fort, named Fort Dufferin by the British. Beyond the fort, she could see Mandalay Hill with its covered stairways snaking up to the pagoda at the top. To the left, the mighty Irrawaddy River was visible as it flowed past the city. In the morning sunlight, the light brown, muddy waters of the river shimmered like molten gold. Sophia heard the whistle of the ferry boat as it announced its departure for Pagan. The faint sound of the huge paddle wheel thrashing and churning the river water reached her as the ferry powered away from the jetty.

Sweet Pea, exhausted from her fruitless chase of the butterflies, now lay in the shade of a rose bush with her legs spread out and her chest and belly resting flat on the cool ground. Suddenly she caught sight of Sophia in the window above, and jumping up, started barking excitedly, imploring Sophia to come down to play.

"No, Sweet Pea, you come up here," Sophia called out, motioning with her hand. The dog stopped barking. With her ears cocked and tail still, she froze for a moment looking up at her mistress. Then she exploded into a mad dash, running through the front door, slipping and sliding on the polished teak floor of the entrance hall, and raced up the steps to Sophia's room.

Devi Lal, back from his morning walk, sat in the drawing room on the ground floor to the right of the entrance hall. He listened intently to the six o'clock English broadcast on the radio from Rangoon. The news about the war was not encouraging and he was worried that the British forces would not be able to prevent the Japanese armies from marching into Burma. He was not fearful for himself as, if he had to, he would stay on in Mandalay — even under Japanese occupation — and help the people who came to him for medical care.

Devi Lal loved Burma. It was his home, and Mandalay his beloved city. These were his people. Many of his patients were farmers and villagers who trusted and respected him. The poor would bring their malnourished and dying children to him and he would treat them, often receiving some vegetables or a chicken in return. To those who had nothing to give, he would say, "Don't worry — I received these medicines as free samples and if not used soon, they would have to be thrown away."

He grieved over the high infant mortality among the poor in the country. Unskilled midwives often used sharp pieces of bamboo or broken pieces of china to sever the umbilical cord of a newborn. Many an infant would contract tetanus and die after suffering horribly. Devi Lal preached the importance of proper diet for expectant mothers and taught the women safe delivery methods. He wrote a book on infant and maternal welfare and had thousands of copies distributed free.

Devi Lal built and furnished a 25-bed maternity hospital in Sein Pun where the poor could come and have their babies delivered safely and free of cost. He also built and donated a home for the elderly in nearby Mingun. Some simple villagers even brought their healthy children to ask Devi Lal just to touch and bless them. News about the kind Indian doctor had spread, and he often worked seven days a week, from early in the morning until late into the evening, totally absorbed.

Recently there had been a spate of burglaries and robberies by a gang of armed thugs who held up the rich in their homes, especially in the outskirts of the city. There had also been two cases of kidnapping followed by ransom demands. But one day, Devi Lal found an unsigned, handwritten note in his mail box. It was in Burmese and said,

"Do not worry — we know of your good work with the poor and the elderly. We will not harm you or any member of your family."

The British Government appointed Devi Lal an Honorary Magistrate in recognition of his civic activities. He held court in the Municipal Court House each Wednesday afternoon, hearing minor civil cases.

"Hello, *Naana*, how are you?"

Devi Lal, deep in thought, was startled. It was his grandson who had walked into the room.

"I'm fine, Neil. I was just listening to the news on the radio."

"I'll see you later. I'm going to ride my bike out front," Neil said over his shoulder, walking out the door.

Devi Lal sighed and turned off the radio. What will happen to my half-Irish grandchildren if the Japanese occupy Burma, he wondered.

He was also anxious about Tim, who was more a son to him than a son-in-law. Perhaps he should send the family to the Sagaing Hills where they should be safe even if Mandalay is bombed. Located across the Irrawaddy River, southwest of the city, these hills were studded with Buddhist monasteries. Devi Lal was very well acquainted with the head *pongyi* of one of the larger monasteries and was sure that his family would receive shelter there. If conditions became worse, he could then send them to wait out the war in Myitkyina, the northernmost town in Burma. God willing, he was going to see to it that his children and grandchildren were kept out of harm's way.

Sweet Pea scampered into Sophia's room and ran excitedly around the bed, barking gleefully, making Mr. Fluffy very, very nervous. Sophia could feel the rabbit's heart thumping wildly against her hands.

"Oh, look what you've done, Sweet Pea. Stop acting silly," she scolded, returning Mr. Fluffy to the cardboard box. "Come on, you naughty dog, let's go down and see what everyone is doing."

Sweet Pea ran down the steps ahead of Sophia and out the front door, attracted by Daw Mu's shrill voice. The old woman was vainly attempting to scold Sher Khan. All the other servants were subservient to Daw Mu's demands and did what she asked. But Sher Khan had a way of haughtily ignoring her, which made her furious. This morning she accused him of not properly polishing the car.

Sher Khan was really quite fond of this grand old lady, but he enjoyed teasing her. The car, a Morris Deluxe, had been purchased in Rangoon only last year and Sher Khan kept it immaculately clean. He had washed the car this morning and polished it to a beautiful shine.

"Look here, Daw Mu," he chided with a mischievous glint in his eye, "I better ask Doctor *Sahib* to have your eyes examined. I don't think you can even see the car, much less any dirt on it."

Sweet Pea seemed to enjoy this banter and started playfully barking at them. Daw Mu shook her fist at Sher Khan and, glaring at the dog, stomped back into the house, just as a *pongyi* draped in the saffron robe of the Buddhist monks walked serenely up the driveway to the house.

"A venerable *pongyi* is at our door, child," Daw Mu informed Khin May who was placing some fruit on the dining table.

"Oh, yes," she answered, "the food is cooked. I'll take it outside."

The monk stood quietly at the front door, clasping a begging bowl, his shaven head bowed and his eyes downcast. Khin May placed some rice and vegetables in the bowl.

No words were spoken: the *pongyi* turned around and, with head bowed, walked out of the gate. The food he begged was all that he would eat that day, after sharing it with other monks who were unable to leave the monastery. The monk did not acknowledge the gift as, according to Buddhist belief, it was the giver who was privileged and should feel grateful to have been provided an occasion to perform a meritorious deed. If no food was offered, the *pongyi* walked away quietly to beg at the next home. Khin May carried out this ritual of giving food to a *pongyi* with reverence each day before her own breakfast.

At seven o'clock, the family gathered for breakfast — all except Neil, who had to be called twice before he appeared.

"Why do I have to eat now?" he complained. "I don't have school."

"You know the rules, son," his mother told him. "We eat our meals together no matter what day of the week."

Breakfast over, Khin May gave hurried instructions to the children before leaving for the clinic with her father.

"Please make sure that you tidy your rooms and don't quarrel with each other. Also, remember, this afternoon we have to go to the railway station to meet Hari."

"Mama, can my friends and I swim in the pool this morning?" Neil asked.

"Yes, Neil, but listen to Daw Mu and don't get into any mischief. I'll see you at lunch time."

"Mama, tell Neil that he and his friends have to get out of the pool by noon," Sophia pleaded. "My friend Rosaline is coming over and we want to be able to swim."

"You heard your sister, Neil. Let the girls have the pool when they want it."

Devi Lal drove the car with Khin May sitting next to him. Turning left onto 84th Street, he wove through the traffic, which became heavier near the Zeygo Market. Bicyclists rang their bells and car and bus horns were being blown at the same time. Pedestrians darted between the traffic. Coolies hurried along with huge baskets and boxes balanced precariously on their heads. The strong odor of dried fish and pungent spices from the stalls of the market mingled with the smell of the dust from the road. A policeman stood on a raised platform in the middle of a congested intersection near the clock tower and vainly tried to direct the chaotic traffic. Scant attention was paid to his waving arms and the sound of his whistle simply blended with the rest of the street noise.

Sophia went up to her room and closed the door behind her. She put the mosquito netting neatly over its canopy and made her bed. Then she reached in her desk drawer and brought out a little black notebook that she kept hidden under several other books. She picked up a pencil and sat down on the window seat. Opening her notebook, she entered the date and started writing.

We went to see the "Wizard of Oz" yesterday and it was wonderful. I liked it so very much. Today is the Festival of Lights. I wish Daddy was coming home. I miss him terribly. Why does there have to be this stupid war? Mama is lonely without Daddy. I can see it. Naana worries about all of us. I hope nothing bad happens.

Then she turned to a back page and started reading a poem she had been writing the previous night. It was simple but touching — about butterflies, flowers, sunshine and rainbows. No one knew of her interest in poetry, as she was shy about it and kept her hobby a secret.

Sophia tried in vain to concentrate, but the laughter and loud voices of Neil and his friends in the swimming pool kept interrupting her thoughts. The boys had tied a rope to a branch high up on a tree at one end of the pool. Holding the rope, they climbed another tree to about ten feet above the ground. Imitating Tarzan from the movies, the boys pounded their fists on their chests, shouting Tarzan's yell. They would then swing, holding to the rope, and drop into the water with a big splash.

"Is your dad coming home for the festival," one of the boys asked Neil.

"No, he's not," Neil answered curtly.

"Why not?" a second boy inquired. "Doesn't he want to be home for the holidays?"

Neil glared at the boys. "It's none of your damn business," he exploded angrily. "Come on, get out. Go home! I don't want any of you to use my pool anymore," he yelled, and ran towards the house.

Sophia returned her notebook to its hiding place in the drawer and started reading a book. Just before noon, she changed into her swim suit and went downstairs. She met her friend Rosaline at the front door and, holding hands, ran with her to the pool.

"Oh, good. The boys are gone," Sophia said, relieved. "They were making so much noise."

"They act so silly, don't they," Rosaline added, "yelling and screaming all the time."

The girls sat on the edge of the pool and chatted, dangling their feet in the water.

"Sophia, what'll you be when you grow up?" Rosaline asked.

"You mean like get married and have children?"

"No, silly," Rosaline laughed. "I mean, what'll you do the rest of your life? What kind of work will you do?"

"Oh, I don't know," Sophia mused. "My grandfather tells me that I mustn't let others decide what I can or can't be just because I'm a girl. He said that God has given each of us a special potential and it's our duty to achieve this potential."

"What does that mean?"

"*Naana* explained that if God has given me the gift to be an artist or a doctor, lawyer or engineer, that's what I should be. He said I shouldn't let others tell me I have to be a secretary or nurse just because I'm a girl. He said girls are as smart as boys and have the freedom to choose whatever they want to do."

"Does he want you to be a doctor like he is?"

"He hasn't said so to me, but I wouldn't mind being like him and help others."

"You love him a lot, don't you?"

"Yes," Sophia answered softly, "I do, very much."

They talked for awhile longer before getting into the water. Sophia swam the length of the pool several times, propelling her body smoothly with graceful strokes of her arms and legs. The two friends were still in the pool when Khin May and Devi Lal returned from the clinic just before one o'clock.

"Mama, Rosaline and I are here in the pool," Sophia called out.

"Hello, Rosaline. Won't you join us for lunch?" Khin May asked, walking towards them.

"Yes, do stay, Rosaline," Sophia added. "It'll be such fun. After lunch we can play in my room." Rosaline was hoping she would be asked.

"Thanks, Auntie Khin May," she answered, "but first I should go tell my mother."

"You don't have to do that, Rosaline. I'll send Swami to let your mother know."

The family sat down to lunch and Sophia and Rosaline chatted happily throughout the meal. Neil appeared morose and kept toying with his food. His mother watched him for some time.

"Is anything the matter, Neil?" she inquired. "Are you feeling all right?"

The boy shrugged his shoulders. "Nothing's the matter," he answered sullenly.

"Aren't you hungry, Neil?" his sister teased.

Neil's face turned red. "Leave me alone, all of you. I'm not hungry." He shoved his chair back and stormed out of the room. Sweet Pea came running towards Neil, wagging her tail, but he kicked her away angrily and raced up the stairs.

Khin May gave her father an anxious look. "Should I go talk to him?" she asked.

"No, wait awhile," he answered. "Give him some time."

A little later, Khin May knocked on her son's door and went in. Neil was lying on his bed, staring at the ceiling.

"What's the matter, son?" she asked softly.

"Nothing," he answered.

"It helps to talk, Neil," she said, gently stroking his head.

"Why isn't he coming home?"

"Your dad?" she asked. "He would have if the Army hadn't canceled all leaves."

"But today is the Festival of Lights, Mama. Why does he have to be in the stinking army? Why can't he stay with us?"

"It's the war, son. Your father is a soldier."

"No, that's not it," Neil continued stubbornly. "He doesn't care for us any more. I hate him." Tears were filling his eyes.

"You mustn't say such things, Neil. That's not true!" Khin May said, taking her son in her arms. "Your father cares for all of us very much."

"Come, wash your face. We'll soon be leaving for the station to fetch Uncle Hari. Later your friends will be over and we'll celebrate *Thadingyut*. Come, my son, cheer up."

Khin May went to her room and locked the door. She felt overcome by a deep sense of sadness. Should she have taken the children and gone to live in Rangoon with Tim? But then the children's education would have been interrupted. Besides, with the war so near, Rangoon would not be safe for them. And now her son was being affected by his father's absence. Oh dear God, what's going to happen, she wondered.

It was almost three o'clock and Daw Mu started reminding everyone to get ready. "We mustn't be late!" she called out. "If the train arrives before we get to the station, Hari will wonder what has happened." Sophia had already changed and wore a white dress with a wide green sash around the waist, tied in a neat bow at the back. Dark brown vines with green leaves and red and yellow flowers were embroidered around the skirt and along the edge of the loose short sleeves of the dress. She had put on her best pair of white leather shoes with little gold-coloured buckles. Her hair had been brushed until it gleamed, and a green satin bow adorned the side of her head.

Devi Lal was in the entry hallway when his granddaughter came down the steps and Daw Mu noticed the look on his face.

"Isn't she a vision from heaven?" she whispered.

"That she is," he answered softly. "That she most certainly is." He often thought that, even at the age of ten, Sophia moved so gracefully — just like Mah Lay, her grandmother, did when he had met and married her 34 years ago. His beloved wife had been dead fifteen years, but Devi Lal had still not recovered from the shock and sorrow. He had thrown himself into his work and looking after his children and grandchildren. But after all these years the hurt was still there.

Khin May was ready and had gone to see if Sher Khan had brought the two cars to the front of the house. Noticing one of the cars there, she was about to go back when she sensed someone standing in the bright sunshine in the middle of the driveway. That was odd: a moment ago the driveway had been empty. She turned sharply and noticed an old man in a strange costume standing in the hot sun and staring at the front door. He wore a faded gold tunic and an ancient crown from the days of the Burmese kings. His hair was long and matted, and he had a scraggly, flowing beard. Khin May felt bewildered. The old man seemed to have materialized out of thin air.

Just then, Sweet Pea came out of the door, her tail wagging excitedly. The dog looked at the old man and froze for an instant. She then started whimpering and, turning around, quickly ran back into the house. That's odd, Khin May thought. Sweet Pea always barks at strangers and sniffs their ankles.

Then the old man spoke, using the style of Burmese from ancient times. "I have come to see the *shwe man khalay*," he said in a scratchy voice.

Khin May was perplexed. The old man had said that he had come to see golden Mandalay's Child.

"Are you looking for my son?" she asked nervously.

"No. I want to see *main-khalay* — the girl-child."

At that moment, Sophia appeared briefly at the doorway and the old man saw her. A toothless grin on his face, he pointed a bent, sinewy finger towards her.

"There she is. Mandalay's child," he beamed. "She is the blessed one. I see her. She has the protection of the *nats*. The Lord *Min Mahagiri* the Spirit of the Great Mountain; *Aungpinle* the Lord Master and keeper of the White Elephants; and the Exalted *Nat Bodaw* Lord Grandfather of Mandalay all favor her. She will cross swift rivers and dangerous mountains and not be harmed. She will walk through infernos and come out unscathed."

Khin May was now most uneasy and wanted this strange man to go away. Thinking that if she made an offering he would leave, she went into the dining room and quickly returned with some fruit.

But the old man had disappeared. Good Lord, where had he gone? There wasn't a trace of him anywhere on the driveway. She felt a cold breeze brush her face and a chill ran through her veins. She looked again where she thought the man had stood. All she could see was some brownish-red dust on the ground. There was a stale, musty odor in the air. She shuddered, and was about to go back into the house when Sher Khan drove up with the second car.

Thank God, she sighed. Sher Khan will know who the strange man was and where he went. "Did you see an old man on the driveway, Sher Khan?"

"No, Daughter. There's no one here," he answered.

Devi Lal came out and got behind the wheel of one of the cars. Sher Khan was to drive the other. Daw Mu quickly climbed into the back seat of Devi Lal's car. "I will not trust my life to the crazy driving of Sher Khan," she muttered. "Come, children, come ride with me," she called out to Neil and Sophia.

Khin May sat next to Sher Khan, deeply preoccupied, wondering if she had imagined the episode of the old man.

The railway station was a huge attraction for the people of Mandalay and the surrounding villages. There was great excitement in the morning when the mail train departed for Rangoon, and once again at four o'clock in the afternoon when the train from Rangoon arrived. Groups of villagers came daily just to gawk at the trains and to enjoy the festive atmosphere of the station. Devi Lal and Sher Khan drove to the parking place for private cars. There were separate areas for buses and for taxis and another area was reserved for bicycle rickshaws. Horse-drawn carts and bullock carts had to wait a little distance away. Stands for bicycles were located close to the entrance. A British army car and two trucks were parked directly in front, perhaps awaiting the arrival of a senior official from Rangoon.

Devi Lal could not understand why so many Britishers in Burma chose to remain isolated in their "Europeans Only" world. Why not absorb this beautiful culture and enjoy these charming people who personify friendliness and hospitality? Maybe some day, when they return to their frigid land, they'll realize what they missed. Devi Lal enjoyed the company of the few Westerners who maintained social contact with "the natives". The Civil Surgeon of the Mandalay General Hospital — the burly Scotsman Dr. Robert McDonald — and the two English head nurses from the hospital were his friends. He frequently played tennis with David O'Connell, a lanky Irishman on the administrative staff of the District Deputy Commissioner.

The grounds in front of the station resembled a carnival. Vendors did a brisk business selling soft drinks, tea and an assortment of snacks. In one corner, several men stood in a circle playing the Burmese game of *Chinlon*. They kept a light cane ball bouncing in the air, striking it skillfully with their legs, knees and shoulders. The object of the game is to pass the ball around between the players, without letting it fall to the ground. In another corner, street shows were performed by puppeteers, musicians, snake charmers, acrobats and magicians. Several fortune tellers and astrologers sat on the ground reading palms and horoscopes.

"Can I buy a glass of sugar cane juice?" Neil asked his mother as they got out of the car.

"Why don't you wait, son," she answered. "We can all have some lemonade from the refreshment room inside the station."

Devi Lal stopped at the ticket office and purchased tickets required to enter the station platforms. Once past the ticket gate, Neil quickly led the rest toward the refreshment room on Platform 1 where the train from Rangoon was to arrive. On one end was the first-class waiting room, next to the railway offices and a mail room. A large waiting area for third-class passengers was located at the opposite end of the platform. A smaller waiting room was reserved for passengers traveling second-class.

Khin May paid for five glasses of lemonade and they drank the cold, sweet refreshing drink while watching the throngs on the platform. Several Englishmen dressed in suits and neckties and some army officers in uniform stood near the entrance to the first-class waiting room. Armed British and Gurkha soldiers with bayonets affixed to their rifles stood at regular intervals on the platform.

The family finished their lemonade and walked toward the area where the second-class train compartments usually stopped. An Englishman who was a judge recognized Devi Lal and greeted him.

Just before four, scores of coolies dressed in red shirts and khaki *longyis* came and stood along the platform where the first and second-class compartments of the train would stop. Periodically necks craned toward the south to see if there were any signs of the train. A distant whistle announced its approach and a hush fell over the crowd.

The faint noise of the steam engine gradually became louder and the huge black engine, spewing a column of dense black smoke from its funnel on top, suddenly loomed in the distance. A buzz of excited conversation spread among the people. The train's whistle gave two short blasts and the engine thundered toward the platform, steam hissing out on both sides. The ground shook as the massive engine rolled past, drowning all noise with its thunderous roar. People at the front of the platform instinctively moved back a few steps.

Heads stuck out of every window of the long line of bright red carriages. Sophia caught sight of her Uncle Hari and, freeing her hand from Daw Mu's, bolted towards the front of the train, dodging between others rushing in different directions. She reached Hari just as he stepped off the train and leapt into his outstretched arms. Next, Hari gave Neil a hug before directing a coolie to bring his suitcase out of the compartment. With Sophia and Neil on each side of him holding onto his hands, Hari walked towards the rest of the family.

An Indian wedding party had also arrived and a brass band started playing loud music in welcome. Members of the wedding party were greeted with garlands of bright yellow marigolds and the bridegroom was showered with red and orange rose petals. A man with a wide grin which exposed his two shiny gold front teeth, held a brass bottle over his head and sprinkled rose-scented water on the wedding party, as well as on anyone else who happened to be near. British and Gurkha soldiers formed a guard of honour, and the visiting dignitary was escorted out of the station before the remaining passengers were allowed to exit.

Hari and the children finally reached their family and Hari embraced each of them. Followed by the coolie with the suitcase balanced on his head, they walked out of the station. Sher Khan and Hari greeted each other warmly.

"Well, son, when are you going to bring a daughter-in-law into our household?" It was the same question Sher Khan asked each time Hari came home.

Hari laughed. "First I have to be able to earn enough money to support myself, let alone a family, Sher Khan. But don't worry — when I do decide to get married you'll be the first to know!"

Hari was slender, tall and fairly good-looking. Although 27 years of age, he hadn't had a serious relationship with a woman. At the hospital he was constantly surrounded by large numbers of young women but somehow had avoided getting to know any one of them well. He was surprised at the behavior of some of his fellow House Surgeons who were having affairs with nurses and female medical students. He was appalled by their constant crude jokes and their free disclosure of their conquests. Lately he had started worrying if there was something wrong with him. He enjoyed his work and proudly walked around the hospital in his white coat and a stethoscope hanging around his neck. He was flattered by the attention he received from the nurses, but, for some reason, shied away from asking them out.

The two cars drove toward *Shanti Gaeha,* negotiating the heavy traffic exiting the railway station. Khin May wanted to ask Hari about Tim but waited till she was able to be alone with him.

"Did you see Tim before leaving?" she asked. "How's he doing?"

"Yes, Sis, I saw him a couple of days ago," Hari said, putting his arm around his sister's shoulders. "He looked fine. You needn't worry about him. He asked if you'd come to visit him at Christmas. It's not likely that he'll be allowed to leave the city."

Khin May and Tim had always been so happy together and very much in love. Tim had been transferred out of Mandalay soon after Sophia was born. At first, Khin May and the children traveled with him from one army post to another. But once Neil and Sophia were of school age, Tim suggested that Khin May remain in Mandalay with her father and that he would come home as often as he could. This arrangement, though beneficial for the children, made Khin May and Tim's relationship difficult. The threat of war had made matters worse, and recently it seemed they were drifting apart. Now the children were being affected.

Khin May made up her mind that she would go and spend Christmas with Tim. They had to work things out and find some way of staying together.

When the family gathered to have tea in the drawing room, Hari brought down several packages he had brought from Rangoon.

"You shouldn't have wasted your money buying all these gifts," Daw Mu admonished him. But then she whispered to Sophia, "I hope he's brought you an expensive gift from the big city."

"Here, Daw Mu, I have something for you," Hari said, offering her a small package.

The old lady looked pleased. "No, no. Give it to your sister. I don't need anything," she said, and then opened the package.

"These are beautiful! Look, Sophia — your uncle brought me prayer beads," she beamed.

"They're from the holy Shwedagon Pagoda in Rangoon," Hari explained.

For his sister he had a gift box containing a bottle of perfume, a tube of lipstick, and a fancy dispenser with talcum powder.

Next, Hari handed his father a package. "Dad, I brought you a stethoscope. It's of the latest design, made in Edinburgh, Scotland. I hope you like it."

"Well, thank you very much, son. I do need a new stethoscope," Devi Lal said with obvious pleasure. "That was very thoughtful of you."

Neil received a kite-making kit, along with a spool of strong thread. Hari's gift to Sophia was a box with a dozen satin bows of different colours, attached to clips. In addition, there was a small book of poems in English.

"How did you know I like poetry?" she asked, giving him a hug.

"Oh, I just took a good guess. After all, Kavita, you are my favorite niece." He sometimes addressed Sophia by her middle name, Kavita, a Sanskrit word meaning poetry.

"She's your only niece, Uncle Hari," Neil joked.

"Well, she's still very special." Then he added, "And so are you, Neil."

The rest of the family exchanged gifts and, later, Daw Mu and Khin May presented gifts to the servants and their families. There were baskets with fruit and sweets, plus a bonus of 20 *rupees* for each servant. The two children of one of the gardeners received toys and the six-year-old daughter of Bahadur, the watchman, received a little bicycle.

The sun went down and dusk was setting in. The family moved out to the front lawn. Together with the servants and their families, they started lighting the hundreds of candles that had been placed all over the house and the grounds. A variety of Burmese and Indian delicacies had been prepared and would be served later. There were deep fried *samosas*, filled with peas and potatoes, and vegetable *pakoras*. There was sliced roast chicken and little Chinese sausages. Platters were heaped with peeled, sliced fruits, as well as Indian sweets.

By eight o'clock, all of the candles were lit and Shanti Gaeha looked magically enchanting. Neil and his friends played on the front lawn, setting off firecrackers. As the first string exploded, Sweet Pea ran into the house and huddled, trembling, under the stairwell in the entry hallway.

Sophia and Rosaline played with long sparklers. Carrying one in each hand, they ran around the driveway swirling them around. Hari bent the wire handles of several sparklers into hooks and threw them high into a tree where they hung from the branches and lit up the tree with their glow. The air was heavy with the acrid smell of firecrackers.

Soon the guests started arriving. Dr. Robert McDonald and his wife, Gwen, drove in bringing with them the two English nurses, Joan Kelly and Laura Hunt. Devi Lal's neighbor, U Ba Kyi, and David O'Connell were there, as were some friends of Khin May and Hari. The house filled with laughter and gaiety. Hari wound up the gramophone in the drawing room and played some of the new records he brought from Rangoon. Devi Lal did not drink alcohol, but offered Scotch whisky and beer to his guests. Daw Mu and Swami brought little plates, napkins and dishes full of snacks and served the guests. Everyone was in a festive mood.

"How are the children, Khin May? How old are they now?" Gwen McDonald inquired.

"They're fine, thank you. Sophia is ten and Neil, twelve."

"I'd like you to meet them," Devi Lal added. "Daw Mu, could you please ask the children to come in?"

Dr. McDonald and U Ba Kyi were discussing British writers. "I say, Robert," U Ba Kyi asked with his eyes twinkling, "tell me about your Mr. Kipling who wrote his poem, 'On the road to Mandalay where flying fishes play'. Tell me — did Mr. Kipling have a drinking problem? Mandalay is 400 miles from the ocean and it's very difficult to see flying fish here."

Everyone started laughing. "Kipling was taking poetic license," Devi Lal explained. "In fact, he must have composed this poem while sailing to Burma. When you come by ship from Calcutta to Rangoon, you do see a lot of flying fish in the Bay of Bengal."

Just then Daw Mu returned, accompanied by Sophia. "Neil is out playing with his friends, *Thakin*. I couldn't find him."

Devi Lal placed his hands on Sophia's shoulders and gently turned her around to face the guests. "I'd like all of you to meet my grand-daughter, Sophia," he said with pride in his voice.

"Hello, Sophia," they all greeted. Sophia nodded shyly.

"I know this young lady very well," Nurse Kelly beamed. "I helped deliver her at Mandalay General Hospital."

"Oh, you're a Mandalay's child, then. Congratulations," said U Ba Kyi.

Khin May turned sharply towards him. "Why are you congratulating her?" she asked.

"It's believed that some Mandalay-born girl-children have special powers," U Ba Kyi answered. "They have the protection of the *nats*."

"Well, to tell you the truth, the day Sophia was born, we all felt that she was indeed a very special child!" Devi Lal added with a smile.

"She certainly has grown into a beautiful, proper little lady," Linda Hunt stated.

"May I go outside now, *Naana*?" Sophia whispered to her grandfather.

"Yes, of course, child, go ahead," he answered, kissing her tenderly on her forehead.

Once Sophia left the room, Khin May turned to U Ba Kyi again. "Tell me more about the *nats* who protect Mandalay-born girls," she asked.

"Well, legend has it that some Mandalay-born female children are blessed by three of the *nats* of our spirit world," U Ba Kyi answered.

"Which are the three *nats*?" Khin May pressed.

Devi Lal looked at his daughter, sensing that something was bothering her.

"I think they are *Aungpinle*, *Min Mahagiri* and the third one I'm not sure but I think it's the *nat* who is considered to be *Bodaw*, the Lord Grandfather of Mandalay," U Ba Kyi answered.

"You don't believe in this mumbo-jumbo, do you, U Ba Kyi?" teased McDonald.

"Well, you are a doctor, Robert. You know better than I. The human mind is extremely powerful. If you believe in something strongly enough, it can happen. The Burmese believe that if a person dies suddenly of unnatural causes — by murder or an accident — and has not performed meritorious deeds like feeding monks and building pagodas — he or she will turn into a ghost. The thirty-seven *nats* worshiped by us are the spirits of kings and queens from ancient times, as well as a few commoners whose end was most gruesome. Many villages and towns adopt a special *nat* as their protector. *Nats* are invoked before we start building a house or upon starting a journey. Festivals are held, called *nat-pwe*, where a woman will dance to loud music. Offerings of green coconuts, bananas, flowers and even whisky, rum and cigarettes are placed in front of the *nat's* statue. The dancer is called *nat-kadaw*, which means 'the wife of the *nat*'. She is like a priestess and often acts as if she were possessed."

The sounds of exploding fire crackers suddenly startled everyone in the room.

"What about you, Devi Lal?" David O'Connell asked, "do you believe in the power of the *nats*?"

"David, I learned a long time ago not to question someone else's faith and beliefs," Devi Lal responded with a smile. "As a child, I remember my mother showing me that when one points a finger at someone else, there are always three pointing back."

"How true that is!" Robert McDonald added.

"Which are some of the better known *nats*?" Linda Hunt asked.

"As I mentioned, there is the *Min Mahagiri*, the Lord of the Great Mountain, called Mount Popa. Then, there is *Aungpinle*, the Lord Master and keeper of the White Elephants. The legend of *Min Mahagiri* is my favourite."

"Oh, would you please tell us the story of this *nat*?" Gwen McDonald pleaded.

Devi Lal glanced at his daughter again. Khin May looked a little pale but was sitting quietly, listening to the conversation.

"Let me warn you," Devi Lal said to his guests, "my friend U Ba Kyi is a superb story teller. He will mesmerize you."

"All right," U Ba Kyi said, making himself comfortable. "I will narrate for you the story of *Min Mahagiri*. It is said that in ancient times a very handsome, tall and powerful man worked as a blacksmith in a village north of Prome. He was so strong that the massive hammer he used in his work shook the earth, producing many earthquakes. This angered the king immensely. The king was married to the blacksmith's younger sister. Yet he ordered his soldiers to tie the blacksmith to a tree and burn him alive. When the soldiers were about to carry out the king's orders, the queen ran to save her brother, but instead was consumed by the flames along with him."

"Oh, how horrible!" Gwen McDonald moaned.

"Well, the brother and sister turned into *nats* and lived in the tree. No one dared walk past it, fearing the anger of the two *nats*. The king, wanting to get rid of them, ordered the tree cut and thrown into the Irrawaddy River. The *nats* cursed the king, who now started losing all of his battles. His soothsayers advised him to seek the forgiveness of the *nats* whose abode he had destroyed and thrown in the river.

"The king at once ordered his soldiers to retrieve the tree from the river. He then engaged master craftsmen and made them carve the trunk of the tree into statues of the two *nats*. A grand temple was built on Mount Popa and the beautiful statues, covered with gold and precious gems, enshrined in it. *Maha*, meaning great, and *giri*, mountain, started the legend of the *Nat Min Mahagiri*, Lord of the Great Mountain."

"How fascinating! Are all of these spirits evil?" Joan Kelly asked.

"Some *nats* are good, Joan. Others are said to get pleasure out of making humans suffer. Victims of the wrath of a *nat* suffer strange accidents. They trip and fall on smooth surfaces. Their homes go up in flames when there is no food being cooked. They get pelted with stones when there's no one near them. Whether you believe in them or not, it is wise not to offend them. Many a brave but foolish person has suffered terribly for offending the Spirits."

"Well, I hope the *nats* protect all of the children should Mandalay be attacked," Joan Kelly sighed. "War does such horrible things."

"Oh, we British will be able to hold off the Japanese. You wait and see," Robert McDonald spoke raising a fist. "Other than these air raid drills and blackouts — which I must say are a bloody nuisance — Mandalay will not be affected. There's no reason for worry."

O'Connell was less optimistic. "Well, I wish you were right, Robert. This is confidential, folks, but the Commissioner has received orders from Rangoon to start making plans to evacuate British families if the Japanese advance threatens Burma. I'm afraid we're all going to have to face some tough times."

"It's amazing how rapidly the Japanese have advanced," U Ba Kyi mused. "They seem like an unstoppable cloud of locusts."

Everyone's mood had turned somber and there was silence in the room. In his mind, Devi Lal agreed with O'Connell: there were indeed going to be some very tough times ahead for all of them. But he did not want the talk of war to dampen this joyous evening. He walked over to the gramophone, wound it, and played another record. The music of Glenn Miller and his orchestra playing *Moonlight Serenade* filled the room. The sound of the children's laughter once again echoed from the front hallway.

"Come, let's go to the dining room," Devi Lal announced, trying to sound cheerful. "Please have some more food." He smiled at his daughter and reached out for her hand. "Come, Khin May, let's go and serve our guests," he said, placing an arm around her shoulders.

Yet, deep in his heart, Devi Lal felt sadness. He wondered if his family and friends would be able to celebrate *Thadingyut* in the beautiful and serene setting of *Shanti Gaeha* ever again.

October 6, 1941
Reflections and Remembrances

*T*he Irrawaddy River bank was a beehive of activity. The Mingun ferry, a double-decker paddle wheel boat, was tied to the shore. Dense black smoke bellowed out of its funnel, and two thick, teak planks connected the lower deck of the boat to the steep, sandy bank. Tea stalls along the shore were crowded with customers. Some sat on wooden stools, while others squatted on the ground drinking hot, sweet tea out of little china cups.

Hawkers sold everything from fresh vegetables and live poultry to items of clothing and snacks. Women carrying large bundles balanced on their heads boarded the ferry, walking cautiously up the narrow planks. Children scampered to find a place along the railing. Everyone seemed in a festive mood. The buzz of conversation was frequently interrupted by bursts of loud laughter.

Khin May had not been able to sleep the previous night. The guests had left by 11 o'clock but she kept mulling over the day's events in her mind. She knew the children were missing their father, but hadn't realized the extent to which Neil was affected. She had also not spoken to anyone about the bizarre vision of the old man.

Khin May went to get a sleeping pill from the bottle she kept under her clothes deep inside a chest of drawers. "Oh, darn it," she moaned. The bottle was empty. I should have remembered: I should have brought some more pills home. She had been using them for some time to help her fall asleep. One of the nurses had seen her taking them out of the large bottle, kept in a locked cabinet in her father's clinic.

"Khin May, be very careful," the nurse had whispered to her. "These can be addicting."

"I only need just a few," she pleaded. "Please don't tell." Now she angrily turned the bottle upside down and thumped it on the palm of her hand. She slumped onto the floor and started sobbing. Towards dawn she crawled back into bed and dozed off.

When she woke up in the morning, her head was throbbing. She took an aspirin and combed her hair. She made up her mind that she was going to cheer up the children, especially Neil. After all, it was the day after the Festival of Lights and, traditionally, on this day the family visited the village of Mingun to deliver gifts to the residents of the home for the elderly which Devi Lal had established. They took a picnic lunch with them and ate it by the river. It was always a fun filled day and she would try to see that it was no different this year.

She came down and helped Daw Mu pack their picnic lunch. They drove to the river shore in two cars. The gift packages and the picnic baskets were loaded onto the ferry by coolies. Sophia and Neil had run ahead of everyone else and quickly climbed to the upper deck.

"Come, Uncle Hari," Sophia called out. "Come and stand with us here at the front."

Khin May helped Daw Mu up the stairs. "Oh, I'm getting too old for all this running around," the old woman complained. "I should have stayed home."

"You're doing great, Daw Mu," Khin May answered. "You know you'd have worried about the children all the time if you hadn't come with us." They sat down on a bench on the upper deck.

"Neil, don't climb the railing," Daw Mu admonished, "and Sophia, dear, stay out of the hot sun. You don't have any *thanaka* paste on your face and the sun will wrinkle your skin."

Daw Mu's face, as well as those of most other women and children, was smeared with a yellowish-white paste. The old woman had prepared the paste by vigorously rubbing a wet piece of the *thanaka* wood onto a stone slab, producing a fragrant, soothing ointment.

"Does the *thanaka* really protect the skin, Daw Mu?" Khin May asked.

The old woman had started lighting a thick white cheroot. "Oh, yes," she answered. "It not only protects it, but also keeps the skin looking young. Why, look at yourself, daughter. I applied *thanaka* on your face and arms each day since you were a baby and you don't look a day older than twenty."

"Thank you, Daw Mu." Khin May laughed. "You certainly know how to flatter a person."

The old woman had closed her eyes. She inhaled deeply and then let out a cloud of bluish-gray smoke. She sat contentedly smoking her cheroot, oblivious to the people and the noise around her.

A group of saffron-robed *pongyis* boarded the ferry. Several Buddhist nuns with shaven heads and wearing pale pink robes also came on board. Shortly after eight o'clock, a blast of the ferry's whistle startled everyone. The last of the passengers ran down from the tea stalls and the two planks were drawn back into the innards of the ferry. Accompanied by the noise of chains rattling and the engine straining, the huge paddle wheel started turning. Gradually the vessel moved away from the shore and powered its way up the river. With the end of the rainy season, the Irrawaddy was flowing full. The ferry inched its way upstream, fighting the strong current.

Numerous boats and rafts of various sizes sailed by the ferry. Massive log islands consisting of hundreds of logs tied together floated downriver to the sawmills of the south. Two or three men tended each of these mammoth islands of timber and guided them downstream. As one such log island floated by, a dog ran the length of it, barking at the ferry, while the men on it waved to the passengers.

Soon the *Sagaing* hills appeared along the west bank of the river and the ferry started edging toward the shore. It docked at the village of Mingun and the passengers hurried off. Devi Lal engaged coolies to carry the gifts to the home for the elderly.

"We'll wait for you by the Mingun Bell, Dad," Khin May told her father.

The children walked on each side of Daw Mu, holding her hands.

Khin May and Hari followed, each carrying a picnic basket.

"Oh look, there's the bell," Hari said. "As often as I've seen it, I'm always awed by its size."

"Neil, come out of there at once!" Khin May yelled at her son who had run under the massive iron bell suspended by steel cables from a huge wooden frame. A painted sign proclaimed it to be the world's largest working bell, and gave its weight as 90 tons.

"Don't worry, Sis," Hari laughed. "That bell's been hanging there for 150 years. It's not gonna fall now!"

"I don't care how long its been hanging," Khin May answered. "I want my son out from underneath it!"

"Neil, get out of there," Sophia pleaded with her brother. "Mama, make him come out at once!"

Neil ducked under the bell and came running out. "Why's everyone so worried about me?" he complained. "I can look after myself."

They walked to the edge of the river and placed the picnic baskets under a large mango tree next to a little white pagoda. The children and Hari took off their shoes and waded in the river up to their knees. They picked up flat stones and tried to skip them on the surface of the water. Close to noon, Devi Lal joined them and they sat under the tree to eat their lunch. It was very peaceful and they chatted pleasantly.

"Well, I should get back to town," Devi Lal said, standing up.

"Can't you stay and return with us, *Naana*?" Sophia pleaded.

"I'd like to, my dear, but there'll be patients waiting at the clinic. You kids enjoy yourselves. I'll see you later at home."

Devi Lal boarded the ferry, pleased that his children and grandchildren were having a good time. He sat down on a bench and looked at the expanse of the river and the shore line gliding by. He liked this river very much and his thoughts went back to almost forty years ago when, as a young man, he had stood on the deck of a ship steaming up this river towards Rangoon. It was the day he had come to Burma for the very first time. So much had happened during these years. Thank you, God, he prayed, thank you for a wonderful life and for all that I have received.

Khin May stayed with Daw Mu in the shade of the tree while Sophia,

Neil and Hari went to look at some of the pagodas nearby. When they returned, it was time to catch the ferry back to Mandalay.

"That was a lot of fun, wasn't it, Mama?" Neil said, climbing to the upper deck of the ferry.

"Yes, it was wonderful, Neil," Khin May answered with a smile, giving her son a hug.

"Oh, don't do that, Mama," the boy complained, freeing himself. "Everyone's watching."

The river shore back at Mandalay was crowded with people, many of whom were shouting slogans. Hari drove the car slowly through the crowds towards the city.

"What's happening, Uncle Hari?" Neil asked.

"I don't know. It seems like some sort of a protest."

After traveling a short distance, they were engulfed by a noisy mob waving Burmese National flags and placards and Hari had to slow the car down to a crawl.

"Oh, it's a protest for independence," Daw Mu said. "I read in the paper that there was going to be a rally today." The noise was now deafening and a man's angry face appeared at their car window.

"Burma is for the Burmese! English, get out of our country!" he screamed, pointing at Neil and Sophia. Several young men began pounding the windows with their fists and other demonstrators started rocking the car.

"What's happening, Mama," Sophia cried out, clinging to her mother.

"Oh my God," Khin May groaned, "they think the children are English."

"You crazy idiots!" Daw Mu screamed at the demonstrators. "We are Burmese. Stop attacking us: we are Burmese!" The car was now being rocked badly.

"Stop! Stop!" another man started yelling and hurriedly pushed the demonstrators away from the car. "Stop! This is the family of Doctor Devi Lal. Let them go." He grabbed and pulled down a boy who had climbed onto the front fender. "This is the family of the good doctor. I know them. Move away, let them go," he kept yelling.

Realizing their mistake, the demonstrators started backing away and parted to allow Hari enough room to slowly drive through.

They had all been shaken badly and Sophia was crying.

"It's all right, honey," Khin May consoled her daughter. "We're safe. Don't worry, sweetheart."

"Those crazy men," Daw Mu said angrily, "they almost killed us!"

"Thank God that man recognized us," Khin May sighed, her voice unsteady. She hugged her daughter closer to her. "Hush, baby, we'll be home soon." She felt so sorry for her children. They had faced discrimination from some English because they were half-Asian, and now these Burmese demonstrators were ready to harm them because they were part British.

Her thoughts were interrupted by sounds of gunfire coming from the direction of the demonstrations.

"Oh, God," Daw Mu moaned. "The police must be shooting at the demonstrators."

Confrontations between Burmese patriots and the British authorities had been going on for some time. Hundreds of young Burmans had been killed over the years, shot by the police and soldiers determined to crush uprisings. Now the British were preoccupied with the war and the Burmese leaders were demanding instant freedom for their nation. Revolutionaries in large numbers had fled to Thailand and were rumoured to have amassed a small army preparing to accompany the Japanese troops attacking Burma. Student dissidents throughout the country were becoming quite bold. Only two days earlier, shots had been exchanged between a group of college students and British soldiers on the outskirts of Mandalay.

As soon as they arrived at home, Neil excitedly told his grandfather all about the demonstration.

"Thank God you're all safe. It must have been a terrifying experience."

"We heard shots, *Naana*," Sophia added, "do you think anyone was killed?"

"Let's hope not, Sophia. The police sometimes try to disperse demonstrators by firing over their heads. Maybe that's what they did today."

"The British should get out of Burma," Neil spoke angrily. "This is not their country. When I grow up, I'm going to join the students and fight for independence!"

"Well, let's hope the country can be freed by peaceful means," Devi Lal said. "Violence is often not the right solution."

"Today was a lot of fun, Uncle Hari," Neil said, his face flushed with excitement. "What should we do tomorrow?"

"Well, whatever you and Sophia want," Hari answered. "I don't have any plans."

"I know what," Sophia spoke up, "let's go to Maymyo."

"Yes, that's a terrific idea," Neil added. "Uncle Hari, will you take us to Maymyo?"

"Sure, if that's what you want."

"That's great," Sophia gushed. "You'll come with us, *Naana*, won't you?"

Devi Lal hesitated. The quaint town up in the hills had too many memories for him. His beloved Mah Lay had been born there, and they were married there. He used to enjoy driving up to Maymyo, but since the death of his wife, he had stayed away.

"No, child, I have my work to attend to," he said. "Take your mother with you and have a nice time."

Later that evening they all gathered in the drawing room.

"Let's play carrom," Neil suggested, bringing out a card table and laying the carrom board on top of it.

"Uncle Hari and I will be partners," Sophia declared, "and, Neil, you are not to cheat."

"I don't cheat," Neil complained. "Come, Mama, you and I will win."

They had barely started playing when they were startled by a loud shrill whistle and then some shouting from the direction of the front gate.

"What's that?" Hari asked, standing up.

"Oh dear God; the blackout," Khin May exclaimed. "We forgot the curtains. Neil, hurry, draw them together."

They could now hear the loud voice of the warden. "Doctor, your lights are showing. Draw your curtains!"

"That's Mr. Donahue," Sophia said, laughing.

"Who's Mr. Donahue?" Hari inquired.

"Oh, he's a teacher at my school," Neil answered, coming back to the carrom board. "He's an ARP warden for our area here in Sein Pun. He takes his work as a warden much too seriously. You should see him in his khaki uniform and pith helmet standing on his skinny legs at the road crossing. He is forever blowing his whistle at cars and stops them to see if their headlights are properly covered with black paint."

"He's very skinny, Uncle Hari," Sophia added. "His upper teeth stick out and he has small, sad red eyes. He looks just like a bunny rabbit." Neil laughed loudly.

"That's not a very nice thing to say, Sophia," Khin May admonished. "We were lucky," she added, "Mr. Donahue spared us tonight. He's been known to deliver long lectures on the dangers of not observing blackouts to anyone caught violating the rules."

They played several games of carrom while Devi Lal sat in a lounge chair reading a newspaper. Sweet Pea lay curled at his feet and Daw Mu sat in one corner of the room with her eyes closed, contentedly puffing on her cheroot.

The next morning Hari came down early to have a cup of tea. Devi Lal was already up. "Would you like to join me for a walk?" he asked his son.

"Sure, Dad," Hari agreed. "We won't be leaving for Maymyo until 8 o'clock."

Devi Lal was pleased that his son had chosen to become a physician. Whenever Hari came home, his father quizzed him about the latest drugs and diagnostic procedures that were being used by the doctors in Rangoon. Hari often wondered what medical education must have been like when his father was a student. Hari, like most young doctors, felt he was well trained and knew all there was about medicine.

Devi Lal's medical education, though sound for when he was a student towards the turn of the century, was quite different from that received by Hari. But over the years Devi Lal had gained great skill as a physician by keeping up with medical literature and by his vast experience in treating an incredible variety of ailments. Yet he was eager to learn more. He also knew that often young doctors learned from their mistakes and, in his son's case, he hoped the mistakes Hari made would not be grave.

Later, Hari drove Sophia, Neil and Khin May to Maymyo. Daw Mu turned down their invitation to accompany them, citing a headache as an excuse. She hated to admit that the steep climb, especially around the sharp hairpin bends in the road, made her deathly sick.

Devi Lal went to his clinic soon after the children left. He returned home a little after one o'clock in the afternoon, tired and depressed. The number of patients who came to see him today was unusually large, something that happened after most holidays. And then he had also been unable to save the life of an infant suffering from severe malnutrition. The four month old little girl had been rushed into his clinic by her distraught parents. The baby was severely emaciated and was having convulsions. She was suffering from an advanced case of beriberi. The disease, a result of malnutrition, was killing so many infants in Burma. Devi Lal gave her injections of Vitamin B1, but it was much too late. In spite of his desperate efforts to save her, the infant died in his arms.

After lunch, he sat down in the drawing room to read the newspaper but could not concentrate. He was exhausted, and for the first time in his life he felt as if his age was catching up with him.

"May I speak with you, Doctor *Sahib*?" Sher Khan asked from the doorway.

"Yes, of course, Sher Khan, come in," Devi Lal replied, putting the newspaper aside.

"Dr. *Sahib*, yesterday when I was waiting at the river shore, a driver of one of the English *sahibs* talked to me. He said that the British Government was making plans to take their women and children out of Burma. Don't you think we should do the same with daughter Khin May and the children?"

"Yes, Sher Khan, I too have been worrying about their safety for the past several months," Devi Lal replied, taking off his reading glasses. "I'm debating whether they should go to the Sagaing Hills or north to

Myitkyina. I'm also very concerned about Hari and Tim. I'd like to... "

The noise of the front door suddenly opening made him stop in mid-sentence. They heard hurried footsteps and a man followed by a woman rushed into the drawing room. Devi Lal was aghast to see the revolvers in the hands of the intruders.

"*Saya wun ji*," the young man spoke respectfully but urgently, "we want you to come with us right now."

Sher Khan had stood, frozen. Now he took a quick step forward. The man pointed his gun straight at Sher Khan.

"Tell your servant not to try anything stupid," he ordered tersely. "We aren't criminals, but we'll shoot him if he interferes with our mission."

"If you're not *dacoits*, who are you?" Devi Lal asked angrily. "How dare you break into my house?"

The girl spoke for the first time. "Doctor, we are students from the Agriculture College in town," she said softly. "Two of our colleagues were injured yesterday near Sagaing in a gun battle against British soldiers. They are in a monastery by the river and need medical attention urgently. We can't bring them to the city as the authorities are searching for us. If they catch us, we'll all be shot."

Devi Lal looked at the girl's face: she seemed so young. Did he know her? She looked familiar. Of course, it came to him, he had treated her once. She was the daughter of the minister of the Baptist church near Amrapura. Her companion he did not recognize, yet he looked like a very nice young man and had spoken courteously.

"Violence is not the answer," Devi Lal said to them. "There are peaceful means of achieving freedom."

"The only way we can get the British to leave is to fight them, Doctor," the man answered.

"But you people are so young. You should be completing your education. You are placing yourselves in such grave danger."

"We'd rather die than remain slaves to foreigners," the girl said softly.

Devi Lal's palms were perspiring and his heart pounding. "Gunshot wounds are very dangerous," he said. "Your colleagues need to be in a hospital."

"No! We can't do that," the man answered firmly. "You'll be able to help them. We trust you. The monks told us about you."

Devi Lal's thoughts went to his own father who, many years ago, had died of gunshot wounds received fighting British soldiers in India. Although Devi Lal was patriotic, he abhorred violence. And these were decent kids from good homes and families.

"You're jeopardizing your whole future," he told them. "You should surrender to the authorities. You'll receive fair trials and will also save the lives of your friends."

"No, it's too late, doctor," the girl said firmly. "We've already gone underground. We don't trust the British. Please help us. You've got to come with us."

Devi Lal stood up. He could not let these kids down. "I'll see what I can do," he said. The man and the girl sighed with relief.

"Doctor, we'll take your car. I'll drive you to the monastery," the man said, giving his gun to the girl who placed it in the shan bag she carried.

Devi Lal turned to Sher Khan. "These are freedom fighters, Sher Khan," he said. "They've placed their lives in jeopardy for the country. They need my help and I'm going with them. Stay at home and wait for my return. I don't want *anyone* to know about this. Put my medical bag in the car."

"Doctor *Sahib*, I should accompany you," Sher Khan persisted.

"No, no. You must come alone, Doctor," the girl said. "Please trust us."

The young man got behind the wheel of the car. He took his revolver from the girl and placed it under his seat. Devi Lal and the girl sat in the back. The car went out of the compound and turned left onto 35th Road, traveling toward the river.

"You recognized me back there, didn't you, Doctor?" the girl asked. "You cared for me when I had broken my leg several years ago."

"Yes, I remember. How is it now?"

"It's fine," she said, smiling.

"What'll you and your companions do?" he asked.

"We plan to go down river to Rangoon and help the Burmese National Army when they come to liberate us."

The young man seemed nervous and kept looking back at the road through the rear view mirror. They were approaching the end of 35th Road near the river.

"Oh, no!" the man groaned. "There's a road block ahead."

"Can we turn back?" the girl asked, nervously. Police constables were visible, stopping cars and horse carriages.

"No, it's too late. They've seen us."

"Let me do the talking," Devi Lal said quietly. "Don't try anything rash."

The man slowed the car and brought it to a stop, his right hand reaching for the revolver under his seat. A police constable walked up to the car and looked inside. Seeing Devi Lal, he smiled.

"*Saya wun ji*. How are you? You don't know me, but you saved the life of one of my children."

Devi Lal smiled back. "I'm fine, thank you. I'm on my way to one of the monasteries along the river to examine an elderly *pongyi* who has been taken ill." Pointing at the girl next to him, he said, "This is my nurse."

The police constable bowed. "Okay, *Saya wun ji*, please proceed."

Tightening his grip on the steering wheel to prevent his hands from trembling, the young man slowly drove forward. He then turned the car left onto a narrow path along the river.

The girl sighed deeply. "Thank you so much, Doctor!" she said, placing her hand on Devi Lal's arm. "Thank you for saving us."

"You needn't thank me," he answered. "It's my duty to help anyone injured or sick. Besides, a long time ago someone very near and dear to me was also killed by British soldiers."

At the monastery, he examined the two freedom fighters and was relieved that their injuries were not life-threatening. He removed a bullet from the shoulder of one of the students. The other had flesh wounds in his thigh and the side of his chest. Devi Lal cleaned and dressed their wounds, and gave the remaining medications and bandages to the girl. Before leaving, he took all the money that he had on him and gave it to the students.

"Here, you can use this. Please take it," he said. He drove back himself, coming out of a small lane on the side of the monastery. He approached 35th Road avoiding the crossing where earlier they had been stopped by the police.

Daw Mu and Sher Khan were waiting at the front gate.

"Are you all right, *Thakin?*" Daw Mu asked urgently as soon as Devi Lal stopped the car. "Did those miscreants harm you in any way?"

"Yes, I'm fine. Just a little tired," he said, getting out. "Don't worry about me. But I want both of you to promise that you will not speak of this to *anyone*. These are brave young men and women, fighting to free the country. We must not put their lives in any additional peril." He looked at each of them. "We'll act as if nothing untoward happened. Sher Khan, I'll rest for an hour, and then I'd like you to drive me to the clinic. I don't want the patients to have to wait."

All through the afternoon he kept thinking about the students, wondering what was going to happen to them. The death of the infant also weighed heavily on his mind. What else could he have done to save the child? Later that evening, when he got back home, he was pleased that the children had returned from Maymyo. Sophia showed her grandfather the pine cones she had brought back.

"When we were driving up, *Naana*, we saw a big python dangling from a tree," Neil recounted excitedly and then continued, "*Naana*, tell us about the gunmen who came and took you. Did you have to pull any bullets out of the wounded?"

Devi Lal looked surprised. "You weren't supposed to have been told about it," he said, turning accusingly at Daw Mu just as the old woman slipped out of the room, averting her face.

Schools were to open the next day and Hari was going back to Rangoon. Khin May went up to her room and sat down at her desk to write a letter to Tim. She told him that she was coming to be with him during Christmas. "*We must work things out, my love,*" she wrote, "*so that the children and I can be with you all the time. My dearest husband, I love you deeply.*" She sealed and addressed the envelope, then sat looking at their wedding photograph in a silver frame on the desk. She was so young then, and so much in love.

She had finished her high school examinations in Mandalay and had enrolled in Rangoon University. She lived in the girls' hostel on the university grounds and at night, after dinner, she and her friends walked on the hostel lawn, enjoying the cool breeze. One night, they heard a soft, sweet voice singing in English. Khin May strained to catch the words and, although she did not recognize the song, she sensed the sadness of the ballad. The following night, the girls again heard the man singing and, this time, Khin May knew the song, "Danny Boy," which she had heard many times before. What a sweet voice, she thought. From the watchman of the hostel, the girls found out that British army barracks were located behind the hostel wall.

One Sunday afternoon, Khin May and her friends had gone to the Shwedagon Pagoda. As they approached the stairway leading up to the pagoda, the girls noticed three young European men dressed in civilian clothes standing at the foot of the steps.

"Look at those rude Britishers," one of the girls complained. "They are staring at us. Khin May, one of them seems to have his eyes glued to you."

"Just ignore them," Khin May answered. "They'll go away."

The girls took off their slippers and left them with an attendant. As Khin May started up the steps, she noticed that one of the foreigners was following her. She felt annoyed, especially when she saw that he had not removed his shoes.

"Excuse me," she said in a cold, angry voice. "This is a holy shrine and even though you are English, you're expected to take off your shoes."

Earlier, the attendant at the foot of the steps had indicated to the Britisher that he should remove his shoes. But the young man had glared at the attendant and kept walking. Now he bowed to the young woman.

"I'm truly sorry. I meant no offense," he said with a smile. "And besides, I'm *not* English."

Khin May looked at him disinterestedly. "Oh, yes? What are you?"

"Actually, I'm Irish."

"Does that make a difference?"

"*I* think it does. Like you, we Irish were ruled by the English for many centuries. It's only recently that we've been able to gain independence for a portion of our country."

"Oh, I see," she answered, in a voice void of any warmth.

The young man smiled. "I'm new to your country," he said, politely. "Will you be so kind as to tell me a little about this pagoda?"

Khin May looked straight ahead and kept climbing. "I do not speak to strangers," she answered.

The young man bowed again. "All right, then," he said. "My name is Timothy Patrick O'Shea. I'm 21 years old and I was born in the small town of Ventry in Ireland. I'm a poor unfortunate Irish soldier in the British Army, with no friends other than those two clowns. And oh — my friends call me Tim. There — now you know all there is to know about me and I'm not a stranger anymore."

Khin May looked at him. "Oh, all right," she smiled shyly. "I'll tell you what I know about the Shwedagon Pagoda."

At first she talked hesitatingly, but gradually opened up a little, encouraged by the young man's soft voice and courteous manner.

Before leaving the pagoda grounds, Tim found out that Khin May was in the first year of college at Rangoon University, that she had lost her mother two years earlier, and that her father and younger brother lived in Mandalay. He also found out she was staying in the girls' hostel behind the army barracks.

"May I come and call upon you at your hostel?" Tim inquired.

"I don't know," she answered. "I don't think it would be proper."

A few days went by and it was the time of the *Thingyan* festival when the Burmese herald the New Year by throwing water on each other. No one is spared from being deluged as people "wash" the old year away. There is music, dancing and food for three full days — and lots and lots of water.

Tables laden with soft drinks and large drums filled with water had been placed outside the girls' hostel. All day, groups of young men came by, playing musical instruments. The girls sang and danced and then they all threw water on each other. Refreshments were served and the young men walked to the next block where another group of girls would welcome them.

"Look, Khin May!" one of her friends pointed excitedly. "There's that British soldier who spoke to you at the Shwedagon Pagoda."

Khin May recognized Tim and tried to look away. But Tim, who was soaking wet, walked right up to her.

"Well, now may I come and see you sometime?" he said, smiling impishly, pointing at his wet clothes. "Has my 'Britishness' been washed away and am I sufficiently cleansed?"

Khin May looked up at him. "No, not quite," she answered seriously. Then, taking a bowl of water, she emptied it over his head. "There, now you are fully cleansed," she said, laughing.

Their courtship was gentle and sweet. Khin May was delighted to find out that this shy Irishman was the one whose melancholy ballads she had loved hearing each evening. "Tell me about yourself," she asked. "I want to know all about you."

Timothy Patrick O'Shea was born in 1906 on a small farm near Ventry in County Kerry, Ireland. His father was a hardy fisherman, sailing out of Dingle Bay, barely able to provide for his small family. Tim's mother grew potatoes and a few other vegetables on their small farm, using most of the crop to feed the family. When Tim was three, his father's fishing boat sank in the icy Atlantic. Like those of many other fishermen lost at sea, his body was never recovered.

Two years later, Tim's mother died of a lung ailment. His father's older sister, Aunt Colleen, took him into her home and raised him. Tim went to school in Ventry, then worked until supper time on a neighbor's farm, for which he received a few pennies and some potatoes.

Aunt Colleen was fond of Tim and raised him lovingly. She made sure he studied his schoolbooks and took him to church each Sunday morning. On Sunday afternoons during the summer months, she would let him go down with his friends to the beach at Ventry, but always cautioned him to stay in the shallow waters. Occasionally, Tim and his friends played atop a high cliff among the purple heather and yellow gorse, looking down upon lush green valleys and the shimmering waters of Dingle Bay.

Tim left school at age 16 and found a job in Tralee, washing dishes in a hotel. His wages were barely enough to pay for his room and board in a nearby rooming house. In 1927, at the age of 21, he and two of his friends from the Dingle Peninsula enlisted in the British Army. After six weeks of intensive training southeast of London, they were shipped out to Burma.

The sea voyage was long and tedious, and it was late March by the time they arrived in Rangoon. The monsoons had not begun and the days were swelteringly hot and humid. Each evening after dinner, Tim and his friends strolled on the lawn behind the barracks, next to the Rangoon University student hostels. And then he had met Khin May.

He was surprised that he had fallen so deeply in love with an Asian girl. When he arrived in Rangoon he thought he'd like to have a fling or two with a few of these native beauties, but had never dreamt of marrying one.

Khin May wrote to her father about Tim and asked if he could come to visit her in Mandalay during the summer holidays. Devi Lal was taken aback. He had known that one day his beautiful young daughter was going to meet a handsome young man and would get married. But Khin May's letter caught him by surprise. To him, the happiness of his children was paramount, but he wasn't sure if marrying a young Irish soldier was in the best interest of his daughter.

In the evening, after dinner, he asked Daw Mu to fetch Sher Khan. "I'd like to talk to you both about a family matter," he said.

"Is everything all right, Doctor *Sahib*?" Sher Khan inquired.

"Well, Sher Khan, I received a letter from Khin May today," Devi Lal answered. "She's met an Irish soldier that she likes. They wish to get married."

"An Irish soldier?" muttered an astounded Sher Khan. "Why? Why does daughter Khin May want to marry a foreigner?"

Daw Mu pointed a finger at Sher Khan, "For once I agree with this man. Why does Khin May want to marry a foreigner — and a mere soldier at that — when there are so many nice, handsome Indian and Burmese young men from wealthy homes?"

"Well, it seems they are very much in love," Devi Lal answered, holding up Khin May's letter. "Besides, if you think about it, I married someone of a different nationality. Khin May's happiness is what matters and that's what I'd like to be assured of."

Daw Mu was adamant. "If you ask my opinion, *Thakin*, I think this will be a mistake. A lot of these foreign soldiers are known for marrying pretty, young native girls. After having a few children, they suddenly decide they need to go back to their own country, and never return. No, I don't think we should expose Khin May to such a fate."

Devi Lal sighed. "Well, Daw Mu, you may be right. Let's think about it some more. We'll talk again tomorrow."

Devi Lal couldn't make up his mind and, in the end, decided that Khin May should at least be allowed to invite the young man to Mandalay.

"Then, if she's absolutely certain this is the man she wants to marry," he told Daw Mu and Sher Khan, "we'll have to agree to let her do so."

Tim came to Mandalay that summer and everyone took a liking to him. Even Daw Mu reluctantly admitted that, "For a foreigner, he's quite a nice young man."

Within a year, Tim and Khin May were married. He was 22 and she, 19, and they were blissfully happy. Tim was able to get himself transferred to Mandalay. One year later, their son was born and they named him Neil Benjamin O'Shea. Khin May was ecstatic but Tim's reaction seemed somewhat restrained.

"Aren't you happy with a son, darling?" she asked.

"Oh, I am. I'm just concerned about the responsibilities of raising children." He did not tell his wife of the relief he felt to see that his son did not look too Asian.

Two years after Neil, Khin May gave birth to a beautiful girl. Tears filled Devi Lal's eyes as he held his little granddaughter in his arms. He had felt joy when his children and grandson were born. But now, holding his little granddaughter seemed to be the ultimate, pure bliss that he had ever experienced. I must be getting old, he mused. Mah Lay would have loved her grandchildren so very much.

Tim and Khin May named their daughter Sophia Kavita O'Shea.

"I often wondered why some adults acted so strangely when they became grandparents," Devi Lal told his friend, U Ba Kyi, "but now I know why."

"Isn't that the truth!" U Ba Kyi laughed. "It's almost as if God created grandchildren to help energize us old people."

"I know what you mean," Devi Lal answered. "I know exactly what you mean."

He would spend long pleasurable periods with his granddaughter lying in his lap. She would gaze at his face with her deep penetrating eyes and he felt that she could see through his very soul.

"Where did I know you before, child?" he'd ask. "In which of my previous existences were you a kin of mine?"

Shortly after Sophia was born, Devi Lal had written a few verses on a piece of paper. He had not shown it to anyone, but had put it away in his desk drawer. Years later, Khin May had found it when she was tidying her father's desk. She had wept as she sat at the desk reading it. He had titled it *"Heaven."* It read:

I know that you came from heaven
  As heaven came to earth with you
I knew what little angels looked like
  From the moment I set eyes on you
I know my life is not the same
  From when I first saw you smile
I knew what paradise felt like
  From the time that I first held you
I know what heaven must be like
  As heaven came to earth with you
If I have wished a thing before
  This is the wish I pray comes true
That you be ever happy and healthy
  With God's grace shining on you
I know one day I'll have to go
  But it surely won't be to heaven
As I know you came from heaven
  And heaven came to earth with you

Khin May gave the sheet of paper to her daughter.

"Oh, it's beautiful, Mama," Sophia had responded tearfully. She kept the poem in her desk drawer as her most treasured possession and took it out periodically to read it.

The Festival of Lights holidays ended and Hari returned to Rangoon. He went to see Tim in the Army barracks and gave him Khin May's letter. Neil and Sophia's schools reopened and the country gradually returned to its preoccupation with the war. Air raid drills and nightly blackouts again became a part of the daily routine in Burma.

Tim wrote and told his wife how pleased he was that she was going to spend Christmas with him. Sophia and Neil also received letters from their father.

"As much as I want to see you and I'm sure you want to see me," he wrote, *"it's best that you not come at this time. Things are a bit hectic here and you'll not be able to enjoy yourself. I love you very much. Hopefully, we'll all be together again soon."*

Sophia wrote to her father at least once a month. She kept a photograph of Tim in his army uniform on her dresser, next to a small silver Celtic cross that he had given her. She loved to hear him sing, which he often did for her whenever he was home.

When they were growing up, Neil and Sophia frequently asked their father questions about his childhood.

"There wasn't anything very exciting about it," he would say. "But one day you'll see Ireland for yourself and you will fall in love with it."

"Tell us about it, Daddy," Sophia would insist.

"Well, there are many beautiful lakes with clear blue waters, and colourful mountains, covered with purple heather. The countryside is bathed with red and orange fuchsia, deep yellow gorse and more shades of green than you can count on both hands."

"Aren't there a lot of castles?" Neil asked.

"Ah, yes, there are. The most famous is the Blarney Castle, where people go to kiss the Blarney stone."

"What happens when you kiss the Blarney stone, Daddy?" Sophia wanted to know.

"It's believed that when you kiss the stone, it gives you the gift of sweet-talking and the art of flattery. Sometimes you'll hear people say that someone is full of blarney."

"You mean like Neil?" Sophia asked, impishly.

Tim laughed. "Aye, Neil does have quite a bit of Irish in him."

"One of my teachers is a priest from Ireland," Neil told his father. "He told us that the English had forcibly ruled Ireland for many years and that the Irish had fought and won their freedom. He mentioned the names of their heroes, Theobold Tone and Robert Emmet, who gave their lives for their country. Did you fight the English, Daddy?"

"No, I was only a lad, just fourteen by the time Ireland gained its freedom in 1921," Tim answered. "Besides, when I was growing up, my hero was Daniel O'Connell who did more for the country with his pen and with reasoning than the others with their guns."

Sophia was interested in Irish legend and never tired of listening to stories about leprechauns. "Sing for me, please, Daddy," she often asked. Tim always obliged his little daughter and sang to her, holding her in his arms.

The children loved their father very much, though Neil at times was overcome with doubts and anger. One winter, when he was nine years old, the family was having dinner and Sophia was telling everyone about the Christmas decorations they had placed in their classroom.

"By the way, I just remembered," Tim said. "There'll be a Christmas party for the families of the soldiers next Saturday."

"Can we go, Daddy?" Sophia asked, eagerly.

"Are we invited, Tim?" Khin May asked before Tim could answer.

"Yes. Families of all the soldiers are invited. It'll be in the Officers Club and there'll be a play staged for the children."

"Will there be lots of food?" Neil wanted to know.

Tim smiled. "Yes, you can be sure of that."

"The Officers Club?" Khin May sounded uncertain, "are you sure it will be all right?"

"Yes. Don't worry. The children will have a great time!" Tim replied.

Sophia and Neil eagerly awaited the party all week. Khin May bought Neil a new pair of shoes and Sophia some ribbons to go with her best dress. The day of the party, everyone got dressed carefully. Daw Mu kept saying how handsome the four of them looked together as a family.

"Come on, Daddy, let's go," Sophia called. "We don't want to be late!"

The Officers Club was decorated with balloons and streamers and an Army band was playing Christmas music. Many families were arriving and lined up in front of a table at the entrance. Tim, Khin May and the children joined the line. When they got to the front, the officer at the table looked at Khin May and beckoned Tim aside. They talked quietly, but Khin May could see that Tim's face was turning red.

He came back to them and took the children by their hands. "Come, we must leave," he said softly.

Sophia held back. "But Daddy, I want to see the play."

Khin May took Sophia's other hand. "No, darling. We'll try and see another play later, some place else. Come. We have to go with Daddy."

No one spoke in the car on the way home. Nearing the market, Tim asked, "Children, would you like some ice cream?"

Before Sophia could answer, Neil angrily yelled, "No. I want to go home right now!" When they reached home, Neil, his eyes brimming with tears, told his mother, "I don't ever want anything to do with the English!"

Devi Lal also felt troubled by this incident, not only because his grandchildren had been turned away for being half Asian, but because of the impression this incident had left on Neil. After a few days, he found an opportunity to be alone with his grandson as they walked along the driveway of *Shanti Gaeha*.

"I'm sorry, my child, that you felt upset after coming back from Mandalay Fort the other day," he said.

Neil visibly tensed before responding. "*Naana*, I hate the English!"

"It's all right to be angry when we see a wrong being done," Devi Lal said gently. "But hating does not harm them. It only hurts us."

Neil looked puzzled. "How's that, *Naana*?" he asked.

"Well, when we hate someone, they don't know about it and it doesn't affect them. However, our minds are so busy with hatred that we forget who we are and can't concentrate on anything else."

Neil remained silent.

"Remember how we talked about our minds being really temples where God resides? We should, therefore, not let hatred for anyone come into our minds."

Without fully comprehending what his grandfather was trying to tell him, Neil still calmed down. "All right, *Naana*, I won't hate the English. But when I grow up, I want to be a freedom fighter like my great grandfather."

Devi Lal smiled. This mixture of Irish and Asian blood has made his grandson a fighter.

The news of the Japanese air attack on the American fleet in Pearl Harbor on 7 December, 1941, shocked the world. On the same day, Japanese armies invaded Thailand and Malaya. Three days later, the British Royal Navy suffered a major defeat when the battleships Prince of Wales and Repulse were attacked and sunk by Japanese war planes. Thousands of lives were lost.

Vast shipments of war supplies were still being poured into Rangoon by the Americans and British. From there, they were transported to China. Fearing that the Japanese might cut off this supply route, Chiang Kai Shek sent large numbers of troops to help defend Burma. The American Army General Joseph Stillwell, nicknamed "Vinegar Joe," was placed in command of the Chinese troops. A group of American pilots formed the American Volunteer Group (AVG) and came to Burma. Commanded by the flying ace Colonel Claire Chennault, the AVG was sent to Rangoon to help defend the city.

When Khin May told her father that she was planning to go to Rangoon for Christmas, he tried to dissuade her, but she was adamant. "I'll be all right, Dad. I need to spend some time with Tim. I'll only be gone four days and nothing is going to happen."

"All right," he relented. "But remember, only if you promise to take the children and go north to Myitkyina when you return."

"Yes, Dad, I'll do that, I promise."

On the morning of 22nd December, Khin May left for Rangoon by train. She was worried about the children and the war but she tried to raise her spirits. She was going to be with her husband and, no matter what else happened, things were going to work out.

44th Street, Rangoon

$\mathcal{T}$im was pacing up and down the Rangoon station platform, anxiously awaiting the train from Mandalay. The last time he had been with his wife was in August and he was so looking forward to seeing her. He had felt very lonely in Rangoon. Earlier, an attractive Anglo-Burmese girl who worked at the Canteen had almost thrown herself into his arms. They had gone out a couple of times but he suffered from guilt, especially when he received Sophia's letter. Now he wanted to be a good husband and, as much as he found the responsibilities of parenthood diffficult, he was also going to try to be a good father.

Every few minutes he looked at his wristwatch. When the train arrived and Khin May stepped off, they held hands briefly. He would have liked to hug and kiss her but they refrained from doing so in deference to Asian custom, which frowns upon public display of affection between men and women.

"How are you, darling?" he whispered.

"I'm well, and so very happy to see you, my dearest."

Since Tim was living in his army barracks, they were to stay with Hari during Khin May's visit to Rangoon. Sitting close to her husband in the taxi, she clung to his arm. "The children asked that I give you their love."

Tim's face softened, "How are they?"

"They miss you very much. Sophia speaks of you often, but Neil doesn't talk much. He's angry and blames the Japanese for keeping you from coming home." Taking a folded paper from her handbag, Khin May gave it to him. "Sophia wrote this letter to you."

Tim read it. "She's an angel!" he said. "Is Neil hard to manage? I wish I could help you with him."

"He's all right. He's just confused. You must feel lonely all by yourself here in Rangoon," she said, pressing her face against his shoulder.

"Yes, it is lonely," he said, pushing aside the guilt that momentarily entered his mind.

"I wish you could leave the army and come to Mandalay."

"I can't do that now, Khin May. Besides, what the hell would I do? How would I support you and the children?"

"We can both work, sweetheart. We can manage."

"I want us to be together, too, darling. Let's wait and see what happens with this damn war," he said, looking out of the taxi window.

Outwardly, Rangoon appeared calm, but there was considerable tension and concern being felt by the people. Japanese planes had recently bombed the southern town of Tavoy and followed it two days later with a damaging bombing attack on Victoria Point at the very southern tip of Burma. Heavy civilian casualties resulted from both raids.

The day of the Victoria Point bombing, sirens went off in Rangoon also, panicking the population. The city's air defenses were mobilized and Royal Air Force fighter planes and the AVG flying Tigers took to the air. No Japanese planes appeared, however, and the city returned to its routine of trying to cope with daily life amidst air raid drills and nightly blackouts. Japanese propaganda, meanwhile, was trying to win the Asian populations over. Slogans such as "Asia for Asians" and "Together let us drive the imperialists out of Asia" were frequently heard in broadcasts by the Japanese from their bases in Thailand.

The taxi entered 44th Street where Hari lived. The street was a conglomeration of people of different nationalities and faiths. Several Burmese families lived on it along with Indians, Chinese, Anglo-Indians, Anglo-Burmans, Italians, Swiss and Armenians. Until very recently, even two Japanese families were among the inhabitants of the street. They had all lived in harmony, getting along well with each other.

Like so many other residential streets of Rangoon, 44th Street was lined on both sides with four-story buildings of almost identical design. A steep stairway led to the upper floors, and each floor consisted of a narrow, long flat. A room at the front served as a combined drawing and dining room, with one or two bedrooms located in the middle. The kitchen and a bathroom were towards the rear. The ground-floor flats opened directly onto the street, but the ones on the upper floors had small, open balconies in the front. As the street was not very wide, people on the balconies across from each other were able to converse easily. Hari liked living on 44th Street.

During the morning, the street was bustling with children leaving for school and adults going to offices or their places of business. During the day, a steady stream of hawkers came through, selling milk, vegetables, clothing, pots and pans and a variety of other wares.

In the evening, the street took on a festive atmosphere. Children played games. Boys kicked footballs and girls drew lines on the pavement with chalk and played hopscotch. The air was filled with the aroma of food cooking and music could be heard coming from open doors. Men and women sat on the steps or in chairs in front of their buildings while others walked around visiting their neighbors. People on the balconies called out to others. Sounds of laughter were everywhere.

Mr. D'Souza, a member of the dance band at the Strand Hotel, often practiced his clarinet on the balcony of his third-floor flat. Mr. Minus, the owner of the bakery near Sule Pagoda, frequently brought tasty little pastries and gave them to the children playing on the street. Hari lived in a third floor, two-bedroom flat. As a student, he had stayed in Prome Hall, one of several hostels on the Rangoon University grounds. When he was appointed a house surgeon, he rented and moved to this comfortable flat.

U Ba Tu, an elderly Burmese gentleman, occupied the ground-floor flat in the same building. He always wore formal Burmese clothes and carried a fancy walking stick. Most of the time he strolled up and down the street talking to people. U Ba Tu had an opinion about all matters and gave advice to young and old, whether they asked for it or not. Everyone got along well with this eccentric old gentleman. Children liked him because he periodically gave them candy and adults found his conversation amusing. Whenever the discussion came around to the war, U Ba Tu would tell his fellow inhabitants of 44th Street not to worry.

"The Japanese, like myself, are Buddhists. They will not harm us. Do not worry. Besides," he contended, "they must know that I am an important person and live on this street. They will not bother us."

Tim directed the driver to stop in front of Hari's building. Just then, U Ba Tu happened to come out of his flat.

"Ah, Corporal O'Shea! Good evening to you," he said, cheerfully. "I see you have brought your charming wife from Mandalay. Please present her to me."

Tim had met U Ba Tu several times before. He said, politely, "U Ba Tu, may I present to you my wife, Khin May."

The old man appeared pleased. Peering at Khin May through his gold-rimmed glasses, he said, "Ah, yes, you are indeed very beautiful; just like the ladies in the court of King Thibaw, where, as you may not know, I was a very important person. I served as an advisor to the king himself and lived in the palace. I have a large house in the country, but live on this street only to help the people when they need my advice. You know, one day they will build a statue in my honour. Actually, my dear child, you are even prettier than the ladies of the court. I am pleased to meet you. But I have to go to attend to a very urgent matter at this time. Later I will tell you about the important advice I used to give to King Thibaw in the Mandalay Palace."

Shortly after six o'clock, Hari arrived. He greeted his sister and brother-in-law warmly.

"You must be tired from your journey, Sis. I can bring some food home for dinner," he offered.

"No, I'm fine — and so glad to be here! Let's go out to eat," Khin May suggested.

"Good, let's do that," Hari answered. "I'd like to take you both to one of the Indian restaurants on Moghul Street. We can have some *samosas* and *biryani*."

"Would you like to have dinner there, Tim?" Khin May asked.

"Yes, that sounds great," Tim answered. "I haven't had Indian food since being home in Mandalay. I've really missed it."

At the restaurant, they sat at a table outside on the pavement by the side of the road and ordered beer. Hari told them about his work at the hospital and the preparations that had been made to handle casualties should the Japanese bomb Rangoon. Their mood soon lightened and they reminisced about happier times when they were all together in Mandalay. Khin May looked radiant and Tim was regretting the turn of events their lives had taken. She was right. Once this war was over, he would leave the army and give his wife and children the attention they deserved.

"That was a superb meal," he said, finishing his second serving of *kulfi*, a rich ice cream-like Indian dessert with pistachio nuts in it. "I couldn't eat another morsel."

"Yes, thanks, Hari," Khin May added. "This has been a truly wonderful evening."

Later, when they returned home and were alone, Tim told Khin May of his decision.

"Oh, I'm so happy, darling. You can't imagine how pleased the children will be. They want so much for us all to be together."

The next morning the sun rose into a brilliant, clear sky. It was Tuesday, December 23rd, and Rangoon awakened to start another busy day. Saffron-robed *pongyis* made their usual rounds carrying begging bowls. Shops opened their doors, although schools and offices were closed for the Christmas holidays. Sounds of children playing on the streets drifted through the air.

Hari went to the hospital to make his morning rounds. Khin May and Tim were relishing this time together and enjoying a late breakfast which Khin May had insisted on preparing. She told Tim about their trip to Mingun but left out the incident of the demonstrators attacking their car. She was about to tell him about the vision of the strange old man when Tim raised his hands.

They could faintly hear an air raid siren begin wailing in the distance. Tim listened intently, his face turning serious. The chilling sound gradually increased in volume, but then became faint, almost inaudible.

"I hope that was the end of it," he said, turning to his wife.

But it started again. The eerie, alternate slow waning and waxing volume of the siren was the message people in Burma had come to dread. A shiver ran through Khin May's body.

"Damn it!" Tim spoke angrily, standing up. "This doesn't sound like a bloody drill. I'm sorry, darling, but my orders are to report back to the barracks as soon as an air raid siren sounds."

"Can I go with you, Tim?"

"No, sweetheart. Stay here. I'll return after the 'all clear'."

"Please be careful, Tim." They embraced and kissed before he ran down the stairs. Khin May followed him and stood on the street joining others who also came out of their flats.

"I hope this is a false alarm," a woman said.

"Let's pray that it is," Khin May answered. Dear God, please let it be a false alarm.

But the siren did not stop and instead became louder, sounding more urgent. Khin May thought she heard the faint sound of airplane engines. Necks craned and they stared at the sky above. The siren was now being drowned by the roar of planes. Then they saw them, flying in formations, streaking across the blue sky.

"It must be the Japanese," a woman moaned. "They are attacking Rangoon."

"No, no, they are British," a man answered. "I saw RAF markings on some of them."

The moment an alarm had been raised by spotters along the Eastern border of Burma that Japanese planes had been sighted flying towards Rangoon, Royal Air Force and the AVG fighter planes had taken off from Mingaladon Airport. They flew southeast of the city to intercept the enemy and soon saw them from a distance. Row upon row of bombers flying in tight "V" formations were headed towards the capital.

Japanese Zero fighters escorting the bombers quickly peeled off from the formations and raced to engage the approaching British and AVG fighters. The American pilots flew with reckless abandon straight at the bomber formations and shot three of the them down during their initial attack. Soon several dogfights were taking place, RAF and AVG fighters locked in battle with the faster Zeros. Planes shot out of the sky fell spiraling to the paddy fields below and exploded into huge balls of fire.

Sheer strength in numbers allowed several of the Japanese bomber formations to reach the city. Two formations headed up the Rangoon River and now switched to flying single file. The roar of their engines was deafening. People in the streets stood dumbfounded, watching the planes flying up the river. Many standing along the river did not believe themselves to be in any danger.

Once the bombers were over the docks, they started releasing their deadly cargo. People below could clearly see the bombs coming out of the bellies of the planes and dropping toward earth in neat rows. The bombs picked up speed as they fell, creating an eerie, whistling sound. Thunderous explosions violently shook the ground when the bombs struck. Buildings crumbled. Wooden structures exploded into searing balls of fire and billowing clouds of black smoke. The entire river front was soon ablaze.

As the sounds of the first exploding bombs reached 44th Street, many more residents rushed out of their flats. Dog fights were now taking place over the city. People stared at each other in disbelief as the terrifying sounds of exploding bombs continued. Children cried and some of the adults started praying. Khin May picked up a little girl and tried to console her. She herself felt dazed.

"My God, what's happening?" a woman screamed.

God, please protect Tim and Hari, Khin May prayed.

Some of the men cautiously walked toward the south to Merchant Street to find out where the bombs were falling. U Ba Tu was out on the street and kept reassuring his neighbors.

"Do not worry. The Japanese will not harm us. You have my word," he kept repeating.

Hari had just finished examining a patient in the children's ward when the siren had sounded. The senior doctors were off for the Christmas holidays and Hari was in charge. He at once ordered the medical students and nurses on duty to take the children out to the trenches.

The little girl he had just examined looked up at him. "Will you carry me out?"

Hari smiled at the child. "Yes, little angel, let's you and I go and see what this excitement is all about."

After leaving the girl in a trench, he ran back to the ward to be with the few patients who were too sick to be moved. He was perspiring and breathing heavily, but felt no fear. That's odd, he thought, but realized that it would hit him later. He knew that soon scores of injured would start arriving. For months they had been preparing for such a crisis. He gave orders to the nurses to get every available bed ready. He then rushed to the operating room to make certain they were ready for the surgeons who would have to perform emergency operations on the critically injured.

After what felt like an eternity, the sound of the exploding bombs stopped and the ground ceased trembling. The "all clear" siren sounded and those who had found trenches to take shelter in came out of them hesitatingly.

"Is it over?" they asked. "Has the bombing stopped?"

Large numbers of people merged toward the river, attracted by the huge columns of dense, black smoke rising from furiously burning buildings. All along the shore, brick buildings had disintegrated and were now piles of rubble. Large wooden warehouses were turned into burning infernos. Scores of injured cried out for help. Mutilated bodies lay all along Strand Road. It appeared that the Japanese had also used some type of anti-personnel bombs which caused the very high number of injuries and deaths. Ambulances, police and army vehicles raced into the area to take the injured to hospitals. The dead were transported to the General Hospital morgue.

Fire engines tried to douse the flames. Next to a partially destroyed brick building, a crowd had gathered. They silently watched the wreckage of two Japanese fighter planes, burning. The charred body of a pilot was partially visible in one of the wrecks. The people watched it unemotionally.

A second formation of Japanese bombers had escaped the British and American fighters and had flown north of the city toward

Mingaladon Airport. It appeared that the Japanese had tried to isolate the capital by destroying the airport as well as the wharves along the river. A few ships on the river were hit, but none were sunk. Many wharves and warehouses, however, were completely destroyed. The airport was damaged and several planes lost.

The human toll had been incredibly high. An estimated two thousand five hundred civilians had been killed and many thousands more were injured. Rangoon was now in a state of panic, with thousands trying to flee the city and head north. All day long, a procession of lorries, buses, private cars, horse carriages and even cycle rickshaws loaded with people and their pitiful belongings headed out of the city. The railway station was packed with people trying to board trains going towards Mandalay and towns beyond. The airport was closed to civilian traffic. With the damage along the river, ferry services were also stopped. But people crowded on to boats or anything else capable of floating and being able to be propelled in a northerly direction.

Hari had been on his feet for the past eight hours, attending to the scores of wounded that had been brought to the hospital. The doctors and nurses worked continuously, cleaning wounds, tying bandages, and taking the more severely injured into the operating rooms. Many of the injured also had severe burns and were in extreme pain. There had been no time for Hari to rest, or even think of the devastation around them.

In the middle of the afternoon Tim had rushed into the hospital. After some difficulty, he located Hari. "Thank goodness I found you, Hari," he said. "I don't have much time. My battalion has been ordered to Moulmein. I'm frantic about not being able to see Khin May before leaving. Can you go and see how she is? I left her in your flat when the damn raid started." Hari could see the anguish in Tim's eyes.

"Sure. I'll go as soon as I can," he answered. "As you can see, we are swamped with the wounded, and they're still coming in. How's it out there? I don't know if 44th Street was hit. I hope to God Sis is okay. When do you leave?"

"We're on our way right now. We're to set up a defensive line should the bloody Japs follow up with a land invasion. I understand most of the bombing was along the river but it's terrible on the streets. People are panicking, trying to flee the city. It must be tough on Khin May. I could only stop here 'cause it's on the way. Hari, get her back to Mandalay right away. Tell her I'll write as soon as I can, and tell her I'm sorry for causing her all this worry and trouble. This damn war."

"I'll do that, Tim. Take care, brother," Hari said, putting his hand out.

"Good luck to you, Hari." The two men shook hands and embraced awkwardly before Tim rushed out to board the army truck waiting for him outside the hospital gate.

By seven o'clock in the evening, all of the wounded that had been brought to the hospital had been attended to and Hari was finally able to leave.

Khin May opened the door before Hari reached the second floor. She embraced him, tears flooding her eyes.

"I'm so glad you're safe, Hari. I was worried sick all day. I didn't know if I should stay here or go looking for you and Tim."

"You did the right thing by staying here, Sis."

"Do you know where Tim is? I hope to God he's safe."

"He's okay. I saw him briefly this afternoon. He stopped by at the hospital to tell me that his battalion was leaving for Moulmein right away. He was very upset about not being able to see you before leaving." Khin May slumped into a chair and started sobbing.

Hari knelt down and took his sister's hands in his. "Tim will be all right. Don't worry, Sis. But he asked me to get you back to Mandalay right away."

"What about you, Hari?" she asked, wiping her tears. "You must leave with me."

Hari stood up. "I'll have to stay back. I'm needed at the hospital. All staff have been ordered to report each day. As a matter of fact, I have to go back tonight. But I'll return early tomorrow morning to take you to the railway station."

In Mandalay, Devi Lal, Sophia and Neil huddled around the radio in the drawing room all evening listening to the news in stunned silence.

"Rangoon was bombed for over an hour this morning," the announcer stated. "Eighty Japanese bombers took part in the raid, inflicting considerable damage to the wharves along the river and to Mingaladon Airport. Over 2600 civilians were killed and thousands more injured. The RAF and the AVG fighters shot down 26 enemy aircraft."

"*Naana*, do you think Mama, Daddy and Uncle Hari are all right?" Sophia asked, her voice trembling.

"I am sure they're fine, my child," Devi Lal answered, hugging his granddaughter. "The bombings were along the river and at the airport. They should be safe."

Later that evening, the Japanese propaganda radio announced that the Japanese Imperial Air Force had delivered a devastating blow to the defenses of Rangoon.

"Soon the Burmese Liberation Army, commanded by Burma's own hero, Aung San, along with the brave Japanese forces, will liberate Burma," the announcer boasted. "Asia will finally be for Asians and foreign domination will be crushed." The broadcast concluded with a strange message. "Citizens of Rangoon: There will be a special Christmas present for you on December 25th."

When Hari returned to the hospital he found that more injured had been brought in. All of the beds were taken and some of the less severely injured lay on mattresses and sheets spread in the corridors. The morgue could not hold any more bodies and an adjacent storage building was being used as a temporary morgue. Family members tried to locate missing loved ones, and heart-rending cries filled the morgue whenever mutilated remains were recognized.

Early the next morning, Hari returned to 44th Street and took his sister to the railway station. It was, as he expected, crowded with people trying to flee Rangoon. The ticket office was closed, but a train, already packed full, was on the platform.

"Come, Khin May. Let me try and get you on it," Hari said, pushing his way through the crowd. They went along the entire length of the train and finally Hari was able to help his sister climb into a compartment.

"You must also leave Rangoon as soon as you can, Hari," she pleaded, gently touching her brother's face.

"Yes I will, Sis. Don't worry about me. Take the children and go north. It may not be safe to remain in Mandalay."

"Good-bye, dear brother. May God protect you," she said softly as the train slowly pulled out of the station.

The day after the bombing, a shocked city tried to collect its wits. Although preparations for an air raid had been going on for months, the magnitude of the attack and the devastation it wrought was something the people of Rangoon had not expected. A mass exodus was taking place as terrified residents fled north. In Mandalay, Sophia and Neil rejoiced to have their mother back home safely. But they all worried about Tim and Hari and prayed for their safety.

Christmas day dawned and the sun rose over Rangoon, a brilliant ball of orange, in a cloudless blue sky.

"Good morning to you, Hari. Are you off to the hospital?" U Ba Tu inquired as he encountered Hari on the street.

"Yes, U Ba Tu. The entire hospital staff has been ordered to report to duty each day."

"Well, you're lucky to be able to perform such meritorious deeds. For myself, today I plan to console my neighbours here on our street."

"Good-bye, U Ba Tu," Hari called out. "I'll see you later."

The distant sounds of church bells summoned worshipers to the eight o'clock service. Hari passed several children dressed in their best clothes, walking with their parents to church. U Ba Tu saw another neighbour come out of a building.

"Ah, good morning to you, Mr. D'Souza. How are you this morning?"

"I guess I'm all right so far, U Ba Tu. Let's hope the Japanese don't return today. The city has already suffered enough."

"Did you not hear their promise to us?" U Ba Tu inquired. "The Japanese radio announcer clearly said there would be a special Christmas gift on the 25th for our city. I tell you, you need not worry. The Japanese will keep their word. They will not harm us."

"I hope you're right, U Ba Tu. I hope to God that you are right."

The church bells had stopped ringing and Christmas services had begun in the churches throughout the city. The air was still and the streets were slowly filling with people. And then the spine-chilling sound of the siren started wailing. Those who had trenches near their homes ran and took shelter in them. Most of the residents of the city simply came out and joined others on the streets to silently gaze at the skies.

On 44th Street, some came out onto their balconies, while others stood in groups on the street, talking nervously. U Ba Tu was again walking up and down the street, talking to his neighbours. The drone of approaching aircraft could now be heard. Small fighter planes were seen streaking over the city. Then loud thunderous explosions were heard and the ground under their feet shook violently as bombs started raining from the skies.

The city was blanketed by an incredible number of planes. Large cumbersome bombers could be seen with holes in their bellies, from which rows of bombs rushed towards the earth. Faster fighter planes raced across the sky, locked in deadly dogfights. Someone on 44th Street noticed a low-flying aircraft in the distance, coming straight down the street, firing its machine guns.

"Look," a man yelled. "That plane is shooting at people on the street."

Some ran into their buildings, but most just stood where they were, horrified. The plane was almost overhead and the roar of its engine was deafening. Machine gun bullets sprayed the street. Children started screaming, women cried out. Within seconds, the plane was over them and gone. Men, women and children struck by bullets were mowed down where they stood on the street and on their balconies. Those not injured appeared dazed and stared at the bloodied bodies around them. No one seemed to have the will to move.

The sound of yet another plane approaching jarred their numb minds. Japanese Zeros, it seemed, were methodically going down each of the residential streets with their guns blazing. Bullets again came streaking down upon them. The pavement along each side of 44th Street was bloodied and strewn with the dead and injured. Torn, bleeding bodies hung draped over the railings of the balconies.

U Ba Tu stood defiantly in the middle of the street. He raised his walking stick and started waving it angrily at yet another approaching plane. "We are Buddhists like you. We believe in nonviolence!" he screamed. "You should not harm us. I am a very important person! I was an advisor in King Thibaw's court. These are my friends. You must not harm them. One day they will build a monument in my honor! I tell you, you must stop and not harm these people anymore. I tell you, one day they will build ..." A bullet tore through his throat and the old man collapsed to the ground. His body convulsed once and then became still.

From a distance, all that was visible of U Ba Tu were his shoulders and head. His gold-rimmed glasses lay on his face, slightly askew. The pink tail of his Burmese silk headdress flapped gently in the breeze. His walking stick was curiously still pointing toward the sky.

The bombing and machine gun attacks, especially of civilian neighborhoods, left Rangoon dazed and devastated. It was a Christmas day that the survivors would long remember. On the same day, the British surrendered Hong Kong to the enemy. Two days earlier, Japan had defeated the American forces in the Pacific, and had captured Wake Island. Soon Guam was also lost. The Japanese propaganda radio continued its attempt to convince the Burmese that Japan's intentions were to expel all non-Asians from Asia. Asians could then rule their own countries. The wanton destruction of their capital and the killing of thousands of civilians was not what the Burmese had expected, however.

The Japanese Air Force had also paid a heavy toll, having lost large numbers of fighters and bombers to the RAF and AVG during the raids on Rangoon. The American pilots soon earned a reputation for their flying skills and daredevil attitude and were feared by the Japanese pilots. The Americans painted the front of their airplanes to resemble fierce sharks, and also painted small Japanese flags on the side of the fuselage for every enemy aircraft they shot down. The number of fighter planes available to the AVG were limited, so they painted their aircraft a different colour each week to mislead the enemy in believing that the AVG force was larger. This, along with the combat skills and daring of the AVG pilots, was enough to have the Japanese suspend daytime raids on Rangoon for a short period.

In Mandalay, Khin May anxiously awaited news from her husband. "You may not hear from him," Devi Lal explained. "With the destruction of Rangoon, the postal service is probably in disarray. Why don't you take the children and go up to Myitkyina?"

"I'm not leaving, Dad, not until I have some news about Tim," Khin May insisted. "For now, we are quite safe here in Mandalay. But as soon as I hear from him, we'll go."

Four days later — incredibly — she received a brief letter from Tim, written from Moulmein. He told her that he was all right, and that she was not to worry about him. He asked her to take the children and go up north. "Wait for me there," he wrote. "If all goes well, I'll see you after the war."

On 3rd January, 1942, Khin May, Neil and Sophia, accompanied by Daw Mu, left by train for Myitkyina. That evening, therefore, they did not hear the news on the radio that Japanese planes had raided the town of Moulmein. Heavy civilian and military casualties had occurred and the town was severely damaged.

On 20th January, the Japanese 15th Army crossed the Thai border and entered southeast Burma, capturing the town of Tavoy. Although the Burmese had already suffered so much, many still welcomed the advancing Japanese troops as liberators. The people were especially pleased to see the Burma Independence Army under the command of their hero, General Aung San, march into Burma along with the Japanese. Yet the Japanese Air Force continued to pound Burmese cities.

Rangoon was subjected to repeated night bombing raids. The population of the city had been reduced to less than a fourth of its original 400,000. Plans were now being made by the British to evacuate all but essential government employees. On 30th January, the Japanese launched a massive ground attack on Moulmein and captured the town.

Rangoon experienced another devastating air attack during the night of 19th February. A full scale evacuation was launched by the Government the next morning. The remaining patients from the hospital were loaded onto a train. Hari and a few other doctors and nurses accompanied them on their journey to Mandalay. Before going to the railway station, Hari rushed to his flat to pack some clothes. To his horror, he found his building, as well as most others on the street, reduced to piles of smoldering rubble.

Devi Lal frantically tried to get a message to his son, asking him to leave Rangoon and return home at once. With the fall of Moulmein, he was also extremely worried about Tim.

He spent the morning at the telegraph office trying to send a telegram to Hari. The clerk at the office was skeptical. "I don't think telegrams are being delivered at the other end in Rangoon. I'll send it, but you may be wasting your money, sir."

Devi Lal then went to the Deputy Commissioner's office, seeking news of Tim. His friend David O'Connell was away and was to return the next day. No one knew the fate of the defenders of Moulmein or of its citizens.

That evening, a tired, despondent Devi Lal sat down alone to have dinner. He did not have much of an appetite and toyed with his food. Oh, God, protect my children. Keep them in the shadow of your love and mercy, he prayed.

Destiny's Decree

*M*orning came and yet there was no news from Hari or Tim. Devi Lal
had decided to go to the Deputy Commissioner's office. He didn't feel
like having breakfast, but at Ko Than's insistence, he sat down to have
a cup of tea and a toast. He was just about finished when Sher Khan
came rushing in.

"Look who's here Doctor *Sahib!*" he said excitedly.

"Dad, can I have some money?" Hari asked from the door. "I need
to pay the rickshaw driver."

A tired, dishevelled Hari was welcomed warmly by his father. Hari
bathed and breakfasted, telling Devi Lal all that had happened in
Rangoon during the past few days. Now, at home and safe, the horror
he had experienced began to hit him. He felt extremely fatigued and
emotionally wrung out.

"I think I'll just stay home and rest, Dad," he said, finishing his
breakfast.

"You do that, Son," Devi Lal answered. "Rest, take it easy. I'll go to
the Deputy Commissioner's office now. They've got to have some news
of Tim."

"Good morning, Devi Lal," David O'Connell said, standing up and
coming around his desk. "Please come in. I'm delighted to see you."

"Hello, David. It's nice to see you, too," Devi Lal replied, shaking
O'Connell's hand.

"I understand you were here yesterday. I was actually up in Maymyo and returned only this morning."

"Yes, they told me that you would return today."

"I apologize for not having come over for tennis during the past couple of weeks, Devi Lal. As you know, things have been a bit hectic and I've been in my office even on Sundays. Let me offer you a cup of tea." He pressed a button on his desk and a peon entered the room.

"Bring some *chai* for the *Sahib*," O'Connell ordered.

"Tell me about Hari. I hope he has come away from Rangoon?"

"Yes, Hari returned only this morning. But David, I'm very worried about my son-in-law Tim. His battalion was moved to Moulmein 23rd December and, other than a brief note to Khin May, we haven't heard from him."

David O'Connell's face turned grim. "Well, I'm afraid the news from Moulmein is not encouraging, Devi Lal. As you know, the Japanese captured the town on 30th January. This is confidential information, but unfortunately we suffered very severe losses. The Japs were able to take almost a thousand British and Asian troops prisoners."

"Did any of the troops get away?"

"I'm afraid not. Elements of the Japanese 15th Army attacked, not only from the east, but they also circled the town and came from the north, thus preventing any escape. Hopefully Tim was taken prisoner."

"Dear God, I hope you are right, David," Devi Lal said. "As you know, Khin May took the children up north to Myitkyina. I want them to wait out the war there. Do you have any information on how the Japanese have treated civilians, especially those who are British or of mixed parentage?"

"From the intelligence reports that have come in, it appears the Japs are treating prisoners of war very brutally. They have not spared European women and children either and have put them into POW camps. They seem not to bother the Burmese population. My advice to you, Devi Lal, is to get Khin May and your grandchildren out of the country. Toungoo was bombed yesterday and it could be our turn here in Mandalay any day now."

"You don't think they'll be safe in Myitkyina?"

David O'Connell sighed. "My friend, I'm afraid we've already given up Burma to the Japanese," he said, lowering his voice. "The invincibility of the British Empire seems to have been just a myth. It's embarrassing, but we'll be pulling out of here to establish fresh defense lines all the way back to the Indian border."

"That's such a pity, David, but how can we leave the country when Rangoon is almost lost? From the news, I hear the Japanese also control all sea lanes out of Burma."

"Well, that's true, my friend. Going out of Rangoon by sea or by air is out of the question. I'm suggesting you consider taking your family over land to India."

"Over land?" Devi Lal asked, aghast. "There's no road between Burma and India! There are impregnable jungles and major mountain ranges between the two countries."

"That's correct, Devi Lal. But a supply route has been carved through the jungles and over the mountains. With the port of Rangoon closed, any fresh troops and supplies coming in to Burma have to use this route. The fact of the matter is, this is the only avenue now available for anyone to escape Burma," O'Connell answered with resignation.

"But how will we find our way, David? How can I ensure that my family will be safe?"

"Give me a couple of days, Devi Lal. I'll gather some information and bring it to you one evening after work."

"Thanks, David, and I hope you'll stay for dinner." O'Connell accepted the invitation and walked his friend back to his car.

Returning home, a disconsolate Devi Lal told Hari about his conversation with David O'Connell and the suggestion that the family trek to India.

"But Dad, you know Khin May won't leave without Tim no matter what we say!"

"Yes, you're right, Hari," Devi Lal sighed. "The best we can hope for now is that Tim is a prisoner of war. We'll have to convince your sister that, for the sake of the children, we must leave — even if it means enduring severe hardships trying to get over the mountains to India."

Two days later, true to his word, David O'Connell visited *Shanti Gaeha*. Accepting a beer from Devi Lal, he pulled out a large brown envelope from his briefcase. He spread the contents of the envelope on the table and showed Devi Lal a map on which he had drawn a red line from Mandalay to the town of Tamu near the border with India.

Taking a sip of his beer, O'Connell said, "We've already started evacuating British dependents, Devi Lal. I'm sure we can make arrangements for you and your family to escape to India through this route."

Tracing a finger along the red line, he continued. "You should travel by car to Sagaing, unless, of course, the Japs destroy the Ava bridge across the Irrawaddy. If they do, then you'll have to get across the river by boat. From Sagaing you will need to go west, perhaps by bus to Monywa. If the Ava bridge is intact, you can drive your cars all the way to Monywa. From there you can catch a steamer going up the Chindwin River to the town of Kalewa."

Devi Lal and Hari listened attentively, bending over the map in front of them. O'Connell took another sip of his beer. "Things, unfortunately, get a little rough from that point on. You'll need to take a tributary of the Chindwin and travel by country boats. The tributary is rather narrow and the boats have to be dragged upstream through some rapids. Then, after that, there is a bullock cart track through the Kabaw Valley and some pretty dense jungle, which leads to the town of Tamu."

Hari turned and looked at his father.

"From Tamu, it's a four to five day trek across fairly rugged mountains to Palel in Assam," O'Connell continued. "The Government is attempting to establish refugee camps along the bullock cart track and the path through the mountains. However, from what I hear, the camps are quite primitive and the going awfully rough."

Devi Lal's face was grave. "David, is there a less treacherous way across? I don't know whether Daw Mu, Khin May and Sophia can handle such an arduous journey."

David O'Connell shook his head. "Unfortunately this is the better of the two routes available. It's really primarily for Europeans and for the military. The second route is from Myitkyina in the north through the Hukwang Valley, all the way to Ledo, through some very, very inhospitable terrain. That route is designated as the Asian route, and I'm afraid thousands will die there in the mountains and the jungles, especially once the monsoons begin. No, your best bet is through Tamu and Palel. I'm sure we can get you a permit to use this European route."

"Thank you, David, thank you so much," Devi Lal said. "You are being so very kind and helpful."

"Don't mention it, Devi Lal. I cherish our friendship, and that's the least I can do for you and the family. In fact, I'm going to miss all of you after you leave."

"What about you, David? It's not going to be safe for you to stay on here. You must leave, too."

"I can't, Devi Lal, at least not now. I have to see to the evacuation of all British Nationals first. Hopefully I'll be out before the Japs get here."

Devi Lal had trouble sleeping that night and kept thinking about the journey that O'Connell had proposed. From Tamu, it would be a four or five day trek across rugged mountains. How would the children, and especially Daw Mu, manage? Besides the impossible terrain, there would most likely be malaria, cholera and other hazards. Where would the children sleep? Should he expose his loved ones to such a dangerous journey, or should they remain in Burma and take their chances with the Japanese?

The next day, at the clinic, he attended to his patients, but his mind was preoccupied. It looked like they had no choice, or did they? What if they all went up north? Was not there even a slim chance that the British would be able to save a part of Burma?

He was relieved when the last patient had been examined and he was able to drive home. Leaving Mandalay was going to be so painful for all of them. This was their home. This is where their friends lived. There were too many wonderful memories to just walk away from.

He stopped the car outside the gate of *Shanti Gaeha*. He could see the graceful lines of their home visible through the garden, framed by the bougainvillea vines and a tamarind tree. His mind flashed back to the many happy moments and memories — the cheerful laughter of his grandchildren as they frolicked in the pool, the music, the festivals, and celebrations with family and friends, the serenity of the gardens. Who will live here when we are gone, he mused.

He sat there for awhile, lost in his thoughts. Then, starting the car, he drove past the house. The river had a way of unclogging his mind and he was now drawn to its shore. He parked the car and climbed up to the high bank of the Irrawaddy. The setting sun cast a magical glow on the rippling waters. He sat down on the grassy slope and felt the breeze from the river soothe his face. The laughter of children playing at the water's edge drifted up to him.

His thoughts went back to his own childhood and to his parents. Once before, many, many years ago, he had to make a difficult choice — a decision that was to so dramatically alter the course of the rest of his life. He was sixteen years of age and had to choose between following the inner yearnings of his heart or adhering to centuries of tradition and custom.

As the eldest son in a *Mohyal* Brahmin family in the Punjab, he was expected to inherit from his father the role as head of the family and chief of his village. He was being groomed for this honor and responsibility. His father, Hem Raj, was a wealthy landowner. A fiery patriot and a freedom fighter, he was a superb horseman. He taught his son to ride and to shoot a rifle. Devi Lal loved his father and admired him greatly. From his mother, Kanti, Devi Lal inherited the traits of compassion, caring, patience and giving. Kanti imbued her oldest son with a deep faith in their religion, as well as acceptance and respect for that of others.

One day, taking a shortcut on his way back to school, Devi Lal had walked into a little village. He found himself among children with open sores on their faces and limbs and dressed in filthy rags. To his horror, he realized these were lepers.

The lepers called their village, *Hari Niwas*, God's Abode and seemed content, accepting their pain and fate. His initial horror and revulsion had been gradually replaced by pity and understanding. He had gone back to the village often, taking fruit and sweetmeats for the children.

There seemed to have been born in his heart an inner yearning that made him want to help and heal the sick. Then one day he met an

English physician who had come to *Hari Niwas* to provide medical care for the lepers. Her name was Sarah Dormsbury Smythe, the wife of an officer of the 11th Bengal Lancers. Sarah asked Devi Lal to interpret for her and they became friends. They worked together, treating the lepers each Sunday afternoon, and occasionally went for walks along the Jhelum River. Young Devi Lal greatly admired "Madam Sarah" and her selfless work. He felt inspired by her to try to become a physician himself. From one of his teachers he learned about a medical school in Lahore and submitted an application for admission.

Upon finishing high school, he made a promise to the lepers. "I shall return one day and, God willing, it will be with the skills of a doctor so that I may repay your friendship and the many lessons you have taught me."

The Medical College in Lahore granted him admission and, as he had stood first in the matric examinations, he also received a full scholarship. The only requirement of the scholarship was that, upon completing his training, he serve as a doctor for the British Government for a period of five years. He spoke to his parents about it. His mother, Kanti, wanted him to do whatever he felt in his heart was right. His father, Hem Raj, was taken aback. "You are my eldest son, Devi Lal," he said, trying to be patient. "You will take my place of honor as the head of the family and as the chief of our village. That is your birthright, your privilege, and a sacred duty."

"I'm very grateful for all I've received, father," Devi Lal answered softly, "but there is so much suffering and disease. As a doctor, I can be of help to many. My brother is only a year younger and is more capable of following in your footsteps."

"You are a Mohyal Brahmin, Devi Lal," his father said, getting a little angry, "a descendent of brave warriors. It is inconceivable that you would agree to touch defiled bodies and sick people. Look, as the eldest son you will inherit all of my land and wealth. If you don't want all of that, then go join the freedom fighters and help rid our country of this oppressive British rule. But forget this nonsense of wanting to become a doctor."

For the next month Devi Lal agonized, trying to make up his mind.

Defying his father was very painful. But in the end, he decided to follow his convictions. Angered by his son's decision, Hem Raj refused to speak to him, and disinherited him. Kanti remained silent but supported her son with her love and encouragement.

Leaving the village of Karyala where he was born and raised, and traveling to Lahore, the largest city in Punjab, was both exciting and frightening for Devi Lal. He missed his family terribly and eagerly looked forward to the letters his mother wrote once a month. He was a good student and worked hard. He stood first in his Medical College examinations and was given a one-year appointment as House Surgeon at the Medical College hospital. A month before completing his assignment, he was asked to see the principal of the Medical College.

Dr. Reginald Jones, a balding, portly Englishman, liked this serious, hard-working Indian physician.

"Well, well, come in Devi Lal!" Dr. Jones said, extending his hand. "I've received splendid reports of your work as house surgeon. That's jolly good but, I dare say, I fully expected that of you. Would you care for a spot of tea? It's beastly hot, but then I have found drinking hot tea actually makes the heat more bearable."

"Thank you, Dr. Jones," Devi Lal had answered politely. "I don't want to bother you."

"It's no bother at all, old chap," Reginald Jones answered, ringing the little bell on top of his desk. An Indian servant quickly materialized through a side door. "*Chai lao*," he was told.

"*Accha Sahib*," the servant answered, bowing.

"Where were we?" Dr. Jones said, turning towards Devi Lal. "Oh, yes. I have exciting news for you, young man," the principal said, picking up an envelope from his desk. "The government is sending you to a town in northern Burma to serve as a District Medical Officer."

"Thank you, Dr. Jones. I'm happy to hear that," Devi Lal replied, although he knew very little about Burma other than what he had read in his geography books in school.

"This position in a remote region of the country will be very good for you, Devi Lal. You will indeed be able to practice the medicine you have learned during the past five years."

Taking a sip of his tea, Jones continued. "I was in Rangoon for a short while several years ago. I must say I found the Burmese to be a rather delightful people. Very friendly and hospitable, you know. I think you'll enjoy working among them."

Handing the envelope to Devi Lal, Dr. Jones said, "Here are your orders, Devi Lal. The Ministry of Health in Delhi has also sent you a train ticket to Calcutta, as well as reservations on a steamer sailing from there for Rangoon."

"When am I to report for duty, Dr. Jones?"

"They've given you two months to complete your journey and settle down, Devi Lal. I dare say, you'll need that much time and more. It's going to be quite an adjustment. You know, I envy you. This will be a great adventure for you. You better watch out for those beautiful Burmese women, though. I'll be surprised if within a year or two one of them doesn't get you to say, 'I do'!" he said, chuckling.

Devi Lal smiled. "No sir, I'll be in no hurry to get married. I'll fulfill my service obligations and return to Punjab as quickly as possible."

"Well, we'll just have to wait and see, won't we?" Dr. Jones replied, still chuckling. "I hear when people go to Burma for any more than a brief period, they become captivated. The next thing you know they talk about settling down there permanently."

Devi Lal thanked the principal and got up to leave.

"Do write and let me know how things turn out, young man. Have a safe journey. God bless."

Devi Lal had not been home nor had he spoken to anyone from his family since leaving his village almost five years ago. He had, however, corresponded with his mother regularly. He wrote and asked her if he could come to see her before leaving for Burma. She replied at once, welcoming him. He traveled to their village and, out of respect for his father's wishes, met his mother, brothers and sisters at the temple. They had not seen each other for five years, but all too soon it was time for Devi Lal to leave.

"Mother, I would like to see our house one more time before I leave."

Kanti nodded and, holding her son's hand, walked towards their home. The door to the courtyard was open. Devi Lal looked in, running his eyes from one end of the house to the other. At first he did not notice his father lying on a *charpai* under the Banyan tree. Hem Raj saw his son standing at the doorway and quickly closed his eyes, feigning sleep. Then Devi Lal saw the *charpai* and his father. He turned to look at his mother. Kanti, understanding her son's desire, nodded.

Devi Lal entered the courtyard and quietly walked toward the *charpai*. He bent down and, so as not to awaken his father, very gently touched his feet. Devi Lal looked at his father's face one last time and folded his hands in silent prayer. Then, as an ultimate act of reverence, he lifted his turban from his head and placed it next to Hem Raj's feet. "I vow not to wear a turban until I receive your forgiveness, my father," he said under his breath. His eyes overflowing, he turned around and walked towards the door. He did not see the drop of tear that rolled down from the corner of his father's eye, nor the hand gently rise to bless him.

On his way back to Lahore, Devi Lal stopped in Jhelum to visit his old school as well as Hari Niwas. He was shocked to see the village destroyed and deserted. From a passerby he found out that the village had been burnt down and many of the lepers had perished. The children who survived had been sent to a leper asylum near Rawalpindi.

Soon after returning to Lahore, Devi Lal left on his long journey to Burma. He had never traveled beyond Lahore before and sat in the train headed for Calcutta, excitedly watching the placid countryside of Punjab flash by. Lush green wheat fields, interspersed with islands of bright yellow mustard, surrounded little villages. Children interrupted their play and waved at the passengers on the train. Grazing cattle paid scant attention as the massive engine, spewing dense black smoke clattered by, pulling its long line of red carriages.

Devi Lal had spoken briefly to the other passengers in the compartment. He wanted to savor every moment of the journey and was disappointed when nightfall blanketed the panorama flashing past his window. Waking early, he sat looking out again. The train rolled over small streams and wide rivers. It sped by smaller towns, racing haughtily past little one-room stations and passengers patiently waiting for slower, local trains. It stopped briefly at larger but not so important towns and hurried away while a passenger or two still scampered to climb aboard.

Around noon, the train reached the holy city of Benares where it would stop a full thirty minutes. A small shrine at one end of the station platform attracted Devi Lal's attention. He left the train and made his way through the crowd. He bowed his head and prayed at the shrine for the well-being of his family in Karyala.

The train crossed the mighty Ganges River. I must return one day to bathe in the holy Ganges, he thought. As the train continued its long journey southeast, the terrain gradually changed. The dry plains of Bihar were replaced by the lush greenery of Bengal. Quaint villages with lotus covered ponds glided past. It had rained during the night and as the sun rose, the morning air was fresh and clear.

After a journey of over 1200 miles, the train with its weary passengers steamed into Howrah Station, across the river from the sprawling city of Calcutta. Devi Lal stayed a night in a small, inexpensive hotel. He was awed by this big city. He walked along the busy Esplanade, lingering to stare wide-eyed at the beautiful shops and the fancy eating places for the rich. He watched a game of cricket played by British dressed in white clothes.

He had only been in small boats on the Jhelum River in Punjab and had never seen a ship before. Arriving at the Outram Ghat, he looked with amazement at the large, sparkling white and red steamer which was to take him to Burma. Rows upon rows of small, round portholes adorned its sides. Little coloured flags fluttered in the breeze, and a large funnel rose imposingly above the ship. Smartly uniformed crew members directed passengers over the gangplank, onto the ship. Devi Lal was assigned a small, second-class cabin on a lower deck. After stowing his luggage in the cabin, he eagerly climbed the steps to the open deck, high above the water.

Below and toward the rear of the ship, the third-class passengers placed their luggage on the open deck to reserve space for themselves. The first-class passengers came on board just before the ship was to sail. The sound of bells signaling came from below. Indian sailors scurried, drawing in the gangplanks and dropped them into the belly of the ship with loud clangs. The passengers on the deck were jolted by the sudden blast of the ship's horn. A pair of tugboats slowly began moving the ship away from the pier.

The river was crowded. Large, unwieldy wooden boats with huge sails sat low in the water, weighed down by incredible piles of gunny sacks filled with grain. Small boats, each tended by a lone man rowing standing up, plied the river, bobbing up and down over the wakes of the larger vessels. A sparkling white Port Commissioner's ship lay at anchor, looking immaculate against the backdrop of cargo ships with peeling paint and rusting hulls.

Once in midstream, the tugboats freed the ship. Soon the crowded city was left behind, and the shores were adorned with stately mansions and coconut palms. Gradually the river widened and the shore line covered with dense greenery. Devi Lal asked a ship's officer where they were.

"We are sailing through the delta formed by the Ganges and Brahmaputra rivers," the man answered. "Those are the Sunderbans."

Devi Lal remembered reading about the mangrove forests of the delta, known for their dreaded man-eating Bengal tigers and huge crocodiles.

By the next morning, the ship was in open sea. The water was a beautiful emerald green and the waves a little larger. The wind had picked up, but the warm air was refreshing and brought sprays of salty water up to the deck. As the day wore on, the ocean's colour darkened to a much deeper green, the waves were higher and capped with crests of white foam. Occasionally the surface was broken by fish which seemed to fly gracefully in silvery arcs, to dive back into the water some distance away.

After dinner, Devi Lal returned to the deck. The skies above him were aglow with an incredible abundance of brilliant stars, and something occurred that night which he would long remember. He had suddenly felt a deep, inexplicable sense of loss. His heart ached and a feeling of sadness overcame him. He saw a shooting star silently streak across the sky. He remembered being told as a child that these streaking lights in the sky were the souls of good people ascending to heaven after their death. He said a silent prayer for the person whose soul had just risen to heaven.

The next morning the ship was rolling and pitching even more. The waters were a very dark blue, and the waves massive. Fewer people came to the dining room for breakfast. Devi Lal spent the day reading a medical book and one about Burma he had brought with him. The third night out at sea, he was awakened from a sound sleep by a persistent knock at his door.

"Yes? Who is it?" he inquired.

A man's voice answered. "Pardon me, Sir, but if you're a medical doctor, could you please come and examine a child who has taken ill?"

"Yes, I am a physician," Devi Lal answered. "Give me a moment to get dressed. I'll go with you."

The young British ship's officer looked anxious. "Thank you, doctor. Please follow me." He quickly led the way up the steps to an upper deck and knocked on a cabin door. It was opened immediately by a lean, tall European.

"Sir, this gentleman is a doctor. He's agreed to examine your daughter," the officer announced.

The man stared at the young Indian at the door. "Is he a qualified physician?" he asked in a clipped English accent. "I don't want any native quack and his voodoo medicine."

"I am a licensed physician," Devi Lal answered calmly, masking his annoyance. "My diploma is from the Lahore Medical College."

"Well then, don't just stand there!" the Englishman said impatiently. "Come in. See what you can do." His face was clean shaven except for a pencil thin mustache which made him look almost sinister. He was dressed in a smartly tailored dark blue suit.

Devi Lal entered the elegantly appointed large cabin. A woman was sitting on a bed next to a little girl. The child's face and golden curls were visible above the blanket covering the rest of her body. The woman stood up. She was slim and elegantly dressed.

"Thank you so much, doctor, for coming." She spoke in a soft voice. "Please help my daughter. She's burning with fever."

Devi Lal sat down at the edge of the bed and began examining the child. She felt very warm to the touch and was breathing with some difficulty.

"How long has your child had this fever?"

"She was fine when we came on board the ship, Doctor. Then, two days ago, she complained of a headache and said her throat hurt. She vomited several times earlier today. She's also complained of an earache."

Devi Lal took the child's hand in his and felt her pulse. He then examined the child's neck. He removed the blanket and opened the top buttons of her night dress. The man stood glaring at him. Devi Lal carefully palpated the girl's abdomen. Then, taking a stethoscope from his medical bag, he listened to her heart. He gently turned the girl on her side and placed the stethoscope on her upper back and listened to her breathing sounds. He then buttoned the child's night dress and covered her with the blanket.

"Your daughter's pulse is fast and the lymph glands in her neck are enlarged. She also has some small red, rash-like eruptions at the base of her neck and along her armpits. I suspect she has scarlet fever," he told the mother.

"What? Are you sure?" the man asked angrily. Then turning to the ship's officer, he demanded, "Isn't there a single European physician on this blasted vessel?"

Devi Lal's face turned red.

"No, sir," the officer answered. "I checked the passenger list. This gentleman is the only doctor aboard."

"What can I do for my child, doctor?" the woman implored, ignoring her husband.

"You can use a cold compress," Devi Lal instructed her, controlling his anger. "Soak a small towel in cold water and apply it to her forehead. I'm going to give you some aspirin powder. Mix it with a little milk and make her drink it. This will relieve her earache and the pain in her throat. I would like to examine her tongue and throat when she wakes up in the morning. In the meantime, please make her drink as much fluid as she will accept. I would also suggest that you fill your bathtub with hot water and leave the bathroom door open to provide more moisture in this room. Please send for me as soon as the child wakes up in the morning. I shall come at once."

The woman placed her hand on Devi Lal's arm. "Thank you so very much, Doctor. You have been most kind," she said, gently.

As Devi Lal was leaving, the man reached into his coat pocket. "How much do you want?"

"It's not necessary to pay me," Devi Lal replied, looking the man in the face. "I am pleased to have been able to help the child."

The pompous swine, Devi Lal thought as he walked back to his cabin. If not for the child, I'd tell him to go to hell.

In the morning, Devi Lal was getting ready to go for breakfast when there was a knock on his door. The same ship's officer who had come to call him earlier in the night told him that the child was awake. Devi Lal went up to the first-class cabin hoping that the child was better and wondering what else he could do to make her comfortable. The little girl was taking sips of a liquid that her mother was feeding her with a spoon. The man was seated at a desk in one corner of the cabin. The woman stood up.

"Good morning, Doctor. Thank you for coming," she said, and then turned to her daughter. "Darling, this man's a doctor. He's here to help you get well."

Devi Lal took her place at the side of the bed and smiled at the child. "I would like to examine you to see how you are doing," he said, unbuttoning the child's night dress. The rash around the base of her neck had spread to the rest of her body. He buttoned the night dress.

"Could you stick your tongue out for me?" he asked. The child's tongue was slightly swollen and a very deep red in colour and her throat appeared congested.

"Well, thank you for letting me examine you," Devi Lal said, smiling at the child. Lowering his voice, he spoke to the mother.

"Yes, your child has scarlet fever. I would like you to give her the aspirin powder three times each day and continue to make her drink as much fluid as she can. The fever seems to be less now, so you need not use the cold compresses. She should be all right in a few days, but you must keep her in bed until she has fully recovered. I would like to see her again tomorrow morning."

The woman thanked Devi Lal profusely. This time the man was less gruff. "Good day to you," he said.

By mid-morning, the ship was rolling and pitching wildly. Ominous dark clouds blanketed the sky and huge waves pounded the sides of the ship. Several third-class passengers became severely seasick. A canvas cover had been stretched over their open deck, but strong winds carrying sprays of sea water added to their discomfort. Devi Lal tended to the sick as best he could. The crew helped move some of the third-class passengers to a more sheltered area of the deck. By noon, the storm worsened. A member of the crew fell and broke his leg while trying to secure a loose canvas awning over a deck. Devi Lal tended the injured man.

By next morning, the storm had abated and the sun rose across a shimmering sea. Flying fish reappeared and knifed through the air in graceful, silvery arcs. The little girl in the first-class cabin was much better and Devi Lal spent an enjoyable day on the open deck. That evening the ship's captain came to the second-class dining room and personally thanked him for having provided medical care to the passengers and the injured crew member.

As the sun rose the following morning, the ship was sailing serenely up the Rangoon River. Devi Lal caught his first glimpse of Burma. Graceful white pagodas, gleaming brilliantly in the morning sun, adorned the landscape on both sides of the river. Coconut palms swayed in the gentle breeze and country boats with huge billowing sails floated lazily up the river. Sleek fishing boats, their large nets spread hungrily over the water, traveled downriver to the Gulf of Martaban to reap the bountiful harvest from the sea. As Devi Lal stood on the deck admiring the scenery, a man and a woman dressed in Burmese clothes came by. They both smiled at him pleasantly.

"Good morning, Sir," the man said. "Is this your first visit to Burma?" They were both slight of build and short in stature. Devi Lal noticed the prayer beads in their hands. He had seen the couple in the second-class dining room several times but had not spoken to them.

"Yes, this is my first visit. I've never been to Burma before," he answered.

"Please permit me to introduce myself," the man said politely. "I am U Maung Hla, and this is my wife, Daw Kyi Kyi. We went to Bodhgaya on a pilgrimage and now are returning home. Are you visiting Burma on business? Will you be staying in our capital city of Rangoon?"

"No, actually I am going to Myitkyina to serve as the District Medical Officer," Devi Lal replied.

U Maung Hla nodded. "Oh, you are going to the northernmost town in Burma, to the land of the Kachin people. You will like it there. Myitkyina is a very pretty town in the foothills of the Himalayan mountains. It will be nice and cool there, not hot and sticky like most of Burma. I myself am a Professor of Burmese history at Rangoon University. Will you be staying in Rangoon before traveling north?"

"No, I'm leaving for Myitkyina later today."

"What a pity. Whenever you happen to come to Rangoon," the man said, "please allow my wife and me the privilege of serving as your hosts and show you our city." He then gave Devi Lal a card with his name and address printed both in Burmese and in English.

"I hope you will have a very nice stay in our country," the woman said softly. They bowed politely and walked away.

In the far distance, a golden spire appeared, ablaze in the brilliant sunshine. A crew member told Devi Lal that it was the Shwedagon Pagoda.

"You are looking at one of the most imposing and beautiful manmade structures in the world," he said.

The city of Rangoon gradually came into view. Suddenly Devi Lal began to feel apprehensive about working and living in a different country. Should he have turned down this assignment and asked to be kept in India. But then he consoled himself that if the Burmese were anything like this couple he had just met, he should be all right.

The river was now narrower and crowded with barges, boats and sampans. The ship slowed down and tugboats gradually eased it along the pier. Thick ropes were tossed out and secured to iron posts. First class passengers were allowed to disembark before the rest and Devi

Lal stood on the deck watching them. He saw the English couple whose little girl he had treated. The woman smiled and waved at him. She said something to the child in her arms and the girl also raised her hand and waved. All he got from the child's father, however, was a blank stare and an imperceptible nod of the head. Devi Lal smiled and waved back to the child.

The pier was a bustling sea of colour, as elegantly dressed English ladies tried to ward off the noonday sun with their silk parasols. Stiffly dressed Englishmen attempted to remain cool and maintain their poise. Indian men with turbans and women in bright *saris* mingled with Burmese women wearing colourful silk *longyis*. Their long black hair piled on top of their heads was adorned with ivory combs and jasmine flowers. Uniformed porters came down the gangplank carrying large sea trunks, elegant leather luggage and fancy wicker baskets. When the passengers traveling second-class were allowed to disembark, Devi Lal followed the porter carrying his suitcase and walked down the gangplank.

Thus it happened that Devi Lal arrived in Rangoon in the summer of 1903 and set foot on Burmese soil for the first time. He was 22 years of age and believed that he would return to Punjab in four short years. Destiny, instead, ordained that four decades would pass, during which time the saga of his life would unfold and intricately bind him forever to the people of this enchanting land.

Now, after all these years, sitting on the shores of the Irrawaddy River, Devi Lal wondered at how quickly time had passed away. Yet the memories were so fresh in his mind and he could clearly recall details of his life as if they had taken place just yesterday.

Upon arriving in Myitkyina, he had written a long letter to his mother giving her details of his journey and describing his new surroundings. Two months later, he received a letter from his brother Mohan Lal, informing him of their father's death. Devi Lal broke down and wept bitterly.

Our father was killed by British soldiers a week after your visit to Karyala, his brother wrote. *He died a brave patriot, riding his horse in battle to free our country.*

My father died while I was at sea between Calcutta and Rangoon,

Devi Lal suddenly realized. Oh God, the shooting star that he had seen — was that his father's soul ascending to heaven. Yes, it had to be, he told himself, tearfully. It must have been.

Our mother has been very courageous, his brother wrote. *She has now become active in the freedom movement and participates in protest marches and demonstrations. I have taken our father's place in the Azad Hind movement as a freedom fighter. Our father's memory will be indelibly etched in all of our minds and will continue to inspire our people.*

Devi Lal felt devastated. For days, he could not sleep nor eat and had stopped going to work. He was overwhelmed with guilt. By disobeying his father, had he let him down? Maybe he should give up medicine and return home. He felt depressed, miserable and lonely. One day, while aimlessly roaming through town, he came across a wine shop. He had never tasted liquor. "It's an evil you mustn't let your lips touch," his father had once told him. But his father was now dead and gone. Devi Lal went in and asked for a drink, and then another. He bought a whole bottle of the potent native brew and took it home. He didn't know how long he remained in a drunken stupor. When he came out of it, he was aghast. How could he have been so weak as to defile the sacred memory of his father with conduct so utterly vile.

Overcome with shame and remorse, he cleansed himself and vowed never to touch alcohol again. He sought solace from his religion and turned once again to the holy book, *Bhagavad Gita*, as he had done so often before, seeking spiritual guidance and answers. He took strength from the powerful passage: "Death is the disassociation of *atman* — the soul — from the physical body. *Atman* continues its journey, assuming another body. We must therefore not grieve."

Later, he received a letter from his mother which he read with tears filling his eyes. She wrote that his father had often spoken about him.

When he was helped off his horse and lay dying, he said that if his doctor son were here, 'he would have saved my life.' The village has built a beautiful monument on the temple grounds in his memory. Many will be inspired by his courage and martyrdom. You, my son, must continue your work of healing. That has to be your way of thanking your Creator and honouring your father's memory.

Time passed, and Devi Lal returned to his work. His commitment to helping those who were ailing and in need of care was now even greater.

As the District Medical Officer, he was provided a comfortable home. The spacious house with a large compound was located on the outskirts of town, next to a mountain stream. Once a month he went on tour, traveling by horseback. He rode to remote villages in the high country, treating patients who were too ill to travel to town.

Soon after his arrival, Devi Lal employed a young Indian to look after the two horses and a mule he used when touring. Sher Khan had left his village in India in 1902 at the age of 16 and had worked for an English army officer who had brought him to Myitkyina. A year later, the officer had gone back to England. Sher Khan had felt abandoned and when he was offered work by Devi Lal, he gratefully accepted it. Sher Khan lived in a room adjacent to the stables in one corner of the compound. He was a devout Muslim and said his prayers five times each day, facing west toward Mecca. He took an instant liking to this gentle young doctor and served him faithfully. Five years younger than his master, Sher Khan was strong like an ox. He grew a mustache and beard which he kept neatly trimmed, and wore a *dhoti* and long shirt, a style of dress common in his native central India.

When Devi Lal went on tours, Sher Khan accompanied him, riding the second horse and leading the mule loaded with medical supplies and their personal belongings needed for the trip. Leopards, tigers and other wild animals were common in these remote hills of North Burma. Both men, therefore, carried rifles.

On one such trip they were passing through a particularly thick jungle where the narrow path was closed in and covered by a canopy of large trees and vines. After a steep climb, they stopped to rest the animals. It was very quiet. A slight movement in a branch above them caught Sher Khan's eye. He looked up and was startled to see a huge python dangling from the branch directly over Devi Lal, about to drop on him.

Quickly swinging his rifle to his shoulder, Sher Khan took aim and fired. The serpent dropped, twisting and writhing, landing on the ground with a loud thud, inches away from Devi Lal's horse. Sher Khan leapt off his horse, bringing with him a three-foot long, sharp Burmese *dah*. With one powerful stroke of the knife, he chopped off the python's head from its 20-foot long wriggling body. While Devi Lal tried to calm his startled horse, Sher Khan used the *dah* to dig a hole on the side of the path and buried the head of the python.

"Thank you! That was a great shot, Sher Khan," Devi Lal had said later. "Tell me, why did you bury the python's head?"

"Well, *Sahib,* I have heard that when a snake is killed by a human, its mate can see the reflection of the killer in the dead snake's eyes, and goes after the person, seeking revenge."

About a year later, on another trip, Devi Lal was attending to sick patients in a remote mountain village. Sher Khan decided to go shoot a jungle fowl to cook for their dinner and walked into the forest, going down a ravine and along a dry gully. After some time he spotted several jungle fowls and shot two. He took out a pocket knife and, in the Muslim tradition of *halaal,* cut their throats and bled them. By the time he left and started climbing out of the ravine, the sun was setting.

Halfway up he suddenly stopped. He had heard the roar of a wild animal. That is either a tiger or a leopard, he thought. He was unable to judge the exact direction the roar had come from. The jungle was dense and the animal could be anywhere. Sher Khan continued on the narrow winding path. The beast roared again. Although Sher Khan was perspiring from the steep climb, he felt a shiver run through his body. This time the animal sounded angrier, and much closer. That's a leopard, he now knew.

A leopard would generally not attack humans unless it had cubs and felt threatened. Sher Khan sensed a slight movement on a rock in front of him. He dropped the jungle fowls, but before he could raise his rifle, the leopard let out a terrifying roar and leapt at him. The beast buried the claws of one paw into Sher Khan's shoulder and sliced his cheek open with the claws of the other. Sher Khan crumbled under the weight of the leopard and slid down the ravine as the beast scrambled away into the jungle. He came to rest wedged next to the trunk of a tree, bruised and bleeding. He was shivering in the cold air and felt faint.

As the sun set and darkness came, Devi Lal became worried. A young boy told him that earlier he had seen a man with a gun walk down toward the ravine. Accompanied by the village headman carrying a lantern, Devi Lal went searching. They found Sher Khan and carried him back to the village. Devi Lal washed and cleaned his wounds and sutured the deep gash on his shoulder and face. They stayed in the village for three days before Sher Khan was able to travel.

Sher Khan knew that if Devi Lal had not found him and treated his wounds, he would have died in the jungle.

Time went by. Devi Lal was enjoying his work and kept busy. One day a neighbour sent word requesting that he stop by to examine a house guest who had sprained an ankle. Returning from the medical clinic that evening, Devi Lal went to his neighbour's house.

"Yes, doctor, thank you for coming over," his neighbour said, meeting him at the door. "This is our guest, Mah Lay, who is visiting us from Maymyo. She hurt her foot this morning."

A young woman was sitting on the edge of the sofa with her legs drawn slightly to one side and her hands in her lap. Devi Lal went down on one knee in front of her and examined her ankle.

"Does this hurt?" he asked, slowly manipulating the joint.

"Yes, just a little," she answered softly.

He could smell the delicate perfume she was wearing. He gently pressed a finger against the bones.

"Do you feel any pain here?"

"No, there's no pain," she answered.

He looked up at her. What an exquisitely beautiful face, he thought. Taking a bandage from his medical bag, he gently wrapped it around her ankle.

"It's a bad sprain, but luckily no bones are broken," he said, standing up. "Please try and stay off the foot as much as possible."

Then he turned to his neighbor. "I'll stop by again tomorrow and examine her."

All evening he kept thinking about the soft, fragile beauty of the young woman. She was so much like the delicate porcelain statues in the shop windows on the Esplanade in Calcutta that he had admired.

He went to see Mah Lay each evening. By the fourth day her ankle was much better and she walked him back to the gate. They talked and she told him about Maymyo, her home town, and her life there. He told her about his family and his work.

Mah Lay had recently graduated from the Teachers Training College in Mandalay and had returned to Maymyo to start teaching at a school for young girls. Her father, also a teacher, had died several years ago and her mother passed away a year back from cancer while Mah Lay was still in college. An only child, she returned to an empty home and tried to put the pieces of her life together. She was a beautiful young woman, poised but shy. Her parents' closest friends had persuaded her to come and visit them in Myitkyina.

Mah Lay's ankle had, by now, almost healed, for it had been only a sprain and there wasn't any need for Devi Lal to continue examining it. Yet he came to see her each day. One evening he shyly asked if she'd like to go for a walk along the river.

"Yes, I'd love that," she answered.

Strolling by the river, she almost stumbled on a pebble. He quickly reached out and took her hand to steady her.

"I'm sorry, that was clumsy of me," she said, but did not free her hand from his.

They walked quietly, not talking. Neither had ever experienced this strange light-headedness and the wild beating of the heart.

At the end of the week, when it was time for Mah Lay to return to Maymyo, they both knew that they were very deeply attracted to each other. They exchanged addresses, promising to write, and reluctantly said farewell with a shy tender embrace. They wrote long letters, once a week. Then Devi Lal asked her to marry him. She replied at once, agreeing.

Devi lal wrote and told his mother. Kanti's reply was prompt. Although she had hoped he would marry a *Mohyal* Brahmin girl from Punjab, she accepted his decision.

My daughter-in-law will be welcome in our house, she wrote. *May God Almighty bless you both with a long, healthy and happy married life.*

A short while later Devi Lal journeyed to Maymyo, accompanied by his neighbours as well as his faithful servant, Sher Khan. Mah Lay and Devi Lal were married with ceremonies from both the Buddhist and Hindu faiths.

Devi Lal took his young bride back to Myitkyina and they were ecstatically happy. He completed the last year of his required government service and was asked to stay on as the District Medical Officer in Myitkyina. Two years after they were married, their first child, a beautiful daughter, was born. They named her Khin May, after Mah Lay's grandmother. They hired Daw Mu to work as an *ayah* and help look after their child.

Devi Lal was then transferred to the town of Kalaw in the Shan States. Much to Mah Lay and Devi Lal's pleasure, both Sher Khan and Daw Mu went with them. Mah Lay gave birth to their second child, a son, in 1914, when Khin May was five years old. They named him Hari, after Devi Lal's maternal grandfather.

Devi Lal remembered the years in Kalaw as the happiest period of his life. Mah Lay was more beautiful than ever, and Devi Lal enjoyed raising their two handsome children. He taught them all he knew about the various religions and cultures around them. He tried to instill in them a sense of compassion and discipline. Having Sher Khan and Daw Mu was also a source of great pleasure for them as, by now, those two were more like members of the family and cared for the children lovingly.

From Devi Lal, his children learned about the Hindu religion. Mah Lay read them the teachings of the Buddha. "The Lord Buddha tells us that we must dispel ignorance and that we must not crave for material objects," she explained to them. "True happiness is achieved when we desire nothing."

Growing up, Khin May and Hari were taught to respect all religions and taken for worship to pagodas and to Hindu temples. They attended schools run by Roman Catholic nuns and thus were exposed to Christianity. They had gone to Sikh temples, and also learned about the Jewish faith from a family in Kalaw who were friends of their parents. In Sher Khan, they had a practicing Muslim.

When Khin May was eight years old, she one day said to her father,

"When I'm at school we go into the chapel and pray in front of a statue of Jesus Christ. Is that all right, Dad?"

"God manifests himself in different places and in different forms," her father told her. "It's all right to worship your creator in a temple, mosque, synagogue, pagoda or a chapel. You must remember that our minds and hearts are also like temples and chapels where God resides. By keeping our minds and thoughts pure, we can worship God, each in our own way. Then, by going to any house of worship, we can pray together with our fellow human beings."

When Hari was young, he asked his father why there had to be so many religions. "Think about God as being on top of a high mountain," Devi Lal patiently explained to him. "We all try and reach Him, but take different paths. Our ultimate goal is the same: we only differ in how we attempt to attain that goal. As long as you believe in God, it doesn't matter what name you call Him or which religion you follow."

Ten years after Hari's birth, the family's idyllic life was shattered when Mah Lay became critically ill. She suffered from severe chest pains and started losing weight rapidly. Devi Lal was baffled and could not diagnose her illness. He took her to Mandalay where she was seen by the Civil Surgeon of the General Hospital. From there, he took her to Rangoon where she was examined by several other physicians. A decision was made to perform an exploratory operation and the worst fears of the surgeons were confirmed. They found cancer of the ovaries with extensive metastasis to the lungs and other internal organs. Devi Lal took Mah Lay back to Kalaw and showered her with loving tender care.

"You must not grieve, my love," Mah Lay told him one day. "We've been blessed with a wonderful life. I'm so grateful for the time I've had with you. Be brave, my husband. The children will now need you more than ever."

Two months later she passed away, leaving behind a grief-stricken family.

Devi Lal could not bear living in Kalaw. He resigned from government service and, with his children, moved to Mandalay. Khin May and Hari became even closer to their father. Daw Mu and Sher Khan showered the children with affection. Devi Lal established a medical practice and threw himself into his work. After two years, he decided to make Mandalay their home and began building *Shanti Gaeha*.

Darkness was setting in and the breeze coming from the river had turned cool. Devi Lal stood up. His legs felt stiff. Hari must be worrying, he thought. I should have returned home earlier. He started his car. He had made up his mind. "We must leave Burma," he said softly, but with resolve. "I must get the children to safety. Their well-being is paramount."

The street lights were not turned on due to the blackout. He had difficulty seeing the road as the headlights were all but painted over in black. Leaving Mandalay was going to be painful. It was ironic, he thought. When he had first come to this country, he was determined to leave as soon as he could. Now, after all these years, he didn't want to go.

Dearest God, he prayed, help us. Guide us, oh Lord, as we prepare for this perilous journey.

The End of Dreams

Khin May, Daw Mu and the children had now been in Myitkyina for over six weeks. They were staying with friends of the family in the same house where, 35 years earlier, her parents had first met. Khin May liked this town in the hills, especially its fresh, cool air. Sophia and Neil began attending a school run by Baptist missionaries from the United States. At first Neil had refused to go.

"It's the middle of the school year," he complained. "How do you expect me to make friends? If you force me, I'll run away to Mandalay," he threatened.

Khin May and Daw Mu talked to him at length. In the end he agreed to try it out for one week. Khin May started working part-time as a volunteer in the same District Medical Clinic where Devi Lal had worked as a young man. When she heard about the fall of Moulmein, she had rushed to the British military authorities in town, frantically seeking information about her husband. No one was able to help her, and all she could do was pray that Tim was safe. She often cried herself to sleep and that, too, only after taking a couple of sleeping pills from the bottle she had removed from her father's clinic the day before leaving Mandalay. My God, she admonished herself. I've even stopped feeling guilty about stealing from my own father. She tried not to let Sophia and Neil worry excessively, but she knew that they did. Sophia missed her grandfather, too. "Why can't *Naana* come and stay with us?"

"Your grandfather is dedicated to his work," her mother answered. "Unless he absolutely has to, he will not leave."

In the evening, Khin May went for long walks while the children did their homework. Daw Mu insisted on accompanying her. "Daughter, it's not safe for you to go alone," she cautioned.

The second evening out, they took a narrow path along the river. As they came around a bend, Daw Mu stopped abruptly and, grabbing Khin May's arm, pulled her back.

"Get down on your knees, daughter," she whispered urgently. "We have to pray."

Khin May also now saw the wooden shrine under a tree. A small figure of an angry-looking man wearing the robes of the Burmese kings was visible within the shrine. Offerings of a green coconut, a bunch of bananas and some rice cakes were placed before the statue.

"Forgive us, oh great *Nat*. We meant no offense," the old lady started chanting, with her head lowered and hands held together in front. "We humbly bow our heads before thee. Permit us safe passage over this path ruled by you, and we shall praise you forever."

She then stood up and slowly backed away from the shrine.

"Your belief in the *Nats* is very strong, isn't it, Daw Mu?" Khin May asked when they were some distance away.

"You mustn't fool with the Spirit world, child!" the old woman answered, staring straight ahead. "If we anger the *Nats* we'll suffer catastrophic consequences."

"A strange thing happened in Mandalay, recently, Daw Mu," Khin May said. "I thought I had a vision of an old man. He said something about coming to see Mandalay's Child." She then briefly narrated the incident. "I must have imagined the whole thing, Daw Mu."

"No, you didn't imagine it," Daw Mu whispered, grabbing Khin May's arm. "You just described the messenger of the *Nats* who sometimes appears mysteriously and carries out the wishes of the Spirits." Breaking into a smile, the old lady continued, "You know, I've always felt there was something special about our Sophia. Being favoured by the *Nats* is a very great blessing. We need to be most thankful."

Khin May received several letters from her father, and also wrote to him. Then she heard the news on the radio that she had been dreading. Mandalay had just been bombed. Japanese planes had flown over the city. Their primary target was the Mandalay Fort, but a few bombs had landed outside on some densely populated neighbourhoods. As most of the homes were constructed of wood, several city blocks burned down. The news broadcast also said that on 15th February, the British authorities surrendered Singapore to the Japanese. Over seventy thousand British troops had been taken prisoners by the enemy. The same day, Khin May received a telegram from her father.

"Please return to Mandalay immediately," the message read. "Must discuss and carry out plans for the children's safety."

The next morning Khin May, Daw Mu and the children left by train for Mandalay.

The Japanese continued to bomb Rangoon. Between 23rd December when the first air attack took place, and 20th February, the city suffered through an incredible 31 days and nights of raids. On 22nd February, Maymyo was attacked. None of the Burmese towns had any defense against enemy air raids. Property damage and casualties were therefore heavy.

The Japanese 15th Army was racing toward Rangoon. In a surprise move, it circled the city from the east and the north. During the first few days of March, demolition crews destroyed all installations the British Government felt could be useful to the Japanese. Much to the annoyance of the Burmese people, the oil refineries in nearby Syriam were blown up. The doors of the city jail were opened and all of the prisoners, many of them hardened criminals, were let loose. The last motor convoy, carrying key members of the British rulers of Burma, quietly slipped out of the city and on 7th March, the Japanese Army marched into the deserted capital. Unlike its vibrant days of the past, Rangoon lay devastated and deserted.

As soon as Khin May and the children arrived home, Devi Lal and Hari tried to convince Khin May that they had to try and escape to India.

"How can I even think about leaving Burma," she answered, tears welling in her eyes, "when I don't even know if Tim is alive."

"We must pray and wait for him in India, just as we would in Myitkyina," her father explained. "David O'Connell has told us that the Japanese are putting British women and children into concentration camps. We must get Sophia and Neil to a safe haven, Khin May," he pleaded.

She resisted all day. In the end, she relented. "All right, I guess we must escape. When do we have to leave?"

"The sooner the better, child," he answered. "As soon as we can get ready."

Devi Lal obtained the necessary permits from the Deputy Commissioner, allowing travel via the European overland route to India.

"Take as much food supplies as you can, Devi Lal," David O'Connell advised. "Also, take your guns and revolvers with you. We've had reports of refugees being robbed on the way by *dacoits*."

"Thank you, David," Devi Lal said, extending his hand. "Thank you very much. I really don't know what we would have done without your help."

"Don't mention it, my friend," O'Connell answered, shaking hands warmly. "I'm really going to miss all of you folks. You've been like family."

"We'll pray that you get away yourself soon, David," Devi Lal said. "Maybe we'll meet in India."

"That'll be wonderful, won't it," O'Connell said, walking Devi Lal to his car. "Good-bye, my friend. God bless," O'Connell called out, waving as Devi Lal drove away.

Devi Lal made arrangements for a Burmese doctor to attend to the patients in his clinic after his departure. With the help of U Ba Kyi, he signed legal documents leaving his clinic and its contents that survived the war to the Home for the Elderly in Mingun.

"I'll be indebted to you, U Ba Kyi, if you could keep an eye on the house. I'm going to tell the servants that, if they wish, they may continue living in their quarters."

"Don't worry, my friend," U Ba Kyi assured Devi Lal. "I'll see to it that your house is safe."

"Thank you, U Ba Kyi," Devi Lal answered, shaking his friend's hand. "God willing, the war will be over soon and we'll return home."

Preparations for the journey, of necessity, were made quickly. Sher Khan was instructed to check the two cars.

"See that the oil is fresh and the radiators full," Devi Lal told him. "Fill the petrol tanks and put two five-gallon tins of petrol in the booth of each of the cars. We'll try to drive all the way to Monywa, Sher Khan. I'm not sure if we'll be able to obtain any petrol on the way."

Hari cleaned his father's four guns and two revolvers and purchased ammunition for each of the weapons. He also replenished his father's and his own medical bags. Khin May and Daw Mu collected a few cooking and eating utensils and packed them in a box. They obtained a ten *viss* bag of rice as well as supplies of salt, oil, tea leaves and sugar.

Khin May prepared six bedrolls for the journey. She bought thin, light mattresses, about an inch thick, pieces of canvas, and mosquito netting. Pillows were made by putting some of the clothing each would need into pillow cases. Each bedroll consisted of the pillow, bed sheet, a light blanket, mosquito-netting sheet, the mattress and a towel. These were wrapped in the canvas sheet and tied with a thin rope. Devi Lal withdrew all the money that he had in the bank and emptied the safe deposit box, bringing home Mah Lay and Khin May's jewelry.

The day before the family was to leave Mandalay, *Shanti Gaeha* was peaceful and quiet. In the morning, as usual, a *pongyi* walked into the compound and stopped at the front door. Khin May placed some freshly prepared rice and vegetables into his begging bowl. Later, the vegetable seller came to the front gate and Ko Than, with Sweet Pea at his heels, walked to the gate and bought vegetables for the day's meals. But everyone was heavyhearted and talked in low voices. Khin May reminded Daw Mu to pack her woolen sweater.

"It's going to be cold going over the mountains, Daw Mu. You'll need to wear warm clothes."

The old woman did not respond but went about quietly helping Sophia and Neil sort out the clothes they were to take. Of the servants, Sher Khan and Bahadur were leaving with the family. The rest had decided to stay back. Neil's friends came over, and they quietly rode their bicycles around the driveway one last time. Devi Lal and Khin May went to the clinic and presented each staff member with three months' salary before saying their sad good-byes to them.

Sophia's friend Rosaline came over around noon and the two walked to the swimming pool, holding hands. They sat with their feet in the water, not saying much. When Khin May returned from the clinic, she once again asked Rosaline to stay for lunch, sending Swami to inform Rosaline's mother. The family sat together and ate quietly.

Khin May's thoughts drifted to Tim and she quickly wiped the tears that threatened to flood her eyes. After lunch, she excused herself and went up to her room. Sophia and Rosaline ate hurriedly and went up to Sophia's room. Sophia brought Mr. Fluffy out of his cardboard box and sat with Rosaline on the window seat, looking out at the city and at faraway Mandalay Hill. Later in the afternoon, Khin May and Devi Lal went to the Maternity Hospital to deliver medical supplies. Devi Lal paid the nurse and the caretaker three months' salary, and once again they said their farewells.

By evening, the two cars were loaded with the meager belongings they were able to take, and were parked on the driveway in front of the house. During the evening, U Ba Kyi and several other neighbours came to say farewell and wish them a safe journey. At dinner, no one spoke. Daw Mu, as usual, stood over Neil and Sophia, occasionally softly brushing their heads with her hands. She briefly looked in turn at Devi Lal, Hari and Khin May and then, excusing herself, retired to her room.

The next morning, each member of the family was preoccupied and hardly spoke as they prepared to leave. Sophia attached a leash to Sweet Pea's collar and brought her down to the front hall. Just before sitting down to breakfast, Khin May asked Ko Than if he had seen Daw Mu.

"I gave her a cup of tea at 5:30, but haven't seen her since," the cook replied.

Neil ran up to her room. "She's not there!" he said, rushing back.

Devi Lal questioned Sher Khan. It seemed no one knew where Daw Mu was.

Sophia was frantic. "*Naana*, we can't leave without her!"

"Don't worry, child. She may have gone to one of our neighbours. I'm sure she'll be back soon."

It was almost eight o'clock and there was no sign of the old woman. Then the owner of the tea shop from down the road came to *Shanti Gaeha*. "*Saya Wun Ji*," he addressed Devi Lal politely, "earlier this morning Daw Mu asked me to hail a horse-carriage for her. She made me promise not to come to you before 8 o'clock."

"Where did she go," Khin May asked, urgently.

"She told me to tell you that she decided not to leave with you, as she would only slow everyone down. She was going to take the eight o'clock ferry to Mingun. She said to tell the children they are to help their mother on the long journey. She will pray for all of you daily."

The family stood there, stunned. Sophia started sobbing.

"Doctor *Sahib*," Sher Khan said, "if you tell me, I'll drive fast to the river shore and try and make it there before the ferry leaves."

"Yes, *Naana*, I'll go with Sher Khan," Neil quickly added. "We'll bring Daw Mu back."

Devi Lal looked at his watch. "It's eight o'clock. The ferry must be getting ready to leave. You will not make it in time, Sher Khan."

Khin May started saying that they would wait and leave the next day, when, from a distance, the wailing sound of the air-raid siren interrupted her. The chilling warning had begun just as the grandfather clock in the hallway finished striking eight. Devi Lal and Hari quickly urged everyone to get into trenches.

The faint drone of airplanes could now be heard clearly. They all sat, huddled together, looking up at the cloudless, blue sky. Sophia held Sweet Pea in her arms. The noise of the planes gradually grew louder and then became deafening as formations of Japanese bombers flew directly overhead. No British planes were there to challenge the bombers, nor any anti-aircraft guns to shoot at them. Sophia desperately wanted to cover her ears but Sweet Pea was squirming in her hands.

Suddenly a thunderous explosion shook the ground and Sophia screamed in terror. Devi Lal put his arm around her and drew her close. Then another explosion, followed by a series of ear shattering explosions, came from the direction of the river, each sounding closer. Dear God, please protect us, Devi Lal prayed.

The Japanese bombers were now criss-crossing the city, selecting their targets and dropping their bombs. Some of the bombs used by them opened up like umbrellas while still in the air and canisters of highly inflammable liquid spewed out in all directions, igniting everything within reach. Homes made of wood exploded into balls of fire. Angry red flames shot up high into the air.

Bombs were now falling all around them and sounded terrifyingly close. Sophia started weeping. A house immediately behind *Shanti Gaeha* received a direct hit and exploded with a thunderous roar. Dust and pebbles shook loose from the sides of the trenches. Devi Lal was perspiring, but his mouth felt dry. Their throats and eyes were burning from the dust-filled air of the trenches.

Then they heard sounds of shattering glass and the crackling of burning wood. A child started crying in one of the other trenches. Devi Lal looked up and, to his horror, saw smoke coming out of one of the upper rooms of their house.

He turned towards Hari. "Get Sher Khan and move the cars!" he yelled. "The entire building might go up in flames."

Hari jumped out and ran towards the cars, calling Sher Khan to follow him. Another bomb dropped further down the road and its explosion shook the ground violently. Several houses were burning and screams of the injured filled the air.

Flames were now coming out of the upper floor of *Shanti Gaeha*. Suddenly Sophia thrust Sweet Pea into Neil's hands and climbed out of the trench. Before anyone realized what was happening, she was running toward the house.

"Sophia, stop!" Khin May screamed. "Come back here at once!"

Sophia slowed down. "Mama, Mr. Fluffy is still in my room," she cried, looking back. "I'm going to get him."

"No. Don't go inside the house," Devi Lal yelled. "Come back here."

Sophia hesitated for a moment, undecided what to do. Suddenly the front and side walls of one of the upstairs rooms exploded in flames, spewing chunks of burning wood and broken glass. One large piece of wood came hurtling down and struck Sophia on her right shoulder, knocking her sprawling to the ground.

"Oh my God, Sophia's hurt!" Khin May screamed.

Before anyone could move, Bahadur, who was in a trench closest to the house, jumped out and ran to Sophia's aid. Picking her up in his arms, he started running back toward his trench. By now the rest of them were out of the trenches and Devi Lal frantically signaled Bahadur to run toward the front gate. Hari opened the back door of one of the cars and helped Sophia get in.

"Are you hurt, Sophia?" Khin May called out, gasping for breath.

"Mama, please help save Mr. Fluffy!" she wept. "I don't want him to die!"

Khin May climbed into the car and took her daughter in her arms. "Hush, child. It's too late. The whole house is in flames. No one can go in now."

A loud explosive sound came from the direction of the house. Devi Lal and the others turned to stare in stunned silence at *Shanti Gaeha*, now burning furiously. Tongues of angry red flames lashed out and even from this distance they could feel the intense heat of the fire. Smoke billowed high above in dark clouds. Tears filled Devi Lal's eyes. Fourteen years of loving memories were being destroyed before their eyes and it hurt so much. Khin May came out of the car and stood next to her father. She placed a hand on his arm. She, too, wept as the raging inferno engulfed their home.

The bombers had left, their gruesome task accomplished. The 'all clear' siren announced their departure, but went unnoticed by the dazed small group huddled near the gate of this once serene dwelling.

"Come. It's time we leave," Devi Lal finally said with a sigh. "There isn't much we can do here."

After one last look at the destruction of their home, they climbed into the cars and drove out of the gate to begin their journey to India.

The Perilous Journey

The two cars turned right and drove along 35th Road. Sher Khan was at the wheel of the car in front. Devi Lal sat next to him, and Khin May was on the back seat, cradling Sophia in her arms. Sweet Pea lay quietly, curled at their feet. Hari drove the second car, with Neil sitting next to him. Bahadur, his wife Surya and their six-year-old daughter Priya sat in the back. Devi Lal felt emotionally drained and physically exhausted.

Several buildings along the road were on fire. A few men and women scurried around with buckets of water, but most stood by, sadly, watching the destruction of their homes. Approaching 84th Street where they would turn right to go towards Sagaing, the cars had to come to a stop as a large crowd had gathered at the intersection watching a house burn.

Devi Lal got out of his car. A bystander informed him that two children were trapped in the house when it had caught fire. "An ARP warden rescued them," he said. "The warden went back to look for the children's mother but, by the time he brought her out, he himself was badly burned. He is there now, lying on the pavement."

Devi Lal peered over the shoulders of the people in front of him. The charred remains of a man lying on the ground were almost beyond recognition. From the lanky body and the gold-rimmed glasses Devi Lal surmised it had to be Mr. Donohue. Heroes come in all shapes and sizes, he thought. May God grant his soul heavenly peace.

"Let's try and drive through, Sher Khan," he said, getting back into the car. "There's nothing much we can do here."

They drove slowly along 84th Street. Buses, cars, horse carriages, bullock carts, bicycles, all laden with people and their belongings, were trying to flee the city.

Leaving Mandalay, they drove by the village of Amarapura, an ancient capital of the Burmese kings. A bus was coming from the opposite direction and Sher Khan signaled the driver to stop. Devi Lal got out and approached the bus.

"Could you please tell me if the Ava bridge is intact?" he asked the driver.

"Yes, *Thakin*, the bridge is fine, though this morning while we were in Sagaing, some Japanese planes fired at it."

He thanked the driver and returned to his car.

Sophia stirred in her mother's arms. "Are you hurt, Sophia?" Khin May asked, alarmed. "Your dress feels damp."

"I don't know, Mama. My shoulder is a little sore."

"Let me see." Khin May turned Sophia around.

"Oh God, you are bleeding. Dad, Sophia is hurt."

"Let me have a look at you, child," Devi Lal said, undoing the buttons on the back of Sophia's dress. There was an inch-long gash on her right shoulder. "We'll take care of this right away," he said reassuringly. "You've been a brave young woman, Sophia."

Hari joined them. "Here, I'll take care of her, Dad," he said. Devi Lal moved aside and watched his son cleanse and dress the wound.

"There. You're as good as new," Hari said, smiling. "Does it hurt? Would you like me to give you some aspirin?"

"No, I'm fine. Thanks, Uncle Hari." They got back into their cars.

"Do you think Daw Mu will be all right, *Naana*? Will we see her again?" Sophia asked.

Devi Lal turned around in his seat. "Yes, child. Daw Mu is better off living comfortably in Mingun. She won't have to go through the rigorous journey we have ahead of us. As soon as the war is over we'll return and she'll be with us again."

Sophia nodded and closed her eyes. They drove on towards Sagaing.

The spans of the Ava bridge loomed in the distance. The approach to the bridge was guarded by armed Indian and British troops. Several large guns were partially visible poking through green and brown camouflage netting and surrounded by sand bag barriers. The wrecked remains of three badly burned army trucks lay on the roadside.

The soldiers stopped the cars and questioned Devi Lal and Hari about their destination; then waved the cars on.

The view from the bridge of the broad river and the pagoda-covered hills on each shore was striking. But today they were preoccupied and paid scant attention to the scenery. The cars entered the outskirts of Sagaing. Devi Lal had hoped they would be able to continue west and reach Monywa before sunset. David O'Connell had warned him that the road was not paved all the way. "Don't drive after dark," he had recommended.

It was past noon and they stopped under a large tree by the river on the outskirts of the town. Ko Than had prepared sandwiches which they shared and ate standing by the water's edge. Soon the two cars drove on, slowly moving along the narrow road heading west. They had gone less than a mile when they were stopped again at an army check post. A British soldier walked up to Devi Lal's side of the car.

"You're not permitted to travel this road today," he said, sternly. "Weren't you told that in Sagaing?"

"No, we came from Mandalay and did not go into Sagaing," Devi Lal replied.

"Well, that's tough, mate. No one's permitted westbound. A flippin' army convoy is traveling east on this road today."

Devi Lal felt irritated but there was nothing he could do.

"Turn your cars around. Go back," the soldier ordered.

"Will we be able to go through tomorrow?" Devi Lal inquired, politely.

"I should think so, unless the bloody Japs decide to get here before you do," he said, now with a smile.

"Thank you," Devi Lal said.

"By the way, you do have permits to travel this route, don't you?" the soldier asked.

"Yes," Devi Lal answered. "We have permits for all of us in both cars."

"Okay," the soldier said, waving. "Come back tomorrow and we'll let you through."

"Are we going back to Mandalay, *Naana*?" Sophia asked when the cars headed back.

"I don't think so, Sophia. That would waste a lot of time," he said. "Besides we wouldn't have any place to stay."

"Can we spend the night somewhere in Sagaing, Dad?" Khin May asked.

"Yes. It just occurred to me," Devi Lal said. "We could seek shelter in one of the Buddhist monasteries in the Sagaing hills. I know the Head Monk of the Tharrawaddy *Pongyi Kyaung*. Let's go there. Sher Khan, stop the car. Tell Hari to follow us to the monastery."

They drove along the river, then turned on to a narrow dirt path that climbed up into the hills. Sher Khan steered the car around boulders and potholes, shifting gears frequently. The motor strained on the steep climb and the car jolted from side to side on the uneven path. The luggage tied to the rooftop carrier swayed precariously. Khin May and Sophia sat on the edge of their seat, holding tightly to the car doors. After a grueling thirty minutes, the cars reached the crest of the hill and entered the monastery grounds.

Devi Lal and his family were welcomed warmly by the *pongyis* and given rooms to sleep in. They spread their bed rolls on the floor.

"We have Daw Mu's bed roll, Dad," Khin May said. "Should I give it to Bahadur? His wife and daughter can use it."

"That's a good idea, Khin May." Devi Lal replied. "How are you doing, child," he asked.

"I'm okay," she answered, averting her eyes.

The view from the monastery of the surrounding hills and the Irrawaddy River was breathtaking. The hills, covered with gleaming white pagodas and huge clusters of bright red and orange bougainvilleas were bathed by the late afternoon sun. Yet looking past the river, they were grimly reminded of the war. The skies over Mandalay were covered with immense black clouds of smoke.

The *pongyis* arranged to have a simple meal prepared for their guests. As the sun set in the west, the Sagaing hills were slowly engulfed by darkness and the magnitude of Mandalay's destruction became more vividly evident. A bright orange glow from the fires still raging lit the entire horizon.

After dinner, Devi Lal came out onto a terrace of the monastery. He tried to imagine what *Shanti Gaeha* must look like. Sophia and Khin May were at the other end of the terrace, also watching the fires consume their beloved city. Devi Lal walked over to them and put his arms around his daughter and granddaughter. Hari and Neil came out and stood next to them. Neil clung to his mother's arm. Sher Khan joined the family.

The flickering glow from the distant fires faintly lit their faces. Their eyes were filled with tears and their hearts ached. Khin May shivered in the cool night air.

"We must get some sleep," Devi Lal said softly. "We have to be rested for the long journey ahead."

They went to their rooms but, instead of lying down on their mattresses, they sat by the windows, heavy-hearted, looking out. No one slept much that night as Mandalay burned.

Morning came and dark clouds of smoke were still visible, lingering over Mandalay. The two cars jolted their way down the hill and onto the road to Monywa. Again, they were stopped at the army check point.

"Oh, you're back." It was the same British soldier who had spoken to them the previous day. Their documents were inspected.

"Jap planes have fired their bloody machine guns at vehicles on this road the last couple of days," the soldier warned them. "If that happens to you blokes, get out of your cars and take whatever cover you find on the side of the road," he advised.

"Thank you. Thank you very much," Devi Lal answered.

"Cheerio, good luck," the soldier called out.

The road was narrow and its surface uneven, forcing the cars to move at a slow pace. Shortly after they left the checkpoint, the unmistakable sound of an air raid siren was heard, coming from the direction of Sagaing. Without looking at his wrist watch, Devi Lal guessed it must be around eight. He wondered why the Japanese bombers seemed to favour this particular hour for their inhumane acts. His prayers went to the people of Sagaing who were about to experience the horrors of war.

Around eleven, they reached the village of Myinmu.

"We can stop here, Sher Khan," Devi Lal said, looking at his watch. "We might as well have lunch now."

The *pongyis* had given them boiled rice, vegetables and some fish sauce, which they all shared. Sophia sat next to Bahadur's daughter Priya and let her play with Sweet Pea.

"Where'll we stay in Monywa, *Naana*?" Neil asked his grandfather.

"I'm not sure, Neil. I did write to a friend who is the Principal of the high school there. Let's hope he can put us up."

"Is that the person you met on the ship when you first came to Burma?" Khin May inquired.

"Yes. U Maung Hla was then a Professor of Burmese History at Rangoon University. He and his wife, Daw Kyi Kyi kept in touch with me over the years. You've met them, Khin May."

"Yes, I remember them."

"He retired recently, but may still be in Monywa."

By now, there was a steady stream of cars and buses driving west, most of them filled with refugees. Sher Khan and Hari eased their cars into the traffic and joined the slow procession toward Monywa.

At the pace they were traveling, Devi Lal figured they would reach Monywa by late afternoon. He turned in his seat to see how his granddaughter was doing. Sophia was reading the poetry book Hari had given her and Khin May sat looking out of the window, her face sad and pensive. Devi Lal's heart went to his daughter: her mind must be in such turmoil, he thought.

As he was about to turn back in his seat, he noticed two little bright spots in the sky, visible through the rear window of the car. Dear God, those look like air planes. With a sinking feeling, he recalled the warning given by the soldier at the checkpoint.

"Pull the car over to the side of the road, Sher Khan. Hurry!" he said, then frantically gestured to his son to also stop.

"Khin May, Sophia, get out of the car. Quick!" he yelled. "Run to those trees and stay underneath them"

Hari was out of his car. "What's the matter, Dad?"

"Japanese planes! They are going to attack us. Get everyone out of the car," Devi Lal yelled.

They all ran towards the trees. Devi Lal almost stumbled when his right knee, which had been sore for the past week, almost gave way. He steadied himself and limped the rest of the way to the trees. Hari waved at the car following his and pointed at the sky behind them, then ran towards the trees. The driver of the car did not understand what Hari had tried to tell him. Instead, he impatiently leaned on his car horn and angrily gestured to Hari to move his car out of the way. The roar of the airplane engines grew louder. Then they heard the popping sound of machine guns.

Two single engine planes flew over the road, firing at the cars and buses. The man who had gestured at Hari to move his car finally realized what was happening when machine gun bullets drilled several neat holes in the bonnet of his car. He and his companions jumped out and raced toward the trees. Halfway there, the man tripped and fell. He lay on his face in the dirt and covered the back of his head with his hands.

The two planes flew west for a few miles and then circled around. Coming back over the road, they fired their guns again before flying away, disappearing towards the east.

Shaken and dazed by the sudden attack, the refugees slowly drifted back to the road. Several cars were burning. Dense black smoke rose straight up in the sky from a number of places on the road. Two men and a woman who had stayed in their car were hit. They lay sprawled on the seats, their eyes staring vacantly. Another man was grazed by a bullet. A young girl fell while running to take shelter and severely bruised her knees. "I'll take care of them, Dad," Hari offered.

Devi Lal noticed that after washing the girl's bruised knees, Hari applied an antiseptic and tied bandages around each knee. Maybe that's what they teach in Medical Schools these days, he thought. In his experience, he had found that leaving minor scratches and bruises uncovered made them heal much quicker. He didn't say anything to Hari, but later when he was alone with the girl's father, Devi Lal advised him to remove the bandages the next day and to see that his daughter receive an anti-tetanus injection.

Several men used wooden sticks and canes to push aside the charred frames of the cars that had burned and were blocking the road. The car in which the three people lay dead was left where it stood. The military authorities would have to deal with it when they came along. Those whose cars were destroyed were given rides by others. It was late in the evening when the weary passengers drove into Monywa.

This sleepy town on the eastern bank of the Chindwin River normally had a population of about twenty thousand, but this number had recently tripled. A large military base had been established to handle war supplies from India. Thousands of refugees trying to escape to India had arrived from Rangoon and other cities. Most were British, but there were also large numbers of Anglo-Burmese, Anglo-Indians, Indians and Burmese, all hoping to receive permits to travel by the European route.

The government had built a refugee transit camp, consisting of rows of bamboo huts. The town was running low on food and medicine. Cholera had been reported and the Health Authorities had started inoculating everyone.

Sher Khan obtained directions to U Maung Hla's house from a police constable.

"Welcome. I'm so glad to see you!" U Maung Hla greeted Devi Lal. "I received your letter, and since then we've been wondering when you would arrive."

Devi Lal had not seen his friend in five years but, to him, U Maung Hla had changed very little. In fact, other than a few gray hairs and a slight paunch, he looked just as he did when Devi Lal first met him forty years back.

"I'm relieved you are still here in Monywa, U Maung Hla. I was worried that after your retirement you may have gone to live with your son in Tongoo."

"No, Monywa is my home now. In fact, because of the war, my son and daughter-in-law have sent their two children to stay with us. Please come in. Let me call my wife."

Daw Kyi Kyi came out of the kitchen. She too had changed very little over the years. "Oh good evening, Doctor. How are you? We are so glad to see you. This is Khin May, right? And your grandchildren. Come, you must be tired. Let me offer you some tea."

U Maung Hla's grandchildren, twelve-year-old Tin Myint, and eleven-year-old Wendy, soon became friends with Neil and Sophia. Tin Myint took Neil to a small stream behind their house to show him his favourite fishing spot. Sophia and Wendy took Priya and Sweet Pea to play on the front lawn.

Daw Kyi Kyi served them tea and then busied herself in the kitchen, preparing dinner. Khin May and Surya helped, and soon the house filled with the aroma of fine Burmese soup and curries.

"I believe you're doing the right thing, Devi Lal," his host said, as they later sat down to have dinner. "Even though the Japanese have promised to give Burma self-rule, I do not believe the conquering armies will treat us kindly. You are being wise in taking your children and grandchildren to India"

"I wouldn't have left but for my grandchildren," Devi Lal answered. "Now I'm worried about the journey through the mountains, and pray the children will be able to cope with it. Tomorrow morning, I'll go to the Deputy Commissioner's office and obtain whatever papers and permits we'll need."

"I shall go with you," U Maung Hla offered.

"I'm very grateful to you for your hospitality, U Maung Hla. I hope we'll not be too much of a burden."

"No, no. It's a pleasure for us to have you stay. We have enjoyed your hospitality on numerous occasions. As close friends, you must consider this your home. Stay here as long as necessary. And please do not in any way feel obligated. As you can see, although sparsely furnished, our house is fairly large and we have no problem whatsoever in accommodating you."

"What about you, U Maung Hla?" Devi Lal asked. "Shouldn't you also escape before the Japanese come?"

"Well, my wife and I are getting on in age," U Maung Hla answered. "We devote most of our time to meditation and going to the Pagoda. We'll stay here and face the consequences. I don't think the Japanese will bother old people like us."

The next morning, accompanied by Hari and U Maung Hla, Devi Lal went to the office of the Deputy Commissioner. After waiting for almost an hour, they were ushered into the office of a Mr. Henry Fisher, an administrative assistant to the Deputy Commissioner. Mr. Fisher, an Anglo-Burman, examined Devi Lal's papers carefully. He was middle aged and wore a crumbled dark blue cotton suit over a white shirt and a red tie.

Henry Fisher had worked very hard all his life and had risen in the British Government service as far as he would ever go as an Anglo-Burman. He knew that the British would never make him Deputy Commissioner. Growing up, he had always considered himself to be English. His father, an Englishman, had died when young Henry was only six. But as he grew older, reality sank in and he felt that he was neither fish nor fowl.

Fisher developed a cynical attitude and went around with a giant chip on his shoulder. But he studied hard in college and, taking advantage of whatever privileges the British were willing to give to those like him, he rose from a mere clerk to an Administrative Assistant. Henry Fisher looked down upon most Asians, as he considered himself superior to them. But then, he was looked down upon by most of the British. He felt insecure and compensated for it by always trying to be very officious.

Henry Fisher scrutinized the papers in his hands and then raised his head to gaze at the Asians sitting in front of him.

"Yes, these look all right. I think I'll permit you to travel to India via Tamu and Palel. Your papers will require an endorsement by our office. Then it will be a question of when we can obtain space for you on the ferry to Kalewa."

Devi Lal felt relieved. He had been afraid that the papers issued in the office in Mandalay might not be acceptable here.

"How many members of the family do you have traveling with you?"

Fisher inquired, although the permits clearly stated the names and ages of everyone.

"I have my son, a daughter and two grandchildren, along with two servants and the wife and daughter of one of the servants."

Fisher peered at Devi Lal above his glasses. "Well, it should be all right for your family, but your servants can't accompany you. As you can see, thousands of refugees are waiting to get permission to travel. This route is designated as a European route, you know."

Devi Lal was dismayed. "Mr. Fisher, I will not leave them behind. If my family is allowed to go, they must also go with us."

"Well, you are a doctor. You're needed here in Burma," Fisher said, tersely. "Why are you trying to get away?"

Before Devi Lal could answer, U Maung Hla spoke up. "My friend Devi Lal is a dedicated doctor and is very well known in Mandalay for his philanthropic work," he said, curtly. "Even your government appointed him an Honorary Magistrate in recognition of his social work. I assure you, Mr. Fisher, that Dr. Devi Lal would not consider leaving Burma but for the fact that his grandchildren, like you, are half-British!"

Henry Fisher was livid by this reference to his background. He was about to retort angrily but changed his mind when he saw the look on U Maung Hla's face. Instead, he shuffled the papers in his hands and spoke in his best official voice.

"Oh, yes, I do see here that your permit from the Mandalay Deputy Commissioner says that your servants can accompany you. I'll still need to endorse these papers. Come back tomorrow and see me at 10:00 o'clock."

Later that evening, Devi Lal talked to U Maung Hla about his two cars. "As you know, I'll have to leave my cars behind."

"Let me show them to the owner of a car repair shop that I know," U Maung Hla suggested. "Perhaps he can help you sell them."

The next morning Devi Lal, Hari and U Maung Hla went back to the Deputy Commissioner's office. This time they found Mr. Fisher to be surprisingly cordial.

"Yes, please come in. Be seated," he said. "Everything's in order, Dr.

Devi Lal. Your permits have been endorsed by the Deputy Commissioner. It seems he has heard about your work in Mandalay. He also received a telegram from a Mr. David O'Connell, asking that every assistance be provided to you."

Devi Lal sighed with relief. Thank you, David, thank you for your thoughtfulness. Aloud, he said, "I'm glad to hear that, Mr. Fisher."

"Do we need permits to carry our firearms with us?" Hari asked.

"Oh yes, you must get permits, or else your guns may be confiscated at any one of the several military check points you'll be passing through." Fisher gave Hari several forms. "fill out one for each gun and I'll approve them."

"Mr. Fisher, what is the earliest that you can get us tickets on the steamer to Kalewa?" Devi Lal asked.

Henry Fisher pulled out a thick file and paged through it. "Only small steamers can go up the Chindwin to Kalewa," he said. "They carry a limited number of passengers. I can get tickets for your group three days from now. If that's agreeable, I'll have the tickets for you when you come to pick up the gun licenses tomorrow."

Devi Lal turned towards his host, but U Maung Hla was already speaking. "That'll be fine," he said. "They'll stay with me as long as necessary."

"Make sure you carry cholera inoculation certificates for the entire party," Fisher cautioned. "You won't be able to board the ferry without them. Well, Doctor, is there anything else I can do for you?"

Devi Lal stood up and put his hand out. "No, thank you Mr. Fisher. You've been most helpful."

Then he remembered, "By the way, my granddaughter has a little dog with her. Will we require a permit for the animal?"

Henry Fisher looked concerned. "I'm sorry, Doctor, but the rules are very strict. Refugees may not take pets with them."

"My grandchild is very attached to her dog. She will be heartbroken if she has to part with it."

Fisher appeared sympathetic but said, "I'm truly sorry, Doctor. She better leave the dog with someone here in Monywa. I'm certain the animal will be taken away from her at the first checkpoint."

Devi Lal sighed. "Well, if that's to be the case, we will have to leave the dog here."

He knew how difficult it was going to be for Sophia to part with Sweet Pea. She had already lost her rabbit, and leaving Mandalay without her father and Daw Mu must be so painful for her.

Devi Lal told Khin May and Daw Kyi Kyi about the Government's policy of not allowing refugees to take their pets with them. "Mr. Fisher has been most helpful — especially after he got the telegram from David O'Connell," Devi Lal concluded. "I'm sure that if there was any way, he would have helped us."

"Doctor, Sophia and Wendy have become good friends," Daw Kyi Kyi said. "If you want, Wendy can keep Sweet Pea. Then, Lord Buddha willing, when all of you return, Sophia can have her pet back."

"Thank you, Daw Kyi Kyi. That might be the only solution," Devi Lal answered. "I'll talk to Sophia tomorrow."

The next morning, Devi Lal took his granddaughter for a stroll to the stream.

"Sophia, how do you like Wendy?" he asked.

"She's a very nice person, *Naana*. I like her a lot."

"We'll be leaving for India in two days. However, there is a small problem."

Sophia looked up at her grandfather. "What, *Naana*?"

"We have been able to get permits for all of us to travel. But it seems the authorities are not allowing any pets."

"Does that mean Sweet Pea can't go with me?" Sophia said, her voice beginning to falter.

Devi Lal put his arm on his granddaughter's shoulder. "I'm sorry, child. Anyway, it might be better for Sweet Pea to stay here in Monywa. The journey will not be safe. None of us would want anything to happen to her."

"Will I be forced to leave her behind?" she asked, trying to fight back her tears.

"It seems Sweet Pea is getting along very well with Wendy," Devi Lal answered softly. "What if you were to give your pet to your new friend?"

"But Sweet Pea is the most precious thing I have left. I don't want to give her away!"

"Giving has true meaning, child, when you give away something that you most cherish," her grandfather said gently.

Tears now welled in her eyes. "All right, *Naana*, if I have to leave Sweet Pea behind, I'd rather give her to Wendy than to anyone else." Devi Lal hugged his granddaughter and they walked back to the house.

The gun permits and the ferry tickets were ready and everyone had been inoculated against cholera. Khin May purchased soap and a few other essentials that they had forgotten to bring from Mandalay. Devi Lal and Hari bought additional medical supplies. They obtained anti-malaria pills as well as a large bottle of potassium permanganate which would be useful to disinfect cooking utensils on the journey.

The jewelry Devi Lal had brought had been carried by Khin May in her shan bag. "I feel very worried about losing it, Dad," she said. They decided that it might be safer for some of the men to hide the jewelry in their clothing. They purchased four men's undershirts, and Khin May sewed pockets onto them. The jewelry was divided and carried by Devi Lal, Hari, Sher Khan and Bahadur.

The auto-repair shop owner came and inspected Devi Lal's cars. He had a buyer for the newer of the two cars. The money received was, however, a fraction of what Devi Lal had paid for it a little more than a year earlier.

"It would please me if you would keep my second car for yourself," Devi Lal told his host.

"Thank you very much, my friend," U Maung Hla replied. "But as you see, I'm retired and already have a small car. You may wish to donate it to the Home for the Elderly here in town. You will earn greater merit for such a charitable deed."

Devi Lal agreed and U Maung Hla arranged for the transfer of the car to the Home for the Elderly.

Their last night in Monywa, Sophia slept with her arms around Sweet Pea. Early the next morning, she took the dog in her arms and held her for a few moments before handing her over to Wendy. She then left the room without uttering a word.

U Maung Hla accompanied his guests to the river shore. The caretaker of the Home for the Elderly was waiting and took possession of the car. Coolies were engaged and started loading their luggage onto the steamer.

"This is such a small steamer, *Naana*," Neil complained.

The steamer they were to take was not only small but also appeared to be quite old. Much of its black paint had peeled off and the metal of the railings and sides of the vessel had rusted. The decks reeked of oil and were cluttered with ropes, several bamboo poles, and the luggage that had been brought aboard.

Suddenly there was a commotion at a small pier just south of where the steamer was anchored. A motor boat had come racing upstream. The two men in it shouted something and several men standing on the pier came running towards the steamer.

"The Japanese have landed at Myingyan," one of them yelled. "They're coming up river in captured motor boats."

The captain of the steamer started yelling orders to his crew. Panicked passengers rushed to get on board. U Maung Hla shook Devi Lal's hand.

"Good-bye, my friend. May Lord Buddha protect all of you on your journey," he said and then hurried up the shore.

No sooner had Devi Lal and his family boarded the steamer when the sailors pulled the gangplanks in. A man and woman came running. "Wait, wait for us," the man yelled. It was too late: the steamer started moving away. The boat strained, fighting the strong current, but was gradually able to move to the middle of the river. A crew member checked their tickets and directed Devi Lal and his family to the upper deck.

"Did we get all the luggage on board?" Khin May asked her brother.

"Yes, we did," Hari answered. "We were lucky to have arrived early."

The few benches on the top deck were already occupied by other passengers who were all British. Sher Khan, Bahadur and his family had been told by the crew to stay on the crowded lower deck. Hari arranged the suitcases so that they could sit upon them. One English family had their two dogs with them. Khin May saw the look on Sophia's face and put her arms around her daughter, drawing her close. Neil glared angrily at the dogs and their owners.

"I hate the English!" he later muttered to his grandfather.

"There are good and bad people everywhere, son," his grandfather explained to him. "There are a lot of very good English and some who are not so nice. There are good as well as evil among all races."

"What about the Japanese, *Naana*?" Sophia asked. "They are so cruel!"

"War does strange things to some people, child. They often behave horribly," Devi Lal told the children. "Yet there are good Japanese, also. Remember Mr. Eto, the photographer who lived in Sein Pun? Wasn't his daughter in school with you, Sophia?"

"Yes, *Naana*, Miyoko was my friend. I was sorry when she left."

"Even if someone does us bodily harm, we should try not to hold them responsible," Devi Lal explained. "Remember that just as we are rewarded by God for our good deeds, we are also punished for our bad deeds. If you think the person harming you to be an instrument of God and is only delivering to you what you have merited through your karmas, then you won't hate that person."

"Do you think the Japanese will catch up with us, *Naana*?" Neil asked.

"Let's hope not, Neil. The British seemed to have lots of soldiers in Monywa. Hopefully they'll be able to stop the Japanese advance."

The banks of the river gradually became higher and thick foliage covered rocky outcrops. The river got narrower and the water a muddy red. Except for an occasional country boat, there was little traffic. After struggling upstream for about three hours, the steamer docked at the little village of Kani. Village women were at the shore, selling a variety of foods.

"Daw Kyi Kyi gave us more than enough food for lunch, Dad," Khin May said. "In fact we'll have quite a bit left over, which we can have for dinner."

"Well, I don't know what'll be available during the rest of the river journey, Khin May. Maybe we should buy something." They purchased a dozen boiled eggs, four fresh papayas, and two dozen small oranges.

They ate their lunch sitting on their suitcases. The steamer left after only a brief stop. The current was now even stronger, and sometimes the entire boat shuddered from the strain of its engines. Just when it appeared that the steamer would lose, it stopped shaking and gradually inched its way up stream.

A little after four, they reached the village of Kin. "The river beyond this point is treacherous," a crew member informed them. "The Chindwin loops sharply to the southwest before turning in a northwesterly direction. We'll dock here for the night."

The gangplanks were set in place and some of the passengers stepped ashore. The crew and the two armed Burmese police constables on board warned them not to wander too far. Several British men wore revolvers attached to their belts. Devi Lal and Hari now did the same, and gave Sher Khan and Bahadur each a rifle.

Their drinking water was running low. "There's a well in our village, a short distance away," a man standing on the shore informed Hari. The two police constables accompanied several passengers and they followed a narrow path through dense jungle. The water from the well appeared clear but had a peculiar smell. "We must boil it for half an hour," Hari cautioned the others. Back on the river shore, the refugees collected wood and lit fires to cook their food and boil the water.

Nightfall came quickly and with it, the air turned cool. The sides of the steamer deck were open and swarms of mosquitoes started pestering the passengers.

"Dad, I'll take turns with Sher Khan and Bahadur," Hari offered. "We'll keep watch throughout the night."

"That's a good idea, son. I'll also take my turn."

They spread their bedrolls on the crammed wooden deck. Sophia lay curled on her side under her mosquito netting, careful not to put pressure on her right shoulder. The wound had healed well, except for the pain she felt when her shoulder rubbed against the thin mattress. She closed her eyes and said her prayers.

God, please look after Daddy, Daw Mu and Sweet Pea. Also, please help us on our journey. Her thoughts kept going back to Mandalay. Finally she fell asleep, but remained restless, dreaming of Mandalay burning and people running.

Devi Lal had taken the first watch and stood at the boat's railing. The night was pitch black. He swatted at a mosquito buzzing irritatingly around his head. He was worried about how his family was going to manage, especially Sophia and Khin May. He knew that they would endure hardships and not complain. He did not know anyone in Kalewa and hoped they would find space in the refugee camp Mr. Fisher had described. Around eleven o'clock, Hari came and stood next to his father.

"I can't sleep, Dad," he whispered. "You go ahead and rest. I'll stay up."

Devi Lal lay down on his bed roll and covered himself with the mosquito net sheet. He felt fatigued. So much has happened in these past few days. Help us dear God. Guide us through this journey, he prayed.

The refugees were awakened in the middle of the night by loud voices coming from the jungle. Devi Lal sat up and pushed the mosquito net away. He picked up his rifle and quickly went to stand next to Hari. Two of the British men also stood up, revolvers in hand. Another voice came from the jungle up river.

"I'm here. It's all right," a man's voice called out.

Several people on the lower deck were also up. "Who are those men?" some one asked.

"I don't know," another replied. "I hope they're not *dacoits*."

"What time is it, Hari?" Devi Lal asked his son.

Hari turned on a flash light. "It's just past two o'clock, Dad."

The voices of the men were heard again, but now seemed to be coming from further away in the jungle. The men on the steamer had difficulty falling asleep. Dawn finally broke and the weary refugees slept for a short while.

The steamer left the village of Kin at eight and powered its way north for about ten miles, negotiating several bends in the river. The current was very strong and several times it seemed as if the boat would not make a sharp turn and, instead, crash into overhanging rocks. It somehow managed to stay clear and move forward. Around ten, the drone of an airplane was heard over the noise of the steamer's engine.

The passengers and crew nervously looked towards the sky, but no aircraft was sighted. At noon, the steamer reached the village of Mingin and made a brief stop.

Late that afternoon, they finally arrived at the town of Kalewa and coolies were available to unload the luggage. A Government refugee office was located near the shore. Devi Lal and Hari stood in line, and when their turn came, a Burmese clerk wrote down the names of their party in a register and stamped and dated their travel papers. He then directed them to the refugee camp.

"You will receive further instructions from the camp officials," he said.

The camp consisted of rows upon rows of newly constructed huts made of bamboo and wood. They were built on posts and sat four feet above the ground. Steps led to an open veranda which ran the entire length of each hut. Six rooms with walls of woven bamboo opened onto the veranda. None of the rooms had any furniture in them but they appeared clean and smelled of freshly cut wood. The camp was crowded with refugees. British families were accommodated in the two front rows of huts and the remaining rows in the back were given to Asians.

After their cholera inoculation certificates had been carefully examined, Devi Lal and his family were assigned two rooms in a hut in the third row. One room was to be occupied by Khin May, Sophia, Bahadur's wife Surya, and their daughter Priya. Devi Lal, Hari and Neil took the second room, while Bahadur and Sher Khan were to sleep on the veranda.

Devi Lal did not want to stay in Kalewa any longer than they had to and, accompanied by Hari, went looking for the camp administrator. The office was in a two-room hut at the entrance to the camp where, upon arrival, their cholera certificates had been checked. A large crowd of refugees was milling around, seeking information about travel to Tamu. Two Burmese clerks seated in one of the rooms were trying to answer their questions. Devi Lal was wondering who he should talk to when a small car drove through the gates and sputtered to a stop near the office. A harried-looking man got out and started walking towards the office. He wore a khaki shirt and trousers and appeared to be in his mid-forties. Devi Lal hailed him.

"Excuse me, but are you the camp administrator?"

"Yes, yes, but right now I'm very busy!" the man answered curtly, wiping his brow with a handkerchief. He was about to enter the office when he happened to look at Devi Lal's face. "You are Dr. Devi Lal of Mandalay, aren't you?" he asked.

"Yes, I am," Devi Lal answered, surprised.

The man smiled and, putting his briefcase down, offered his hand. "My name is Tommy Carroll. You don't know me, but several years ago I watched you save my father's life in Mandalay."

Devi Lal remembered the Subdivisional Officer, an Anglo-Indian, who, while touring his district, had been bitten by a wild monkey and had contracted rabies. Devi Lal was able to get anti-rabies vaccine from the Mandalay General Hospital and had given the man a series of four-teen injections. Devi Lal was not sure the man would survive, but after suffering through the painful injections, given under the skin of the abdomen, he had recovered.

"Yes, I remember your father. How is he?"

"He's fine. In fact, since his retirement four years ago, he and my mother have been living with me here in Kalewa."

"This is my son, Hari, Mr. Carroll," Devi Lal said.

"Pleased to meet you," Tommy Carroll said, shaking Hari's hand.

"Come in, Doctor. Come into my office." He offered them the two rickety wooden chairs in front of his cluttered desk. "You must be traveling to India," he said, collecting several files from his desk and stacking them on the floor behind him.

"Yes, we are attempting to get to India and will appreciate whatever you can do to assist us," Devi Lal said, sitting down on one of the chairs.

"I'll be pleased to help you," Tommy Carroll said, taking a map from his desk drawer and placing it on the table. "Let me show you the route you'll need to follow to get to the border, Doctor. Here's the town of Tamu on the border with India. As you see, it's quite some distance north of Kalewa and to the west of us. This high mountain range runs north-south between here and Tamu and is very difficult to cross. This is the Kabaw Valley and, as you can see, it also runs north-south between this mountain range and another to the west of it. The best way to get to Tamu, then, is through this valley. Although almost totally covered with malaria-infested, dense jungle, there is a narrow bullock cart trail that runs the entire length of the valley."

Devi Lal studied the map carefully. "How do we get to the valley from here?" he asked. Pointing at a thin brown line, Tommy Carroll continued. "There's a narrow gorge that runs west from Kalewa to the village of Nat Kyi Gon and a tributary of the Chindwin flows through the gorge. As you can see, the Kabaw Valley starts just north of this village. The tributary has two sets of treacherous rapids, but local boatmen are able to pull their boats through them. Although the gorge is only fifteen miles long, the trip through it takes about a day and a half. The boats stop overnight on a sandy beach a little beyond the halfway point."

"Will it be safe for us to travel by this route?" Hari asked.

"So far we haven't had any reports of major mishaps with the boats going through the rapids. Police patrols do go through the gorge periodically, but unfortunately there have been a few incidents of local gangs of *dacoits* attacking and looting refugees," Tommy Carroll said, putting the map back into his desk drawer.

"Between my son, our two servants and me, we have four guns and two revolvers. I guess we will have to take our chances," Devi Lal answered.

"It's good that you have some arms, Doctor. You never know when you may need them. I suggest that you see the boat owners right away and reserve the number you need. If you walk through the town to its southern edge, you will come to the tributary. You should bargain with them and not pay more than 200 rupees per boat. If you need my assistance, let me know. I have to process several British families today, but perhaps tomorrow morning I can be of further assistance."

"You've been very helpful already, Mr. Carroll." Devi Lal said, standing up. "Yes, we're most grateful," Hari added.

They returned to their hut to tell Khin May that they were going into town to reserve the boats. Devi Lal asked Sher Khan to accompany them.

Both sides of the road leading into town were crowded with mostly Indian refugees camped in the open. It seemed that some of the routes to Kalewa had not been guarded particularly well and large numbers of Asians had been able to reach the town. Initially, the authorities denied them permission to use the Tamu-Palel route. But after several days of protests and near riots, they relented and allowed small numbers of Asians to take the European route each day.

"*Salaam*, Sher Khan," a man standing on the side of the road hailed. "It is I, Hashim." Sher Khan looked at him, surprised.

"Ah yes, Hashim," he answered. "What are you doing here?"

"We are on our way to India," the man said, walking over. "I and twenty-four of my fellow teashop owners left Mandalay the day after the bombing."

By now several of Hashim's companions had joined him and they greeted Devi Lal respectfully.

"We have finally received permits to travel this route, Doctor *Sahib*. We leave the day after tomorrow," Hashim said politely. "Doctor *Sahib*, we will be very grateful if you would permit us to travel with you. We are simple people and do not speak the English language. Your guidance on the journey will be most helpful to us."

"I know these men well, Doctor *Sahib*," Sher Khan whispered to Devi Lal. "Many of them come from the same village in India as I do. They are honest, hardworking people. They'll be of no trouble to us."

"You may join us," Devi Lal told Hashim. "We plan to take country boats from here to the village of Nat Kyi Gon. If you wish, I can hire boats for you also."

"Thank you very much Doctor *Sahib*. That'll be wonderful," several of them said, smiling. "We are most grateful."

Tommy Carroll was right. The head boatman, a short stockily-built man who introduced himself as Zaw, began by asking 500 rupees per boat. At first he was very adamant and would not budge, but after twenty minutes of haggling, the price was settled at 200 rupees. Devi Lal reserved four boats and, at Zaw's insistence, paid a deposit of 100 rupees. They were to leave two days later at seven in the morning. On the way back, Devi Lal informed Hashim about the arrangements for the boats.

"Thank you, Doctor *Sahib*," Hashim answered with a broad grin. "We'll be ready. Thank you very much."

Dusk was settling in by the time they got back to the camp. Several fires had been lit in the open and the refugees were preparing their food. Khin May, Surya and Bahadur had cooked a simple meal of rice and vegetables. They all sat and ate their dinner by the light of the cooking fires.

"It'll be good having Hashim and his men with us, Dad," Hari said in a lowered voice. "The larger our group, the safer we should be."

"That's right, Son," Devi Lal answered softly. "Tommy Carroll spoke of refugees being attacked by *dacoits* during the boat trip. We'll have to be very vigilant. I'll talk to everyone before we leave. There's no point in alarming them now."

"Are we safe in this camp, *Naana*?" Sophia asked, seeing the worried look on her grandfather's face.

"Oh yes, Sophia, we're quite safe here. Mr. Carroll told us that the camp is guarded by armed police constables who patrol the grounds day and night."

"Good, then we can sleep peacefully," she said, smiling.

"Well, we should all be going to bed now," Khin May said, standing up.

"It's so peaceful and quiet here, Mama," Sophia said. "Can't we stay up just a little longer?"

"All right, a few more minutes. It's almost ten o'clock."

"But we don't have any school tomorrow, Mama," Neil joked.

"You're right, Neil," Hari said, laughing. "But we have to check our supplies tomorrow and prepare for the journey ahead."

Khin May swallowed a sleeping pill when no one was watching, and lay down on her bedroll. The rest fell asleep quickly. The fatigue of the past few days and the relief of being in a safe camp made them sleep soundly. Towards the early part of the morning, the cries of a woman shattered the quiet of the camp. After a moment the woman screamed again.

Sher Khan got up and, picking up his gun and a flashlight, ran toward the hut from where the screams had come. He returned shortly.

"Doctor *Sahib*," he called urgently, "an English *Sahib* has been bitten on his foot by something. He's in great pain."

Others in their hut had also awakened.

"I'll come right away," Devi Lal answered.

"I'll go with you, Dad," Hari offered. They picked up their medical bags and rushed out. Two constables and several refugees were by now at the hut Sher Kahn led them to. A middle-aged Englishman was lying on the floor, his head cradled in the arms of a harried woman sitting behind him. The man was perspiring profusely and breathing very fast. It appeared that he was having convulsions.

"My son and I are physicians," Devi Lal said to the woman, moving the hurricane lantern on the floor closer to the man's foot. He noticed a tiny puncture wound on the outside of the big toe. He took a rubber strap out of his medical bag and tied it around the man's leg, just above the knee.

"Could you tell me what happened?" he asked the woman.

"We were asleep, Doctor. I think my husband got up to go to the bathroom. He suddenly screamed and said that he had been bitten on his foot." Devi Lal examined the wound closely. He lowered his voice and whispered to Hari.

"This doesn't look like a snake bite, nor that of a centipede. It must have been a scorpion. I'll prepare a serum injection."

"Are you sure, Dad?" Hari whispered. "It might have been a snake."

"No, I don't think so, Son," Devi Lal answered softly, giving the prostrate man an injection. "I noticed a single puncture wound. With snakes and centipedes there'd be two wounds, like a bite mark."

Hari took the flashlight from Sher Khan and pointed the beam around the floor. In his mind he was trying to remember what he had learned in Medical School about snake bites. A pair of bedroom slippers were lying next to the man's foot. Hari gingerly picked up the right one and, turning it over, shook it violently. A black scorpion fell out and landed on the floor. It at once raised its tail and curled it up defiantly. Hari quickly stomped on it with his shoe and, twisting his foot several times, crushed it.

"Oh God, what was that?" the woman asked, shuddering. "I hope you killed it."

"It was a scorpion," Hari answered. "It's dead now."

"Could you get me some water, please?" Devi Lal asked the woman.

He took a bottle of ammonia from the medical bag and washed the sting site. Then he loosened the tourniquet for a few minutes before tightening it again.

Within an hour, the man seemed to breathe a little easier. The tourniquet had been removed. "If you have any brandy or whiskey, I'd like you to give some to your husband," Devi Lal told the woman.

The woman produced a small bottle of brandy and poured a little into a glass. With her hands trembling, she held the glass at her husband's lips.

"I think your husband will be all right," Devi Lal said, closing his medical bag. "We'll return in the morning to see him." They walked back to their hut.

"Let me carry your medical bag, Dad," Hari offered.

"What was it, *Naana*?" Sophia and Neil asked excitedly. "Why did the lady scream?" Hari told them what had happened.

"The poor man," Khin May said. "Is he going to be all right?"

"Yes," Hari answered, "Dad saved his life."

"Well, we were lucky," Devi Lal said. "In the confined space inside the slipper, the scorpion did not have room to strike with force. That saved the man's life."

"It seems the poor chap came to Burma only four months ago," Hari added. "He was asked to come out of retirement and manage the oil refinery in Syriam. Not having lived in the tropics, he didn't know that you don't stick a foot into a shoe without first turning it over and shaking it."

"Weren't you scared when you crunched the scorpion?" Neil wanted to know.

"Well, I didn't have much time to think about it," Hari answered.

Sophia looked at the floor around her mattress, and tucked her feet under her bedsheet.

The next morning, Tommy Carroll came to see them.

"Thank you very much, Doctor," he said. "Thank you for treating the Englishman last night. I understand you saved his life."

"Hari and I were happy to be able to help," Devi Lal replied.

"Doctor, I would like to ask you a very big favor," Tommy Carroll said. "Will you please let my parents accompany you to India? I have to stay in Kalewa until the very end, but I'd like them to get away as soon as possible."

"Certainly. That'll be fine, Mr. Carroll. We'll do whatever we can to help them. We may need to hire one more boat. I only reserved four for my family and some other refugees who asked to join us."

"Oh, thank you so much, Doctor! I'm so relieved," Tommy Carroll said. "I'll arrange for the boat. I'll also talk to the boatmen and make sure that they look after all of you very well throughout the journey."

Later, Devi Lal went to see the Englishman again and found him to be resting comfortably.

"I don't know how to thank you, Doctor," his wife said, shaking his hand. "You're truly an angel of mercy!"

The refugees spent the day preparing for the boat journey. Additional food supplies were purchased. "Hari, remember to buy several boxes of matches," Devi Lal told his son.

"Why do we need so many matches, *Naana*?" Neil asked.

"We've been warned that the jungle is full of leeches," Devi Lal explained, "and the best way to get rid of them, I'm told, is to hold a burning match stick against their body."

"Wow, that's exciting," Neil exclaimed.

"Oh, how horrible," Sophia moaned, shuddering.

By nightfall, all preparations had been completed. Yet Devi Lal felt obsessed with the dangers his family was to face — the boat ride on the treacherous tributary through the mountain gorge, the bullock cart journey through the dense jungles of the Kabaw Valley. It all seemed so impossible!

He watched Khin May sitting on the steps of the hut, combing Sophia's hair. In the gentle glow of a hurricane lantern, they both looked so vulnerable. What will tomorrow bring for them, he wondered. We must make it through safely, he resolved. With God's help I must get them to India.

Dangerous Gorge

*T*he refugees arrived at the confluence of the Nat Kyi Gon tributary and the Chindwin River just before seven in the morning. Several country boats were anchored to the shore and a group of men sat around a small fire on the sandy beach, drinking tea. Zaw, the head boatman, stood up and came forward. A wide grin split his face.

"Yes, *Thakin*, your boats are ready," he said. "We'll see to it that you and your party get through the gorge safely." Zaw wore a *longyi* and shirt. A towel was wrapped around his head.

"Good. I'm glad to hear that," Devi Lal answered, moving his hand away from his right thigh so that the revolver in its holster was clearly visible.

Zaw appeared surprised upon seeing the more than a couple of dozen men in Devi Lal's party. Hari, Sher Khan and Bahadur carried rifles in their hands. Hashim and his men held stout sticks and some carried spears.

"Will these men accompany you," Zaw asked, "or are they in a separate party?"

"No, they're all traveling with us," Devi Lal answered.

The head boatman looked uncomfortable. Then he became downright distraught when he saw the refugee camp administrator, Tommy Carroll, coming down the bank. An elderly couple and two coolies carrying luggage accompanied him.

"What brings you to our boats so early in the morning, *Thakin*

Carroll?" Zaw asked, bowing. "Everything's all right here. There's no problem."

"Zaw, these are my parents," Carroll spoke sternly. "They'll be accompanying the Doctor's party."

"No, no, *Thakin*! Today would not be a good day for your honorable parents to leave. It is in fact a very inauspicious day. Please bring them back in three days when I will personally take them in my boat."

Tommy Carroll raised his voice. "Look, Zaw, you scoundrel—either my parents go today and you look after them or I'll call the constables right now and have all of your boats confiscated. Then I'll have you thrown into jail."

The man was visibly shaken. "No, no, *Thakin*. "That will not be necessary! I will see that your parents are delivered safely beyond the gorge." He then yelled at the other men.

"Get up, you lazy rascals. Load the luggage into the boats. We don't have all day. Look, *Thakin* Carroll is here. Get moving!"

"Doctor, I'm Johnny Carroll. This is my wife Martha. You remember us?"

"Yes, most certainly. How are you, Mr. Carroll?" Devi Lal answered, shaking the hand offered to him.

"I'm well, thank you."

"Thank you for taking us along, Doctor," Martha Carroll added.

"It's my pleasure, Mrs. Carroll. I'm happy to have you both accompany us."

The wooden boats were 25 feet in length and no more than six feet at their widest in the middle. A canopy of woven bamboo arched over the middle to provide cover from the hot sun. A piece of canvas at each end of the canopy could be dropped at night to provide protection from mosquitoes and the cold. Devi Lal divided their group into five and assigned them to the boats. He, Khin May, Sophia and Priya took one boat. Neil and Hari were with Johnny and Martha Carroll in a second. Bahadur and Surya, along with Sher Khan and Hashim were in the third and the rest of Hashim's companions rode in the remaining two.

The tributary at this point was wide and its current not too strong.

The three men tending each of the boats were able to move them smoothly upstream. Two of the men used long bamboo poles to push the boat while the third sat at the back and steered with a single long oar. Gradually the stream became narrower, the shores covered with rocks and boulders. The current now was stronger and the boatmen strained against their poles.

After about four hours, a narrow strip of sand appeared along the southern edge of the stream. The boats pulled in and tied to the shore, grouped together.

"We shall rest here for an hour, *Thakin*," Zaw informed Devi Lal. "Then we will tackle the first set of rapids."

"It feels good to stretch my legs," Neil said, leaping off the boat.

"Yes, that was a long time to sit in one position, especially for a young active man like you," Martha beamed as Neil helped her off the boat.

Martha Carroll had a gentle round face and wore glasses. Her hair was completely gray, giving her a very grandmotherly appearance. "Careful, Johnny," she called out to her husband, "wait 'til this fine young man helps you get off."

Johnny Carroll was tall, but his skin was pale and he appeared tired. "Oh, I can manage, Martha," he answered, slowly climbing out of the boat.

Devi Lal looked around the shore and beckoned his son. "Hari, take Sher Khan with you," he said softly. "Go up to the top of those rocks and see what's there in each direction."

Hari and Sher Khan picked up their rifles and started climbing. Neil ran and joined them. The tallest rock was about sixty feet high and from there, they had a clear view of the reddish-brown waters in both directions. They could hear a faint roar coming from upstream.

"Could those be the rapids, Uncle Hari?" Neil asked.

"Yes, that's what it sounds like," Hari answered.

"Wow. It'll be exciting going through them," Neil exclaimed, scampering up another rock.

Behind them, as far as the eye could see, was thick, impenetrable jungle. They climbed down and Hari told his father what they had seen.

"Tell Hashim to assemble his men, Hari. I'm suspicious about Zaw's intentions." The men gathered at one end of the narrow strip of sand.

"We need to be extremely alert on this journey," Devi Lal told the men. "Several refugees have been attacked by *dacoits* in this gorge. When we stop for the night, we'll post guards. We'll stay up all night in groups of five."

Later, he spoke to Bahadur, Sher Khan and Hari, "If we are attacked by *dacoits*, shoot them — but aim for their legs and knees. There's no need to kill them."

After resting for about an hour, the men got the boats moving again. They went around a bend in the tributary and the roar of the rapids became much louder. Large boulders could be seen strewn across the stream with the waters noisily gushing around them. The boats were again poled towards the shore and tied to overhanging branches just below the rapids.

Oh God! Khin May thought. How're we going to get through those rocks?

The boatmen tied a thick rope to the front of the first boat. They took off their shirts and, pulling the lower end of their *longyis* between their legs, tucked them into the folds of the garment behind their waists. Zaw and several of his men jumped into the shallow water. Pulling the rope, they gradually started towing the boat forward. The men on board used their poles to keep the boat from hitting the rocks.

Zaw and his men strained, pulling on the rope, leaning forward, trying to maintain footholds on the slippery rocks. Zaw kept calling out instructions to his companions. His muscular shoulders glistened with perspiration and the spray of the rapids. Suddenly the boat rocked and, jerking to one side, slammed into a large rock. Khin May, Sophia and Priya were thrown against the bamboo canopy. A boatman quickly leapt onto the rock and, bracing his shoulder against the boat, started pushing it away. They got the boat moving again.

The men had been labouring for half an hour and appeared exhausted. They now wrapped the front end of the rope around a projecting boulder and rested, standing in the hip-deep water. After a few minutes, they began pulling again. There were fewer rocks now and the men were able to get the boat to calmer waters and to a sandy beach.

Anchoring the boat to the shore, they untied their rope and walked back, hugging the shore, at times wading through the water and then climbing over rocks. They reached the remaining boats and pulled them safely through the rapids, one after another. By the time the last boat had been made fast to the beach, it was past four o'clock. The exhausted boatmen sprawled on the sand.

"You and your companions did well, Zaw," Devi Lal said, feeling a sense of respect for these hard-working men. Perhaps I've been too hasty, thinking they intend to rob us, he thought.

"We'll camp on this beach for the night, *Thakin*," Zaw replied. "The second set of rapids are even more hazardous. We'll need at least half a day to get all of the boats through them, that is if all goes well."

Hari and Sher Khan walked to the edge of the beach away from the water. They found a narrow path that wound its way between some boulders, headed deep into the jungle.

"The trees and bushes are very dense, but this path is well-worn," Sher Khan commented. "We'll have to keep an eye on it."

The boatmen collected driftwood and started preparing their meal in one corner of the beach. The refugees did the same. Later, Devi Lal instructed Hashim and his men to collect as much driftwood and dried brush as they could find.

"We must keep a bonfire burning all night," he instructed. "If we're going to be attacked, we have to be prepared."

Devi Lal took his revolver belt off. "Hashim, I'll show you how to work the safety catch and fire the weapon. Wear it around your waist."

"Thank you Doctor *Sahib*," the man replied, beaming. I'll use it most carefully and only when you direct me."

Tying the belt around his waist, Hashim swaggered towards his men.

"Be vigilant at all times," he ordered them. "Pay attention to what the Doctor *Sahib* asks us to do."

Dusk had set in and the refugees had finished eating. They sat conversing in quiet voices. Khin May had taken an instant liking to Martha and Johnny Carroll.

"I'm so pleased you've joined us," she said to them.

"Oh, it's our good fortune, my dear, that you all came along," Martha answered, hugging Khin May.

Devi Lal beckoned Hari and Sher Khan aside. "I've been thinking. We'll have to guard the path coming from the jungle," he spoke softly. "In addition, we must watch the tributary for any approaching boats. The fire has to be kept going all night, and we should also keep an eye on the boatmen as I'm not sure if we can trust them."

"Bahadur, Hari and I will take turns staying up through the night, Doctor *Sahib*," Sher Khan offered. "You should rest tonight. We'll also have Hashim and his men join us to keep watch."

"Thank you, Sher Khan. If anything suspicious happens, wake all of us up. I don't want us to be caught by surprise."

Darkness came quickly and except for the chirping of crickets and the croaking of a few frogs, the night was very still. Sleeping in the crammed boats was difficult and many of the men opted instead to sleep on the soft sand of the beach. Sophia lay awake, her mind wandering over the events of the past few weeks. She finally dozed off, lulled by the lapping of the water against the side of the boat, but she had disturbing dreams of bombs, fires and children getting hurt. Khin May slipped a sleeping pill into her mouth. Devi Lal felt tired. His knee was still sore and now there was a burning sensation in his stomach. He was going to have to take some medicine if it persisted. He turned on his side and tried to fall asleep.

Sher Khan, accompanied by four of Hashim's companions, slowly walked up and down the beach. The flames from the bonfire created eerie patterns on the dense foliage behind them. Occasionally Sher Khan directed the powerful beam of a flashlight down the path through the jungle. The boatmen lay curled in their blankets and seemed to be asleep.

It was close to midnight and, so far, everything had been quiet. Just as Sher Khan was about to wake Bahadur up to take the next watch, he heard a whistle, like the call of a bird, coming from the direction of the water. He froze, listening intently. Then he clearly heard a whistling sound, this time from the jungle. Sher Khan gently shook Bahadur's shoulder.

"Get up," he whispered. "Go wake up Hari. There's something going on. I'll inform Doctor *Sahib*."

Sher Khan then turned to the four men with him. "Wake up your companions," he said urgently. "Tell them to be very quiet. They are not to do anything but await Doctor *Sahib*'s instructions." He then rushed to Devi Lal's boat.

"Doctor *Sahib*, please wake up," he said softly.

Devi Lal climbed out of his boat. Before Sher Khan could tell him what was happening, they heard a whistle come from where the boatmen were sleeping.

"Moments ago, there were similar sounds from the jungle and the water, Doctor *Sahib*," Sher Khan whispered.

"Perhaps the *dacoits* plan to attack us from both sides," Devi Lal mused. "The boatmen must be signaling them. Bahadur, take four or five men with you and stand guard over the boatmen. Don't let any of them get up."

"*Achha, Sahib*," Bahadur replied, patting the razor sharp *kukhri* hanging at his waist.

Hari had been peering into the darkness upstream. "Dad, I can make out a boat. There are several men in it," he said urgently.

"Hari and I will fire a few rounds over the heads of the men coming downstream," Devi Lal quickly instructed Sher Khan. "When we do that, I want you to fire a couple of rounds into the path through the jungle. Tell the rest of the men that when they hear the shots, they should make as much noise as they can. Hurry. We don't have much time."

Neil came out of his boat. "What's happening, *Naana*?" he asked, excitedly.

"Hush! Go, quietly wake up the rest" his grandfather told him. "Tell them to stay in their boats."

Devi Lal nodded to his son and they both fired their guns, aiming a few feet above the outline of the approaching boat that was now clearly visible. The loud sound of the guns echoed explosively through the gorge. Sher Khan fired his gun toward the path and Hashim's men started screaming, making an infernal racket beating on pots and pans.

The boatmen on the beach suddenly sat up and Zaw leapt to his feet. Then he saw Bahadur standing next to him, grinning, slowly brandishing a large *kukhri*. Zaw had seen a Gurkha at a large religious festival behead a full-grown water buffalo with a single slash of the lethal knife. The head boatman quickly sat down on the ground.

The boat coming downstream had slowed down. Then, to the sound of furious paddling, it reversed its direction and quickly moved back upstream. Devi Lal fired another round over the fast-retreating boat before it disappeared into the darkness. The last echo of the rifle shots slowly faded and Hashim's men quieted down. All that could be heard now was the gurgling of the water in the tributary.

"*Thakin Gyi*, those must have been the *dacoits* who prey on the refugees in this gorge," Zaw said sheepishly, walking up to Devi Lal. "It was very good that you were able to scare them away."

"Yes, this time we shot over their heads," Devi Lal answered sternly. "But if they return, I'll instruct my men to shoot straight at them and at anyone else who helps them!"

"That is right, *Thakin Gyi*," the head boatman said avoiding his eyes. "You should kill these scoundrels."

Dawn broke and in the rays of the rising sun the gorge once again appeared peaceful. The boatmen went about their business as if nothing untoward had happened.

"It's best we not ask them too many questions," Devi Lal told Hari and the rest of the men. "We need their help to make it through the gorge."

"Well, they haven't abandoned us," Hari added. "At least not as yet."

The boats took off again around seven o'clock, with the boatmen poling and rowing upstream. After about an hour, the roar of rapids ahead became deafening. The gorge was narrower, the sheer granite walls on each side higher.

Once again, the boats were guided to the shore and tied to overhanging trees. The thick rope was fastened to the front of the first boat. The boatmen scampered over rocks and, entering the water, pulled the boat through the rapids. The two men with poles kept the boat from being buffeted against the rocks. Now and then, the wooden hull hit hard against a rock, jarring the boat, making the people on it very edgy.

Three boats had made it safely through the rapids. The boatmen began bringing the fourth boat through, on which Hashim's men were sitting. Suddenly the tow rope snapped. The boat started hurtling downstream. It hit a boulder with a jarring motion, throwing the two men with the poles into the water. The boat bounced from one rock to another, spinning crazily in the churning waters. The third boatman fortunately kept his balance and frantically worked the oar, trying to steer through the rocks. Hashim's men sat stern-faced, tightly clutching any handhold they could find. After several terrifying minutes, the lone boatman succeeded in getting the boat clear of the rocks and steered it towards the shore.

The men who had fallen into the water, slowly made their way back downstream to the boats at the shore. The frayed end of the rope was cut off and the last two boats were then pulled through the rapids safely. The exhausted boatmen lay on a grassy slope by the water. The refugees stood on the shore, dazed, but very grateful that they had all survived.

"All right, *Thakin*," Zaw said, standing up. "We can now take you to the end of this journey."

As the boats moved upstream over smoother waters, Devi Lal looked back at the raging waters. Thank you, God, thank you so much, he prayed silently.

The boats pulled to the shore and came to a stop, side by side. Zaw was the first to climb out.

"Here we are, *Thakin Gyi*," he said, bowing to Devi Lal. "We have safely made it to our destination. We are in Nat Kyi Gon."

Several villagers offered to carry the luggage and led the refugees to the camp just beyond their village. Devi Lal paid Zaw for the boats at the prearranged price of 200 rupees each. He then gave him an additional 300 rupees to be shared by all of the boatmen. Zaw was pleased and bowed repeatedly.

"These men are so nice, aren't they, *Naana*?" Sophia asked her grandfather as she walked along, holding his hand.

"Well, they worked very hard," he replied. "They brought us safely through the gorge. For that we should be thankful."

The British authorities had only recently begun building refugee camps through the Kabaw Valley. This camp at its southern end was the first and consisted of forty huts of the same design as those in Kalewa. The rooms in the huts did not have any furniture, neither did the openings in their walls have any doors or windows that could be shut. Two Burmese employees of the Government were responsible for the construction and the supervision of the camp. Men and women from the surrounding villages were hired to extract bamboo from the jungle and build the huts. Most huts were already occupied by refugees who had arrived in several groups the previous day. Devi Lal's party was given three huts.

"I am U Ba Thein, the camp supervisor," the older of the two government employees said to Devi Lal. "I see that you have many men in your group, as well as guns. That's good. We've had problems with gangs of robbers in the valley."

With the experiences of the past two days, Devi Lal and the men in his group seemed more self-assured. Sher Khan, Bahadur, Hari and Devi Lal wore their guns slung behind their backs. Bahadur, additionally, wore his *kukhri* at his side. Hashim swaggered around, with the revolver attached to his belt. His companions boldly carried their spears and long stout canes.

The other refugees, numbering about sixty, looked at these new arrivals with curiosity. The people already in the camp included two British couples, one Chinese family of five, several Anglo-Indian and Anglo-Burmese families, and about twenty Indian men who had worked in the teak forests of eastern Burma.

"How many days will it take us to journey to Tamu?" Devi Lal asked U Ba Thein.

"You will most likely need to stop for five nights," the supervisor answered.

"Are there camps such as this on the way? We'll be very grateful for your advice and assistance."

"No, Doctor, this is the first camp we are building," the man answered. "As you can see, we still have to install doors and window shutters. Shortly my companion and I will move north into the valley to start construction on additional camps. I'll help you hire bullock carts. During the middle of the day, it gets extremely hot in the valley. So the bullock carts usually leave early and then stop for two to three hours during the middle of the afternoon."

"Will it be safe for the women and children to sleep in the carts on the way?" Hari asked.

"They will have to manage as best they can," the camp supervisor answered. "You must post guards. The Deputy Commissioner of our area has arranged for the police in Tamu to provide patrols on horseback and constables ride through the valley periodically. But the jungle is very dense and bands of miscreants have been bothering refugees."

"Thank you very much for the information," Devi Lal said. "I'll be very grateful if you could arrange for bullock carts for our party. We are a total of thirty-six men, women and children. We also have our food supplies and other luggage. If possible, we would like to leave tomorrow morning."

"I think you'll need twelve carts," U Ba Thein answered. "I shouldn't have trouble getting them for you. The villagers around here are anxious to earn money. I see no reason why your party could not leave by eight tomorrow morning."

When Devi Lal returned to his assigned hut, several of the other refugees were waiting for him,

"Sir, we arrived here yesterday," one of the men addressed Devi Lal. "Some of us were robbed on the way. We're all very nervous about the trip to Tamu. We'll be most grateful if you would allow us to join your group."

"I'm sorry to hear about the attack," Devi Lal responded. "We were also going to be robbed, but were able to scare the *dacoits* away. It'll be all right for any of you to come with us. In fact, the larger the group, the better it might be for all of us. We plan to leave tomorrow morning by eight o'clock."

The men quickly went back to tell their companions and to arrange for bullock carts for themselves. The word got around rapidly and the remaining families also decided to leave the next morning. Nightfall came quickly. Except for the narrow path which led to the village of Nat Kyi Gon and another that came in from the west, the camp appeared to be surrounded by dense jungle. The refugees prepared their food and ate by the light of the cooking fires and a few lanterns. Women and children went into the huts to bed down for the night.

Sophia sat on her mattress and was trying to write in her diary, but the light from the hurricane lantern was too weak. She closed the diary and put it away in the shan bag she had brought with her from Mandalay.

It was a dark, moonless night and the eerie silence of the surroundings was broken only by the sounds of crickets and an occasional hooting of a night owl. The camp supervisor was talking to Devi Lal and was about to leave when some drums started beating in the distance. The sharp piercing sound of reed instruments joined in, playing a strange, haunting tune.

"What's that?" Sophia asked, turning to her mother.

"I don't know," Khin May answered, getting up and walking out onto the veranda. Sophia and Neil followed and stood next to her.

"The inhabitants of a village up in the hills about two miles west of here called Hontha are conducting a *nat-pwe*," U Ba Thein explained to Devi Lal. "Tonight they'll put on their exotic costumes and dance to the music. There'll be a lot of drinking and eating all night as they worship the Spirit that protects their village." The supervisor then left saying, "I'll see you tomorrow morning, *Thakin*."

The strange music was making all of the refugees very nervous. Sophia clung to her mother's arm. Devi Lal, Hari, Sher Khan and Bahadur were standing next to a cooking fire which they planned to keep lit all night.

"I want us to post guards again tonight, Sher Khan," Devi Lal spoke softly. "In fact, we must do so each night for the rest of the journey."

"That's a good idea, Doctor *Sahib*," Sher Khan answered. "I'll speak to Hashim and his men. Bahadur and I will work out the details."

Hari was about to say something when they heard a shuffling noise from the direction of the narrow path coming from the west. Suddenly three men appeared, emerging out of the darkness of the jungle. They wore cotton *longyis* and were bare-chested. The light from the flames of the cooking fire drew dancing designs on their faces.

Hari placed his hand over the revolver at his waist and Sher Khan quickly bent down to pick up his rifle lying on the ground. The men stopped a short distance from Devi Lal and looked at him with expressionless faces. Their eyes appeared glazed and stared vacantly.

Then the one in the middle spoke. "We have been told you are from Mandalay town," he said in Burmese, his voice slurred and slow.

"Yes, we're from Mandalay," Devi Lal answered.

"You have a Mandalay-born girl child," the same man continued, "we ask that she come with us."

"No! Go away. Go back to your village." Hari said firmly, his mouth going dry and his palms beginning to perspire.

"The *Min Mahagiri*, the Lord of the Great Mount Popa, is the protector of our village," the man was saying. "The Lord who favors Mandalay-born female children will be pleased by the presence of such a child at our festival. No harm will come to her."

"No, no! No one will be taken from this camp," Devi Lal spoke angrily. "You're being warned. Leave here at once," he threatened.

The men seemed to be in a trance and stood staring at Devi Lal. "We must take her," one of them repeated stubbornly.

Back on the darkened veranda, Sophia shuddered. She didn't know what was going on but felt strangely agitated. "I want to go in, Mama," she whispered, pressing her face against her mother's arm. Khin May led her back inside and Sophia lay down on her mattress with her head cradled in her mother's lap.

Devi Lal signaled to Bahadur and Sher Khan. The two started advancing towards the villagers. "Get going," Sher Khan said curtly, raising his rifle. They pushed the three men towards the jungle path.

"You have angered the Spirits," one of the villagers yelled, pointing a finger at Devi Lal. "You have drawn their wrath upon yourself."

No one spoke for some time after the villagers disappeared into the darkness.

Devi Lal's heart was racing and he felt weak. The gnawing dull pain in his stomach was back again, making him grimace.

They doubled the guards and put more logs on the fire. The drums and the strange music continued eerily throughout the night. Khin May slept with her arm across Sophia's shoulders. With the breaking of dawn, the music stopped and the surrounding jungle appeared less frightening. The refugees quickly prepared their morning meal and broke camp.

They waited for the bullock carts, but by eight o'clock, only half the promised number had arrived. U Ba Thein assured everyone that the rest would come soon.

"There's nothing to worry about," the camp supervisor kept repeating. "They'll be here." It was almost noon by the time the rest of the carts showed up. The refugees quickly loaded their belongings onto them.

"*Thakin*, this is Aung Tin," the camp supervisor said, pointing at a small thin man with close-cropped gray hair. "He's the leader of the cart drivers."

One by one the bullock carts moved onto the narrow path leading away from the camp and rolled north towards the dense jungle ahead. No one spoke of the events of the previous night. That was behind them. Now their journey to Tamu through the dreaded Kabaw Valley had begun.

Valley of Kabaw

*L*ike the boats of the Nat Kyi Gon tributary, the bullock carts also had arched woven bamboo canopies which kept the hot rays of the sun away. But there was barely enough room in the middle, behind the driver, for three people to sit cross legged, and two more could sit with their feet dangling over the rear. With their luggage occupying some of the space, the refugees rode crammed, sitting on the hard wooden floor. Compared to the boats, the ride in these carts was hell.

Devi Lal, Hari and Neil rode in the first cart driven by Aung Tin, the leader of the drivers. Khin May, Sophia, Surya and Priya were in the second. Mr. and Mrs. Carroll occupied the third. Devi Lal told Sher Khan, Hashim and two of his men to ride in the last cart.

"If there's a problem, Sher Khan, and you wish to signal us," Devi Lal instructed, "fire two shots in the air. Bahadur, you and the rest of Hashim's men should spread out among the other carts in the middle."

The narrow, uneven dirt path consisted of two ruts carved out of the hard ground by the wheels of the carts and the hooves of the bullocks pulling them. Frequently branches from the trees of the jungle scraped the sides and top of the cart canopies. The crudely made carts squeaked and jolted erratically, tossing the passengers sitting crowded together in the confined space. Some men chose to walk between the carts. A choking cloud of reddish-brown dust, stirred up from the dry surface of the path, engulfed the carts and rose into the trees. The refugees covered their faces with handkerchiefs and towels. The intense heat was unbearable.

Two hours after leaving the Nat Kyi Gon camp, they arrived at a small clearing.

"We'll rest here for an hour, *Thakin*," Aung Tin announced, stopping the carts.

"Good," Devi Lal answered. "It's past two o'clock. The children must be hungry."

"Oh, I'm so stiff," Sophia moaned, climbing down. "My whole body aches."

"Stretch your arms and legs, Sophia," Khin May advised her daughter.

The drivers unharnessed the bullocks and let them graze at the side of the clearing. The refugees ate the food they had cooked the previous evening.

The camp supervisor had assured Devi Lal that the bullock cart drivers were reliable. "They can be trusted," he had said. "These are simple villagers who survive by farming small parcels of land carved out of the jungle and are now trying to earn a little extra money."

Devi Lal nevertheless cautioned the men. "Remain alert," he said.

Soon Aung Tin instructed his drivers to round up their bullocks and the refugees climbed back into the carts.

"Come on, you lazy bulls," Aung Tin yelled, striking each of the beasts with a thin bamboo cane. "Move. Get going."

The carts started rolling and gradually picked up speed.

"Are there any wild animals in this jungle?" Hari asked the driver.

Yes, there are, *Thakin*, " Aung Tin replied. "There are tigers and elephants. But generally they do not bother us."

"Will we see any on the way?" Neil wanted to know.

"I hope not!" Aung Tin replied, laughing. Then he added, "Several months ago one of our bullocks was taken at night by a tiger."

"Where will we camp for the night?" Devi Lal asked.

"There's a clearing in the jungle, *Thakin*, next to a stream, about three hours away. We'll stop there."

The afternoon heat was searing. The constant jolting and the dust added to their misery. The boiled water they carried was also running low.

Dear God, when will this ride end, Khin May wondered.

They had been traveling for nearly three hours. Suddenly the bullocks quickened their pace and started running: the bells around their necks jingled loudly. The men who were walking had to rush and climb onto the carts.

"The beasts have sensed that they are close to water, *Thakin*," Aung Tin explained. "That's why they are running."

The sun was setting as they arrived at a large clearing in the jungle.

"Ho, ho," Aung Tin tried to soothe the restless bullocks. "I'll free you in just a moment."

As soon as the drivers released the harnesses, the bullocks stampeded to the nearby stream. The authorities had cleared the jungle around the edge of the stream in preparation for the establishment of a refugee camp. Firewood was stacked in several rows along the edge of the clearing. Soon several cooking fires were lit.

Darkness came quickly and a few kerosene hurricane lanterns provided meager light. Swarms of mosquitoes buzzed around as the people prepared to bed down for the night. Some slept inside the carts while others lay down on their suitcases placed below the carts. A few opted to sleep in the open. Once again, the men divided themselves into groups to keep watch throughout the night.

"Mama, do you think we'll ever see Daddy again?" Sophia asked softly as they lay on the hard surface of the cart.

Khin May caught her breath. The same thought had occurred to her moments earlier while she had said her prayers.

"Let's hope and pray the war ends soon," she answered quickly. "With the grace of God we'll all be together again."

"I hope so, Mama," Sophia sighed.

"Everything will be all right, child. Sleep well."

The camp was quiet except for the crackling sound of the large fire that would be kept burning all night. Periodically the soft conversations of the men on guard penetrated the foggy minds of those trying to fall asleep. Later, the night air was momentarily pierced by the distant agonizing screams of an animal as a predator dealt its prey a death blow.

Dawn broke and cooking fires were lit to make tea from the water taken from the stream and to prepare their noon meal.

The night had been relatively peaceful, and now the sun's rays broke over the mountains to the east, lighting up the valley. "We'll leave promptly at sunrise," Devi Lal had alerted everyone the previous evening. The refugees seemed a little less tense. Hashim's men joked with each other. Children could be heard laughing.

"We've gone a couple of days without problems," Devi Lal told Hari and Sher Khan. "That's good, but I don't want the men to drop their guard."

"That's right, Doctor *Sahib*," Sher Khan said. "I'll speak to them about it at the next stop."

One by one, the carts rolled out of the camp, maintaining the same order as the previous day. The bullocks were rested and moved briskly. The path wound down a small hill and the bullocks started running, the carts bouncing behind them. Children shrieked happily as they were tossed around. Suddenly a woman screamed.

"Stop the carts," a man yelled. "Stop the carts."

The cart drivers called out to each other and pulled on the reins. Hari jumped out and ran back to where the screams had come from. A young girl sitting at the rear of a cart had fallen off. Miraculously, the pounding hooves of the bullocks and the heavy wheels of the cart following the one she fell from missed her. The little girl lay crying in the middle of the path.

Hari picked her up gently and carried her to her mother.

"Is she all right?" the woman wept. "Is my baby hurt?"

"She's fine," Hari replied. "Just a little scared. She's not hurt."

The rest of the morning passed uneventfully, and they stopped during the hottest part of the afternoon. The carts started moving again around three o'clock. After traveling for about two hours, they arrived at a small clearing.

"We'll camp here for the night," Aung Tin announced. "We have plenty of water."

A small pool was fed by water cascading down a twenty-foot waterfall. A narrow stream ran from the pool, winding its way into the jungle.

"Why are we stopping here?" Devi Lal inquired. "The supervisor of the camp told us we were to spend the second night in the village of Kontha."

Aung Tin started unhitching the cart. Averting his eyes, he answered, "Kontha is a full hour's ride away. This is a good spot, *Thakin*."

The other drivers also started unhitching their bullocks.

"I don't like this place," Devi Lal confided to Hari. "The clearing is too small. No more than half of our carts will fit here."

"Aung Tin, this place does not look safe," Hari told the head driver. "We should go on to the village."

"No, no, it's quite all right, *Thakin*," the man answered, shuffling his feet. He then walked over to where some of the other drivers were standing and started talking to them in a quiet voice.

"They're hiding something from us, Dad," Hari said softly. "We must find out what it is."

Sher Khan had joined them and the three men walked over to the cart drivers. "Look, Aung Tin," Devi Lal spoke sternly. "What are you hiding from us? Tell me what it is, man. Speak up."

Aung Tin appeared very uneasy and looked at his companions, a troubled expression on his face.

"Forgive me, *Thakin Gyi*, forgive me!" he blurted out. "My fellow drivers and I have done wrong. We were ordered by a gang of *dacoits* to stop here tonight. We are simple, poor villagers," he moaned. "They have threatened to burn our village and kill all of us if we do not cooperate. May Lord Buddha forgive me for my sinful deed, but we're very afraid of them. They are many in number and have guns."

Devi Lal's initial reaction was that of anger. But then he realized that the villagers were at the mercy of the bandits.

"Do you know when and from what direction they plan to attack?" he asked patiently.

"*Thakin Gyi*, they will be coming down from their hideouts in the mountains to the west," the driver answered softly. "They will cross the stream and attack after everyone in the camp is asleep."

"How many men do you think will there be?" Hari asked angrily.

"About twenty or so, *Thakin*. They'll have guns and some may be on horseback."

Devi Lal's voice was now calm. "What do the *dacoits* expect you and the other drivers to do?"

"We are supposed to go back and stay behind the last cart," Aung Tin said, pointing to the rear of the column of carts. "But, *Thakin Gyi*, we will not help them! I'll speak to my men. We will stand with you and fight them with our *dahs* and sticks."

"No, that won't be necessary," Devi Lal answered. "You people have to live here. We don't want these outlaws to carry out reprisals against you and your families. You've been helpful by warning us — we'll try and fight them ourselves."

Devi Lal conferred with Hari, Sher Khan and some of the other refugees. "Why don't we force the drivers at gun-point to take us to the village," someone suggested.

"The *dacoits* will still be able to follow us and attack us there," Johnny Carroll countered.

"We'll have a slight advantage by staying here," Devi Lal stated. "They won't suspect that we are aware of their plans."

"Isn't this dangerous?" another refugee wanted to know. "Wouldn't it be better to hand over our money to them when they come?"

"Yes, there is danger in what we are planning to do," Devi Lal responded. "But by shooting at them first, we might be able to scare them off. Besides, even if we agreed to hand over our valuables, we can't be sure they wouldn't harm us, especially the women and children."

"You're right," one of the Englishmen added. "I say we defend ourselves. We'll teach these blighters a good lesson!"

Several other men agreed. "We'd rather fight than simply give up."

"All right, it's agreed," Devi Lal declared. "That's what we'll do. Aung Tin, have six carts brought into the clearing. Line them up side by side, facing the stream."

"Yes, *Thakin*," the head driver answered, relieved. "Should the bullocks be left hitched?"

"No, no," Devi Lal instructed. "Move all the bullocks away to the rear. Sher Khan, get several suitcases placed inside each cart towards the front. Hari, have all the women and children moved to the last few carts. Instruct them to stay there. Also, collect any flashlights others may have."

Hari led the women and children to the carts at the end of the column. "Here, Sis, keep this. Use it if you have to," Hari said softly, giving his revolver to his sister. Khin May placed it in her shan bag.

"Can I do anything, Doctor?" Johnny Carroll offered.

"Yes, perhaps you could ask the other refugees if they have any firearms?"

"Certainly, I'll do that right away."

Soon five men came forward with rifles and two revolvers.

Darkness was setting in and the men all assembled in the clearing.

"According to our cart drivers," Devi Lal told them, "the gang is supposed to attack after we go to sleep — perhaps around ten or eleven o'clock. Those of us with rifles should tie flashlights to the barrels. We'll get behind the suitcases in the carts and wait."

To Hashim's companions and the other men without guns, Devi Lal said, "I would like to have all of you stay back near the remaining carts and deal as best you can with any of the miscreants who get close to you."

The night was pitch black. The men with the guns were in their places in the front row of carts. Devi Lal felt surprisingly calm. He walked back to where the women and children were sitting.

"What's happening, *Naana?*" Sophia whispered. "Will we be all right?"

"Yes, Sophia. Don't you worry. Everything will be fine." Then he added, "If there's any shooting, I want all of you to lie down flat in your carts. Don't come out until we ask you to."

"Dad, please be careful," Khin May said softly.

"I will, Khin May. We'll be fine."

He was about to return to the carts facing the stream when he stopped. He thought he heard the neigh of a horse coming from the direction of the village. Then he heard the hooves of several horses.

Devi Lal tensed, wondering if the drivers had deceived them. He was told the attack would come from across the stream. But the *dacoits* seemed to be coming from the village up ahead. Should he run and tell Hari and the others with guns to move to the path leading from the village?

It was too late. The darkness around them was pierced with the beams of several powerful flashlights.

"Hello, is Dr. Devi Lal's family in this group?" a man's loud voice called out in English, startling the refugees. Hari and Sher Khan had come running and stood next to Devi Lal.

"Who are you?" Hari yelled back.

By now, the riders had drawn close. Devi Lal, Sher Khan and Hari held their rifles ready.

"I'm John Harris, Deputy Commissioner from Tamu."

Devi Lal and Hari both sighed with relief and lowered their guns just as the group of horsemen rode up to them. Devi Lal stepped forward.

"I am Dr. Devi Lal. My family is here with me. We also have several other refugees who joined us at the camp in Nat Gyi Gon."

"What are you people doing here?" the Deputy Commissioner asked, getting off his horse. "Why haven't you gone on to Kontha?"

Devi Lal told him what had happened. "We thought you and your men were the *dacoits*. We're all very relieved to see you, Mr. Harris."

"I received a telegram from David O'Connell in Mandalay and then Tommy Carroll called me on the radio from Kalewa," the Deputy Commissioner said. "They asked me to give you assistance. I'm on my way to Nat Kyi Gon on an inspection tour. Once we've taken care of the *dacoits*, I'll deal severely with these bullock cart drivers."

"No, no — please do not punish them," Devi Lal pleaded. "They have helped us by warning us of the attack. Aung Tin, the head driver, even volunteered to have his men help defend us."

"All right, if you say so, Doctor, these men won't be punished," John Harris said. "Now I want all of you to go and stay in your carts in the rear. My constables will take care of matters here."

The constables — about thirty in number — were well-armed. Several carried Sten guns. John Harris gave orders to the head constable in Burmese. The men dismounted, and led their horses back a short distance toward the village and tied their reins to trees. The constables then fanned out on each side of the six front bullock carts and took positions behind large boulders and tree trunks. Harris drew his revolver and joined his men. Devi Lal and the rest of the refugees retreated to the carts in the rear and waited.

They could not see the carts in the clearing. It was deadly quiet.

Shortly after ten o'clock, the silence was shattered by an angry loud voice.

"This is the Deputy Commissioner. You are surrounded! Put down your guns quietly. If not, you'll all be killed."

Not expecting any opposition, the *dacoits* had come down on foot from their hiding places and had walked boldly towards the stream. Powerful flashlight beams blinded them.

One of them fired his rifle in the direction of the Deputy Commissioner. He was sprayed by a burst from a Sten gun held by one of the constables. The rest threw their weapons down quickly and raised their hands. It was over in a few moments. The refugees heard the Deputy Commissioner order his constables to handcuff the crooks and chain them together. John Harris then came and spoke to Devi Lal.

"Everything's fine, Doctor. We've captured the scoundrels. They're being taken back to Tamu in chains by some of my constables."

John Harris did not want to alarm the refugees and did not tell them that four of his men were digging a shallow grave across the stream to bury the dead *dacoit*.

"You might as well camp here for the night, Doctor. The village is still a good distance away. I'll leave two of my constables to accompany you all the way to Tamu. There are already about twenty carts with refugees up ahead in Kontha. I've sent word to them. They are to wait for your group tomorrow morning. All of you can travel together to Tamu."

"We're all so very grateful to you, Mr. Harris," Devi Lal said. "It was very fortunate that you came by. I don't know how we would have fared on our own."

"Glad to have been of help, Doctor," Harris answered.

"We've never met before, but I've heard about you, Mr. Harris. They say you are admired greatly by the people of your district. Now I know why."

"A lot of exaggeration, Doctor," Harris said modestly. "I just do my work."

He now turned his attention to the bullock cart drivers. "Who is the head driver? Come here at once!" he ordered.

Aung Tin came running and, folding his hands, knelt down in front the Deputy Commissioner.

"Please forgive us, *Thakin Gyi*," he said meekly. "We were afraid of the *dacoits*. That's why we did not drive on to Kontha. I beg you not to punish us."

"You saved yourself by telling the truth to the Doctor," John Harris said, his voice now less stern. "I want you and your men to look after these people very well. Do you hear me?"

All of the cart drivers spoke up quickly. "Yes, *Thakin Gyi*, we'll do exactly as you say."

John Harris extended his hand to Devi Lal. "I'll ride on now to Nat Kyi Gon, Doctor. I'll be back in Tamu about the same time you arrive there. Come and see me in my office."

"Thank you, thank you," the refugees called out as the Deputy Commissioner rode away towards the south, followed by his constables.

John Harris had come to Burma as a young man from his home town of Welling, Kent, in South East England. He hadn't planned to spend the rest of his life in this country, but had fallen in love with Burma and its people. He had returned to England once many years ago, but felt almost like a stranger. His parents were dead and there wasn't much there to keep him. Now the war, of course, had changed everything. He didn't know what the future had in store for him, but in the meantime, he had a job to do.

The next morning fifty-two bullock carts left the village of Kontha after Devi Lal's group joined the twenty carts already in the village. The refugees were now in much better spirits. Although the journey was still very difficult, they felt secure having the two armed constables on horseback accompanying them. And then, the *dacoits* had also been dealt with. The drivers were cheerful and did everything they could to help the refugees.

The horse ridden by one of the constables was a white stallion. Devi Lal was reminded of his father's horse in Punjab — also a handsome white stallion — that his father had named *Kamaan*, a warrior's bow.

"That's a very fine horse," Devi Lal said to the constable.

"Would you like to ride him, *Thakin?*" the man asked, offering the reins to Devi Lal.

"May I? You can have him back in a few moments."

"No, no, *Thakin*. Please ride him all the way to Tamu," the constable insisted, climbing into the last cart with Sher Khan and Hashim. Many of the men walked together, chatting. Some of the children rode in carts together, playing and laughing.

The next two days went by quickly. Other than sore bodies from the constant jolting of the carts, the refugees seemed to be faring well.

Khin May was more wistful. Oh, where are you my dearest husband, she kept thinking, and prayed for his safety. She also fretted over her daughter. Each night Sophia seemed to suffer nightmares and would toss around and moan until her mother gently shook her shoulders.

The fifth and last evening of the journey through the Kabaw Valley, the carts stopped in a large clearing near a stream. There was still some daylight left.

"Could you take us into the jungle to shoot some jungle fowls?" Sher Khan asked Aung Tin.

"Yes, most assuredly," the cart driver responded enthusiastically. "I know a spot not far from here where there are bound to be many birds."

While the rest of the refugees chatted and made preparations for the evening meal, Sher Khan, Hari and one of the Englishmen followed Aung Tin into the jungle. Several shots rang out and the men returned with over a dozen fowls. That night, the refugees enjoyed a veritable feast!

The next morning they all felt excited. "We'll be in Tamu by midafternoon," the drivers told them.

"Great!" many exclaimed. "This tiresome journey will be over."

Yes, but what lies ahead, Devi Lal thought. His friend, David O'Connell, in Mandalay had warned him about the dangers of the trek across the rugged mountains between Burma and India. They had come this far, he told himself, with God's grace, they would make it through the rest of the journey.

"The jungle in this part of the valley is particularly dense, *Thakin*," Aung Tin informed Devi Lal.

"Will we have any problems?" Hari asked.

"No, everything should be fine," the driver replied. "In fact, the path is more level. We should make good progress."

The carts rolled out of the clearing at sunrise. Everything seemed to be going well. They had been traveling about two hours. The dust was bothersome but the heat was not as yet intense.

"We'll make a stop in about an hour, *Thakin*," Aung Tin said to Devi Lal who rode alongside on the constable's horse. "Then from there it'll be only about a four-hour ride to Tamu."

"That's great," Devi Lal answered.

Aung Tin abruptly stood up in the cart. Turning around, he frantically gestured to the drivers following him to stop. Then pulling on the reins, he brought his own cart to a halt.

"Please ask everyone to be very quiet," he said softly. Devi Lal stopped his horse.

"What's the matter, Aung Tin?" he asked.

"I think there are elephants ahead, *Thakin*. I heard their trumpeting."

Hari climbed down from the cart and ran back to caution the others.

"Shall I ride ahead to check?"

"No, no, *Thakin*. It may be dangerous. I'll go."

The second constable rode up to see why they had stopped. Aung Tin handed him the reins of his bullocks. He then ran along the path and disappeared from sight.

In the silence the refugees could now hear the elephants trumpeting and the crackling sound of branches being torn from trees.

"They seem to be quite close, *Naana*, don't they?" Neil said softly.

"Sound travels a long way in forests," Devi Lal replied. "Let's wait and see what Aung Tin finds out."

Twenty minutes later the cart driver returned. "There's a herd of wild elephants feeding in the jungle next to the path, *Thakin*," he said. "They seem to be moving farther away, but until they've gone some distance from the path, we must not proceed."

"Should we just wait here?" Devi Lal asked.

"I think everyone should get off the carts and move to the back, *Thakin*. If the bullocks get the smell of the elephants, they may be difficult to control."

The refugees got down and walked back behind the last cart. The drivers talked soothingly in low tones to the bullocks. One of the constables stayed with Aung Tin's team. The head driver once again crept towards the elephant herd. Almost two hours had gone by since they had stopped. The sounds of the herd gradually faded away.

Aung Tin came running back. "The herd has moved far enough into the jungle," he announced. "We can proceed."

The refugees quietly climbed back into their carts.

"Is it safe?" Devi Lal asked. "The herd won't turn around and come back?"

"I don't think so, *Thakin*. We should be all right."

Yet everyone sat in the carts, nervously listening for sounds from the jungle. Shortly, they came to the area where the elephants had crossed the path. Trees lay torn down and bushes trampled on both sides of the path. The refugees nervously looked out of the carts, praying that the wild beasts had indeed gone deep into the jungle.

After an hour, they reached the clearing and stopped for a brief rest. The near encounter with the wild elephants had abated their jubilation of the past day. Now their thoughts focused on the journey ahead — beyond Tamu.

Later that evening, the fifty-two bullock carts rolled into the town of Tamu and proceeded towards the refugee camp. A typical sleepy border village, Tamu had mushroomed into a noisy crowded frontier town. British, Indian and American soldiers were everywhere, as were the refugees fleeing Burma. Hundreds of Naga tribesmen from the mountainous region of eastern India were also in town to hire out as porters and guide the refugees through the rugged mountains.

The people in Tamu stared with curiosity at this long row of carts and the armed band of refugees, led by the grey-haired man on horseback. The carts pulled up in front of the camp.

"*Saya wun Ji*, my colleagues and I will pray daily to Lord Buddha for you and your family," Aung Tin said, bowing.

"Thank you very much, Aung Tin," Devi Lal replied. "You and your men looked after all of us very well. We'll all long remember you with gratitude."

The luggage was unloaded and the cart drivers paid. The camp was new and well-constructed. The two huts assigned to Devi Lal's party even had doors and windows that could be closed.

"What luxury!" Khin May said, smiling.

They slept that night feeling secure. There was no need for them to post guards.

In the morning, Devi Lal and Hari went to the Deputy Commissioner's office and were greeted pleasantly by Harris. "I hope the rest of your journey to Tamu was uneventful?" he said, shaking their hands.

"We didn't have any problems," Devi Lal replied. "We were only delayed a little by a herd of wild elephants feeding near the path. Eventually, they moved deeper into the jungle and we were able to proceed. We arrived here yesterday evening."

"I also arrived late last night," Harris answered. "I'm glad you told me about the elephants. I'll have my Forest Rangers follow the herd and get them further away from the bullock cart path. How many people do you have in your group, Doctor?"

Devi Lal produced the travel papers given to him in Mandalay, along with those for Hashim and his men, plus Mr. and Mrs. Carroll.

"Thirty-six of us have traveled as a group from Kalewa," he answered. "If possible, we'd like to continue together for the rest of our journey."

Harris barely glanced at the travel permits. "That shouldn't be a problem. I'll stamp and sign these papers for you right away. We're permitting a thousand refugees to travel each day. You should be able to leave as early as the day after tomorrow. That should give you some time to stock up your provisions and to be rested. The journey through the mountains to Palel on the Indian side of the border is quite exhausting."

"Mr. Harris, how far is Palel from here?" Hari inquired. "And, are there camps on the way?"

"The actual distance is only about forty-four miles, but you'll be crossing several mountain ranges and the trail is quite steep in places. Camps have been built along the route. You should be able to stay in them at night. My office will assign you the required number of Naga coolies, as well as any chairs you may need."

"What type of chairs are these?" Devi Lal asked.

"Actually, they're crude palanquins made of bamboo and carried by four Naga coolies. You can decide how many you'll need and let my administrative assistant know. He'll arrange for the coolies and chairs. They'll be at your camp early in the morning, the day after tomorrow."

Devi Lal and Hari stood up. "You've been most kind, Mr. Harris. I don't know how to thank you," Devi Lal said shaking the Englishman's hand.

"You don't have to, Doctor," the Deputy Commissioner responded. "I'm delighted to have been of help. I've heard of your work in Mandalay and I'm pleased to have met you. I wish you and your family a safe journey to India. If there's anything else at all that I can do before you leave, Doctor, please see me."

Back at the camp, Devi Lal and Hari discussed the plans for the journey to Palel with the family and the other refugees.

"I'm not riding in a chair, *Naana*," Sophia objected. "You've told me before that girls can do anything they want. Well, if you, Uncle Hari and Neil walk, so can I."

"I don't need a chair either, Dad," Khin May added. "Sitting in the bullock carts for the past five days was enough for me!"

Devi Lal felt relieved. This was the second time in the past two days he had seen his daughter smile, though he knew that inside she must be torn apart.

"All right, ladies," Devi Lal acquiesced. "We'll order only one chair for you, Martha. If Priya gets tired, she can ride with you."

The rest of the day was taken up washing clothes and resting.

"Mr. Carroll looked a little pale so I took his blood pressure, Dad," Hari told his father later that day. "It's slightly elevated. I told him to rest."

"Good, Hari. Keep an eye on him."

During the evening, the two English couples who had traveled with them from Nat Kyi Gon came to say goodbye. They were leaving for Palel in the morning. The next day the refugees bought food supplies and other essentials for the journey. Hari had worn a hole in the sole of one of his shoes and bought himself a pair of khaki canvas boots.

After dinner, they sat talking in front of their hut.

"This is perhaps our last evening in Burma," Martha sighed. "By this time tomorrow we'll probably be on the Indian side of the border."

"Oh, I'm so sorry dear," she quickly added, noticing the look on Khin May's face. "I shouldn't have been so thoughtless. Forgive me, dear."

"That's all right, Martha," Khin May answered, brushing off a tear. "The sooner all of this is over, the better it'll be."

"Yes, Khin May," Martha piped, trying to sound cheerful. "Tomorrow is another day. Before you know what's happening, the war will be over and we'll all be back in Burma."

"By the way, did you see the Naga coolies in town the other day?" Martha continued, changing the subject. "They look tough, don't they? I understand we'll have twenty of them to carry our luggage."

"Yes, I saw them," Khin May replied.

"Are they Indians? I thought some of them had oriental features."

"The Nagas are from a Tibetan-Burmese tribe, although their homes are in India," Khin May answered. Then, smiling, she added, "I also read that at one time they practiced head-hunting."

"Are you serious?" Martha asked aghast.

"Yes," Khin May laughed. "But I understand they've given up the practice all-together. The photographs that I saw in a magazine showing shrunken heads hanging from the doorways of Naga huts were all old and faded."

"Goodness me," Martha moaned. "I'm going to have trouble falling asleep tonight!"

The next morning, John Harris' administrative assistant arrived at the camp promptly at five o'clock, accompanied by twenty Naga coolies.

"Good morning, Doctor," the administrative assistant greeted Devi Lal. "This is Suraj, your guide and head coolie."

"*Namaste, Doctor Ji*," the young Naga said in Hindi.

"He also speaks Burmese," the administrative assistant explained. "Doctor, you can trust these men implicitly."

"Thank you very much," Devi Lal answered. "That is reassuring."

The coolies carried all of the luggage from the huts and put them into large straw baskets they had brought with them. They put the straps of the baskets across their foreheads and hoisted the heavy loads onto their backs. Another group of refugees, consisting of eight Indian and Anglo-Indian families with sixteen Naga coolies, had joined Devi Lal's group. Three women from this group were riding chairs.

Martha Carroll looked at the chair she was supposed to ride in. "My, that thing doesn't look very comfortable," she said. "Maybe for now, I'll also walk."

Suraj gave a signal and the coolies lined up in a row behind him. "We are ready, Sir," he told Devi Lal. "We're ready to take you to Palel."

Devi Lal nodded. Suraj raised his voice and said something in the Naga language. The coolies slowly marched out of the camp in single file. The refugees followed, to begin this, perhaps, the most arduous portion of their journey.

The Hazardous Trek

Now far behind them, the town of Tamu disappeared from sight and the refugees walked slowly along a narrow path which climbed gradually. The Naga coolies had started a strange chant. "Hey ho, hey ho, hey ho," they sang.

"Why do the coolies keep repeating those words, *Naana*?" Sophia inquired.

"I think it helps them concentrate," Devi Lal answered. "It probably diverts their minds from the heavy loads on their backs."

The chant of the coolies had an almost hypnotic effect on the refugees. They, also, tried to walk to the continuous intonation of "hey ho, hey ho, hey ho."

Johnny Carroll was walking, conversing with Khin May and Martha.

"Mr. Carroll seems to be feeling better, Dad," Hari commented.

"We'll have to watch him, Hari," his father warned. "If he shows any signs of fatigue, we'll have to insist he ride the chair."

After about four miles, they reached a small open space where the side of the hill had been carved away. Suraj raised his hand and called out something in the Naga language. The coolies repeated the word in unison and stopped. They lowered their baskets to the ground and removed the straps from their foreheads.

"*Sahib*, we shall rest here for a few minutes," Suraj informed Devi Lal. "Then we'll start climbing the first mountain."

The Naga coolies were all powerfully built and wore short skirt-like *longyis* and shirts. They were all bare feet. Some of them had strings of bright coloured beads tied around their ankles. Suraj, their leader, was a good-looking young man in his early twenties.

The sun had risen behind them. Many of the refugees sat down along the path.

"*Naana*, see, I am not at all tired," Sophia informed her grandfather. "I'll walk all the way."

"That's great," her grandfather replied with a smile. "I'm very proud of you, Sophia."

Neil discovered there were two boys about his age in the other group of refugees. The three of them were soon busy conversing. Two young girls kept watching Hari. The four day old beard on his face and the rifle slung behind his back made him look ruggedly handsome.

"Don't look now, Hari, but there are a couple of pretty girls who can't stop looking at you!" Khin May teased.

"Oh, those two?" Hari answered, blushing a little. "They're just kids."

Suraj gave a signal and the coolies stood up. They placed the straps of the straw baskets on their foreheads and lifted the suitcases and trunks onto their backs.

"Martha, why don't you ride the chair now?" Johnny Carroll asked his wife. "You must be exhausted."

"All right, dear, maybe I will," she agreed. "But if you feel even a little tired, let me know. You can take my place." Martha climbed into the chair. The four coolies looked pleased and, smiling broadly, hoisted the chair onto their shoulders. Starting their rhythmic chant again, the coolies began climbing.

The path was steep and narrow, not more than six feet wide and it hugged the side of the mountain. There was a sheer granite wall on one side and a deep ravine on the other. The refugees walked close to the inside of the path, away from what appeared to be a bottomless chasm. The coolies continued their climb, however, unconcerned. Martha sat stiffly in the chair, her eyes focused straight ahead. The chair swayed slightly from side to side. She wished her coolies would move away from the edge of the path.

Many among the refugees were showing signs of fatigue. There was little conversation. Leaning on their canes and sticks, they concentrated on moving up the path. Johnny Carroll was walking laboriously with one hand resting on Khin May's shoulder. He almost stumbled and Khin May quickly put her arm around his waist and steadied him.

"Some of the people seem to be tiring," Hari informed Suraj. "Can we take a brief rest?"

"Yes, *Sahib*," the Naga answered, without breaking his stride. "We'll reach the top in a few minutes. That'll be a good place to stop."

Gradually the path widened and the refugees slowly climbed the last few feet to reach a small grassy knoll. The coolies eased the loads off their backs. Men and women slumped down on the grass.

"There's Tamu and Burma," Suraj declared, pointing in the direction they had come from. "We've now crossed over into India."

The refugees looked back, most showing little emotion. Khin May stood up and walked to the edge of the clearing. Her eyes searched the horizon and she raised a hand, as if reaching out. Tears slowly rolled down her face. Her father walked up to her and placed his arm around her shoulders, drawing her close. In their hearts, each bid farewell to their loved ones left behind and to their land.

"Johnny, are you all right?" Martha asked her husband.

"I'm fine," he responded, trying to sound cheerful. "Don't you worry about me."

She looked at him closely. "If you get tired, take my place in the chair."

"No, I'm okay. I can manage."

A young Indian from the group of refugees who had joined them came to speak to Devi Lal.

"Doctor *Ji*, my name is Chand Prakash," he said politely. "The coolies told me you are a doctor."

"Yes, my son and I are physicians."

"I'm very worried about my wife Neelam," the man continued. "She is expecting our first child, and I think the strain of the journey might be too much for her."

"Do you know the expected date of her delivery?"

"We're not sure, but I thought it wasn't for another two weeks. We talked about staying on in Tongoo. But my wife wanted to give birth in her parent's home in India. We would have reached there in time but, unfortunately, we were held up for more than a week in Monywa."

"If you like," Devi Lal offered, "I can examine your wife when we reach camp."

"Thank you, Doctor *Ji*," the man answered, relieved. "That'll be very nice."

The stiff climb and exertion of the past few hours had exhausted them and their throats felt parched. They had been warned of the scarcity of water on this part of the trek and drank only a few sips from their water bottles. After resting for about twenty minutes, the coolies stood up. The refugees got up much more slowly. The path now began winding its way down into a valley.

"You have to be careful and not slip," Suraj advised the refugees. "The path here is covered with gravel."

"Going downhill must be a little easier for you and your companions, Suraj," Hari commented to the head coolie.

"No, actually, *Sahib*, it's easier carrying loads up hill. This is more tiring."

At one point the path took a sharp bend. Turning sideways, the coolies took short steps and slowly edged their way down, all the while continuing their chant. Going around the sharp bend was particularly frightening for those riding chairs. Martha shut her eyes and gripped the sides of the chair tightly.

"When the monsoons come," Suraj explained, "we have a lot of difficulty traveling this route."

"I can well imagine that," Hari agreed.

At last they reached the bottom of the valley. It was almost two in the afternoon.

"We'll rest here for one hour," Suraj informed Devi Lal. The refugees slumped down to the ground.

"Ah, that feels good," Johnny Carroll exclaimed, taking off his shoes and massaging his feet. "Oh no, I think I'm getting a blister," he added.

"Hari can give you some sticking plaster tape for it," Khin May suggested.

There was no time to cook a meal and they ate the food they had brought from Tamu. Their water bottles were by now empty.

Sophia lay down on her side, pillowing her head with her arm.

"Are you all right, Sophia?" Khin May asked her daughter.

"I'm fine, Mama. I just want to rest for awhile."

The valley was peaceful and quiet and the air filled with the fragrance of pine trees. Sophia closed her eyes. She wasn't tired but had felt sad all day. Now the image of her father came to her mind. She imagined him singing her favorite song to her. She knew the words so well.

> *O Danny Boy, the pipes, the pipes are calling*
> *From glen to glen and down the mountain side*
> *The summer's gone and all the flowers are dying*
> *'Tis you, 'tis you must go and I must bide*
> *But come you back when summer's in the meadow*
> *Or when the valley's hushed and white with snow*
> *'Tis I'll be there in sunshine or in shadow*
> *O Danny Boy, O Danny Boy, I love you so.*
> *And if you come when all the flowers are dying*
> *And I am dead, as dead I well may be*
> *You'll come and find the place where I am lying*
> *And kneel and say an "ave" there for me*
> *And I shall hear, tho' soft you tread above me*
> *And all my dreams will warm and sweeter be*
> *If you will not fail to tell me that you love me*
> *Then I simply sleep in peace until you come to me.*

Tears filled her eyes, and lying in the desolate, remote mountain valley, the young girl sobbed silently. She prayed for her father, her tears overflowing.

Johnny Carroll was sitting on the side of the path with his eyes closed. Martha was next to her husband, looking at him with concern. The few refugees who were conversing were doing so very softly, as if trying to conserve energy.

Suddenly voices were heard, coming from somewhere up ahead. Devi Lal and Hari stood up.

"Who can those men be?" Hari whispered. Bahadur and Sher Khan joined them.

"Let's not take any chances," Devi Lal answered softly. "Let's move up a little and spread out. Get behind tree trunks."

Hashim and his men also spread out across the narrow valley. Suraj crept forward, holding a long sharp *dah*.

"I don't think these are *dacoits*, Doctor *Sahib*," he whispered, standing next to Devi Lal. "We have not had any problems in this valley before. They could be soldiers bringing supplies from Palel, but it's wise that we take precautions."

The men's voices grew nearer. "They are talking in Hindi," Suraj said. Four men in army uniforms, carrying submachine guns, came into view and waved to the refugees. Devi Lal and the others came out from behind the trees. The soldiers told them they were an advance patrol of an army supply column of mules, headed toward Tamu.

"Our orders are to stop any refugees from proceeding until the supply mules have gone through," one of the soldiers informed them. "It's good that we came across you in this valley. If it had been further back we would have had to stop you from proceeding."

"How far is the camp from here?" Devi Lal asked.

"It's at the end of the valley, about two hours' march."

"Is there any drinking water there?" Hari asked.

"Yes, there's a stream next to the camp. Our supply column will be arriving there later this evening and will spend the night."

The refugees started walking again and arrived at the camp a little after five. Although the sun had not set, the valley was in deep shadow.

"Don't drink the water from the stream without first boiling it," Devi Lal and Hari warned their companions. Their advice was not heeded by every one and several men and women quickly cupped their hands, scooping up mouthfuls of the cool water.

The camp was in a large clearing. Four long narrow bamboo huts had been constructed and ran the entire length of the camp. The front of each hut was open and there were no doors or windows. Along the back wall of each hut, a narrow bamboo platform provided a surface for sleeping. Those unable to find space on the platform would have to sleep on the dirt floor.

The authorities had placed piles of firewood near the huts. The refugees quickly started fires to prepare their meals and to boil water for the next day's journey. Shortly, the army supply convoy arrived. The soldiers, with over a hundred mules, camped for the night by the stream. The refugees were relieved to see them. We'll all be able to sleep safely tonight, was their thought.

"Perhaps I should examine the young pregnant woman now," Devi Lal said to his daughter. "Why don't you come with me, Khin May?"

"All right, Dad," she agreed.

Hari felt slighted that his father had not asked him to help. He knew how to deliver babies. He had done three cases as a medical student. Maybe Dad asked Khin May so that the woman doesn't feel embarrassed by having two male doctors help her, he consoled himself.

By the light of a hurricane lantern held by Khin May, Devi Lal examined Neelam.

"Your wife could deliver her baby any time now," he later told the anxious husband. "Everything appears normal. Make her rest as much as she can." Then he added, "I'll speak to Suraj. The coolies should be careful not to jolt her chair."

Shortly after dinner, Johnny Carroll experienced a tightness in his chest and was having difficulty breathing. He blamed it on the food he had eaten and decided not to bother anyone. With nightfall came the usual swarm of mosquitoes, as well as a chill in the air. The refugees slept curled in their blankets. The coolies slept around a huge fire they kept burning all night.

Khin May lay under her blanket with troubling thoughts clouding her mind. She wondered what was going to happen to them. "Once we reach Karyala, we'll have to decide where to live," her father had said. She had been to her father's ancestral home in Karyala. But how will Neil and Sophia adjust to their new life in a small village? Hari and she spoke Hindi quite well but her children were able to speak the language only a little.

Her thoughts went to Tim and she felt overcome with a sense of hopelessness. Ever since leaving Mandalay, she had stubbornly avoided thinking about the possibility that she might not ever see him again. Now, as she lay in this remote wilderness, crying, she couldn't blot the thought out of her mind.

Sophia murmured and tossed around. Khin May shook her daughter gently. Sophia sighed deeply, woke up for an instant and then fell asleep again.

The morning air was chilly. The refugees quickly prepared their meals and boiled water for drinking. By seven, they had eaten their meager breakfast and were ready to leave.

They walked out of the valley, again following a narrow climbing path, clinging to the side of a mountain. The morning air was cool, yet the refugees were perspiring. Johnny Carroll was having a difficult time and was walking slowly, leaning on a cane for support. After climbing for almost two hours, Suraj called a brief rest. The refugees slumped down in the middle of the path.

The sun was now high in the cloudless sky and the air had turned warm. The valley below was very quiet. Except for an eagle lazily soaring against the deep blue sky, nothing stirred. The mountains looked like a brightly coloured delicate painting. Sophia followed the eagle's flight through half-closed eyes as she lay on the ground, inhaling deeply of the sweet pine and eucalyptus-scented air.

I wish I could fly and soar with the eagle. I'd glide through the air and look down upon the mountains, valleys and streams. Her thoughts were interrupted by the faint drone of airplanes and she sat up. A moment of panic was soon replaced by indifference. Why would anyone harm them in this distant place. Sophia relaxed and lay down again.

Several aircraft appeared coming from the northwest. They were very high and kept flying toward the southeast.

It was time to get up and start walking but Johnny Carroll stayed on the ground, his face pale and covered with perspiration.

"How are you feeling, Mr. Carroll?" Khin May asked.

"I'm a little tired," he answered.

"You don't look well at all, Johnny," Martha said. "I want you to ride in the chair now. Come on. Let me help you."

Johnny Carroll did not object as his wife and Khin May helped him into the chair.

"This particular day's march to the next camp is the longest," Suraj had warned them that morning. "There's no water available on the way."

The sun beat down upon them. The coolies laboured under their loads. The refugees panted and sweated as they slowly inched their way up the mountain. Thirst was becoming a particular woe.

"Oh, it'll be wonderful to reach the top," Sophia exclaimed.

"Yes, it'll be great, won't it," her mother added. "Let's hope this is the last mountain we have to climb."

Sophia ran up ahead. "Oh, no," she moaned, reaching the top. "There are more mountains ahead of us, Mama!"

"Two more days of walking after this," Hari said encouragingly, "and we'll be in Palel!"

They sat down and ate the food left over from the previous night. Most of the water in their bottles was gone.

Khin May walked to where Neelam was sitting, resting against a boulder. "Hello, Neelam. How do you feel?"

"I feel a little better now," the young woman answered. "Earlier, my stomach had started hurting a little."

"You'll be just fine," Khin May said, patting her hand.

The trek down into the next valley was particularly tiring.

"I wish there was a cloud or two," Martha said, looking anxiously at her husband's perspiring face.

An elderly Indian refugee stumbled and fell and lay on the path, gasping. Two other men quickly went to his aid. They lifted him and put his arms over their shoulders, helping him to walk.

The water was now all gone. Throats felt raw, their bodies ached. Finally, mercifully, they reached the valley floor.

"Oh, what a heavenly feeling to be in the shade," Khin May sighed.

Even before Suraj could announce they would rest for half an hour, the refugees dropped down. Johnny Carroll remained seated in his chair. Devi Lal propped his rifle against a tree and wiped his brow with a handkerchief. He walked over to Johnny Carroll. "How do you feel?" he asked.

Carroll grimaced. Placing his hand on his chest, he replied, "I seem to have some pain here."

"I'm going to give you some pills. I'd like you to take one every three hours," Devi Lal said. "You must not walk. When we reach camp, I want you to lie down and take complete rest. Do you have any water left?"

Carroll looked at his wife.

"I'm afraid not. It's all gone," Martha answered. She stood by her husband, gently wiping his brow with a handkerchief.

Time passed much too soon and the refugees slowly got up and followed the coolies through the valley. The camp was still almost three hours away. Thirst had become their worst enemy. Devi Lal walked up to Suraj.

"Is there any chance of finding even a little water before reaching camp?" he asked.

"There is a *nallah* about two miles ahead, a little to the side of this path, *Sahib*. It fills up in the rainy season. But now there'll most likely not be any water in it."

"Will it be worth going and looking?" Devi Lal persisted. "The children, especially, are suffering. We also have a sick man who needs to take his medicine."

"There is a small pool just beyond the *nallah* by the side of the mountain," one of the other coolies told Suraj. "But the jungle is quite thick around it."

The children must have water, Devi Lal decided. Turning to his son, he said. "Hari, take Sher Khan with you and look for the pool. If you find water, fire two shots as a signal. If you are not successful, then proceed on to the camp."

Hari and Sher Khan collected six empty water bottles each and quickly moved ahead. Although tired, they walked briskly, going deep into the valley. They walked about two miles and then, following the coolie's instructions, turned sharply to the left and entered the jungle.

"We can cover more ground if we separate," Hari suggested. "Let's each go in a circle, Sher Khan. If you come across water, fire one shot." Hari turned to the left and Sher Khan to the right.

The floor of the jungle was covered with fallen branches and leaves. The rays of the sun barely penetrated the dense canopy of trees. Hari was walking quickly and, stepping over a fallen branch, he didn't realize that the ground ahead of him sloped down into a ravine. He lost his footing, slipped, and fell headlong, tumbling down the slope. The water bottles and the rifle fell out of his hands. He continued to slide down, finally coming to a stop, flat on his back, at the bottom of the narrow ravine.

Out of breath and angry at his own carelessness, he painfully raised himself onto his elbows. Just as he was about to sit up, he heard a soft hissing sound. From the corner of his eye, he saw a huge serpent not more than four or five feet from him. The snake's head, spread into a hood, was raised threateningly. Hari froze. With a sickening feeling, he realized that it was a cobra. The snake was slowly swaying from side to side. Hari could see its black tongue dart in and out and its eyes staring unblinkingly at him. He knew that if he made any sudden movement the cobra would strike. Judging by the size of the serpent, the bite undoubtedly would be fatal.

His arms and neck were getting tired. A sharp stone was digging into the middle of his back. Cold sweat covered his body. He didn't know how long he could lie there without having to move. Hari was astounded by the size of the serpent. Its massive head, about the size of a coconut, stood at least three feet above the ground. He had only seen a cobra this large once before, and that was on Mount Popa.

He wondered where Sher Khan was. He regretted not having his revolver on him. With it, at least he may have had a chance of hitting the cobra before it could strike. The smell of the damp mud and rotting leaves filled his nostrils as he lay there, his life in peril. His arms and elbows ached agonizingly. The sweat from his brow flowed into his eyes, blurring his vision.

Hari thought about his life. Was it going to end in this desolate jungle? He felt a sharp cramp in his arm muscle and one of his elbows slipped a little. In a flash, the cobra jerked its head back to strike. Then a loud explosion shattered the quiet of the ravine and echoed against the mountains. Hari's elbows gave way and his head and shoulders fell back onto the jungle floor. Through blurry eyes, he thought he saw the serpent's head fly straight up into the air. He had no strength left. He lay there, spent, unable to move, his eyes filled with sweat and tears.

Then he faintly heard Sher Khan call his name. The sound of someone walking through the jungle reached him. Soon he was being pulled up onto his feet. He felt dazed and his knees buckled under him. A strong arm steadied him. Slowly the fear in his heart subsided and his eyes cleared a little.

Sher Khan helped Hari climb out of the ravine and sat him down on a fallen tree. He then went back down into the ravine. Drawing his dagger from his belt, he dug a hole in the soft earth and buried the cobra's head. He then retrieved Hari's rifle and some of the water bottles. When he returned, Hari spoke to him haltingly.

"You saved me from a horrible death, Sher Khan. I owe you my life."

Sher Khan patted Hari's shoulder. "You would've done the same for me, son. Now let's go and join the rest before they start worrying about us."

The refugees had heard the single gun shot in the distance and wondered what had happened. Devi Lal was confident about Sher Khan and Hari's ability to look after each other. He had spent many hours with them, tracking through the jungles in northern Burma. But why a single shot, he questioned.

The refugees continued their slow march through the valley. As the sun set, they finally reached the camp, completely exhausted. Suraj pointed to a rocky area to the side of the camp. "There, there's the mountain stream, Sahib," he said. Many of the men and women stumbled toward the stream and drank deeply of the cool, clear water.

Devi Lal had hoped to find Hari and Sher Khan at the camp. Disappointed, he asked Bahadur and Suraj to accompany him to search for them.

"There they are, *Naana!*" Neil yelled excitedly. "I can see Uncle Hari and Sher Khan coming."

Sophia and Neil ran to meet them. As they came closer, Devi Lal noticed Hari's soiled clothes and bleeding elbows.

"What happened, Son?" he asked.

Hari briefly told him of his fall and the encounter with the serpent. "Sher Khan saved my life, Dad. If he hadn't shot the cobra, I would have died in the jungle."

Devi Lal turned toward Sher Khan but saw him quickly walk away.

"Thank God you were not harmed, Son!" he said. "Now we both owe our lives to Sher Khan. Many years ago, he also saved my life in the jungle around Myitkyina. Come, let me dress your wounds."

Later that evening, Hari examined Johnny Carroll and was relieved to see that he was feeling better. The two young girls had been following Hari with their eyes all evening. At one point the older of the two walked past him.

"Meet me at 10 o'clock, by the stream," she whispered.

Hari, taken aback, mumbled something about being tired, but was not sure if she had heard him. I can't meet her. I don't even know her, he told himself. Perhaps he should see her just so she wouldn't feel hurt. But when the time came, Hari could not make himself go, and went to bed instead. Why couldn't he be like other men his age? Was there something wrong with him, he wondered.

Through the early part of the night, people in the hut could hear Neelam groan periodically as her labour pains became more intense. About two in the morning, Chand Prakash came to fetch Devi Lal.

"Doctor *Ji*, please come. I think my wife is about to have the baby."

Devi Lal and Khin May rushed to the young woman's side. They stayed with her, helping her through her labour. At one point, they heard the roar of a wild beast.

"That sounds like a tiger," Devi Lal said in a whisper.

"It sounds close by," Khin May said, alarmed.

Around four, the rest of the camp woke to the loud cries of a baby. Martha and Surya prepared tea. Dawn was breaking as Devi Lal stood by the fire, exhausted but relieved there had been no complications. Chand Prakash walked up to him.

"Doctor *Ji*, I have no words to thank you enough for all that you and your daughter did for Neelam and our newborn son," he said gratefully. "Will she be able to travel safely so soon after giving birth?"

"A day's rest would have been very good for her, but by morning she should be able to manage."

Hari had joined his father. "Dad, why don't we do just that — rest here for an additional day. You and Khin May stayed up most of the night. Everyone else could also use a day off before going on."

Devi Lal thought for a moment. "It certainly would be good for all of us. But I think we should first talk to Suraj and see whether the coolies will agree. We must, of course, pay them for the extra day. There's also the question about other refugees who may arrive here later today. They'll need to sleep in the camp."

"This camp is large enough. When they arrive, and if there isn't enough room, we men can sleep out in the open," Hari said encouragingly.

"You're right. We should be able to manage. Why don't I talk to Suraj and see what he says? Then we can speak to the others in our group and get their opinions."

The coolies agreed to spend an additional day on the journey when Suraj told them they would be paid extra. Members of Devi Lal's group also gladly agreed to rest for the day. Soon word spread throughout the camp.

The other groups of refugees who had also arrived the previous evening were now getting ready to leave. Three British couples from among them approached Devi Lal and asked if they could accompany his group.

"I have no objections," he responded. "You're welcome to join us."

The refugees who stayed on spent the day resting, almost in a festive mood. They gathered around their cooking fires, drinking tea. Later, Chand Prakash brought out his newborn son for everyone to see. Martha Carroll asked to hold the baby.

"Have you selected a name for this handsome young man?"

"Yes, Neelam and I talked about it," Chand Prakash replied. "We've named him Devi Prakash, after Doctor *Ji*." Everyone agreed it was a very nice idea.

"That was not necessary," Devi Lal said, taken aback, "but I'm honoured."

"Oh, look at his little fingers!" Sophia said. "They're so cute. Mrs. Carroll, may I please hold him?"

"Certainly, Sophia, but you'll have to be careful."

Sophia carried the baby in her arms and gently rocked him. "*Naana,*" she called, "Come and see. He has his eyes open and he's looking at me."

Later, many of them washed their clothes and children ran around and played. Some of Hashim's men took their spears and waded into the stream. They tried to spear fish, but their attempts were more comical than successful. Two of them slipped and fell into the stream. The Naga coolies laughed loudly at their ineptness. One man even tried catching fish with his bare hands. Carried away with his enthusiasm, he suddenly found himself in deeper water. He floundered and started yelling for help. Suraj dove into the stream and, grabbing the man by the collar, pulled him out.

Suraj then cut a thin branch from a tree and sharpened one of its ends. Within thirty minutes, he speared half a dozen fish and gave them to the astonished refugees. Sher Khan noticed huge paw prints in the soft, muddy shore of the stream on the other side of the camp. He recognized them as those of a tiger. He called Neil and the other boys to come and see the footprints.

In honour of the birth of the baby, several Indian women got together and prepared a special sweet called *halwa*. Late in the afternoon, Chand Prakash again brought his son out of the hut. The refugees and the coolies gathered to welcome and bless the newborn. The four coolies who carried Neelam's chair grinned broadly. The women distributed *halwa* to everyone, including the English couples who had joined the group. One of the Englishmen brought out a bottle of Scotch whisky and offered some to anyone who wanted a drink.

During the afternoon, the coolies started a wrestling contest. The coolies, it seemed, belonged to two adjacent Naga villages and frequently competed in friendly matches. Eight of the strongest-looking Nagas took off their shirts and, pairing off, started wrestling. Their powerful muscular bodies glistened with perspiration as they tried to grapple and throw each other to the ground. The refugees stood watching with admiration. The remaining coolies applauded and called encouragement to the wrestlers. At the end, everyone applauded without knowing which village had won. The wrestlers shook hands and slapped each other's shoulders.

As the sun set, the valley became cloaked in shadows. Another large group of exhausted refugees arrived. They looked at the inhabitants of the camp with curiosity, surprised by the festive mood of this group of Asians and Europeans who seemed to behave like one big, happy family.

Sophia sat by the hurricane lantern on her mattress on the bamboo platform. Taking out her diary, she started entering the day's events. After so many days of problems, she finally had some happy thoughts to write. She wrote about the birth of the child and the joy she felt when she carried the baby in her arms. *I wish we could stay forever in a peaceful valley such as this. The war is so far away and everyone is nice to one another. Why do people have to be mean and fight and kill each other?*

"Sophia, say your prayers and go to sleep," her mother urged her. "We have to wake up early tomorrow morning."

"Yes, Mama, all I have to do is enter tomorrow's date and then I can sleep." Sophia suddenly smiled. "Do you know what day it is tomorrow? It's April first — April Fool's Day."

Neil, who was almost asleep, sat up. He looked at his sister and mother, a mischievous grin on his face.

"Oh no, you won't!" his mother admonished, reading his mind. "You're *not* to try any of your silly pranks tomorrow. We have enough to worry about without you bothering others with your April Fool's tricks."

"Oh, Mother," Neil groaned, "will I have to wait one whole year to have some fun? I had already thought of a great trick to fool Sher Khan and Bahadur."

Not seeing any change in his mother's expression, Neil muttered under his breath and, turning his back towards his mother and sister, went back to sleep.

Tragedy and death, the refugees discovered, had not been left behind with the war. An elderly Anglo-Indian woman, accompanied by her two young grandchildren, had arrived the previous evening. She had died during the night in her sleep, apparently of a heart attack. The children, a boy of four and a girl of five, looked pathetic, standing outside the hut. An elderly English couple took the children under their care, promising to deliver them to the British authorities in India. Several men from her group carried the woman's body across the stream. With the help of their coolies, they dug a grave and buried her.

The death of the woman cast a gloom over the entire camp. Devi Lal's group of refugees walked out of the camp quietly. Even the coolies marched without their chant.

The sky was overcast. Although the monsoons were not due for another four weeks, the travelers sensed that it was going to rain. They had been climbing toward the top of a mountain for the past hour and a half. A strong wind blew, making walking up the narrow path even more difficult. By eleven, a cold drizzle started and strong gusts of wind blew the rain into their faces.

Chand Prakash opened a large black umbrella for his wife. Neelam held it in one hand while cradling her son with the other, holding him close. The wind periodically tried to snatch the umbrella from her hand. She hunched over her child to protect him from the rain and wind.

They reached the top around noon and rested for a few minutes before descending into the next valley. The rain was now heavier, but mercifully the wind had died down. Those who had umbrellas were able to protect themselves from being completely drenched. Sophia's clothes were soaking wet. She clung to her grandfather's hand and walked along. No one spoke. There was nothing to say. They were too miserable.

After passing through a valley, the path started gradually climbing again. The rain was now coming down in sheets and the path turned to a sea of ankle-deep mud. One of the coolies suddenly lost his footing and, falling sideways, he slithered over the edge of the path. The strap of his basket slipped off his forehead and onto his neck, yanking him down. The heavy trunk, still in the basket, rapidly slid down the hill, dragging the helpless coolie. As the man disappeared from sight, Khin May screamed.

Suraj turned around. "Keep walking. Don't stop!" he yelled. "If we stop, more of the group will be in danger!"

"After we reach camp," he told Devi Lal, "I and my companions will return to look for him."

Darkness was setting in by the time the exhausted refugees crawled into the camp. Most were completely drenched and all of them were hungry and cold. The huts provided some shelter from the rain. Without wasting any time, Suraj and three other coolies left, taking with them a flashlight and a hurricane lantern the refugees gave them. Khin May said a silent prayer for their safety, and for the poor coolie whom they were going to try to find. Cooking a meal in the rain was impossible. The refugees changed into dry clothes and sat huddled in their huts, eating whatever little cooked food they had with them.

It was almost midnight when Suraj and the three coolies returned. They had found their companion deep in a ravine, his body bruised and bleeding. His right leg had been broken. The man was unconscious, but moaned when they tried to move him. They carried him and the trunk up onto the path and back to the camp.

Devi Lal and Hari examined the man's leg. It was shattered, with the jagged edge of the thigh bone sticking out through the skin. An angry red welt had formed along the front of the man's neck where the strap of his straw basket had choked him.

"We'll need several canes to use as splints," Devi Lal informed Suraj. After cleaning the wounds on the leg, Devi Lal instructed Suraj to grasp the injured man under his armpits. "My son and I will pull on his leg to set the broken bone," he explained. As they pulled, the man regained consciousness and screamed. To their relief, the broken edges of the bone came together with the first attempt. They placed pieces of cane around the leg and wrapped them with a bandage made of strips of a bedsheet that they had torn.

The rain finally stopped and Bahadur found enough dry wood somewhere to light a fire and make some tea. Suraj and the coolies now sat near the fire drinking the hot, sweet liquid.

"Doctor *Sahib*, tomorrow, late in the afternoon, we'll be in Palel," Suraj said smiling. "This tiring journey will be over."

"You and your men have looked after us very well, Suraj," Devi Lal replied. "You must see that your companion is taken to a hospital. He'll need to have a proper cast put around his leg."

The refugees woke up to a glorious morning. The view around them was breathtaking. The camp was on a hill overlooking a lush green valley. Terraced fields gently climbed up to the next hill on which a little village sat with several huts standing in a semicircle. Trees with bright red and yellow blossoms blanketed the slopes. The air felt clean and invigorating.

A radiant double rainbow adorned a distant hill. The fragrance of the rain-soaked earth filled the air. The refugees stood outside their camp, taking deep breaths. The clouds above them began breaking up and the rays of the rising sun added to the magnificent panorama.

Soon they had to start preparing for their departure. With most of the food supplies already consumed, the coolies were able to redistribute their loads. The trunk carried by the injured coolie was picked up by another. Two of the women with chairs offered to take turns walking. The injured coolie was made to sit in one of the chairs in spite of his loud protestations.

"It's amazing how well he looks this morning in spite of his near-death experience of only a few hours earlier," Hari commented to his father.

The injured man said something to Suraj in their language. The four coolies who were to carry him laughingly protested, shaking their heads and hands. Later, Devi Lal asked Suraj what had happened.

"The injured man was so concerned about being a burden to the others that he offered to carry the trunk if they placed it on his lap!" Suraj said laughing. "The coolies who were to carry him did not think it was such a good idea. They told him that he was heavy enough without the trunk. They teased him, saying he would owe them each at least one fat chicken when they returned to their village."

Devi Lal examined Neelam and her baby before leaving. They were both doing fine. Johnny Carroll, however, had not slept well. He had developed a bad cold and again looked pale and distressed. One of Hashim's men was also ill with severe chills and a high fever.

"Looks like Malaria," Hari said to his father, and gave the man some quinine tablets. The clouds gradually disappeared. The rays of the sun warmed the chilled refugees as they marched along through the valley toward the next hill.

After an arduous climb, they reached the top of the hill and Suraj called a brief stop. The ground around them was still wet and muddy so they rested standing up. The injured coolie sat in his chair, quiet.

He must be in considerable pain, Devi Lal thought, and gave the man some medication. He also gave Johnny Carroll more pills.

"Take one now," he suggested.

Looking ahead, Devi Lal asked Suraj, "Are there many more hills before we reach Palel?"

"Just one more hill to cross, Doctor *Sahib*. We may encounter some difficulty in the last valley, though. Water gets trapped there when it rains heavily. If the water across the path is too deep, we may have to wait for it to drain away."

Going down the hill was once again difficult and dangerous. The path was covered with slippery, slushy mud which occasionally sucked off the shoes from the feet of the travelers. Since they had walked with wet shoes for some time, many had open sores on their feet. Some removed their shoes and walked barefoot.

Suraj's fears were soon confirmed. Their path was blocked by a pool of muddy water that had accumulated at the bottom of the valley. Several long logs and wooden planks were stacked by the path on the other side of the water, about forty feet away.

"The British authorities are constructing a bridge across this narrow part of the valley," Suraj told Devi Lal. "For now, however," he said, "the only way to get across is to wade through this water, provided it's not too deep." Suraj lowered the basket from his back. "I'll try to go across, Doctor *Sahib*. "I'll see how deep it is."

The refugees watched anxiously as Suraj stepped into the muddy water and slowly started, feeling his way across with his feet. By the time he had gone about a third of the way, the water was up to his waist. Raising his arms above his head, he kept moving. When he reached the middle, the water came almost up to his chin. Soon he came out on the opposite side and started slapping his legs.

"Leeches," he yelled back. "We can cross, Doctor *Sahib*," he announced. "We'll have to bring the luggage on the chairs. The women and children will all have to be carried over."

The coolies carrying Johnny Carroll went across first. Placing the chair poles on their shoulders, they slowly stepped into the water, inching their way to the middle. As the water got deeper, they lifted the chair above their heads in unison. The muscles of their arms and shoulders strained under the weight. They kept moving and lowered the chair poles back onto their shoulders only when they were back in waist deep water.

Devi Lal had given Carroll several match boxes and the coolies used the matches to burn off leeches attached to their bodies. Suraj took the place of one of the coolies and helped bring the chair back. Neelam and her baby were carried across. Chand Prakash waded into the water, accompanying his wife and son. Martha, with Priya in her lap, went next, followed by Sophia, Khin May and the other women and children. Hashim's sick companion and the injured coolie were also carried across.

It took over two hours for all the refugees and the last piece of luggage to be taken to the other side. The exhausted coolies stood leaning against trees and boulders.

After just a brief rest, they picked up their loads and once again started climbing the next hill. The refugees trudged along, wondering when this ordeal would end. Exhaustion had numbed their bodies and their minds were confused. It was late in the afternoon when the group crested the hill.

They looked in disbelief. To their astonishment, there in front of them in the valley, was the sight for which their eyes had thirsted for so long. A bustling little town of streets, bazaars and neat little cottages with gardens. And more incredibly, several buses lined up, waiting. Devi Lal quickly looked at Suraj. The young Naga smiled.

"Yes, *Sahib*," he beamed. "It is Palel. Those are the buses the authorities are providing to take refugees to the large camp in Imphal."

Devi Lal could hardly believe it. He did not notice his son and daughter come and stand next to him. All the planning, worrying and the dangers of the past weeks — they are over, he sighed, and by the grace of God, we made it safely through this incredible trek.

Sophia and Neil came and stood in front of their grandfather. Devi Lal put his arms on their shoulders and drew them close. Sophia looked up at him.

"*Naana,* have we reached the end of our journey?"

"Yes, my child," he answered, his voice a little shaky. "Yes, we have."

Their spirits raised, they walked down into the valley and to the town of Palel.

The trek out of Burma was completed safely. But now — what lay ahead? What grand design was karma weaving for them? They did not know. But for the present, they were relieved and very, very grateful!

Farewells and Uncertainties

𝐵ritish authorities and the people of Palel welcomed the refugees. Food and cups of hot tea awaited them. Their luggage was loaded onto buses. They paid the Naga coolies not only the agreed amount, but whatever extra each could afford. All they had time for was to gratefully shake the hands of the coolies. Then the refugees climbed aboard the buses and were whisked away.

They sat in their seats, their minds numbed by the sudden change in their circumstances. Few noticed the rolling hills and scenic valleys. Nor were they bothered by the jolting of the bus as it traveled over the rough road. The thirty-mile distance to Imphal was covered in a little over an hour and a half. Just as the sun was setting, the buses drove into the compound of a large refugee camp.

Once again, their reception was heartwarming. Local civic and religious groups provided food, clothing and blankets to anyone needing them. There were some official formalities to be completed and travel documents to be checked.

The authorities required the refugees to surrender their guns and revolvers to the police. The owners received monetary compensation for the arms. Devi Lal was pleased to get rid of the firearms.

"We won't have any use for them now," he told Hari. "Besides, the money will help pay for the rest of our travel."

Devi Lal decided that, on the way to Punjab, they would stop in the city of Lucknow.

"We're almost out of money," he told Khin May and Hari. "We'll need to sell some of the jewelry, and pay Sher Khan and Bahadur. From Lucknow, Sher Khan's village is not far. And Bahadur and his family can travel to Nepal by train."

"I hate the thought of parting from them," Khin May said softly.

"Yes, they've been like family to us," Devi Lal agreed.

After dinner that night, Sophia made an entry in her diary.

Today is April 2, 1942. We have finally reached India. Naana is very relieved the long journey is over. I'm going to miss Daddy, Daw Mu and Sweet Pea even more. I think my Mama cries a lot but she doesn't let us see her tears. I'm afraid of tomorrow. I don't know what it will bring and where it will take us. God, please look after my Daddy, Daw Mu and Sweet Pea. Also, bless all of us here in this camp.

The next morning, the time came for them to bid farewell to the Carrolls. Johnny Carroll was going to be admitted to the local hospital. Later, he and Martha were to travel to Calcutta, where they planned to stay with her sister and brother-in-law.

"I believe Mr. Carroll suffered a heart attack on the journey," Devi Lal told the camp doctor. "It's good that he can be treated in the hospital here in Imphal."

Martha Carroll's eyes filled with tears. "I shall miss you all so very much!" she said, embracing Khin May and then Sophia.

"You will come and see us soon, Aunty Martha, won't you?" Sophia asked, her voice unsteady.

"Yes my child, we will — very soon," Martha answered softly. "You've become very dear to me. We'll see you again!"

Johnny Carroll shook Hari and Devi Lal's hands warmly. "All of you have been very kind to us. We both will always remember you gratefully."

The rest of the refugees boarded the buses that were to take them to Kohima, seventy miles away. From there, they would travel another fifty miles to the railhead town of Dimapur. The three English couples were going to Bombay, from where they planned to sail for England. Chand Prakash, Neelam and their newborn son were going to Bangalore where Neelam's parents lived. Hashim and his companions were returning to their village near Benares.

Leaving Imphal, they drove past terraced plantations and pine and eucalyptus groves. The sun shone brightly and the deep blue sky was adorned with clusters of fluffy white clouds. The air smelled fresh and carried the scent of the eucalyptus trees. The refugees looked at the scenery around them, but their minds were still troubled. Each wrestled with the memories left behind and the uncertainties of the future.

The buses stopped in Kohima for an hour and here, also, the townsfolk provided them with refreshments. It was around three in the afternoon when they reached Dimapur. The bus had to slow to a crawl as the town was bustling, crowded with local residents and refugees. Additionally, hundreds of British and Indian army personnel drove around in their military vehicles. Neil and Sophia looked out of the bus, wide-eyed. Sophia tugged at her grandfather's shirt sleeve.

"Is all of India this crowded, *Naana?*" she asked.

"Yes, my child," he answered with a smile. "India has a lot of people. Most cities will be like this."

The refugees were relieved to find that special waiting areas had been provided for them at the railway station. The tea planters of Assam had arranged for them to be fed. Clothing and blankets were also available to anyone who needed them. Khin May and Surya washed some clothes for the family. Then they all sat and ate their evening meal together.

The next morning, more farewells were said. Devi Lal and his group boarded the train and sat together in a crowded third-class compartment.

After stops at Lumding and Kampur, the train pulled into the city of Gauhati on the banks of the river Brahmaputra. Other passengers started leaving the train. A railway employee spoke to the refugees.

"You must all get off here. You'll be taken across the Brahmaputra by ferry. Pick up your luggage and leave the train. Hurry."

"Why do we have to take a ferry, *Naana?*" Sophia inquired.

"I don't know," her grandfather replied. "It must be that they don't have a rail bridge over the river." They were rushed to the river's shore. A large double-decker ferry was waiting.

"This is just like the Mingun ferry," Sophia commented.

"It's bigger," Neil added.

"*Naana*, can we go up to the top deck?" Sophia asked.

"Yes, if there is room," he answered, thinking that the children were correct, this is almost like being on the Mingun ferry. He tried to imagine what Mandalay must look like after the bombing raids and the fires.

Khin May said something to her father.

"I'm sorry, child," he answered. "My mind was preoccupied. I didn't hear what you said."

"I just asked where we'll stay in Lucknow."

"I do have an old medical college friend who lives there. But I don't think we should impose on him. Perhaps there'll be a refugee camp where we could spend a couple of nights."

Arriving at the shore, they were directed to another train and boarded it. They rode in it all evening and night, sleeping sitting up in the crowded compartment. Early in the morning, they reached Lucknow. They got off and bid farewell to Hashim and his companions who were to take another train to their village.

Owners of the many sugar mills in the city had made arrangements to assist the refugees coming from Burma. Devi Lal and his family were assigned rooms in the guest house of one of the sugar mills on Sita Pur Road near the Gomti River. They were driven there in three horse-drawn *tongas* provided by the sugar mill owners. Arriving at the guest house, Neil and Sophia jumped out of the *tonga* and entered the building. A covered veranda ran all along the sides and front of the red brick bungalow and there was even a small flower garden in front.

"Mama, come quickly!" Sophia yelled urgently.

Khin May was getting off the *tonga*. "What's the matter, Sophia," she called back.

"Come in here. Hurry!" Sophia called from inside the guest house.

"What's the matter, child? Are you all right?" Khin May asked, running in.

"Look, Mama," Sophia pointed. "Real furniture and bedrooms and bathrooms!"

"Oh my God, you're right. I can't remember the last time I took a proper bath!"

They bathed and changed their clothes. Lunch was prepared for them and they ate sitting on chairs at a table.

"Oh, this is wonderful," Sophia sighed, leaning back in her chair.

Hari, Bahadur and Sher Khan gave Devi Lal the jewelry that they had carried for him all the way from Monywa.

"Some of this is the jewelry your mother wore," Devi Lal told his daughter. "When she was taken ill, she asked that I keep it for you and Hari and for grandchildren that we might have. I don't know how I can sell this jewelry."

"The children don't need the jewelry, Dad, and neither do Hari and I," Khin May assured her father. "We need money to complete our travel and to live on. Besides, you also have to pay Sher Khan and Bahadur."

Devi Lal reluctantly agreed and sorted out the jewelry they would sell.

"It will be easier if we can get someone from this city to help us," he said. "Hari, let's see if my medical college classmate is still here in Lucknow." They spoke to the guest house caretaker.

"Yes, Doctor *Ji*," the caretaker informed them. "There is a clinic on Amina Bad Road belonging to a Dr. Shiv Kapoor."

Devi Lal was not sure if, after all these years, his friend would recognize him. But Shiv Kapoor welcomed his old classmate and Hari warmly.

"I've been thinking about you since the refugees started coming from Burma," he said, embracing his friend. "I hoped that, should you come to Lucknow, you would seek me out." He was short of stature and dark complexioned. Devi Lal noticed that his friend had become quite obese.

"I'm pleased that you are still in Lucknow, Shiv," he said. "I was afraid you might have retired and moved out of the city."

"Where are you staying?" Shiv Kapoor asked. "Why don't you move into my house? As you know, my wife passed away five years ago and the house is empty. Stay with me. I insist."

"That's very kind of you, but we are quite comfortable in the guest house of one of the sugar mills. We intend to leave for Punjab as soon as we can. I'll be very grateful, though, if you could help me sell some jewelry that I have. The cash that we brought with us is all gone."

"You needn't sell your jewelry," Shiv Kapoor said softly. "Why don't you let me lend you some money? You may return it whenever you can."

"That's most generous of you, Shiv, but I can't do that," Devi Lal answered. "I don't know whether I'll be able to earn enough to support my family. I must sell some of the jewelry."

"I understand. There's a jeweler that I know whose shop is just down the road. I have one more patient to see. We'll walk over after that and take care of this matter. How about bringing the family over to my house for dinner tonight?"

"I would like to do that. But the two servants who have accompanied us will be leaving for their homes tomorrow. We'd like to be with them this evening. If it's all right, perhaps we can come and visit you tomorrow evening."

"Good! It's settled," Shiv Kapoor agreed. "I shall look forward to meeting your daughter and grandchildren too."

The jewelry was sold and Devi Lal and Hari returned to the guest house with the money. After dinner, Devi Lal spoke to his servants.

"You've both been very loyal and close to the family," he said to Sher Khan and Bahadur. "However, now I don't have the means to employ you. I would like each of you to have this money, which is about four months of your salary."

Sher Khan raised his hands. "No, Doctor *Sahib*. What I've received from you and the children, no amount of money can buy. I do not wish to take more. I'd rather have you use this money on the children."

"Yes, *Sahib*," Bahadur added. "You've already bought tickets for us to take us to our village in Nepal. I also do not wish to take this money."

"No, you mustn't refuse," Devi Lal insisted. "Take this money — you'll need it. I have enough left over for the children."

The time came next morning for them to say good-bye. Sophia and Priya sobbed uncontrollably. Surya and Bahadur, their eyes brimming with tears, bowed down and touched Devi Lal's feet. Taking their daughter's hands, they walked through the gate of the guest house to the *tonga* that was to take them to the railway station.

Sher Khan came to the children to say farewell. Tears streaming down his rugged face, he tenderly placed his hands on Sophia and Neil's heads as they both clung to him, sobbing bitterly. Khin May and Hari stood by, tears filling their eyes. Sher Khan did not know how to say farewell to them. He looked at them through his tears. His voice choking, he simply said, "May *Allah* protect you wherever you go."

Hari and Khin May each embraced him. "You'll always be in our prayers, Sher Khan," Khin May cried.

Sher Khan now turned to face his master and bent down to touch his feet. Devi Lal held him up and, instead, embraced him.

"You, Sher Khan, have been more like a brother to me," he said, his voice breaking. "I shall always be in your debt."

Unable to speak, Sher Khan walked to the door with his head bowed and hands folded in front of him. He turned, and looking at his family for the last time, softly prayed, "*Inshah Allah*, these eyes shall see you again before I die."

Devi Lal had not had any time to talk to his children about the family's future plans. "We need to make some decisions now," he told Khin May and Hari. "The money we have remaining will pay for our journey to Punjab and for us to live on for two to three months," he said. "We can stay in Karyala in my mother's house. But Karyala is a small village. We'll need to move to a city where Sophia and Neil can attend good schools and I can set up my practice."

"I'll seek work right away, Dad," Hari offered. "I understand there is a medical college here in Lucknow. I was thinking of going there to see if they'll hire me."

"I can also find work, Dad," Khin May added. "If necessary, we can sell the rest of the jewelry."

"We'll do that only as a last resort, Khin May," Devi Lal said. "I felt bad enough selling some of it yesterday."

"Which is the nearest large city from Karyala?" Hari asked.

"Rawalpindi is not far," Devi Lal answered. "It also has many schools."

"Well, first we need to get to Karyala," Khin May said. "Then you have to rest for a few days, Dad."

Later, Hari left for the medical college. "I'll be back soon," he said.

Khin May went to see the caretaker. She returned and spoke to her father. "Dad, the caretaker told me that the British Army has an Area Headquarters Office here in Lucknow. I'd like to go there and inquire about Tim."

"All right," Devi Lal answered. "I'll go with you, child."

Leaving Neil and Sophia with the caretaker's wife, they went to the British Army offices. The English Lieutenant into whose office they were ushered was sympathetic.

He went through a thick file containing a large number of papers. "I'm very sorry, Mrs. O'Shea," he finally said. "The British and Indian troops in Moulmein at the time of its fall were either killed or taken prisoner. We can be certain of each soldier's fate only when the war is over. I'm sorry — that's all I can tell you now." Deeply disappointed, Khin May returned to the guest house with her father.

Later, Hari came back. "The Medical College didn't have any vacancies," he said. "But recruiters from the Indian Army were there, trying to hire doctors and I spoke to one of them. He said I could apply and gave me an application form. After six weeks training, for which they will pay me, I'll be commissioned as a Captain."

"How long will you have to sign up for, Son?" Devi Lal asked.

"I'll have to serve a minimum of three years. Then, if I wish, I can apply for a permanent commission."

"Hari Uncle, that's great!" Neil said excitedly. "Will you be given a uniform? Will all the soldiers have to salute you?"

"First, I have to decide whether or not I am applying," Hari answered, chuckling. "Then, if accepted, I'll have to go through training and most likely learn how to salute others before I receive my uniform and rank."

"Hari Uncle," Sophia asked sadly, "will you, also, be leaving us?"

"Well, it'll be just like when I used to go to Rangoon and then came back, Sophia," Hari answered gently. "I'm sure they'll let me come home for a visit as soon as my training is over."

That evening, Devi Lal and his family were treated to a lavish meal at the elegant home of Dr. Shiv Kapoor. Several servants ran around looking to their every need.

"Hari is thinking of joining the Army Medical Corps," Devi Lal informed his host. "What do you think about it, Shiv?"

"Many young doctors are joining the Indian Army," Shiv Kapoor replied. "After their training, most are being sent to Assam to treat wounded soldiers coming out of Burma. Getting a job at a hospital in India is very difficult, Hari. The few positions they have are given primarily to their own graduates. Would you find working at an Army hospital interesting?"

"Yes, I think I would. And it's only for three years," Hari explained. "By then, hopefully, the war will be over and we can return to Burma."

That night Sophia again made an entry in her diary.

I feel sad saying good-bye to so many people. It's so unfair! Today, everyone was sad. I cried all day. Priya and her mother and father went to their home. I miss them. Why did Sher Khan have to leave? He loves us so much. It hurts to think that he is no longer with us. I love you, Sher Khan. I'll pray for you each day.

Tomorrow morning we'll say good-bye to Uncle Hari, and leave for Karyala. He has promised to come and see us when his Army training is over. I am sure he will look most handsome in his uniform! We will leave by train in the morning. Mama says that my great grandmother will be glad to see us. I hope we are not a bother to her. She is very old. God, please bless and protect my Daddy, Daw Mu, Sweet Pea, Sher Khan and all of us here.

They boarded the train the next morning for the last leg of their journey to Punjab. Hari came to see them off. He was going to stay with Dr. Kapoor for the next few days. The Army recruiter had told him that, once his application had been processed, he would be sent to a training camp near Calcutta.

Although it was early in the day, the heat in the crowded third-class compartment was oppressive. The children sat on the wooden seats looking out of the window. No one spoke much as the train rattled on all day. During the night, Devi Lal and Khin May tried to sleep sitting up. Sophia and Neil curled up in the space they had. Their clothes were soaked through with perspiration.

The train made many stops and pulled into Lahore the next morning.

"Look, *Naana*," Sophia said, pointing at a newspaper held by a vendor. "Calcutta was bombed."

Devi Lal bought an English language paper, *The Statesmen*. There were several photographs and an extensive write-up about this first air raid of an Indian city. The main target of the Japanese planes had been the bridge connecting the railway station and the city, across the Hooghly river, but the bridge was not damaged.

A smaller headline on the front page read, "*Mandalay Devastated By Yet Another Japanese Air Raid*." The entire city, it seemed, had burned. According to an eye witness, nothing was left standing from one end of the city to the other. Heavy civilian casualties had resulted.

They got off at Mandra Junction and took a local train for the brief ride to Chakwal. From there they engaged a *tonga* for the six mile trip to Karyala. Memories flooded Devi Lal's mind. He had traveled this way so many times. The vision of his father, Hem Raj, proudly riding his white stallion, *Kamaan*, was vivid before his eyes. He had not seen his mother, Kanti, for six years. She was now over eighty years of age. Of his brothers and sisters, only Mohan Lal remained in their village.

The *tonga* stopped at the outskirts of Karyala and the driver helped carry their luggage. They climbed the winding cobblestone lane that Devi Lal used to run up and down as a boy. Their large house, built of red bricks, at the top of the hill, was next to the village temple. It was a comfortable home, with several rooms downstairs as well as on the second floor, next to a large terrace.

Devi Lal opened the door and looked around the spacious courtyard. His mother was sitting on a *charpai* under the banyan tree. She looked frail, and at first did not recognize him as he bent down to touch her feet.

"Mother, it is me, Devi Lal."

Kanti's eyes filled with tears. She held her son's face in her hands. "I am so happy to see you, my son! God has answered my prayers. Your brother has been telling me about the war in Burma. I have been praying that you and the children would remain safe."

"My daughter and grandchildren are here with me, Mother."

Khin May was amazed. How dainty and dignified grandmother looks. What an incredibly beautiful woman she must have been in her youth, she thought.

Kanti tried to stand up. Devi Lal's hand steadied her. "Where are the children? I want to see them," she said.

Khin May came forward. "Grandma, I'm Khin May."

Kanti embraced her granddaughter. "I am so pleased to see you, my child. You're even prettier than the last time I saw you. Now let me meet your children."

Sophia and Neil, who had heard so much about their great-grandmother, stood looking at her in awe. They now came forward and Kanti embraced them tenderly.

"May God, Almighty, grant you a very long, healthy and happy life," she blessed them.

"Where is my grandson Hari?" Kanti wanted to know.

"Mother, Hari stayed in Lucknow," Devi Lal answered. "He's going to join the Indian Army as a doctor."

"Oh, I'm so disappointed," Kanti complained, "I would like to have seen him. He's going in the Army you said? Well as long as he is working for the British only to save lives, I suppose it's all right."

Just then, Mohan Lal and his wife, Kumari, entered the courtyard.

"I'm so pleased that you and the children are safe," Mohan Lal said, embracing his brother. "We were very worried about your safety." Khin May noted how much his face resembled her father's, although he was shorter in height.

"I'm sorry I did not write, lately," Devi Lal apologized. "Once we decided to leave Burma, we were very busy making preparations."

Kanti hailed her daughter-in-law. "Kumari, Devi Lal and the children must be thirsty. Offer them water. Also, prepare tea for them."

"Yes, Mata Ji, I'll do so at once," Kumari answered, quickly pulling her *dupatta* to shield her face from her brother-in-law. This she did in keeping with the tradition of village women in Punjab who consider it disrespectful to let a male elder see their face.

Kumari did all of the house work, including washing clothes and cooking their meals, but did not mind it. As a daughter-in-law, it was expected of her and was the custom of their culture. She had raised her children, gotten them married and doted upon her grandchildren. But now as she walked to the kitchen, she wished the old woman would not order her around in front of others.

Kanti turned to Devi Lal. "I need to sit down, my son. Come and sit next to me. Tell me about your journey." Mohan Lal fetched some chairs from the veranda.

Devi Lal sat down next to his mother on the *charpai*. "We came by the overland route," he told her. "We traveled at different times by cars, boats and bullock carts. Then, for the last four days, we walked to a small town in Assam. From there, we came by bus and train."

"The journey must have been dangerous. How did the children manage?" Kanti inquired.

"They did very well, Mother. They walked the entire distance through the mountains."

"Come, Child," Kanti invited her granddaughter. "Come to me."

Khin May knelt down in front of her grandmother.

"I'm so grateful to God for letting me see you again, and for letting me see my great grandchildren before I die," Kanti said tenderly, touching her granddaughter's face.

"I'm also so very pleased to see you, Grandma," Khin May said, hugging her grandmother.

Kanti next turned to her great grandchildren. "Come, children, sit next to me and tell me about yourselves." Sophia and Neil sat on each side of their great grandmother.

"*Naana* has told us a lot about Karyala and about you," Sophia said. "I've been wanting to see you for a long time, Great Grandmother."

"And I've been wanting to see you, my dear child," Kanti said quietly.

"*Naana* has also told us about our great grandfather," Neil added, "how he fought bravely as a freedom fighter. Great Grandmother, I'm going to be like him. I'll become a freedom fighter."

Kanti's eyes softened. "Yes, your grandfather has left us with a glorious legacy. I know that you and Sophia have in you the noble traits of your Mohyal ancestry. I'm sure one day the nation will be proud of the brave deeds of you and your sister."

"Can we go to see the monument built in honour of our great grandfather?" Sophia asked.

"Yes, child, after you have your tea, your Uncle Mohan Lal will take you to the temple. I am a little tired. I think I'll rest."

Kumari started preparing the evening meal. She was a slim petite woman. Her gray hair was tied in a tight knot behind her head, making her face look stern. Her mind was racing. Why have they come to Karyala? Does he now want to take over as head of the family? After her husband had looked after his parents, the farmlands and the house for all these years? How dare he even think about it. Not only does he show up, but he brings these half-breeds with him. The nerve of the man. And then her husband was being so stupid, welcoming them, ready to give up everything. She would talk to him tonight and drum some sense into his head. She thought about her children and grandchildren and her eyes softened. She must see to it that they weren't deprived of their rightful claim to the family's properties.

Mohan Lal took his brother, Khin May and the children to the temple where they prayed together. Then they walked to the monument built by the village in memory of Hem Raj, their revered martyr.

"*Naana* told us that our great grandfather died fighting British soldiers," Neil said to Mohan Lal.

"Yes, that's true. He was a courageous freedom fighter. He went to the aid of six young Indians who were about to be captured by British soldiers for having attacked a military supply convoy."

"Did the men get away?" Neil asked.

"They did, only because your great grandfather rode his horse between them and the soldiers chasing them. He galloped straight toward the soldiers and started shooting at them. He was hit with three bullets. His horse brought him back to the house where he died in the courtyard."

Devi Lal tenderly ran his fingers over the inscription carved in the stone monument. The others stood respectfully, their heads bowed.

After dinner, the two brothers sat in the courtyard talking.

"It's good to have you and the children home," Mohan Lal said. "As the eldest son of our parents, my brother, this house is yours."

"No, Mohan," Devi Lal replied. "It's our mother's. After her, the house and the farm lands can be divided equally between all of us brothers and sisters."

"You will, of course, live here, won't you?" Mohan Lal asked. "There's ample room for all of us. My children are married and settled in other parts of Punjab. It will be good to have you, Khin May and the children stay with us."

"We will stay here just a few days, Mohan, but I'll need to go to a larger city where I can establish my medical practice. I've been thinking about Rawalpindi. It's not far from here. There must also be schools in the city where the medium of education is English. Sophia and Neil can speak Hindi, but can't read and write it."

"Yes, Rawalpindi is a large city and has many schools," Mohan Lal agreed. "The leader of the *Azad Hind* organization there, Bir Singh, is very well known to me. Our father and his father, you'll remember, were very close friends and fought side by side against the British. I'm sure he'll give you assistance in finding a house and setting up your clinic. I'll write him a letter and give it to you to take."

"Yes, I remember meeting him once when I accompanied father to Peshawar," Devi Lal answered. "I think I'll leave for Rawalpindi tomorrow."

Kumari waited for the opportunity to speak to her husband. "Have you gone mad?" she angrily whispered to him in their room. "What are you trying to do, turn your children and grandchildren into paupers?"

"What do you mean, Kumari?" Mohan Lal asked, puzzled. "What are you talking about?"

"I'm talking about your being so syrupy towards them. Can't you see he's here to take over the properties?"

"That's not true," Mohan Lal protested. "My brother is not like that. In fact, he's planning to live in Rawalpindi. I'm going to write and ask Bir Singh to help him."

"Good! Get rid of them. The sooner the better," Kumari said relieved. She made up her mind, however, if her husband didn't get rid of them she would have to think about somehow doing it herself.

The next morning, Devi Lal left for Rawalpindi.

"Shouldn't you rest for a couple of days, Dad?" Khin May had asked her father.

"No, I'm fine," Devi Lal answered. "The children's education has been interrupted long enough. We must get them enrolled in schools right away."

Khin May felt depressed all day. Sophia and Neil had made friends with some of the other children from the neighborhood and were busy playing with them. What was going to happen to them, Khin May kept wondering. Moving to a strange city and trying to set up a home with little money was going to be so very difficult. Nightfall made her feel even more panicky. She would take three of the sleeping pills tonight.

"Oh, God, it can't be," she moaned softly, finding the bottle empty. She must have taken the last ones the night before. What am I going to do, she pondered, twisting and turning the empty bottle in her hand. Even if she had the money, there weren't any chemist shops in this village. She crept into bed and shut her eyes, but sleep would not come and she tossed and turned all night.

The next day she was very irritable and paced about the courtyard nervously rubbing her hands together. Her mind felt numb. She could not eat and felt nauseous. She tried to throw up several times. At one point she even snapped at the children. Oh God, I must be having withdrawal symptoms, she moaned.

She suffered through a second night of sleeplessness. Towards morning she dozed off but woke up with a start. Oh what a horrible nightmare. How was she going to continue. I've got to do something about it, she groaned, or it's going to kill me. She prayed to God for help.

Devi Lal got off the train at Rawalpindi and engaged a *tonga* to take him to Moti Bazaar. The city had grown in size since his last visit and the traffic was very heavy. A herd of water buffalos slowly ambled along the road, tended by three young boys wielding small canes and shouting at the top of their lungs.

Shortly, the *tonga* came to a stop at the edge of a bustling bazaar. Scores of small shops were crowded together along narrow lanes. Devi Lal paid the driver and walked into the first lane. Stopping at a small shop, he asked the owner for directions to the luggage shop of Bir Singh. The shopkeeper looked at him suspiciously.

"I don't know any Bir Singh," he answered gruffly. "Who are you?"

By now, two other men from adjacent shops came and stood staring at Devi Lal.

"I've come from the village of Karyala. I have a letter for Bir Singh from my younger brother, Mohan Lal."

The man looked surprised. "Are you the son of *Shaheed* Hem Raj?"

"Yes, I am."

The attitude of the three men changed at once. "I'm sorry, brother, for acting so rudely," the first shopkeeper said courteously. "I was misled by your western clothes. We'll take you to Bir Singh."

"Thank you," Devi Lal answered. "I am a refugee from Burma and have just arrived in Punjab."

Bir Singh received Devi Lal warmly and invited him to his small flat above the shop. He was a Sikh and as a requirement of his religion, did not cut his hair nor shave his face. He wore a turban over his hair which was knotted on top of his head.

"I'm honoured to welcome you to my house," he said respectfully. "I'll give you whatever assistance you need."

Devi Lal explained his desire to find a small house to rent. "I'd like to look at areas near schools for my grandchildren."

"After we have some tea, Doctor *Ji*, I'll take you to see the owner of a to-let service right here in Moti Bazaar. This agent will be able to give you information about houses for rent throughout the city."

Bir Singh's wife, Kulvant, served them tea and snacks while her two young children stood staring at Devi Lal.

The to-let agent seemed to be very well informed about all types of property available for rent or sale.

"We'll start with an area east of Murree Road where there are two good schools. If you're able to ride a bicycle, Doctor *Ji*, we can go there today. Then, if you like, tomorrow I can show you some other areas."

Devi Lal climbed onto the bicycle and followed the agent through the crowded street. They crossed Murree Road and stopped at the edge of a play field next to a large building. "This is the D.A.V. High School for boys," the agent pointed out. "It's indeed very good, Doctor *Ji*. About half a mile north on Murree Road, there's a girls' school called St. Brigid's Convent which is run by British nuns. Many of the rich Indians send their daughters to that school."

The agent then took Devi Lal to a residential area. "Here's a house for sale, but the owner is willing to give it on rent."

Riding their bikes another five minutes, they stopped in front of a single-story house. "Here's another house available for rent. It has four rooms, all on the ground floor."

"My resources are limited," Devi Lal told the agent. "The rents on these houses will most likely be more than I can afford."

"Let me show you two more homes. Then we'll return to my office and I'll look up the rents."

Devi Lal was right. Renting a house was going to be out of the question.

The next morning, he accompanied the agent on foot. They looked at several flats in a low rent neighbourhood. Devi Lal finally rented a small three room flat on the top floor of a three-story building on a street called Mandir Gallie. The owner of the building operated a sweet-meat shop on the first floor, and lived with his family above it. Mandir Gallie — so named because of a Hindu temple on it — originated adjacent to a crowded section of Murree Road. The street was narrow and seemed to run forever, meandering deep into the inner city bazaars.

Devi Lal felt depressed. Khin May and the children will not complain, but he wished he could have been able to afford something better.

He returned to Moti Bazaar. "Bir Singh, I need to purchase some used furniture for the flat," he told his host.

"I'll take you to the second-hand furniture shops in Raja Bazaar, Doctor *Ji*," Bir Singh answered.

Late that afternoon, two coolies with a pushcart loaded with four *charpais*, a small table and four chairs accompanied Devi Lal to the flat. The coolies carried the furniture up the steep, narrow stairway to the third floor.

The flat had a small open terrace, from which a door led into a room. Two smaller rooms on either side could only be entered through the larger middle room. Doors to a small kitchen and a bathroom also opened onto the terrace. An open wooden staircase provided access to the latrine on the roof of the building. Each of the rooms had one small window — all opening toward the front of the building.

The air in the flat was unbearably hot and Devi Lal quickly opened the three windows. The noise from the street filled the rooms. The heavy smell of frying food drifted in through the windows. The few pieces of furniture did not alter the dingy appearance of the flat. I must get the walls whitewashed, he decided.

The landlord had taken two months rent as an advance. After paying for the furniture, there was barely enough money left for their train tickets to Rawalpindi. We'll need to buy utensils: the children will require books and clothes. We will have to sell more of the jewelry, he sadly concluded. The next day Devi Lal returned to Karyala.

Sophia and Neil had been very happy staying with their great grandmother. This morning, when leaving for Rawalpindi, they embraced her fondly.

"Couldn't we have stayed on in Karyala, *Naana*?" Sophia asked as they boarded the train for Rawalpindi. "I'm going to miss great grandmother terribly."

"We need to be in a larger city, Sophia, where you and Neil can attend good schools."

In his heart, Devi Lal felt deeply troubled. How will I be able to provide for Khin May and the children, he kept wondering. Will people come to a doctor they did not know? What will life be like, especially for my daughter and grandchildren, in a strange large city? He tried to dispel the doubts about their future from his mind, but he couldn't stop worrying.

God, Almighty, give me the wisdom and courage to do what is right! Give my children and grandchildren the protection of your mercy and love, he prayed.

A New Beginning

*T*he train station was crowded and noisy and the heat intense. Devi Lal engaged a *tonga*. Sophia sat on the back seat between Neil and Khin May. Her grandfather climbed into the front next to the driver. Devi Lal had tried to prepare the children for life in the large, congested city.

"We'll be among strangers, but I know you'll soon make friends and get accustomed to living in Rawalpindi."

"Tell us about our new house, *Naana*," Neil asked.

"I'm afraid we won't be able to afford a proper house for some time, Neil. I've rented a flat on the top floor of a three-story building."

"I hope I'll have a lawn to play on," he complained.

"No, Son, there isn't a lawn," Devi Lal answered, his voice showing some of the strain he was under.

"Neil, your school will have a playground," his mother offered. "You'll be able to play there." She would talk to her son later to be less demanding and show some understanding.

The *tonga* moved slowly through the congested traffic. Turning onto Murree Road, it picked up a little speed. But soon it had to come to a stop as a large number of goats, shepherded by an old man, started crossing the road. Their continuous bleating added to the din of the loud piercing horns of cars and buses and the incessant ringing of bicycle bells.

"Look children," Devi Lal pointed out, "see what's coming down the road!"

Sophia and Neil stared wide-eyed. An elephant was lumbering towards them, a large bell hanging from its neck ringing loudly in rhythm with its lolling gait. Two saffron-robed Hindu holy men rode the huge animal. The heavy traffic quickly moved out of the way and the elephant shuffled along, contentedly chewing on a piece of sugar cane.

The *tonga* stopped at the entrance to Mandir Gallie. Crowded with pedestrians and bicycles, the gallie was too narrow for a *tonga*. They carried their luggage up the narrow stairs. Entering the flat, Devi Lal quickly opened the three windows.

"This is a nice flat, *Naana*," Sophia said, trying to sound cheerful.

"Oh, it's hot in here," Neil said with a frown on his face.

"This is going to be just fine," Khin May added quickly. "As soon as we open our suitcases and the bedrolls, we'll be quite comfortable."

Each of the rooms had one electric wall fixture. "I'll go and buy some bulbs," Devi Lal offered.

"Dad, could you also get some milk and a vegetable I could cook for dinner?" Khin May asked. "We can have it with the *naans* we brought from Karyala."

"Sure, I'll get them," he answered, walking out of the flat.

With her father gone, Khin May decided to talk to her son. "Neil, I'd like to have a word with you," she said, placing an arm around his shoulders.

"Now what is it, Mother?" he asked, starting to be irritated.

"Come, let's sit down here," she said, patting a step of the stairs going up to the terrace.

"What did I do?" he asked angrily.

"You need to be less demanding and show a little more appreciation, Son. We lost everything in Burma and this is the best your grandfather can provide for us. We should be gracious and be grateful for what we have."

"We shouldn't have left Karyala," Neil blurted out. "At least there I had some place to play. You don't worry about me, do you! All you worry about is Dad and he doesn't even care about any of us. I hate everyone," he cried and ran up the stairs to the roof top.

Sophia had witnessed her brother's outburst. "Mama, make him come down, please. I don't want to see him cry," she pleaded.

Khin May sighed but got up and climbed the stairs. She tried to put her arm around her son's shoulders.

"Leave me alone," Neil said angrily, moving away.

"We all love you, Neil. We care about you very much," Khin May spoke softly.

"No you don't," her son answered, stubbornly.

"Tell me, do you love your *Naana*?"

"Yes, I do," he answered softly.

"Do you think your grandfather loves you and Sophia?"

"Yes, he does," Neil answered, calming down a little.

"He now needs your help, Son. He's in his sixties. He's getting old. You've got to look after him." Neil did not answer.

"Come, Son, come. Let's go and make some tea," she said, taking his hand in hers. Neil wiped his tears and allowed his mother to lead him down the staircase.

Devi Lal walked down the steps, heavy hearted. It was going to be so very difficult, especially for the children. But then he thanked God for bringing them all safely through their long journey, for the roof over their heads — no matter how humble — and for the continued well-being of his family. He prayed especially for Tim.

A young man stood leaning against a doorway. "You have just arrived here, *Babu Ji*?" he said as Devi Lal came out onto the gallie. "My name is Raju. If you need any help, just let me know."

Devi Lal looked at the slightly built man dressed in a white *salwar* and *kameez*. His swarthy face displayed a pencil-thin mustache. A gold chain hung around his neck, and he wore small gold earrings. His gleaming black hair was plastered down with oil.

"Yes, I have moved into this building, but I don't need any help, thank you," Devi Lal answered, turning and walking down the gallie. The young man joined him.

"Where have you come from, *Babu Ji*?"

Devi Lal felt irritated by the man's persistence. Not wanting to sound rude, he replied, "We are refugees from Burma."

The man grinned, showing a row of beetlenut stained teeth.

"I've heard that the people from Burma bring a lot of jewelry with them." Devi Lal did not answer and, turning, walked away.

Mandir Gallie was lined with small shops selling vegetables, clothing, utensils, sweetmeats and milk, clay pots, spices, flowers and toys. There were also tailor, barber and chemist shops. Additionally, hawkers selling a variety of wares daily plied the street adding to the heavy traffic and din. Devi Lal bought four light bulbs and some onions, tomatoes and potatoes.

Walking back, he was relieved that the man who called himself Raju was nowhere in sight. Karam Singh, the owner of the building from whom Devi Lal had rented the flat, sat cross-legged to one side of the front of his sweetmeat shop. He was stirring the milk boiling in a large metal pan over a red hot charcoal stove. A burly man with a thick beard covering his face, he wore a blue turban and white *salwar* and *kameez* which were soiled with perspiration and the dust from the gallie. Metal platters piled high with a variety of sweetmeats were displayed at the front of the shop. The aroma of the sweetmeats mingled with the smell of *samosas* being fried at a food shop across the gallie.

"*Namaste*, Doctor Ji. Welcome to our neighbourhood," Karam Singh greeted Devi Lal warmly. "Have your children come with you this time?"

"*Namaste*, Karam Singh," Devi Lal answered. "Yes, my daughter and grandchildren are here. We arrived a short while ago. I'd like to buy some milk, but first I'll need to get a container."

"I'll give you a pan, Doctor *Ji*. You can return it tomorrow. How much milk would you like?"

"One *seer* should be enough. How much do I owe you?"

"Don't worry, Doctor *Ji*. I'll enter the amount in the *khatta* under your name. You can pay me once a month. Also, I'll tell my wife Jeet that your daughter and grandchildren are here. She'll be most pleased to help them in any way that she can."

"That's very kind of you. My daughter and grandchildren have never lived outside of Burma. They'll be grateful for your wife's assistance. By the way, a man calling himself Raju approached me a little while ago. Do you know him?"

Karam Singh's face turned angry. "That scoundrel is a *gunda*, the leader of a band of miscreants who prey on the shopkeepers of this area. They steal, rob and pester everyone. This man also works for a Pathan moneylender and helps him extort exorbitant interest for the money poor people borrow from him. Do not have any dealings with him, Doctor *Ji*. He's a dog of the lowest breed!"

When Devi Lal returned to the flat, Sophia greeted him warmly but Neil appeared subdued. He had helped light a fire in the single woodburning *angithi* in the kitchen, and Khin May had put some water to boil for tea. Devi Lal told his daughter about his conversation with Karam Singh and the offer of help from his wife, but said nothing about meeting Raju.

Sophia picked up the bedrolls. "I'll make the beds, Mama. How are we going to sleep?" she asked.

Before Khin May could answer, Neil spoke up. "I'll sleep in the middle room," he offered. "You should have one of the bedrooms, *Naana*, and Sophia and Mama can have the other."

Khin May looked at her son, pleasantly surprised, overcome with a feeling of maternal love. Her son was all right. He was just hurting like the rest of them. She cooked the potatoes into a curry. A little later, Karam Singh's twelve-year-old daughter, Kiran, brought a bowl of vegetable curry made from peas and bell peppers as a welcoming gift. Kanti had given them six brass *thaalis* and Khin May used four of them to serve their dinner which they ate together at the small table.

The only source of water in the flat was a slow-flowing tap in the bathroom. After dinner, Khin May started washing the dishes. The tap made a gurgling sound and the water stopped flowing. It was an hour before the water came back on again.

"Sophia, let's fill all the pots and pans we have," Khin May told her daughter, "just in case it stops again."

They would soon discover that the electricity was also prone to go off at different times almost every day.

Sophia sat on her bed with her diary in her lap. She entered the date — *13th April, Monday, 1942*. She had a pensive look on her face. Then she started writing.

Today we are in our new home. It's different, but it's ours. I miss Daddy,

Daw Mu, Sweet Pea and Mr. Fluffy. I also miss Uncle Hari and Sher Khan. If they were all here, it would be so much nicer. Tomorrow Neil and I are going to our new schools. I hope I'll find a good friend. Naana worries so much about us. He is the best grandfather in the whole world. God, please bless him and bless Daddy, Mommy, Neil, Uncle Hari, Great Grandmother and all our relatives.

They slept fitfully through the night as it was unbearably hot in the rooms. Devi Lal woke up around four and went out to the terrace where it was a little better.

The only way to sleep at night, he thought, will be to put the beds here on the terrace. Quietly changing his clothes, he went down the stairs and turned towards Murree Road.

There wasn't much traffic at this early hour. A municipal water truck had just gone by, sprinkling the road. A gentle breeze was blowing and the air smelled fresh. Devi Lal walked north, going away from the center of the city. He enjoyed walking, especially in the morning when his mind was clear and there were few distractions. He started making plans. First, they would get the children enrolled in schools. He also needed to find a place to set up his practice. They would have to sell more of the jewelry.

Walking along deep in thought, his eyes happened to catch sight of a small signboard at the side of the road. The lettering, painted in black next to a red arrow pointing in the direction of a narrow lane, read "*Leper Asylum.*" He came to an abrupt stop and stared at the sign. The past came flooding back and his thoughts went to the lepers living near his school in Jhelum.

Dear God, did you bring me to this city so that I may fulfill my promise to the leper children? He wondered.

As he stood there lost in his thoughts, a leper woman appeared, pushing a crudely made wooden cart with a grotesquely deformed man lying on it. The woman was moving quickly so as to get to the temple and beg for alms from early morning worshipers. The cart rattled by: the man greeted Devi Lal. "*Jai Ram Ji Ki,*" he called out.

Devi Lal stood with the palms of his hands held together, unable to speak. Could these have been two of the children he had known in

Hari Niwas? I must keep my promise, he decided. I must serve them.

On his return, approaching Mandir Gallie, Devi Lal noticed Raju and three of his friends standing at the corner.

"Oh, *Babu Ji,* I've learnt that you're a doctor," Raju said with a broad smile. "That's good. I may need your help sometime."

"I haven't opened my clinic as yet," Devi Lal replied, his face stern. "When I do, and if you're ill and come to the clinic, I'll treat you like any other patient."

As he walked by, he did not see Raju turn to his friends and wink.

After breakfast Devi Lal, Khin May, Sophia and Neil walked to St. Brigid's Convent School. Sophia wore her best clothes, a white cotton dress and socks, and her hair was neatly braided and tied with a ribbon. She had been looking forward to starting school but now felt apprehensive. She reached for her mother's arm and held it with both her hands. Although it was still early in the day, it had gotten quite hot.

The school was located in a walled compound next to a large church on the east side of Murree Road. A uniformed guard opened the iron gate and directed them to the principal's office. The two-story brick building was large, and painted a pale pink. The doors and window frames were stained dark brown and a deep covered veranda ran around the entire building. There was a large playground, a well-tended garden, and a green lawn. School was in session, but other than the soft, murmuring sounds coming from the classrooms, the compound was peaceful and quiet.

"*Naana,* this may be a very expensive school," Sophia whispered to her grandfather. "I don't have to go here."

"Well, let's meet the principal and find out what the fees are," Devi Lal answered, placing his arm around his granddaughter's shoulder. "Besides, there aren't any other good girls' schools in this part of the city."

Sister Margaret Rose, the principal, welcomed them into her clean, spacious office. A ceiling fan slowly whirled overhead, making the room quite pleasant in contrast to the searing heat outside. Sister Margaret Rose was in her mid-fifties and had spent the past fourteen years at St.

Brigid's. She was a tall imposing woman with a surprisingly soft voice.

"The school year is over," she informed them. "The students are taking the last of their final examinations today. I'll be happy to accept an application for classes starting in July, after the summer vacation is over."

"That'll be good, Sister," Khin May answered. "Sophia has been away from school for over two months and can do some reading at home during the summer. Will it be possible for her to come and meet her teacher before school starts?"

"Yes, certainly, that can be arranged," the principal agreed. "Sister Anna Marie is the sixth standard teacher. I'll speak to her. Sophia should be able to meet her any day next week. I would like you to take these application forms with you and fill them out."

Sister Margaret Rose also gave them a pamphlet. "This describes the uniform the girls are required to wear, as well as other rules they have to observe. The fee for the sixth standard is 600 rupees for the year. Half of this sum will have to be paid before school starts."

Sophia quickly glanced at her grandfather and he smiled at her. The moment they were out of the principal's office, Sophia grabbed her grandfather's hand. "Is that all right, *Naana*? The fees are not too high?"

"No, they're fine, child," Devi Lal answered, masking the concern he felt about his ability to earn enough to support the family.

Next they went to the D.A.V. High School for Boys. The headmaster agreed to allow Neil to attend the eighth standard after the summer vacation and gave them an application which Devi Lal filled out before they left. The fees at this school were only 200 rupees a year.

When they arrived back home, Sophia and Neil ran up the steps.

"Can we afford their school fees, Dad?" Khin May whispered. "How will we manage?"

"We'll sell more of the jewelry, Khin May, and I'll also set up my practice right away. With God's grace, we'll manage."

From Karam Singh, Devi Lal found out that Sarafa Bazaar had many jewelry shops. He walked through the narrow lanes to the bazaar, with one hand covering his pants pocket in which he was carrying the jewelry, wrapped in a handkerchief. Unknown to him, one of the young men who earlier had stood on the street corner with Raju was following him.

Devi Lal went to four different shops and was disappointed that none of the shopkeepers were willing to give him what he considered fair value for the jewelry. He finally sold it at the last shop, where he was offered the most money. Putting the cash into his pocket, he walked briskly toward the College Road post office near Moti Bazaar. He opened a passbook savings account and deposited all but 200 *rupees*. With the passbook in his hand and the money in his pocket, he walked back home. The young man who had been following him went looking for Raju.

That afternoon, Devi Lal rented a small room in Bohr Bazaar near several chemists' shops. The room was on the ground floor of an old building on a narrow street. The traffic outside was heavy and noisy. He would have to paint the walls, and since there were no windows, he would need a table fan. He purchased a desk, two chairs and a wooden examination table from the same secondhand furniture store in Raja Bazaar where he had bought the furniture for the flat. The electric fan would have to wait. Neil went with his grandfather and swept the floor of the clinic and helped arrange the furniture in the small room. Devi Lal then ordered a signboard painted with his name on it, along with the hours the clinic would be open, seven days each week.

While Neil and Devi Lal were at the clinic, Sophia was at home with her mother, sorting out their clothes. There was a knock at the door from the stairs.

"Who is it?" Khin May called out in a loud voice.

"*Bibi Ji*, it is me — the sweeper woman," a voice answered.

"Oh, she must be the cleaning woman," Khin May said and, followed by Sophia, went to open the door. The woman came in, carrying a flat, circular cane basket on her head and a similar one in her arms. She was a slim, tall woman with a dark complexion and pockmarked face. A large round red *bindi* was painted on her forehead as a symbol of her Hindu faith and married status. Her *salwar* and *kameez* were soiled and torn, her *dupatta* consisted of a dirty rag and she was barefooted.

"The *Bibi Ji* downstairs told me to come and clean your latrine each day," she said. "Is it all right for me to come about this time in the afternoon?"

"Yes, that'll be fine," Khin May answered, making a mental note to ask Jeet how much she should pay the woman. The sweeper woman placed the basket from her hands in a corner of the terrace, and climbed the wooden staircase to the rooftop to clean the latrine.

Khin May returned to her bedroom but Sophia stayed out on the terrace. She looked at the basket the woman had placed in the corner and was surprised to see a little baby lying in it, happily kicking its arms and legs.

"Oh, what a cute little baby you are!" she said softly, walking over and kneeling down next to the basket.

The infant smiled and kicked its limbs faster. Sophia put her hand out, and the baby grasped a finger.

"Oh, *Bibi Ji*, please don't touch my child!" the sweeper woman cried, hurrying down the staircase. "I need this work and I'll be fired if anybody sees you. Please, please, don't do that! Go quickly, take a bath or at least wash your hands with soap and water!"

Sophia was startled. She looked at the woman, puzzled.

"Why must I wash my hands? I'd like to carry your baby in my arms. Can I do that?"

"No! You don't know!" the woman frantically pleaded. "You mustn't touch us. We are *achoots* — untouchables."

The woman picked up the basket with the baby and quickly walked down the stairs. Sophia didn't understand why the woman had acted so strangely. She bolted the door and went into the bedroom.

"Mama, who are *achoots*? Why do they consider themselves untouchable?" she asked her mother.

"Oh, the sweeper woman must have told you that. Well, it is terrible. In the Hindu caste system, these people supposedly belong to the lowest caste," Khin May explained to her daughter. "They earn their livelihood by sweeping streets and cleaning latrines."

"But mother, isn't that wrong? Why should they have to do this work? And why did she ask me to take a bath?"

"Yes, it's very wrong, child, but upper class Hindus consider physical contact with the *achoots* defiling. They take a bath if they even accidently touch them."

"That's not fair! I will not take a bath all day!" Sophia said angrily.

"No, you don't have to bathe, Sophia," Khin May smiled. "Not because you touched the baby. But I do hope you'll take a bath before dinner, anyway."

That evening Sophia asked her grandfather about the untouchables.

"This is one of the sad ills of Hinduism, my child. Some of our leaders are trying to correct it," he explained. "Mahatma Gandhi, for example, calls the untouchables *Harijans*, God's children. He has been trying to break the caste system. He uses a very ingenious method to get upper class Hindus to come into the areas where the untouchables live."

"What does he do, *Naana*?" Neil asked.

"Well, each day, thousands of Indians go to see Mahatma Gandhi and attend his prayer meeting. Often, Gandhi Ji moves in and lives with the *Harijans*. The people who want to see him have to enter the villages and homes of these so-called lower-caste Hindus."

"*Naana*, have you ever seen Mahatma Gandhi?" Sophia asked.

"Yes, Gandhi Ji came to Burma in 1934, and I took your mother with me to the railway station in Mandalay. The platform was packed with thousands of people and there was great excitement when the train arrived. The moment Mahatma Gandhi appeared in the doorway of his third-class compartment, a hush fell over the crowd. I remember a strange sensation going through my mind. I realized that we were in the presence of someone truly great."

"Can we go to see him if he should come to Rawalpindi, *Naana*?"

"Yes, most certainly. We'll do that."

Soon they settled into a daily routine. Neil accompanied his grandfather each morning to help open the clinic and wipe the furniture clean of dust. Sophia helped her mother at home. Each day, they bought a vegetable which Sophia washed and cut and then observed her mother cook. Karam Singh's wife, Jeet, showed Khin May how to knead wheat flour and then took her to a food shop down the gallie. The shopkeeper shaped the wheat dough into flattened, round *naans* and, for a fee of four *annas,* baked them in a hot tandoor.

Neil had moved the four *charpais* out of the rooms and onto the small terrace, and they were able to sleep at night a little more comfortably. In the morning, Neil placed three of the *charpais* on their sides in one corner of the terrace. Khin May purchased a length of rope from one of the shops and Neil helped her string it across the terrace. Sophia then hung the clothes out to dry that her mother washed under the tap.

A week after first visiting St. Brigid's Convent, Sophia returned to meet her teacher. Sister Anna Marie Kelly welcomed her warmly. She was Irish, born and raised in Rathdrum, a town south of Dublin in County Wicklow. She was a slim attractive young woman, 32 years of age, vibrant and committed to her work. She smiled a lot and spoke with a soft gentle voice.

They chatted and Sophia briefly told her about her school in Mandalay and their journey to India.

"That's so interesting," the nun said, walking Sophia to the school gate. "I've truly enjoyed our conversation. You must come and see me again."

Sophia saw Sister Anna Marie several times during the summer holidays. Khin May or Neil walked her to the Convent gate and, later, one of them returned to accompany her home.

On Sundays, Devi Lal, Khin May and the children went to the Arya Samaj temple for a prayer meeting in the morning. After lunch and a brief rest, Devi Lal would then open his clinic at three o'clock and stay there until eight in the evening.

"I was thinking of going with Neil and Sophia to College Road, Dad," Khin May told her father one day. "I thought we might look at school uniforms for Sophia. The brochure the principal gave has the address of the tailor shop."

"Can we stop and see your clinic on the way, *Naana*?" Sophia inquired.

"That'll be nice, Sophia," her grandfather answered. "It's only one room, but I'd like you to see it."

After preparing their evening meal, Khin May locked the door to the rooms, as well as the one leading from the stairs to the terrace. She, Neil and Sophia walked through the winding lanes toward the center of the city. Sophia was wearing a white cotton *salwar* and *kameez* her mother had purchased for her from a shop on Mandir Gallie. At five feet, three inches, she was tall for her age and looked more mature than an eleven-year-old. Neil was also tall and his mother had noticed that his voice was changing.

When they entered the small room in which Devi Lal had his clinic, Khin May's thoughts went back to her father's well-appointed large clinic in Mandalay which now must be in ruins. She knew her father was a good physician and sooner or later the word would get around and people would come to him for treatment.

"You'll be home by eight, Dad?" she asked.

"Well, just a little after that, Khin May," he answered. "I'll keep the clinic open until eight."

They found the tailor shop on College Road. St. Brigid's Convent School required its pupils to wear a white blouse with a little red necktie, dark blue pinafore and a red belt. Their socks had to be white, worn with black or brown leather shoes. Khin May looked at the price labels, and mentally added them up. The clothes were going to cost much more than she had anticipated. They were going to have to sell the rest of the jewelry, and she would also have to find some work right away.

"Will we be able to buy the uniforms before school starts, Mama?" Sophia inquired as they came out of the shop. "Everything looked so expensive."

"We should be able to manage it, Sophia. You've got to have the clothes required by the school."

They started walking back towards Mandir Gallie and by the time they reached their flat, it was almost 6:30. Khin May at once sensed there was something wrong when she saw that the door leading to the terrace was open. Neil ran up the stairs and, reaching the door leading into the rooms, he yelled,

"Mama, come quickly! Our flat's been broken into!"

"Oh my God!" Khin May moaned, entering the middle room. Their suitcases had been opened and the contents strewn all over the floor. Their clothes and personal belongings were scattered throughout the three rooms. "Why would any one rob us?" she cried. "We don't have anything of value."

Then she thought about the jewelry her father kept in his tin trunk and ran to his room. The trunk was lying on its side with its lock broken. The jewelry in the trunk must have been what the thieves were after, she thought, with a sickening feeling. She frantically rummaged through the clothes scattered on the bed and on the floor. Dejected, she sat down on the floor and tears filled her eyes.

Sophia put her arms around her mother. "Don't cry, Mama. We'll straighten the rooms and put everything away."

"I'll kill the dogs who did this to us!" Neil muttered, his voice shaking with anger.

"Mama, you and Sophia stay here," he continued. "I'm going to fetch *Naana*. I'll also tell Mr. Karam Singh downstairs. I want you to bolt the door to the terrace and don't open it until I return."

The police arrived, summoned by Karam Singh. A small crowd gathered in front of the building. A constable asked bystanders if they had noticed anything suspicious. Devi Lal hurried back with his grandson. Khin May went to her father.

"I'm sorry Dad. I should have stayed home and not gone out with the children. The jewelry is gone."

"It's good you weren't at home, child. I'm glad no harm came to you," Devi Lal answered, placing his arm around his daughter's shoulders. "Material objects can eventually be replaced."

The police were sympathetic but unable to help. They promised to continue their investigation and suggested that stronger locks be put on both the terrace door and the door leading into the rooms.

Khin May blamed herself for the theft of the jewelry and felt terribly depressed. That night she was unable to fall asleep. She had not taken any sleeping pills since running out of them in Karyala. There, she had suffered terribly for several days, but then resolved never to take them again. If only she had some with her now, she wished.

For the next few days, Devi Lal also felt deeply disturbed. With the jewelry gone, he worried about his ability to provide for his daughter and grandchildren. He was sixty-one, and if something were to happen to him, who would take care of the children? He thought about asking his brother if they could sell some of their ancestral lands. If his practice did not pick up soon, he would journey to Karyala and talk to Mohan Lal.

Devi Lal started visiting the leper asylum once a week, providing whatever medical care he could. The turmoil in his mind ebbed somewhat when he was with his daughter and grandchildren, and whenever he attended to the lepers.

Sophia had started reading a book on the life of Mahatma Gandhi her grandfather brought for her from the city library. In the afternoons, she waited for the sweeper woman to come and played with the baby while the mother went to clean the latrine. One day she took a banana which she had saved and placed it in the basket next to the baby.

"*Bibi Ji*, please don't do that," the sweeper woman pleaded. "I'll be accused of stealing."

"If you eat the banana now," Sophia answered. "Nobody will say that you stole it." The woman had not eaten since morning. She looked around to see if anyone was watching and quickly peeled the banana and ate it.

"Where do you live?" Sophia asked.

"We live outside the city in our village by Rawal Lake, next to the cremation grounds."

"Why do you have to do this work?"

"Well, we're of the lowest caste, *Bibi Ji*. We are expected to clean latrines and sweep streets."

"But you don't have to do it. You could do something else. You could sell vegetables," Sophia persisted.

"We are *achoots, Bibi Ji*. Untouchables. No one would buy them."

"You can change things, can't you? Why don't you and your husband go to another town where no one knows you?"

The woman thought for a moment. "That will not work, *Bibi Ji*. It's our karma to do what we do. How can we change that?"

Sophia felt confused. No one should be forced into any type of work because of their caste, she thought angrily. But the woman seemed to be content with her life. Sophia had even heard her humming a tune while sweeping the floors.

"What's your daughter's name?" she asked.

"My husband and I named her Jyoti"

"That's a very pretty name. It means light, doesn't it?"

"Yes, it does," she replied, smiling. "When she was born, my husband said she had brightened our lives, so we named her Jyoti."

"May I pick Jyoti up?"

The woman looked concerned, but noticing that the door from the stairs was bolted, she said, "All right, *Bibi Ji*, but only for a short while. I have to clean several more latrines before evening."

Sophia picked up the infant and, gently rocking her, walked back and forth on the terrace. She tenderly embraced the baby before placing her back in the basket.

Devi Lal's medical practice started growing slowly. A large community of Mohyals lived in the city and when the word got around who Devi Lal was, many started coming to him for their medical needs. In addition to the leper asylum, he started going to a nearby orphanage once a week to provide medical care to the children.

Occasionally Devi Lal bought an English newspaper and brought it home, and the family followed the news of the war with great interest. British forces had retreated rapidly, pursued by the advancing Japanese armies. One Burmese town after another fell in rapid succession. All the Allies could do, it seemed, was to hurriedly destroy essential installations and flee.

During the middle of April, the British Army destroyed the oil fields at Yenangyaung. They demolished oil rigs and machinery and blew up thousands of barrels of crude oil. Six thousand oil wells were left burning. The exploding oil barrels shook up neighboring towns and villages and the night skies were lit for weeks by the flames from the burning oil. The Burmese people were deeply angered by the destruction of their country from a war they wanted no part of. Yet fleeing British and Indian troops were often helped and treated kindly by the natives.

On 20th April the town of Lashio fell. By the 29th, the last of the British troops had crossed over to the western side of the Irrawaddy River. As columns of Japanese tanks advanced rapidly, the British blew up the Ava bridge near Mandalay. Two spans of this, the only bridge across the Irrawaddy, fell into the river, temporarily slowing the Japanese advance. The city of Mandalay lay besieged and was captured by the enemy on 1 May.

As Japan consolidated its hold on Burma, the Burmese were horrified by the wanton brutality with which the Japanese treated their prisoners of war. Wounded, captured soldiers were seen being used for bayonet practice. Captured British officers were treated with unmentionable, humiliating torture before being executed by the Japanese using their ceremonial swords. The Burmese were expecting to be liberated, but instead found themselves ruled by a cruel master.

On 8 May, the Japanese entered the northern town of Myitkyina. Thousands of refugees tried to flee to India through the dreaded Hukwang Valley. British Civil Service employees valiantly attempted to help them. With the onset of the monsoons, however, thousands perished in what came to be known as the Valley of Death. The American General Joseph Stilwell made the headlines by leading a band of about one hundred multinationals, marching towards India in the middle of the monsoons. His group included an American surgeon, Dr. Gordon Seagrave, and several of his Burmese nurses. General Stilwell got his group to India safely, vowing to soon return to Burma. By 12 May, the last elements of the British Army had withdrawn to Kalewa, and by the 19th, they had fled Tamu, and escaped toward Palel and India. By 20th May, the Japanese armies had completed their conquest of Burma.

Sophia had been looking forward to attending St. Brigid's and was pleased when summer vacations were over and schools reopened. Her mother had not been able to find work, but started serving at the orphanage as a volunteer. Khin May walked Sophia to school each morning and then went on to the orphanage to work until noon. She met Sophia at the school gate at 3:30 and accompanied her back home.

One day Sister Anna Marie asked Sophia to tell the class about Burma and their trek to India. Standing in front of her class, Sophia spoke about Mandalay and some of the towns and places of interest around the city. When she came to the part about the war and the bombings, she stopped.

Turning to her teacher, she pleaded, "I don't want to talk about it, Sister."

"You don't have to," Sister Anna Marie said gently. "I'm very sorry that I asked you."

Sophia had become friends with Nusreen Bhutt, a Muslim girl in her class who was the daughter of a wealthy building contractor. She and her parents lived in a large comfortable home in an affluent area near St. Brigid's Convent. She was Sophia's age, but at four feet ten inches, was considerably shorter. Her black hair was fashionably cut shoulder length and her school uniforms were made of expensive silk fabrics. She was fair complexioned but was conscious of her aquiline nose and had developed a habit of holding her right hand in front of her face. She was an only child but had remained unspoiled in spite of her doting parents. On Saturdays, school ended at noon and Nusreen had asked Sophia to spend the afternoon with her at her home. Khin May agreed to let her daughter go. "I'll come to your friend's place at three o'clock to walk you back home," she said.

Nusreen's mother was waiting at the school gate in a car driven by a chauffeur. Following lunch, the two friends went up to Nusreen's bedroom. The room was elegantly furnished and had a large window with a seat along it covered with a thick cushion.

"What a great view you have from here," Sophia said, thinking about her own room in *Shanti Gaeha*. "Is that a lake there beyond the fields?"

"Yes, that's Rawal Lake," Nusreen replied. "I love sitting here and looking at it, especially at night when the moon is full."

"Have you been near it?" Sophia asked.

"No, I'm not allowed to go out there."

"Who lives in those huts next to the lake?" she asked.

"Oh, that's the village of the *harijans*, the untouchables," Nusreen answered.

"Oh, yes," Sophia said, "our sweeper woman told me that she lived near Rawal Lake. You know, I'd like to see the village."

"Why do you want to see it?" Nusreen asked perplexed. "It's probably not very nice."

"I just want to," Sophia said, getting up. "Should we go?"

"You mean, you want to go there now?"

"Yes. It's so close. We'd be back in a few minutes."

Nusreen hesitated a moment. "Okay, let's do it," she said excitedly. "Let's sneak out."

The girls walked down the steps and quietly slipped out the front door. Holding hands and giggling, they ran along a narrow path through the fields. The lake was further away than it looked from her window, and Nusreen started worrying. Then in the distance, she saw the lake and the small huts crowded together near the water's edge. The girls ran faster and as they got closer, they heard a woman wailing.

"What was that?" Sophia asked, slowing down.

"I don't know," Nusreen answered. "It seems to be coming from those huts."

The girls walked towards the village, drawn by the woman's crying. Then they saw a tall giant of a man, wearing a grey *salwar kameez* and a white turban, standing in front of one of the huts. He held a knife in one hand and had a foot planted on the chest of a frail-looking figure lying on the ground.

"Please, please don't harm me!" the prostrate man pleaded. "I'll return your money with full interest. I just need a little time, but I promise I'll return every *paisa*."

The woman cowering at the door of the hut suddenly noticed Sophia. "What are you doing here, *Bibi Ji*?" she cried. "Please get away. Go back! Run! You mustn't come here!"

The big man turned around and angrily stared at the two girls. Then, noticing the beautiful tall girl with the golden hair in the Convent School uniform, he smiled. He had a long mustache and his face was unshaven. A front upper tooth was covered with a gold cap with a small heart-shaped opening in it.

"Let's go, Sophia," Nusreen whispered urgently, pulling Sophia's hand. The girls ran and did not stop until they were back in Nusreen's house.

The smile left the man's face and he pushed down hard on the chest of the untouchable whimpering on the ground. "All right, I'll give you one more week, but no more. If you haven't paid up by then, I'll have to kill you."

He flicked his knife closed and started walking rapidly in the direction the young girls had taken.

"How could you have done such a thing, Sophia?" Khin May scolded. "You should have known better than to have gone looking for trouble. Your grandfather will be very angry with you. You must never do a stupid thing like this again!"

Sophia's eyes filled with tears. "But Mama, that evil man was hurting the sweeper woman's husband. We must help them. Please give her the money they owe. If not, this man said he would kill her husband."

Later, Devi Lal was also angry, but patiently explained to Sophia that it was not safe for her to go off, even with her friend, without grownups.

"I promise, *Naana*, I'll never ever do it again. But we must give the sweeper woman the money her husband owes," she pleaded.

The next day when the sweeper woman came, Devi Lal spoke to her. "Sophia told us that a man was threatening your husband and demanding money. Who is this person, and how much do you owe him?"

"What can I say, *Babu Ji*," the woman moaned. "My husband needed money to get his young sister married. We borrowed fifty rupees from the money lender. Now we owe him an additional forty rupees in interest."

"Who's this man? How much time has he given you?"

The woman started weeping softly. "His name is Kassim. He comes from Peshawar. He's a very bad man. I know that if we don't pay him he's going to kill my husband. We have six days before he'll be back."

"Do you have any money at all?"

"My husband will have twenty rupees saved by next week."

Devi Lal thought for a moment. "All right. I'll get you the rest tomorrow."

"Thank you, *Babu Ji*, thank you! May Krishan Bhagwan bless you and your family. My husband and I will return the money to you as soon as we can."

That evening, Sophia had just finished setting the four *thaalis* and glasses on the table for dinner when there was a knock on the terrace door.

"Who is it?" she asked.

"Who do you think it is?" a familiar voice responded. "Hurry up, Sophia, open the door and let me in!"

Sophia flung the door open and leapt into Hari's arms.

"*Naana*, Neil, Mama — come quickly! Uncle Hari is here!" They all came running.

"Oh, you look so handsome in your uniform, Uncle Hari!" Sophia said, standing back. Hari, indeed, looked handsome in his khaki bush shirt, trousers and British Army cap with the insignia of the Medical Corps on it. He was deeply tanned and his hair had been cut quite short.

"Well, my training is over and now that I'm a full-fledged officer, I'm required to wear a uniform."

"How are you, Son? It's so good to see you," Devi Lal said, hugging him.

"I'm fine, Dad. It's great to be home."

"How long can you stay, Uncle Hari?" Neil asked.

"You'll have to see my school tomorrow," Sophia added before Hari could answer Neil.

"Children, slow down!" Khin May said laughing. "Let him catch his breath. We were about to have dinner, Hari. Neil, go down and borrow a chair from Mr. Karam Singh."

They chatted during dinner and Hari told them about his training.

"Have you received your orders, Son?" his father asked.

"Yes, Dad, I've been assigned to the Military Hospital in Imphal."

That's so close to the front, Devi Lal worried.

"This is the first time we are having dinner together since leaving Lucknow," Sophia commented. "How long are you going to stay with us, Uncle Hari?"

"Well, I am here for two nights, but will try and come back soon," Hari said, and then added, "Tell me, how are all of you doing? How's your practice, Dad?"

"It's picking up slowly, Hari. I keep busy by going once a week to an orphanage and to a leper asylum."

"How about you, Sis? How do you spend your time?"

"Well, I work as a volunteer at the orphanage until noon. I'm at home the rest of the time."

"How do you like your school, Neil?" Hari asked his nephew.

"It's a good school, Uncle Hari. I've joined the R.S.S. We have to wear uniforms and learn self-defense. I can twirl a six-foot bamboo lathi and fight off several men."

"What's the R.S.S.?" Hari asked.

It stands for Rashtriya Swayamsevak Sangh," Devi Lal explained. "It's a nationwide organization where young Hindu men and boys learn about discipline and self-defense and help with the freedom movement."

"That's great," Hari answered. "You must get a lot of exercise."

"That he does," Khin May spoke up. "They are forever going for long marches."

"We also read a lot about India's struggle for freedom and about the many leaders who sacrificed their lives to try and free the country," Neil added.

Later they borrowed a *charpai* from Karam Singh and sat on the terrace talking late into the night.

The next day was Sunday and the family attended a prayer service at the Arya Samaj temple. Sophia and Neil then took Hari to show him their schools. In the afternoon, they hired a *tonga* and Hari took them sightseeing.

He felt depressed over the small flat the family was staying in. He also felt sorry for his sister. She looked pale and he knew that she must miss and worry about Tim terribly. He had avoided asking any questions. If there was any news, his sister would have told him. Later that evening, he forced Khin May to accept two hundred rupees he had brought with him.

"Please use it for the children," he pleaded. "I know Dad won't take it. I'm paid well and really have little to spend it on."

Hari left the next morning, and the family returned to its routine. A few days later, Khin May found work as a teacher in a nursery school. She taught the children how to recite the English alphabet and kept them occupied with games. Sophia started reading a second book on the life of Mahatma Gandhi and found it fascinating.

Gandhi's philosophy of nonviolent resistance greatly appealed to Sophia, as she herself abhorred violence. She had not known about the long-standing animosity between Hindus and Muslims and the blood that had periodically been shed over the past few centuries by one faction attacking the other. She was deeply impressed by Gandhi's preaching of love and understanding between people of all faiths, and was fascinated reading about the famous salt march that Gandhi had undertaken in 1930. The British government had imposed a tax on salt, and declared that only official government plants could produce it. Gandhi felt this policy was wrong and led his followers on a two hundred mile march to the sea shore to defy the government's ban. Thousands of people joined him on the way and newspaper reporters came from all over the world to write about this simple, nonviolent act. It was strange that a small frail old man could pick up a fistful of salt on the remote shores of an ocean and let the whole world know of India's plight and struggle for independence.

The British were perplexed and didn't know how to deal with these strange tactics. They arrested Gandhi and other Indian leaders, and put them all in prison. This only further inflamed the people and nonviolent civil disobedience became the order of the day. Indians throughout the country started making salt. Gandhi asked the people to get rid of their western clothes. He instructed them to wear clothes made from *khadi*, a fabric made from cotton thread woven on home spinning wheels.

The British Government invited Gandhi to London. Gandhi went, dressed in a white cotton loincloth and sandals. He traveled all over England and drew large crowds. He refused to stay in hotels and instead, stayed with a poor family in a crowded slum of London. He was invited to Buckingham Palace to have tea with King George the fifth, and with Queen Mary. Gandhi went dressed the way he always did, in his *dhoti* and a shawl. Asked later by a reporter why he had not put on more clothes, he reputedly responded with a smile that the King was really wearing enough clothes for both of them.

Gandhi met with George Bernard Shaw, Charlie Chaplin, and church and political leaders. The only person who refused to see him was Winston Churchill.

The British Government was adamant and would not consider giving India its freedom. Shortly after his return to India, Gandhi was once again arrested and thrown into prison. He and his fellow leaders continued their struggle for independence from within the prison walls.

The British Government was frustrated by the events in India. The political situation in Europe was worsening. When Britain declared war on Germany in 1939, the British Viceroy in Delhi announced that India was also at war with Germany. The Indian leaders and people could not understand Britain's determined waging of war in Europe to defend democracy, while continuing to maintain its colonial strangle hold on India's throat. Indian leaders were also angry with many of the nearly six hundred rajas and maharajas in India. These rulers of princely states offered their support to the Allies in Europe while continuing to bleed their own subjects at home.

Gandhi and his fellow leaders were appalled by the barbaric and inhumane acts committed by Hitler and his Nazis. Gandhi spoke passionately against fascism and the Nazis. The Indian leaders and people were further infuriated when they found out that their eight thousand-year-old symbol of Aryan Hindu civilization and culture, the swastika, had been distorted and was being used by the Nazis as their emblem, representing their heinous plans. To the Hindus, their swastika signified prayers for success and accomplishments, a symbol of good luck and nobility.

President Franklin Roosevelt and the government of the United States tried to persuade Winston Churchill and the British government to grant India its freedom. Churchill remained adamant. Gandhi continued to preach nonviolence and noncooperation as a means of ridding India of British rule.

Now, in 1942, Gandhi introduced a new slogan which he asked the people to adopt. It simply said, "Quit India," a call to the British to leave. "If Indian soldiers are to die in this war," Gandhi said, "then let them die for a free India."

Yet Gandhi wanted the people to protest without resorting to violence. The "Quit India" movement picked up speedy momentum and spread throughout the land. Not all the leaders were willing to remain nonviolent. Many freedom fighters believed they had to continue the fight with swords and guns. One charismatic leader, Subash Bose, escaped from the British police and managed to reach Japan. With the help of the Indian population in Southeast Asia, he formed the Indian National Army, made up of volunteers and Indians of the British Army held prisoners of war by the Japanese.

Rumor had it that in Rawalpindi, the freedom fighters planned to intensify their activities. Neil had taken part in protests and demonstrations but was anxious to get involved in something more exciting and adventurous. Not yet fourteen, he was taller than the other boys his age and was trying to find some outlet for the anger he held bottled up inside him. On his way home from an R.S.S. meeting, he went to Moti Bazaar to see Bir Singh.

"I want to become a freedom fighter," he said. "Could you please tell me what I can do?"

"You're much too young to get involved in our activities, Son," Bir Singh answered. "Does Doctor *Ji* know of your coming to see me?" he asked.

"No, he doesn't," Neil answered.

"Why don't you wait awhile. Perhaps in a few years you can join us."

"Isn't there anything at all I can do to help?" Neil persisted.

"All right, I'll contact you when something comes up," Bir Singh answered, hoping the boy would soon forget the whole thing. "Convey my respects to your grandfather. How's he doing?"

"He's doing all right. I'll give him your message," Neil said, leaving. But when he got home he found that his grandfather was very distraught. Earlier that afternoon a telegram was delivered to the flat. Mohan Lal wired that their mother, Kanti, had died peacefully during the night. Devi Lal's eyes had filled with tears.

"I must go to Karyala" he told his daughter. "Will you and the children be all right by yourselves?"

"Yes, Dad, please don't worry about us," Khin May answered, tears running down her face. "Let me help you pack."

Devi Lal left for Karyala later that evening, knowing that his mother's funeral must already be over. His thoughts went back to his childhood. He was so very close to his mother and worshiped her. She had loved and supported him even when he had defied his father. He felt guilt-ridden. As the eldest son, he should have been at her cremation to recite prayers and help light the pyre, just as he should have been at his father's funeral. Early the next morning, he went to the cremation grounds and, tears overflowing his eyes, stood there for a long time.

On the fourth day following Kanti's death, her ashes were collected and placed in a brass urn. Devi Lal returned to Rawalpindi, but planned to go back to Karyala again on the thirteenth day after his mother's death. He and his brother would then take her ashes to the holy city of Haridwar, and put them in the waters of the river Ganges.

Khin May and the children had also been deeply affected by Kanti's death. They took turns reading the verses in the *Gita* dealing with death and sorrow and prayed together. The morning after her father had left for Karyala, Khin May came out of their building with the children to walk Sophia to school. Raju and his friends were standing at the end of the gallie.

"You ladies from Burma are looking exceptionally beautiful today," Raju said with a broad smile.

Neil's face turned red and he stopped.

"Ignore the dog, Neil," his mother whispered, grabbing his arm. "You'll only encourage him by reacting to his taunts."

The boy started walking, but swore under his breath that one day he would take care of this *gunda*.

Devi Lal returned to Rawalpindi and then went back to Karyala when it was time to take his mother's ashes to Haridwar. A Brahmin priest there performed a religious ceremony, and the two brothers placed their mother's ashes into the holy river. A cold drizzle had started falling by the time they returned to Karyala late in the evening. Winter would soon be upon them and the children did not have any warm clothes. Devi Lal started worrying.

The next morning, before leaving, he spoke to his brother. "The jewelry we had was stolen," he explained. "Mohan, I need to buy the children winter clothing and pay for their schooling. I would like to see if we can sell a portion of our ancestral land."

His brother agreed. Kumari, who had heard a portion of their conversation, was irate.

"Don't sell any of the land," she later told her husband. "I knew he was going to try and get half-share of everything we have. Tell him the land is all ours and you don't plan to part with it!"

"Look, my brother lost everything," Mohan Lal pleaded with his wife. "The children will freeze in the winter without warm clothes. He's only asking for us to sell a small portion of the land."

"Yes, but that's just the beginning. Next he'll demand half-share of all of the buildings. Think about our own children and grandchildren. I would give my life for them, but you don't seem to care."

"Of course I'm concerned about our children and their families, but Kumari, be reasonable and for God's sake show some pity towards my brother," her husband moaned. "Besides, he's only asking for a fifth share."

"Why does he want only a fifth?"

"Well, he wants everything divided equally between we brothers and sisters."

"Oh. All right, that's a little better," Kumari said, calming down a little. "You can send him his one-fifth share, but I'll be damned if anyone else gets a *paisa* from the rest."

Devi Lal returned to Rawalpindi and slowly got back into his daily routine. He woke up at four o'clock and, after returning from his walk, sat and read a medical journal that he had subscribed to, and medical books he borrowed from the library. But now his eyesight was deteriorating and he started having difficult reading. Sophia noticed her grandfather rubbing his eyes one morning. "Are your eyes sore, *Naana,*" she asked.

"Only when I read, my child, they hurt a little," he answered.

"Then let me read to you, *Naana,*" Sophia offered.

"Well, all right, if that's what you want," Devi Lal replied with a smile. "It will be very nice to have you read to me."

From the next day, therefore, it became a ritual for Sophia to wake up early and read to her grandfather. At first she had trouble pronouncing some of the medical terms and laughed at herself when her grandfather explained to her that the letter 'p' in pneumonia was silent and was not pronounced phonetically.

Winter was approaching and it was getting dark earlier in the evenings. After closing his clinic, Devi Lal had to walk back home through the dimly lit, narrow lanes. One evening he tripped over a loose stone and fell, hurting his knee. From then on, each evening, Neil took a hurricane lantern and walked his grandfather back home from his clinic.

At his daughter's insistence, Devi Lal went to the General Hospital to have his eyes examined. The doctors told him that he had developed cataracts in both eyes. The one in the right eye needed to be removed right away. Devi Lal underwent surgery for the removal of the cataract. The eye operation was successful but, unfortunately, an infection set in while he was recuperating, damaging his eye irreparably. The vision in his right eye was completely lost.

He took his setback in stride, continuing with his life and work as well as he could. He attended to the medical needs of the children in the orphanage and the lepers, and worked in his clinic until late each evening. But he was now totally dependent upon his granddaughter to read his books and journals to him in the morning, and on his grandson to guide him home at night through the dark gallies of the city.

He often recited in his mind a poem written by the great Indian poet Tagore, that he had memorized.

> *Let me not pray to be sheltered from dangers, but to be fearless*
> *in facing them.*
> *Let me not beg for the stilling of my pain, but for the heart to*
> *conquer it.*
> *Let me not look for allies in life's battlefield, but to my own*
> *strength.*
> *Let me not crave in anxious fear to be saved, but hope for the*
> *patience to win my freedom.*
> *Grant me that I may not be a coward, feeling your mercy in my*
> *success alone; but let me find the grasp of your hand in*
> *my failure.*

Friends and Foes

*W*inter was upon them and bone-chilling cold winds from the north brought the temperatures down to below freezing. It was difficult to imagine that only a few short months ago people were dying of heat stroke. None of the family had any winter clothes. Devi Lal thought about borrowing money, but where could he go?

Then, to his great relief, he received a money order from his brother. "This is your fifth share from the sale of our land adjacent to Karyala," he wrote.

Devi Lal bought blankets, woolen sweaters and scarves for all of them. He wished he could have bought something elegant for Khin May and Sophia, perhaps the fine Kashimiri pashmina shawls from the fancy shops of Kalan Bazaar. But those were expensive, something his meager funds could definitely not afford.

Christmas holidays for schools were two days away, and political organizations as well as religious groups in the city had called for a one day general strike. Office and factory workers stayed away and school and university students walked out of their classrooms. Businesses closed their doors, and that afternoon, a rally was to be held near Moti Bazaar. It would be followed by a procession along College Road and end with a sit-in in front of the British Government office buildings on Murree Road, across the Leh River.

The Government buildings were located in an area of the city referred to as the Cantonment, where the British had built their comfortable homes and offices, along tree-lined, clean wide roads. Cantonments could be found close to most Indian cities and towns. Natives were not allowed to live there except for those who worked as servants and were given servants' quarters behind the homes of their masters.

Neil had joined the thousands gathered near Moti Bazaar. Flags and banners fluttered in the cool air. The bright sunshine felt good and warmed those who were able to stay out of the shade. Parents bought balloons for their children. The mood of the people was defiant but festive.

"*Inkalab Zindabad*—Long live Freedom!" they chanted.

"Release our leaders. Free our country!" they demanded. Speeches were made and patriotic songs sung.

In other parts of India, many demonstrations had turned violent, with crowds attacking government installations. A few post offices had been set on fire and railway traffic was disrupted. The bolder Freedom fighters cut telegraph wires between cities and raided police stations and army posts. In Rawalpindi, today's rally was planned as a peaceful protest. Hindus, Muslims, and Sikhs stood side by side, shouting slogans urging their fellow countrymen to boycott everything that was British. The procession started and the people began moving along College Road. The orange, white and green Indian National flag was everywhere. Children held hands and walked in rows.

Neil marched in a column of boys dressed in their khaki R.S.S. shirts and shorts. He felt his body tingle with excitement. They were followed by young Muslim men dressed in black *salwar* and *kameez* and a piece of cloth, representing their shroud, wrapped around their head, symbolic of their readiness to die for the country. Yellow-robed Sikh holy men marched carrying their steel *kirpans* and spears.

As the procession proceeded along College Road, more people joined it and soon the entire road was packed with a sea of humanity. At the front of the procession, the leaders were approaching the bridge across the Leh River. Hundreds of police constables and armed soldiers stood in the middle of the bridge, blocking it. The leaders of the procession appeared not to be affected by the presence of the authorities and kept marching.

"Halt. You are not allowed to cross this bridge," a British Army officer commanded, using a loud speaker. "Go back. Return to your homes."

The warning seemed to only further inflame the protestors and they started chanting their slogans even louder. The officer issued a second order to disperse, but by now the marchers were already at the bridge. Suddenly dozens of police constables rushed forward and plowed into the marchers, wielding their heavy sticks. They beat men and women who, other than raising their arms to protect themselves, did not retaliate. Many fell with bleeding skulls and broken limbs. Children started weeping. When the constables reached the young marchers and started hitting them, fights broke out. The angry youths tried to wrestle the sticks away from the constables.

A police officer swung his cane at Neil. Raising his hand, Neil took the blow on his arm. He wrenched the cane out of the officer's hand and threw it over the side of the bridge into the river. Finding himself surrounded by several angry young men, the officer drew his revolver from its holster. He pointed the weapon toward the youth, and quickly retreated to the safety of the bridge and the armed soldiers.

The police constables were meeting greater resistance now. The R.S.S. members and the Muslim and Sikh youths fought back. The voice of the British officer once again crackled over the loudspeaker, ordering the marchers to disperse. The warning was ignored. A dozen armed soldiers quickly formed a line across the bridge and raised their rifles. They received a command and fired over the heads of the crowd. There was a moment of silence and then men and women started screaming. Those who could get away ran to take shelter. More constables rushed into the crowd, beating everyone within reach and arresting those who could not escape.

The helpless marchers were being routed. The road near the bridge resembled a battlefield with the injured lying sprawled every where. Men and even some women were being handcuffed and dragged away. There was complete pandemonium. The soldiers fired over the heads of the marchers again.

Neil and one of his companions went to the aid of a man carrying a flag who had been knocked down by the police. Neil held the flag with one hand and, aided by the other boy, dragged the man into a side street. Doctors and nurses from the General Hospital had set up a first-aid station and tended to the injured.

It was past seven o'clock by the time Neil returned home. "Oh God, there's blood on your shirt! What happened, Neil?" Khin May asked, alarmed. "Have you been injured? I told you to leave the march at once if there was trouble."

"I'm okay, Mama. The blood isn't mine. It's that of a man I helped to the first-aid station."

"Neil, what happened to your arm?" Sophia asked her brother.

Neil looked at the angry welt across his arm where he had been hit by the police officer's cane. "Oh, it's nothing—I'll be fine. I have to leave now. *Naana* must be ready to return home."

Devi Lal was perplexed and wasn't sure what advice to give his grandson. Although concerned about Neil's safety, he didn't wish to suppress his sense of patriotism. During dinner, they talked about the protest march. All he said, in the end, was "Be careful, son—I don't want you to get hurt."

Khin May later learned from Karam Singh that her father and some of the other doctors from Bohr Bazaar had spent the afternoon attending to the wounded. One elderly man had died of a skull fracture, while hundreds had been injured.

The last day of school before the Christmas holidays, St. Brigid's Convent School was to open only half a day. Sophia took a small silk handkerchief she had brought from Burma, and gave it to her teacher as a gift.

"Why, this is truly beautiful!" Sister Anna Marie exclaimed. "Thank you very much, Sophia. Will you be going away for the Christmas holidays?"

"No, we can't afford to travel," Sophia answered.

"Perhaps you could come and visit me in the Convent," the nun said quickly. "I can show you photographs of my home in Ireland."

Sophia's face lit up. "That would be very nice, Sister!" she said. "I'd like to do that."

During the middle of the Christmas holidays, Sophia had gone to visit Sister Anna Marie at the convent. Neil accompanied her to the school gate, and to his annoyance, saw Raju and his friends standing as usual at the corner of the gallie. Neil knew he'd have to listen to Raju's taunts and wished he could settle matters with this *gunda* once and for all.

"Well, there goes the little *mem sahib*!" Raju called out. "She is too haughty to respond to our greetings."

"Please, Neil," Sophia whispered, "don't say anything. Mama told you to ignore him." Neil gritted his teeth and kept walking.

The doorman at the convent gate let Sophia in. Neil left, telling his sister that he would be back at eleven. When he reached the corner of Murree Road and Mandir Gallie, he was confronted by Raju and his friends.

"What do you want?" Neil asked angrily.

"You people are so very proud," Raju sneered, grabbing Neil's shoulder. "I think you need to be given a lesson on how to be friendly."

Neil brushed Raju's hand off his shoulder and pushed his way past him. Two of the thugs were about to go after Neil but Raju stopped them.

"No, this isn't the place. We'll get him later."

"I'm so happy to see you, Sophia," Sister Anna Marie said with a smile. "Would you like a glass of milk?" The nun had taken a genuine liking to this serious young girl who was a very good student and always so polite.

"No, thank you, Sister. I had breakfast just before coming."

"It's much warmer outside in the sunlight. Should we go and walk in the garden?" the nun asked.

"Yes, that'll be nice, Sister," Sophia answered. It was indeed pleasant outside. The flower beds were in full bloom with roses, daisies, marigolds and chrysanthemums. Butterflies fluttered among the brightly coloured flowers and the air was filled with the fragrance of the blossoms.

"I understand your father is Irish."

"Yes, Sister, he was born in Ventry in County Kerry and came to Burma many years ago. He's in the British Army, but we haven't heard from him for many months. I don't know what's happened to him."

"Oh, I'm sorry," Sister Anna Marie said, putting her arm around Sophia's shoulders. "I hope and pray he's safe and is reunited with you very soon."

"Thank you, Sister. Have you been to Ventry?"

"No, I haven't, but I understand it's a very lovely place."

"My father told me one day I should go to Ireland, and that my Aunt Colleen will show me all of the sights. What part of Ireland are you from, Sister?"

"I was born in a town called Rathdrum in County Wicklow along the eastern coast of Ireland, just south of Dublin. It's quite pretty, full of beautiful valleys, lakes and mountains. Some call it the Garden of Ireland."

"Rathdrum must be a famous town."

"Not really. But there is a well known place just north of there called Glendalough which has the remnants of monastic settlements dating back, I think, to the sixth century."

"Did you live in Rathdrum before you came to India?"

"Well, my parents moved to Dublin when I was eleven years old. I attended high school and later went to college there."

They had reached a wooden bench at the edge of the garden. "Let's sit here," Sister Anna Marie suggested.

"May I ask you a question, Sister?"

"Yes, of course."

"Why did you become a nun?"

Sister Anna Marie smiled. "Well, I'll tell you—as a young girl, I was very much influenced reading about the life of Saint Brigid who founded many churches and established convents and monasteries in Ireland."

"Is our school named after her?"

"Yes. It was a bit of a coincidence that I should come to serve in a church and a school halfway around the world, named in honour of the saint whose life so influenced my decision to become a nun."

Sophia looked up at her. "I think you're very nice, Sister. Maybe some day you will be a saint."

Sister Anna Marie laughed out loud. "No, I don't think so, Sophia. Indeed, I am sure I will not! Come, let's go in. If you wish, I'll show you my photographs."

They sat down at a table in the visitor's room of the Convent. Sister Anna Marie opened a photo album.

"This is our Motherhouse in Dublin in an area called Donnybrook," she said. "Here's a photograph of three other nuns and me standing in the garden of our House."

"The garden looks very beautiful, Sister. My grandfather's house in Mandalay also had a very nice garden."

"Do you miss Mandalay?"

"Yes, I do, but our house burned down the day Mandalay was bombed."

Remembering the difficulty Sophia had talking about the war in front of the class, the nun quickly changed the subject. "Oh, here are some pictures of Glendalough," she said, pointing to several photographs on the page. "Here you can see some Celtic crosses."

"Why is the Celtic cross different? Why do they have this circle at the top?" Sophia asked.

"I'm not sure of its origin. The early Celts worshipped many gods, and I believe when St. Patrick brought Christianity to Ireland, he combined the Christian cross with the symbol used by the Celts for the sun. At least that's the explanation I read somewhere," Sister Anna Marie answered, laughing.

"My father gave me a small Celtic cross made of stone."

"Do you still have it?"

"Yes, it's at home. I'll bring it and show it to you next time."

"I'd like to see it. Here's a photograph of the central mall of Trinity College and this is a picture postcard that I bought in the library of the college, showing the Book of Kells."

"What's the Book of Kells, Sister?"

"It's a very rare book that was written by monks in a monastery in the town of Kells, many centuries ago. The monks drew pretty designs, lettering and paintings, using bright colours, and described several historical events, legends and heroes. Parts of the Bible are also described in it."

Soon it was eleven and Sister Anna Marie walked Sophia to the gate. "The time passed so quickly, Sophia. I'm very glad you came. Perhaps we can do this again sometime soon."

"I enjoyed myself, Sister," Sophia smiled. "Thanks.

Neil was waiting at the gate of the convent and walked his sister home. That evening, when he left to fetch his grandfather from the clinic, he had a feeling of being followed. Looking over his shoulder, he noticed two of Raju's men coming towards him. Neil sprinted and ran fast down the gallie with the men in pursuit. Coming around a sharp bend, he slowed down. Two more of Raju's thugs were ahead of him, blocking his path.

He was suddenly grabbed from behind by the men chasing him. He tried to struggle but was overpowered and held firmly with his arms twisted and pinned behind his back. The lantern he was holding had fallen to the ground. One of the men grabbed Neil's hair and snapped his head to one side just as Raju stepped out of a doorway.

"Well, well, well—what do we have here?" he said, swaggering over. "What does our *Sahib* from Burma have to say now?"

Neil glared back and suddenly Raju slapped him across the face.

"I'll get you for this," Neil whispered.

Raju laughed and, swinging his arm, hit Neil in the stomach with his fist several times. Neil felt a wave of nausea before the pain shot through his stomach.

"Let him go," Raju told his companions.

Gasping for breath, Neil doubled over, clutching his middle. Raju and his friends turned and walked away, laughing loudly at something one of them said. The pain in Neil's stomach gradually subsided. He picked up the lantern and, burning with anger, started walking quickly towards his grandfather's clinic, worrying that he was late and his grandfather would be wondering what had happened.

Devi Lal worked long hours at his clinic and also attended to the medical needs of the lepers and the children at the orphanage. He tried to overcome his physical handicaps as best he could, and cherished the care and attention given to him by his daughter and grandchildren. Sophia continued to read his medical journals to him each morning, and frequently read the newspaper to him in the evenings. Devi Lal's right knee remained sore most of the time and he now walked with a slight limp. Neil not only walked him home each night, but also accompanied him, holding a lantern, whenever Devi Lal was called to see a sick patient at night.

Hari sent a money order from Imphal, this time for three hundred rupees. *"I'm paid well and have not much to spend it on,"* he wrote. *"I'm busy at the hospital and finding out how much there is to learn."* Devi Lal insisted that his daughter use the money to buy clothes for the children and for herself.

Khin May again asked her father to accompany her to the British Army Headquarters office in the Cantonment. Once more she was disappointed and came away without receiving any news about Tim. She busied herself working at the nursery and looking after the family.

During February, the newspapers contained reports of a 21-day fast Mahatma Gandhi had undertaken in prison. The people were concerned about the health of their frail, 74-year-old leader. The Freedom fighters intensified their attacks on police and military installations.

Neil's anger at Raju simmered and he planned his revenge. All he wanted was to be able to fight the gangster one-on-one. He confided in his closest friend, Ashok, who was in his R.S.S. troop as well as in his class at school. Ashok was the oldest of seven children and lived with his parents in a small home near the school. His father owned a dry cleaning store and his mother taught in a girl's school. Ashok was almost as tall as Neil, and like him, was very good at the games they played and the martial arts they learned as members of the R.S.S. The two felt confident that, twirling their *lathis*, they could handle Raju and his gang. For three days, Neil and Ashok returned together from their troop meetings, hoping to run into Raju. On the fourth day, they saw him, as usual, standing on the corner of Mandir Gallie surrounded by his friends. As they walked by, Raju's sarcastic voice rang out.

"Here are two boys with their little sticks, trying to act tough."

Neil's plan was to draw Raju into one of the isolated, narrow lanes. He suddenly poked Raju in the stomach with his *lathi* and, followed by Ashok, ran quickly down the gallie. Raju was taken by surprise. The sharp pain in his stomach made his eyes water. He uttered several profanities and turned to his companions. "Get the swine," he screamed.

The boys bolted through the winding lanes and, entering one of the side gallies, slowed down, allowing their pursuers to catch up to them. The two boys stopped and with their backs to each other, began slowly twirling their *lathis*.

"Well, little Burma boy—you didn't learn from your last encounter with us. This time you're gonna be taught a better lesson."

"It's easy for you to talk big with four of your friends helping you," Neil answered, still twirling the *lathi*. "Why don't you act like a man? Fight me alone."

"So the little boy wants to fight like a man. Why not?" Raju smiled. "Come on, put your stick down and I'll break every bone in your body with my bare hands."

Neil put his *lathi* down and stepped forward. Then he saw the long-bladed knife in Raju's hand. Neil quickly looked at the other men. They, too, now held knives in their hands. The five men, brandishing their knives, gradually circled and surrounded Neil and Ashok. One of them picked up Neil's *lathi* and tossed it away.

Neil wet his lips. He crouched down a little, holding his hands in front of him. Ashok was twirling his *lathi* faster and suddenly leapt forward. He hit one of the men on the shin of his right leg. The man screamed and, dropping his knife, fell to the ground. Raju lunged forward and slashed with his knife. Neil quickly moved to one side, but the tip of the knife grazed his left arm, inflicting a long, shallow cut. Raju raised his hand to strike again.

"Stop right there!" a man's voice rang out. "If you move a muscle, I'll put a bullet through your stomach."

Neil quickly glanced over his shoulder and breathed a sigh of relief. It was Bir Singh standing a few feet away, holding a revolver in his hand. Two of Raju's men took off, running as quickly as their legs could carry them. Bir Singh pointed the revolver at Raju and his companion standing next to him. "Put your knives down on the ground," he ordered, and both men complied at once. Bir Singh turned to Neil. "What happened, son—why are these men attacking you?"

"They've been bothering my sister and mother. I want to teach this *gunda* a lesson."

"Are you cut badly?" Bir Singh asked, noticing the blood on Neil's arm. "Let me take you to your grandfather's clinic."

"No, no—it's only a scratch," Neil answered quickly. "Besides, I need to settle my score with this man."

Raju made a move to pick up his knife, but Bir Singh stepped forward and kicked the knife away. "For once you're going to have to fight like a man, you son of a sow."

"Pick up the knives and throw them in the gutter," Bir Singh told Ashok. "These crooks won't be needing them." Then turning to Neil, he said, "All right, son, go ahead. Settle your score."

Before Neil could react, Raju rushed at him. Neil quickly employed one of the defensive moves he had learned. Placing his hands on Raju's shoulders, he fell backwards to the ground and flipped Raju over his own head, sending him sprawling.

Raju jumped up and lunged again. Neil quickly sidestepped and hit him on the side of the head with his fist. Raju stumbled and fell, but jumped to his feet again, only to have Neil hit him with three or four solid blows, dropping him to his knees. Raju's nose now bled as Neil hit him once more on the side of the chin, knocking him to the ground. Raju lay there in the dirt, gasping for breath.

Bir Singh lowered himself on his haunches. "Well, Mister Brave Man, have you had enough?" Raju lay panting. Bir Singh grabbed the man's hair and jerked his head up. "I asked you a question, you imbecile. Have you had enough?"

Raju nodded. "Yes," he said with difficulty.

Bir Singh pressed the barrel of the revolver against Raju's teeth. "If you so much as touch a hair of this young man or of any member of his family, I swear by the Gurus, you will be flushed out of every rat hole in which you hide and I will kill you with my own hands. Do you understand?"

Raju closed his eyes and nodded his head. Bir Singh looked at Raju's two associates.

"This is also a warning to all of you. If any of you even says something insulting to this boy or his family, I, Bir Singh, will come and cut your tongue out with my *kirpan*. Is that understood?"

The two men silently nodded, their eyes downcast.

"How's your wound, son?" Bir Singh asked. "Does it need to be attended to?"

Neil had wiped the blood off his arm with a handkerchief. "No, its nothing. I'll go home and wash it."

"All right, son—you and your friend can go ahead. Don't worry about these rats. They'll not bother you any more."

Sophia noticed the cut on her brother's arm as soon as he reached home. "Neil, you're bleeding! What happened to your arm?"

"Oh, it's only a scratch," Neil answered. "Don't tell Mama or *Naana*."

"I'm not going to lie to them," Sophia answered.

"No one is asking you to lie, Sophia. Just don't go blabbing about it if they don't ask," Neil persisted.

"All right, I'll be quiet," Sophia agreed reluctantly. "But only this one time."

The Japanese had been in Burma for a year and were reported to be treating it as their conquered land. The Burmese people, as well as the Burma Independence Army which had fought alongside the Japanese to liberate Burma, were becoming disillusioned, finding themselves being ruled by a different master. Japanese soldiers were often cruel. *Kempei*—the Japanese military police—soon came to be dreaded by the people.

By capturing Burma, the Japanese had achieved their objective of cutting off the Burma Road. The Allies had to look for other ways to send war supplies to the Chinese, and the U.S. Airforce established a 500-mile air link between rapidly constructed airfields in Assam and the city of Kunming in China. As a result, large numbers of American military personnel came to be stationed all over northeast India.

The pilots of the American Transport Command (ATC) took off from these airfields in Assam and flew northeast across the mountain ranges of the Himalayas. Skirting the higher peaks and flying over dense jungle-covered gorges, they flew over the mountains north of Burma and then southeast to their destination in China. The pilots named this route "The Hump." The terrain they had to cross was most inhospitable, and the weather always unpredictable. They were also frequently attacked by Japanese fighter planes based in Myitkyina.

By February, 1943, the Americans had captured Guadalcanal. In London, the United States and Britain began to develop plans for the invasion of Europe. By July, Allied bombers were raiding German cities, inflicting heavy damage. Mussolini was deposed in Italy. In India, the struggle for independence continued.

The final examinations were over, and summer holidays had begun. Sophia busied herself reading books she borrowed from the library. She also started working as a volunteer at the orphanage for a few hours each morning, supervising young children at play. She visited Sister Anna Marie and learned more about Irish history and culture. The heat during this particular summer in Punjab was very intense. The hospitals were filled with people suffering from heat stroke and several had died. The little flat on Mandir Gallie during the day was like an oven.

One day Sophia received a note from Nusreen, sent through a servant.

My parents and I are going to Murree for one whole week, she wrote. *My mother asked me to invite you. Please come, Sophia. It'll be such fun.*

Oh, to spend a week up in the mountains, that will be like heaven, but then Sophia started thinking about her mother, grandfather and brother.

"Perhaps I can wait until we can all go together, Mama," she told her mother.

"No, go ahead, Sophia. It'll be cool in the mountains. The change will be good for you," Khin May encouraged her. "Neil's busy with his R.S.S. activities and your *Naana* will not wish to leave his clinic unattended. Perhaps next year we'll all visit the hills."

Reluctantly, Sophia agreed, and the day she was to leave, Khin May and Neil walked her to Nusreen's house. When they got to Murree Road, Neil noticed Raju and his friends standing in their usual spot on the street corner. But as he had done since their fight, the moment Raju saw them he quickly turned and, followed by his companions, walked away.

Raju had learned his lesson. He was well aware of Bir Singh's underground network of fanatic Freedom fighters. He fully believed that Bir Singh had meant what he said. Raju was a practical man and knew when to back away. Although he had his gang and could count on Kassim, the money lender's support, they would be no match against these crazed Freedom fighters.

In his line of work, Raju rarely had to resort to violence. In fact, he was mortally afraid of getting hurt and painfully remembered the beating he received from Neil. Only once before had matters gotten out of hand when several years ago he had decided to discipline a rickshaw puller. The man used to wait at the end of Mandir Gallie for customers and was required to pay Raju five rupees each month. One month he had not paid up, so Raju and two of his friends told him to give them a ride. The poor man strained, pulling the rickshaw with the load of three passengers, and when they got to the outskirts of the city, Raju and his two thugs beat him up. They left him lying on the side of the road and had walked back, only to learn later that the man had died.

Raju had grown up on the streets, somehow surviving, sleeping on sidewalks and anywhere else he could find shelter. He had never known his parents and was raised as a child by a couple living in a hut in a shanty town outside the city. He worked at a tea stall when he was six years old, washing dishes and carrying tea to the rickshaw pullers. He was often beaten and abused. At eight, he ran away and joined other boys, mostly older, begging, stealing and occasionally finding some menial work that paid a few *paisas*. He gradually fought and clawed his way to the top and had, for some time now, headed a gang of about six hooligans. They lived in the same shanty town where he had been raised, but their two huts were more spacious and covered with corrugated tin sheets they had stolen from the government *godown* in the city.

Raju couldn't understand why some of his countrymen were so anxious to get rid of the British. He personally was willing to let them rule the country as long as they left him alone, allowing him to lead his own life. Between the protection money he received from some of the shopkeepers and rickshaw drivers and the occasional payments from Kassim for helping collect his interest, Raju led a comfortable existence. He didn't have to work hard and enjoyed the power he wielded over the shopkeepers, *harijans* and labourers. If these Indian politicians took over the country, he knew they would force him to change his ways. Raju was deathly afraid of Bir Singh and his men. He was therefore most assuredly not going to bother these people from Burma anymore.

Nusreen's parents owned a quaint bungalow in Murree on a lane lined with fruit trees and overlooking a beautiful valley. A servant had come running to open the gate. Although not cold, a log fire was burning in the fireplace and lunch was ready and served by another servant.

After eating, Nusreen had taken Sophia for a walk on the Mall. Flowers were in bloom everywhere and the mountain air was refreshingly cool. The Mall was not crowded at this hour, but later many would come, dressed fashionably, and parade up and down this main street of town. It was the in-thing to do, especially for the British. Then, at sunset they would retreat to their 'Europeans only' club to enjoy their Sherries, Scotch and sodas and talk incessantly about the "beastly heat" down in the plains.

Sophia and Nusreen walked holding hands and chatting about school, their teachers and boys.

"Sophia, do you know who you'll marry when you grow up?" Nusreen asked.

"What a strange question, Nusreen!" Sophia answered, laughing. "I've no idea at all. Besides, it won't be for at least another ten or fifteen years. I'm only twelve."

"But when you do, will your mother let you marry anyone you wish, or will she pick your future husband for you?" Nusreen inquired, leaping to pick an apple from a tree.

"Well, I haven't thought about it. I think my mother and grandfather will let me marry someone of my choosing. After all, my grandfather allowed my mother to marry an Irishman."

"Do you miss your father very much, Sophia?"

"Yes, I do," Sophia answered, turning her face away. "It's been almost two years since I last saw him."

"Do you know where he is?"

"He was in a town called Moulmein when the Japanese captured it. My mother has gone to the British Army office several times but hasn't been able to get any news."

"How about you, Nusreen," Sophia asked, trying to sound cheerful. "Who will you marry when you grow up?"

"I think my parents are going to get me married to my cousin Akram."

"How can that be?" Sophia asked, surprised. "You can't marry your cousin. That wouldn't be right."

"No, marriages between cousins are permitted among Muslims. We think it's okay."

"How do you know you'll marry your cousin?"

"My uncle and aunt and their children visited us from Karachi last winter. I overheard my parents talking to Akram's parents about how good a match this would make."

"Do you like your cousin?"

"Oh, he's all right. He's fifteen and quite good looking, but sometimes he acts silly. I'm so glad you're my friend," Nusreen added. "You're like a sister to me."

"I'm very glad, also," Sophia answered. "You are my best friend."

The week had gone by much too quickly and soon it was time to return to the heat and dust of Rawalpindi. "You have to accompany us every time we come to the hills, Sophia," Nusreen insisted. Sophia didn't answer.

Driving back, they had to once again slow down on the outskirts of Rawalpindi where the road was being repaired. Scores of workers toiled unprotected under the glare of the noonday sun. The traffic came to a standstill and Sophia looked out of the car window.

A woman labourer sitting on the ground by the side of the road was using a hammer to pound a large rock, breaking it into smaller stones. Her face, streaked with perspiration, was covered with dust from the stones and the passing traffic. Three children, the youngest no more than a year old, sat near her in the dust, all dressed in rags barely covering their bodies. The children were staring at the cars and the people in them, but the woman sat swinging the hammer, immersed in her labour. She was paid according to the size of the pile of small stones she produced, and couldn't afford to be distracted from her work. The traffic started moving again, and Sophia did not talk much for the rest of the journey. She kept seeing in her mind the face of the woman and the look in the eyes of the children.

Why was life so unfair, she mused. Why was God so unkind to some? Dear God, why?

Growing Up

$\mathcal{A}$ year had gone by and Sophia was now entering the seventh standard. She was going to miss Sister Anna Marie as her teacher.

"Could I still come and see you, Sister?"

"Yes, of course, Sophia," the nun had answered. "I'll be most disappointed if you don't."

On the first day after summer vacation, Khin May, as usual, walked her daughter to school. "I'll meet you here at 3:30, Sophia," she said.

"No, Mama, there's no need for you to come to fetch me. I'll soon be thirteen. I can easily walk back by myself."

Khin May was reluctant. "I don't think I should let you do that, Sophia. None of the other girls walk home alone."

"Oh, Mama, you worry too much! I'll be okay. I'll walk straight home, so please don't come," Sophia pleaded.

Khin May hesitated. "All right. We'll try it for a day or two. But you must promise you'll not talk to anyone on the way. Come straight home."

Sophia smiled, and waving at her mother, ran through the gate. "I promise, Mama," she called out.

Sister Catherine, the seventh standard teacher, was considerably older than Sister Anna Marie. She peered at her students over the reading glasses she wore low on the bridge of her nose. She kept her head tilted down so she could look at the entire class without having to take her glasses off. Sister Catherine was short of stature and very thin, but made

253

up for her small physique by her powerful voice. She informed her students most authoritatively that she expected them to complete their homework each day.

"You are also to conduct yourselves like ladies at all times," she reminded them. Some of the girls found that to be amusing and started giggling. The nun quickly came out from behind her desk and admonished them.

Once Sister Catherine had established her authority, the day progressed rapidly. She covered different subjects and gave out homework assignments. When the bell rang at 3:30 to announce the end of the school day, Sophia and Nusreen ran out of the classroom hand in hand. Coming out of the school gate, Nusreen waved to her friend and climbed into the car waiting for her.

Sophia turned and was about to walk towards home when she collided with someone. "Oh, I'm sorry," she said, and tried to side-step but was restrained by a pair of strong hands clutching her shoulders. She got a whiff of stale perspiration, and quickly looked up. It was the same man she had seen at the village of the *harijans*. Sophia gasped and froze with fear. The man was looking at her with a strange wide grin. She could see his stained teeth and the gold cap on a front tooth.

She struggled and wrenched herself free. Clutching her books tightly in her arm, she started running and did not slow down until she reached Mandir Gallie. Karam Singh was sitting at his usual place in the front of his sweetmeat shop.

"Daughter, what's the matter?" he asked.

"A man tried to grab me," Sophia answered, gasping for breath.

"Who was he?" the Sikh said, standing up.

"He was a big man in a white turban," Sophia answered. "I ran as fast as I could."

Karam Singh picked up the *kirpan*, lying beside him. "You go up to your flat and don't worry, child. I'll take care of him."

Running on to Murree Road, Karam Singh looked around. He went toward the Convent School, but didn't see anyone fitting the description Sophia had given him.

"That is it, young lady," Khin May scolded her daughter. "From now on you're not to leave this flat alone! Thank God you were not harmed."

"All right, I won't ever walk back alone, Mama," Sophia agreed, "but please don't tell *Naana*: he'll worry needlessly."

Devi Lal's practice was continuing to build, and now the nuns of St. Brigid's Convent sought treatment from him as did some of the teachers from Neil's school. That evening, as the family was about to sit down to have dinner, a man came running up the steps.

"My name is Feroze Khan," he told Devi Lal. "I'm the caretaker of St. Brigid's Church grounds. Doctor *Sahib*, my son is gravely ill. Please help me!"

Devi Lal fetched his medical bag and followed the man down the steps. "Doctor *Sahib*, I beg of you, please save my child's life," the man pleaded as they walked quickly towards the church.

"I'll do whatever I can. Tell me what's the matter with the child and how old is he?"

"*Hazoor*, Iftikar is just four years old. His body is burning with fever and he has vomited several times. His whole body shakes even though we have covered him with blankets. He does not seem to be able to move his head or legs."

"How long has your child been ill?"

"He fell ill suddenly three days ago. My wife showed him to a local *hakeem*, who gave a paste to rub on his chest and a talisman to tie around his arm. When the Padre *Sahib* saw my son, he became alarmed and said I should come to fetch you right away."

The caretaker lived in a small hut toward the side of the church grounds. The room Devi Lal entered was hot and stuffy. He found the child lying on a small cot in a corner against the wall. His distraught mother, who had been sitting on the floor near the bed, stood up.

Devi Lal knelt down next to the bed and, removing the blankets, started to examine the child. The boy's pulse was very fast, his chest covered with several small red lesions. He was lying with his legs drawn up. When Devi Lal tried to straighten them, the boy screamed with pain. He reacted similarly when his head was moved. The top of the child's forehead showed a slight bulge.

"Did your son get an infection earlier, or did he hurt himself in any way?" Devi Lal asked, standing up.

"About ten days ago he was playing on the front steps of the church," Feroze Khan answered. "He fell, hitting his head on the cement."

"Did you take him to the hospital? Was an x-ray taken?"

"No. After crying for awhile, he seemed to have been all right," the man answered.

"I'm afraid your son's illness is very serious," Devi Lal said softly.

"What's the matter with him, Doctor *Sahib*? Please, you must save him," Feroze Khan pleaded. "I'll be grateful to you for the rest of my life."

"I think an infection has gone to the child's brain," Devi Lal said gently. "He must receive treatment at once. We'll need to put him in the hospital."

The caretaker placed his hands together in front of his face. "Doctor *Sahib*, I'm a poor man. I have no money."

"Don't worry. Right now the important thing is for your son to receive immediate treatment." He instructed the father to wrap the boy in a blanket and led the way out to the road. Hailing a *tonga*, they took the child to the General Hospital.

Devi Lal stayed at the hospital past midnight, much to the relief of the young house surgeon on duty. Working together, the two doctors performed a spinal puncture and sent the cloudy liquid that came out for microscopic examination. They placed a catheter to relieve the child's distended bladder. He was given sulfonamides and an intravenous drip to combat the dehydration caused by the fever and vomiting.

When Devi Lal returned to the hospital at six the next morning, he was met by Father Finnegan of St. Brigid's church.

"Thank you so much, Doctor, for helping Feroze Khan," the priest said. "What do you think the young lad has?"

"I think it's meningitis," Devi Lal answered. "It possibly resulted from an infection that occurred at the time of his skull injury."

"Will he be all right?" Father Finnegan asked.

"I hope we were able to start treatment in time," Devi Lal answered. "Unless there are complications from excessive pressure of the fluids on his brain, I believe he should recover in due course. He must stay in the hospital for a few days though, even after his symptoms subside. I'll continue to come to see him."

Young Iftikar's life remained in the balance for another day and a night before the effects of the treatment took hold and he started showing signs of recovery. Devi Lal visited the hospital each day, and his tentative diagnosis was confirmed by the test results.

A month later, Devi Lal had just returned from his clinic when Feroze Khan again knocked on the door. This time, he came carrying a basket full of fruit and flowers, followed by his wife carrying Iftikar in her arms. Feroze Khan and his wife bowed, and placed the gift basket at Devi Lal's feet.

"Doctor *Sahib*, my wife and I will always be thankful to you. We pray that Allah protect you and your family for having snatched my son from the jaws of death."

He then took two 10 rupee notes from his pocket. "I am a poor man, *hazoor*. This is all I have to give you."

Devi Lal accepted the fruit and flowers, but not the money.

"I've been amply rewarded by your son's recovery, Feroze Khan," he answered. "It was God Almighty who heard your prayers and spared your son's life."

Winter was approaching and Neil was getting restless. He had not seen or heard from Bir Singh since the day he had fought Raju. When am I going to get something important to do, he kept wondering. Then one day as he left school, he heard a young man walking alongside him whisper, "Be at the entrance to the mosque on Purana Qila Bazaar Road. Nine o'clock tonight. Alone. Bir Singh wants to see you."

Neil felt excited all day and in the evening, he went to his grandfather's clinic early. As soon as the last patient left, he quickly helped lock up the clinic, and lighting the hurricane lamp, walked his grandfather back to their flat. He gulped down the food his mother served.

"I'm late for my R.S.S. meeting," he said, and ran out. It was already close to nine o'clock and he sprinted down the narrow dark lanes toward the inner city, eventually emerging onto Sarafa Bazaar Road. Slowing down a little, he turned right onto Purana Qila Bazaar Road and approached the mosque, hoping he was not late. He stood, gasping for breath, and barely heard a voice behind him whisper, "Follow me."

He turned around and saw a man enter a narrow alley next to the mosque. Neil followed, hoping that was the one who had whispered to him. He sensed that there was another person walking close behind him. After entering another lane, the man in front stopped.

"We'll have to blindfold you," he said, reaching into his *kurta* pocket.

Before Neil could object, a cloth was tied around his eyes and the two men slowly turned him around several times. They led him by the hand down one alley, then through another, before entering a doorway and helping him climb several steps. It seemed to Neil that they had crossed over two or three terraces and then climbed down several stairs to reach another narrow lane.

They entered a doorway and climbed more steps, then stopped. The men untied the blindfold and Neil tried to peer around him in the dimly lit room. His eyes gradually adjusted to the light from a lantern and he saw several men seated in a circle on the ground in a large room. Neil recognized Bir Singh.

"Sorry we had to bring you to our headquarters blindfolded, but it's our policy not to take chances. We trust you, but we don't want the police to force you to divulge our location."

Awed by the experience so far, Neil just nodded his head. Bir Singh gestured for him to sit down.

"We need the help of your group of volunteers, Neil. How many young men do you have in your R.S.S. troop who are completely trustworthy?"

"I'm the leader of my troop of twenty. They'll do whatever I ask."

"That's good! We need to have you create a diversion for us next Sunday evening in front of the police outpost on Grand Trunk Road. I want you to have your troop march slowly in front of the police outpost, calling out slogans."

"But there are only twenty of us. Will that be enough?"

"There'll be local people from the area who will join you. You and your troop must make as much noise as you can. After exactly thirty minutes, you should disperse and get to your homes as quickly as possible. Can you handle that?"

"Yes, most certainly," Neil responded eagerly.

He was led back, blindfolded, following the same procedures and path taken in bringing him in. He felt a little disappointed that his role was going to be somewhat insignificant. But he consoled himself that at least he had been brought into the secret headquarters of the organization.

The R.S.S. youth carried out their assignment effectively, creating the diversion needed by the Freedom fighters. After half an hour of shouting slogans at the top of their lungs, the boys left in small groups and returned home. Two days later, an item in the local newspapers stated that the police outpost on Grand Trunk Road, next to the race course, had been broken into sometime during Sunday evening, and several rifles and a large quantity of ammunition stolen.

Neil now felt quite proud of being actively involved in the fight for the country's freedom even if it was only to create a diversion for Bir Singh and his men. He tried to cover the Irish half of his identity and had stopped using O'Shea as his last name. Instead, he insisted on being called Neil Lal. Although fair-skinned people are common among North Indians, Neil was pleased with the deep tan he had acquired. He had grown tall and mostly wore a *salwar* and *kameez*.

For some time now, he had been aware of a young girl who lived a few doors away. She had large luminous eyes and a dazzling smile. She often appeared at the second floor balcony of her home and smiled at him whenever she saw him walk by. Only a few days ago he had seen her on the street. She had coyly waved at him but he had been too nervous to stop and talk. The next time we meet, I must at least find out her name, he decided. Today he was also excited with the news he heard at the R.S.S. meeting that Mahatma Gandhi was coming to Rawalpindi, and all R.S.S. volunteers were to assist with preparations for the revered leader's visit.

Gandhi, who had been imprisoned once again, had undertaken a 21-day fast. The British government, expecting him to die, had quietly made preparations to cremate him on the prison grounds, but he miraculously survived. On 22nd February, 1944, the nation mourned the passing away of Kasturbai, Gandhi's wife and companion for sixty years. Gandhi was released from prison and once again started traveling, continuing his mission, preaching love and understanding among Indians. He called for nonviolent noncooperation with the British as a means of gaining freedom.

Devi Lal took Khin May, Sophia and her friend Nusreen to attend the morning prayer meeting at which Gandhi was to speak in their city.

Sophia craned her neck to look over the heads of the multitudes sitting on the ground in front of her. As was his custom, Gandhi was staying in the home of a *harijan*, in their village near Rawal Lake and those who wanted to see and hear him had to come and mingle with the Untouchables. A wooden platform was constructed next to the village and a loud speaker system installed. Neil and his R.S.S. volunteers, along with men and women from several religious organizations, worked for several days clearing a large area to make room for the thousands who were expected to attend daily prayer meetings. This morning the volunteers had been there since six, helping control and direct the large crowds as they arrived. Earlier, municipal water trucks had sprinkled the ground to settle the dust. Nusreen and Sophia sat cross-legged on the hard ground between Devi Lal and Khin May.

"I'm glad we came early," Sophia told her grandfather. "Look at the crowd behind us. All of Rawalpindi must be here." The cleared area was already packed and people were still arriving. The latecomers spilled over onto adjacent fields, trampling some of the crops. Others packed the streets approaching the *harijan's* village.

At eight, the frail figure of Mahatma Gandhi, surrounded by the supporters who traveled with him, appeared at the edge of the village. The people near the front stood up and in unison called out, "Mahatma Gandhi *Ki Jai!*" Gandhi, clad in his white *dhoti*, climbed up the platform and was greeted with thunderous applause from the masses waiting to get a glimpse of him. The atmosphere was electrifying. Sophia stood mesmerized, finding it difficult to believe that she was at last in the presence of the great one about whom she had heard and read so much.

Gandhi sat down on the wooden platform, and the prayer services began. Several hymns were sung and verses and passages read from the *Gita*, the *Koran*, and the *Bible*. Then Gandhi spoke, urging greater understanding and love among the people.

"Hindus, Muslims and Sikhs must put their differences aside and work together as brothers and sisters, united for the common cause of freeing the country," he said. "We must remain nonviolent even towards the foreigners. We can achieve freedom from slavery by firmly adhering to what we hold to be noble and the truth."

He urged his listeners to adopt simple ways of life by wearing homespun *khadi*, not eating meat, and treating everyone with respect and equality — especially his hosts, the *harijans*, the children of God.

Sophia listened to every word intently. As the prayer meeting ended, she and Nusreen surged forward with the crowd towards the platform. A path had been created by volunteers holding hands and Gandhi walked through the people, stopping periodically to bless them. Sophia and Nusreen found themselves standing at the edge of the path. They looked in astonishment as the Mahatma, with a small group of his followers, walked towards them. "May God bless you, especially you, the children. You are the future of our country and the salvation of our people. God bless you," he said gently placing his hand on Sophia's head.

Sophia stood in a trance, her palms held together in front of her face. She felt a strange tingling sensation race through her body, and was overcome by a feeling of peace and tranquility. Tears filled her eyes. She didn't know how long she stood there among the crowd.

She felt Nusreen tugging on her arm. "Come, Sophia, let's go find your mother and *naana*. They must be worrying about us."

All day long Sophia kept thinking about Mahatma Gandhi's message. She would follow his teachings. She would do her part, of that she became convinced. Before dinner that evening, she spoke to her mother.

"I've decided to give up eating meat, Mama. I'll also wear clothes made only from *khadi*."

Khin May was not too surprised. "Okay, Sophia, if that's what you want," she answered gently.

By December 1943, the Americans had occupied parts of the Gilbert

Islands in the Pacific. Italy surrendered and the Russians recaptured Kiev. On the Burma front, several attacks by British troops had failed to dislodge the Japanese. Newspapers carried accounts of raids in central Burma, behind enemy lines, by a band of British, Gurkha and Burmese soldiers, led by Orde Wingate, an English Brigadier. This small force, named the Chindits after their emblem showing the lion-like mythical beasts seen in front of Burmese pagodas, was air-dropped behind enemy held positions. Their mission was to sever Japanese communication and supply lines, and to panic the enemy. They met with only limited success and returned to India, having suffered heavy casualties.

Wingate and his Chindits carried out a second campaign behind enemy lines deep inside Burma. This time, they were aided by American Air Commandos, headed by their ace fighter pilot, Philip Cochran. Gliders laden with soldiers, supplies and mules were towed and landed in a clearing named "Broadway," in the jungles of central Burma. This daring campaign brought ten thousand Chindits along with Cochran's fighter planes to the heart of Burma. The Chindits played havoc upon the Japanese, cutting their lines of communication and supplies. General Wingate died 24th March in a plane crash near Imphal, but his bold plan significantly affected the morale of the Japanese troops and the eventual course of the war.

Early in March 1944, the Japanese launched a major offensive, attempting to capture the Indian towns of Imphal and Dimapur. Sophia read for her grandfather the newspaper accounts of the threat to Imphal, and they all worried about Hari.

"Hospitals are a safe place to be in during war," Devi Lal tried to reassure Khin May and the children, though he himself felt gravely concerned about his son's safety.

The village of Kohima, sitting high atop a mountain between Impahl and Dimapur, became a major battle ground. A small contingent of Indian and British troops defending the village was surrounded by a force of twenty thousand Japanese soldiers. Fierce hand-to-hand combat took place around a tennis court of a British official in the village. The Japanese tossed hand grenades, and then charged with their bayonets, but the Allies held on.

Imphal was surrounded by a massive Japanese force and relied on supplies air-dropped by Allied planes. Toward the end of June, the will of the Japanese army started to wilt and the siege of Imphal ended.

Devi Lal, Khin May and the children, who had spent several very tense months awaiting news from Hari, finally received a letter from him. He wrote to say that he was safe and well. Much of the letter, however, had been made illegible by army censors, who had blacked out several paragraphs with heavy ink.

Their inability to capture Kohima and Imphal, plus the heavy losses they suffered, proved to be utterly demoralizing for the Japanese. The remnants of their once powerful army were now in chaotic retreat. Over thirty thousand Japanese soldiers died around Imphal, and thousands more fell victim to the mountains and jungles of Burma as they tried to retreat before the advancing British, Indian and American troops.

American troops under the command of General Joseph Stilwell also conducted deep penetrations into enemy-held territories. The Americans, three thousand strong, were nicknamed "Merrill's Marauders" after their commander, Brigadier General Frank Merrill. They left their base in Ledo and entered the Hukawng Valley where they engaged and routed the Japanese, often in hand-to-hand bayonet combat. They continued their advance through inhospitable jungles and over mountain ranges. Helped by Chinese troops and local Kachin guerrillas of Burma, Merrill's Marauders captured Myitkyina airport on 17th May.

The Americans were also paying a heavy toll. They were not only facing stubborn resistance from the Japanese holding the town of Myitkyina, but were also falling prey to the mosquitoes and leeches in the jungles. The American surgeon, Gordon Seagrave, established a hospital at Myitkyina airport. He and his team performed operations on wounded soldiers, using makeshift beds out in the open, right next to the airstrip. That summer the Japanese finally surrendered the town of Myitkyina to the Americans.

June 6, 1944 brought the long-awaited news that the Allies had landed on the beaches of Normandy. Two days earlier Rome had been liberated. Soviet, American and British troops were winning the war in Europe.

Great Britain was, therefore, now able to divert some of its attention to the problems in India, and appointed Lord Archibald Wavell as Viceroy. The Indian people and their leaders felt frustrated and were losing their patience. Hundreds of thousands of patriots had given their lives to free India since 1784 when the Government in London took over the colonial interests from their East India Company and established their rule. Now, additional thousands were dying as soldiers in the British Army trying to save the crumbling British Empire. The Indians demanded their freedom and wanted it immediately. Lord Wavell began negotiations with some of the Indian leaders.

Muhammad Ali Jinnah, the head of the Muslim League party of India, used the age old, deep-rooted antagonism that existed between Hindus and Muslims and demanded that India be partitioned. He told the British that the Hindus could have India but a new nation of Pakistan must be created for Muslims. Many Muslims disagreed with him and fought for a united free India.

In Rawalpindi, not having any news about her husband was taking its toll on Khin May, and she appeared more frail than before. Lately, she had also expressed concerns to her father about Neil.

"He's taking part in too many marches and demonstrations, Dad," she confided.

"Yes, I've also been worrying about him, Khin May. I've wondered what we should do." Then, with a faint smile, he added, "Perhaps it's the fault of the mixture of his Punjabi Mohyal and Irish blood which has turned him into a rebel."

Khin May smiled, grateful that her father was always able to somewhat ease her worries.

"How about you, Daughter? You're working much too hard," he said.

"I'm all right, Dad. Don't worry about me," she answered. "Besides, the work keeps me busy."

"Anyway, there's no need now for you to wash the clothes," he said. "I spoke to Mr. Ali Bhutt yesterday. He's promised to send their *dhobi* to see us. We'll give the clothes to him for washing and ironing."

Summer of 1944 was upon them and school was over. Nusreen again asked Sophia to accompany her to the hills, but this time Sophia declined her invitation.

"Thanks, Nusreen," she said. "But I need to stay back and help my mother with the housework."

The first week of the holidays, Sophia went to visit Sister Anna Marie. They were now very good friends and chatted freely. "You seem always to be so calm, Sister. Is your mind at peace at all times?" Sophia asked.

They were sitting on a bench under a large tamarind tree. The nun was no longer surprised by the questions her young friend asked.

"Whenever I'm bothered by anything, I turn to prayer," she responded. That makes me feel much better."

"There's so much suffering around us," Sophia commented. "I wish something could be done to help the poor and the sick. My grandfather tells me that all of us have to pay for our past sins — perhaps that's why there is so much suffering."

"You're very fond of your grandfather, aren't you?"

Sophia's eyes softened. "Yes, I love him very much. I wish I could be just a little bit like him. He's a very special person."

Well, you're also a very special person, my friend, Sister Anna Marie thought.

"Would you like to see a poem called 'Heaven' my grandfather wrote when I was born?" Sophia asked.

"Yes, I'd like to very much."

Sophia took out her diary from the shan bag she carried with her and removed a folded sheet of paper. Sister Anna Marie took the fragile-looking paper and carefully unfolded it. The ink of the handwritten poem was faded and the paper frayed. She read the poem slowly.

"Why, this is simply beautiful! I can see why you love him so much," she said softly.

"Can we go into the church, Sister?"

"Yes, of course," the nun answered.

The two walked through the convent gardens and entered the church compound. The interior of the church was cool and dark. Sophia walked into the smaller chapel of the Virgin Mary. She stood there, looking up at the serene face of the beautiful statue, and then said a silent prayer for her family, and for the poor and the sick.

"Sister, may I ask you something?" she said, coming out of the church.

"Yes, certainly Sophia."

"I've been thinking about asking my mother and grandfather to allow me to transfer to an Indian school. Do you think that would be the right thing to do?"

"Why would you want to do that, Sophia?"

"I think it's wrong for one country to rule another and let them remain so poor. Mahatma Gandhi has asked the people to boycott everything English and to wear clothes made from *khadi*."

"What Mahatma Gandhi said is right. People should not impose their will on others. I'd like you to stay on at St. Brigid's, however, since ours is an Irish order. As you know, Ireland was also under English rule for a long time. Perhaps you could have your school uniform made from *khadi*."

"That's a good idea, Sister," Sophia answered, smiling. "I think I'll do that."

Later, Khin May came to fetch her daughter and, as they walked home, neither noticed Kassim standing on the opposite side of the road. The money-lender followed them, his eyes glued to the girl's beautiful, shiny golden hair and young body. He saw them turn onto Mandir Gallie and slowed down. He smiled to himself. Now at least he knew the street where the young convent school girl lived.

Shortly after Khin May and Sophia returned, Neil came bounding up the steps and, entering the terrace, quickly bolted the door behind him.

"What happened, Son? What's the matter?" Khin May asked, coming out of the kitchen.

"Oh nothing, Mama," Neil answered, sitting down on a *charpai*. "I was being chased by two stupid policemen, but I eluded them."

"Why were they chasing you, Neil?" Sophia asked quickly.

Neil hesitated. "Oh, it was nothing serious."

"Tell me anyway," his mother insisted.

"Well, three policemen caught one of Bir Singh's associates near Moti Bazaar," Neil said impatiently. "They were trying to drag him away to the police station when Ashok and I came by. We knew they would torture the man and get the names of the Freedom fighters."

"What did you do?" Khin May asked sternly.

"Well, we couldn't just let them take him. So Ashok and I jumped the policemen. It was fun," he continued with a smile. "We drew them away from the Freedom fighter and some bystanders helped us so that the man was able to escape. A crowd gathered and started threatening the policemen. Ashok and I were also able to slip away. The constables tried to chase us, but were not able to keep up. We separated and ran to our homes."

"Neil, don't you get involved in such activities! I don't want you to get arrested and taken to jail," Khin May said angrily. "Taking part in protests and processions is fine, but attacking police constables? Why, that's inviting trouble."

"Don't worry about me, Mama. I can take care of myself," Neil answered, getting up and going into his room.

Two days later there was a knock at the door at seven o'clock in the morning. "Who is it?" Devi Lal asked.

"This is the police," a man's voice answered, angrily. "Open the door."

An Anglo-Indian police inspector, accompanied by two Indian constables, entered the terrace. The officer was short and portly, and held a cane tucked under one arm. His khaki uniform was crumpled and wet around the armpits. He took a handkerchief out of his pocket and, removing his cap, wiped his brow and balding head.

"What do you want?" Devi Lal asked.

"I'm Inspector Jimmy Smith," he answered angrily. "Two of my constables were attacked by some young thugs near Gordon College last night. We have reason to believe that a youth from this neighborhood was involved. I've been informed that you have a young man living in this flat."

"My grandson is only fifteen. Last night he came to my clinic at 7:30 and we walked back home together a little after eight."

"Well, where was he after that?" the inspector asked gruffly.

By now, Khin May had come out of the kitchen. Sophia and Neil also came to the terrace and stood next to their grandfather.

"My son was with us at home all evening," Khin May answered. "He did not leave the house."

"I can see your boy was not involved," the inspector conceded. "Witnesses described the miscreants as dark-complexioned and shorter in height than him."

Then, noticing Neil's uniform, he continued. "I see he's an R.S.S. *gunda*. You better advise him to stay out of trouble if he knows what's good for him."

Devi Lal felt angered. "My grandson is not a *gunda*, Inspector," he said, controlling his voice. "He's a responsible young man who does not want to remain a slave to the English like some others."

The inspector glared at Devi Lal and then angrily stomped down the steps, followed by the constables.

The next morning, Devi Lal had left for his walk and Sophia started tidying the rooms. She picked up Neil's *kurta* lying on a chair next to his bed and was surprised by the weight of something in the pocket. The heavy object slipped out and fell to the floor. Sophia looked at it, stunned. It was a small, shiny revolver. She bent down to pick it up, when Neil awoke. He quickly grabbed the gun from the floor and slipped it under his pillow.

"Don't you breathe anything about this to Mama or to *Naana*," he whispered urgently.

"What are you doing with a revolver, Neil?" Sophia whispered back. "That's very dangerous. You'll get into serious trouble!"

"It's not my gun," Neil answered, getting out of bed. "I'm only delivering it for Bir Singh to one of his associates at the Gordon College Hostel. Please, Sophia," he pleaded, "I beg of you — don't say anything to Mama and *Naana*. I'll deliver it this morning. Promise me you won't let me down."

Khin May came into the room from the kitchen. "What are you two whispering about?" she asked, smiling.

"Oh, nothing, Mama," Neil quickly answered. "Sophia was nagging me to get out of bed."

"Well, you should. It's past six o'clock," she said, going into her bedroom.

As soon as they finished breakfast, Sophia glared at her brother, making urgent gestures with her hand. Neil nodded and left, taking the revolver with him.

Later, Sophia helped her mother clear up and wash the breakfast dishes. The two then sat on a *charpai* on the terrace while Khin May combed and brushed her daughter's long hair.

"Mother, will we ever see Daddy again?" Sophia asked.

Khin May stopped the brush in mid-stroke. "I hope we do, child," she answered gently. "As soon as the war is over, we'll go back to Burma. With the grace of God, we'll find him hale and hearty."

Khin May started brushing her daughter's hair again.

"Sister Anna Marie has gramophone records of some of the Irish songs Daddy used to sing. She played them for me once. I miss him very much."

Khin May's eyes filled with tears. She was relieved that her daughter's back was toward her. She started braiding Sophia's hair into a plait.

"Mama, after attending Mahatma Gandhi's prayer meeting, I was going to ask you to let me transfer to an Indian school. But Sister Anna Marie told me that St. Brigid's is really an Irish school and I shouldn't leave. But I'd like to start wearing clothes made of *khadi*. Sister Anna Marie suggested I could even have my school uniform made of *khadi*. Could we do that? I know the tailor will do it. Nusreen has her uniform made out of silk. I'll need new uniforms soon anyway, when I start eighth standard."

"Your teacher is right, Sophia. There's no reason for you to transfer from St. Brigid's," Khin May answered. "We can go to the tailor's shop and ask him to stitch a couple of sets of uniforms for you in *khadi*. He may have to get the fabric dyed the right colour, but I'm sure that can be done."

They heard someone coming up the steps. An envelope appeared, pushed through the space below the door.

"Oh, look. It's a letter, Mama," Sophia said, picking it up. "It's from Uncle Hari!" she added, excitedly. "It's addressed to you."

Khin May opened it and started reading.

"What does it say, Mama? Let me read, too," Sophia said, peering over her mother's shoulder.

Khin May chuckled. "It seems he's interested in an American nurse he met in Imphal. He says she's very friendly and attractive."

"Wow! Do you think he's going to marry her?" Sophia asked.

"Well, they've probably known each other for just a short while," Khin May answered, still smiling. "Why don't you write and ask him?"

"Mama, how long did you and Daddy know each other before you got married?"

"Oh, I think it was about a year from the time we first met. But things are different now. With the war going on, for all we know, in his next letter Hari may tell us they are already married!"

Sophia laughed, "No, Uncle Hari wouldn't do that. I'm sure he'll want all of us to be at his wedding. Nusreen told me that her parents plan to get her married to her cousin Akram. When I grow up, will I be able to marry anyone I want, Mama?"

Now it was Khin May's turn to laugh. "Certainly, Sophia, as long as he's a good person and is approved by me, your grandfather, Uncle Hari and Neil."

Sophia looked alarmed. "You're not serious, are you Mama?"

Khin May laughed again. "No, I am not," she said. "All I want is for you to be happy."

The summer of 1944 also saw the Allies make significant advances in Europe, liberating Paris and, later, Brussels. The valiant uprising of Polish patriots in Warsaw had been brutally suppressed by the Nazis. But the U.S. armies had crossed into Germany. In Asia, the Americans kept their promise to return, and landed in the Philippines on 20th October. They dealt a major blow to the Japanese fleet, destroying several aircraft carriers and other battleships.

British and American victories continued into 1945 with the liberation of Warsaw and the landing of U.S. troops on Iwo Jima. In Burma, the Allies advanced rapidly, and by early March the newspapers reported that divisions of the British 14th Army had surrounded Mandalay. Devi Lal and Khin May couldn't believe that their beloved city was about to be liberated. They anxiously searched the newspaper each day for accounts of Allied gains.

Maymyo was captured, and bitter fighting ensued to wrest control of Mandalay Hill from well-entrenched Japanese troops. After several unsuccessful attempts, the hill was captured on 11th March by Gurkha troops. They reportedly climbed the hill on a dark moonlit night and, with their dreaded *kukhri* knives, killed every Japanese soldier on the hill. Mandalay was finally captured after several days of bitter street by street fighting. But the Japanese stubbornly held on to Fort Dufferin. The ramparts of the fort were eventually breached by continuous heavy shelling and bombings, and on 20th March, the entire city of Mandalay came under Allied occupation. Devi Lal and his family were jubilant. Khin May bought a small cake from a bakery shop on College Road to help celebrate.

Newspapers were now full with accounts of Allied victories as the 14th Army continued its rush to capture Rangoon. The Burmese Independence Army made contact with the British, and turned against the Japanese. Monsoons breaking early slowed down the advancing 14th Army, but the occupation of Rangoon was carried out on 3rd May by Gurkha paratroopers and amphibious landings by British troops coming from the sea up the Rangoon River.

The remnants of the seemingly invincible Japanese armies were in chaotic retreat, chased and killed not only by the British, but also by some enraged Burmese who had suffered through their brutal regime for the past three years.

In Europe, Mussolini had been killed. Hitler committed suicide and Germany officially surrendered on 7th May. World War II came to an end, at least in Europe.

Reading about the Allied victory in Burma and the recapture of

Rangoon, Khin May now eagerly awaited news about Tim. Still, she was apprehensive, fearing the worst, but prayed and hoped for the best, which was that Tim had been held a prisoner of war. She went back to the British Army Headquarters office in the Cantonment, again to be told there was no news. The officer who saw her said it might be some time before every soldier missing in action could be accounted for.

The daily strain of hoping and praying was taking its toll and Khin May's already frail body looked weaker, causing her father great concern. Then, it arrived — a simple brown envelope with an official seal addressed to Mrs. Khin May O'Shea. The letter inside carried the regrets of His Majesty's Government for the loss in battle of her husband, Corporal Timothy Patrick O'Shea, on or about 30th January, 1942, during the defense of Moulmein.

Khin May crumbled to the terrace floor, unable to read the letter further, and her body shook with pitiful heart-rending sobs. Karam Singh's wife Jeet heard the mournful cries coming from the open terrace door and came running. Not knowing what had happened, she gently helped Khin May to the *charpai* and brought her a glass of water from the kitchen. She held her in her arms and made her drink a few sips. Khin May tried to control her sobs.

"My husband is dead," she wept.

Jeet ran down to ask her husband to inform Devi Lal. She then came back and once again sat, holding Khin May in her arms.

Devi Lal came up the steps quickly and Khin May ran into his arms. "I knew all along, Dad, I knew Tim was dead. But I didn't want to believe it. What am I going to tell Neil and Sophia? They'll be devastated."

Devi Lal held his daughter tenderly in his arms, rocking her gently as tears filled his own eyes.

"You'll need to be strong, my child, so you can ease the pain the children will feel. We must all rely on prayers. Have faith in God and accept His actions, no matter how painful."

Neil had wept and then his tears turned to anger. Sophia was inconsolable and cried her heart out. They sent a telegram to Hari and he took the next train to Rawalpindi. Sophia went to St. Brigid's to pray with Sister Anna Marie in the chapel of the Virgin Mary. After Hari arrived, they all went to the Arya Samaj temple, where special prayers were said for Devi Lal and his family, and for the loved one they had lost.

Before returning to Imphal, Hari spoke to his father and sister about their future plans. "The war in Asia will soon be over," Hari said. "Once things settle down, you should go back to Burma."

Khin May looked up nervously. "No, I don't want to go back — at least not yet. Besides, Sophia should finish her Senior Cambridge examinations before we move her from her school."

During early July, the United States government attempted to get the Japanese to surrender, but to no avail. Then the world was shaken by the news of the devastation unleashed on 6th August when an American airplane dropped a single atomic bomb on the Japanese city of Hiroshima. This was followed by an equally devastating bomb blast over Nagasaki on 9th August. The incredible destruction caused by the two bombs and the loss of thousands of lives finally brought the Japanese government to its knees. The world rejoiced when news of the formal surrender of Japan was announced. On 2nd September, 1945, Japanese commanders handed their swords to General MacArthur aboard the U.S.S. Missouri, bringing the Second World War officially to an end.

With the end of the war, Britain elected a new government and the leader of the Labour Party, Clement Attlee, became Prime Minister. More sympathetic to the plight of the Indians, the Labour Government agreed to gradually transfer power to the Indians, eventually giving them self-rule. Although the Indian leaders were pleased at these recent declarations by the government in London, the masses and the Freedom fighters were skeptical. They had been made promises before, and did not trust British intentions. Angered by the fact that hundreds of thousands of young Indian soldiers serving in the British Army had lost their lives helping Britain win the war, the Freedom fighters intensified their attacks on British military installations.

Neil passed the matric examinations and enrolled as a student in Gordon College. He was pleased to at last be in the middle of a large group of student activists. At age sixteen, he was already a trusted member of Bir Singh's *Azad Hind* organization. He now spent more time away from home, and occasionally stayed the night in the students' hostel. Handsome and tall, he had grown a mustache and looked quite mature. He soon moved into the top circle of the militant students.

Sophia had entered the eighth standard and was now maturing into a strikingly beautiful girl. She was to take the Junior Cambridge examinations later that year and kept preparing for them. Results would not be available for two months as the answer sheets had to be shipped to Cambridge University in England. The Senior Cambridge examinations could only be taken two years after successfully completing the Junior level examinations.

Sophia now wore clothes made only of *khadi*, and had completely given up eating meat. She continued her volunteer work at the orphanage and, in addition to watching the young children at play, had started helping in the kitchen. She visited Nusreen's home and periodically went to see Sister Anna Marie. Khin May always made sure that she or Neil accompanied her daughter wherever she went, although Sophia had not faced any problems since being stopped by the big man in front of her school.

Kassim had not been able to keep the image of the beautiful young convent girl with the long golden hair out of his mind. He came to Rawalpindi often, and waited across the road from St. Brigid's Convent School. He would look at Sophia with hungry eyes as she came out and walked home with her mother.

Kassim was forty-two, and lived on the outskirts of Peshawar with his wife and four children. He traveled, mostly by train, between Peshawar and Lahore, stopping at various towns collecting interest for the money he loaned. Kassim, like other money lenders, established his own interest rates and required prompt payment. He considered himself a man of principle and did not tolerate those who failed to keep their promise to him. Coercing, and sometimes resorting to beatings, was part of his business, as far as he was concerned — a perfectly acceptable practice. He did not discriminate against people for their religion. He lent money to all who needed it and then extracted the interest and the loan even-handedly from Hindus, Muslims and Sikhs.

Kassim finally made up his mind that he had to possess this jewel of a girl, no matter what the cost. He was a patient man and willing to bide his time. He was going to plan his strategy methodically. After giving the matter a great deal of thought, he arrived at what he considered a simple solution. He would kidnap the girl and take her with him to Peshawar. How he would accomplish this, his simple mind had not worked out. He decided he would get help from one of the *gundas* of Rawalpindi who occasionally assisted him in collecting money owed to him.

From the description that the money lender gave, Raju at once recognized who Kassim was planning to kidnap. Raju's eyes lit up at what he thought was a brilliant idea. Oh, how sweet his revenge would be when the girl was kidnapped and taken away! Raju had not forgotten the humiliating beating he had received from the girl's brother. Although he drew satisfaction from the jewelry he had stolen from their flat, his hatred for Neil had consumed his innards. He would have liked nothing better than to stick his knife into the boy's back, but fear of Bir Singh and his words kept him from fulfilling this desire.

The thought of Bir Singh suddenly jolted Raju out of his pleasant daydreams and the smile disappeared from his face.

"No, no, Khan *Sahib*," he said, patronizingly, "forget the convent girl. Don't even go near her. She and her family are protected by the crazy Freedom fighters. Believe me — should anything happen to the girl or her family, you and I will pay a price a million times more than the pleasure you would derive from possessing her."

Kassim knew Raju to be a coward, but could not understand why he was afraid of helping with such a simple scheme. "You'll be paid handsomely, you jackal," Kassim said, controlling his anger. "Don't worry about those Freedom fighters."

"No, Khan *Sahib* — please keep me out of this," Raju now pleaded. "I'll do anything else for you, but you don't know the wrath of these fanatics. Forget this girl. Perhaps I'll help you find another one equally desirable."

Kassim spat on the ground. Muttering obscenities, he turned and walked away.

After returning to Imphal, Hari wrote to his sister each week and tried to cheer her up. He told her about his work and about the people at the hospital. Now that the war was over, he was able to write detailed accounts of the siege of Imphal and the courage of the defenders of the town. He told her about the Americans and some of their crazy antics. *Their favorite pastime,* he wrote, *was to have a rickshaw race down the main street of town with the surprised rickshaw pullers made to sit in them and the Americans pulling the rickshaws.* He wrote that his friend had returned with her army hospital unit to the United States and that he was missing her a lot.

By the way, I don't know if I've told you, her name is Stephanie Brown. She's from a small town called Racine in the state of Wisconsin, he wrote. *Sis, next to you, she's the most beautiful woman I've ever met.*

Three months later, Hari wrote to his father, this time to tell him that he was leaving the army and wanted to go to the United States to specialize in surgery. He said the staff of the American hospital unit he had worked with in Imphal had returned home, and were going to help him get into the residency program at the University of Chicago. He added that after he was discharged from the Army, he would come to Rawalpindi before leaving for the United States.

Hari came home and stayed for a week. It was during the Christmas holidays and the children were home. There was not much rejoicing, though. It was almost as if Hari had already left. The second day that he was home, Sophia went to visit Sister Anna Marie and Neil walked her to the Convent gate. Khin May stayed with her brother during the afternoons after she returned from work. Neil often went to see his friends. They talked during dinner but it was not the same as before. It was as if they wanted to get on with their lives.

Sophia cried when Hari embraced her before leaving. "I'll write to you often," he promised. "I'll return as soon as I can."

Neil shook his uncle's hand and drew away. Khin May hugged her brother but seemed to have run out of tears to shed, though her heart ached terribly.

Devi Lal felt tired and emotionally wrung out. America was so far away and his son was leaving to go there. His daughter was a widow at such a young age and was wasting away before his eyes. Where was his grandson headed? To be martyred like his grandfather? And what was going to happen to dear, sweet, gentle Sophia?

Doubts filled his mind. What sort of decisions had he made in his lifetime? Those that affected him, he didn't care about. But those that were affecting his loved ones, if only he could somehow undo some of them. He was proud that his son was going to become a surgeon. But would he ever see him again? Could he have stopped his son now from going so far away? Should he have? After all, he, in his own youth, had also left his home to go to a faraway land.

In the end, he could only turn to prayer. Almighty God, protect my son through all of life's journeys and shower him with Your love and mercy. Be with my loved ones in their trials and tribulations. Give me the courage and will to look after those that are, with Your grace, yet with me.

Independence and Partition

The night was pitch dark. Icy cold January winds blew in from the hills and chilled Neil's bones. He was sitting crouched next to a large boulder, looking intently in the direction from which the train was to come. He drew his coat collar tightly around his neck and waited, huddled next to several other students. In the faint glow from the stars, he could see the rail line that had been pried away from the wooden sleepers.

The students had been given information by a railway employee that a train carrying British troops was coming southeast from Peshawar on its way to Delhi. The militant students' leaders decided this would be a great opportunity to inflict a dramatic blow to the British by derailing the train.

They had stolen huge wrenches, hammers and crowbars from the railway workshop. Several of them had toiled for the past three hours and were finally able to dislodge one of the iron rails, pushing it out away from the track. The informant also told them that the train at this point, just outside the city, would be traveling at a slow speed as it negotiated a curve. They expected to produce a spectacular accident without injuring anyone severely.

Neil's *kurta* had become damp with perspiration while he had laboured, taking his turn wielding the huge hammer. Now he felt as if his shoulders and back were covered with ice. He pressed his back against the boulder they were huddled next to. Then he heard the faint hoosh-

hoosh, hoosh-hoosh of the train, coming from a distance. He thought his heart was going to explode out of his chest, and took several deep breaths. The sound of the train was now louder and he could see a dim glow over a hill in the direction from which it was coming. But it didn't seem to be slowing down. The noise from the steam engine was getting much louder and he could even hear the clatter of the train's wheels.

A powerful beam of light knifed through the night sky and the train came into view. The ground beneath them started shaking. The sudden piercing whistle of the engine made the boys jump. "Come on, slow down," Neil muttered. God, it's travelling so fast. The monstrous black engine was almost at the curve. Then there was an ear-shattering noise and the engine's powerful light eerily danced around. The front end of the carriage immediately behind the engine shot off to one side. The rest of the carriages surprisingly remained on or near the tracks but, accompanied by the sickening sounds of shattering wood and metal scraping against metal, several of them rammed into each other.

"Oh my God," Neil moaned, his body trembling. The night air was now quiet except for the hissing of steam escaping from the engine which lay on its side next to the tracks.

"Come on, let's go," one of the boys whispered, grabbing Neil's hand. They crouched low and ran. They could hear screams and orders being yelled behind them. They kept running. Two hours later, scared and exhausted, they got back to Gordon College and stole into the hostel.

Police informants had for some time been trying to infiltrate student organizations at Gordon College, and a week earlier the authorities had been alerted that the students were planning 'something big'. Early in the morning after the train derailment, scores of police raided the College's hostel. Those students known to be leaders were dragged away to jail. Only a few were able to escape.

In the evening Devi Lal waited in his clinic. It was almost eight o'clock, and he wondered why Neil had not come to walk him back home. Just then, an elderly man came in and asked to have his eyes examined. "I have a message from Bir Singh," the man whispered as he lay down on the examination table. "He asked me to tell you that your grandson is in hiding with four other students. They escaped from their hostel this morning. The police were going to arrest them as suspects in the train derailment."

"How do you know this?" Devi Lal asked, taken aback. "Where's my grandson?"

"I don't know where he is. Bir Singh said to tell you not to worry — your grandson is safe."

Rumors had been abuzz all day and people were talking about the train derailment. It was said that, although no one was killed, many had been seriously injured. Devi Lal had been afraid something like this might happen. After the old man left, he closed the clinic and started toward his home through the dark gallies, trying to see his way as best he could. As he approached his building deep in thought, he was greeted by Karam Singh seated cross-legged at his usual place in front of his sweetmeat shop.

"Doctor Ji, how come you are alone today? Where's Neil?"

Devi Lal trusted his landlord, but was not sure if he should tell anyone what had happened. "Neil was delayed at his college. I decided not to wait for him," he answered, quickly climbing up to his flat.

"Oh my God," Khin May cried, "what's going to happen to my son now?"

Devi Lal tried to sound reassuring. "Bir Singh and his Freedom fighters are very well organized. I'm sure they'll be able to protect him."

Sophia had been listening. "*Naana*, is my brother a fugitive?" she asked. "What will the police do to him if they catch him?"

"He's in hiding, child," he answered. "What we can do now is pray that he remains safe. I'm sure Bir Singh will get in touch with us as soon as he has more news."

Early the next morning, a police truck stopped at the entrance to Mandir Gallie and Inspector Jimmy Smith came up the steps, followed by three constables.

"Where's your *gunda* grandson?" he demanded, glaring at Devi Lal. "We are here to arrest him."

"My grandson is not here," Devi Lal answered quietly. "We don't know where he is."

The inspector signaled to his constables who quickly went through the flat, searching. "Do you people realize that he committed treason?" Inspector Smith said, nodding his head, a grim look on his face. "Do you know the penalty for crimes against the crown? Why, he could be sent to the gallows, or in the least, be sentenced to hard labour for life, and rot in jail."

Devi Lal did not answer. Sophia stood clinging to her mother's arm. The constables looked in the rooms and kitchen. One of them climbed up to the rooftop latrine. They returned, shaking their heads.

"Your grandson is a criminal," the inspector said angrily. "He can't escape. We'll catch him and throw him in jail where he belongs."

Sophia fretted all day. Why did Neil have to get involved in the train derailment? People should not resort to violence. One after another, those she loved and cared for all her life were being taken away from her.

"Please God, please look after my brother, and also my Mama, Uncle Hari and *Naana*." she prayed.

Khin May seemed to have drawn some inner strength and, although she looked pale, remained calm. She tried to console her daughter and support her father. Word spread quickly and soon everyone on Mandir Gallie learnt of Neil's involvement in the train derailment. Karam Singh and the other shopkeepers worked out arrangements and each evening one of them took a lantern and walked Devi Lal back from his clinic.

A week had gone by with no more news about Neil. Then the same old man came back to the clinic. "Your grandson and the other boys have been taken to the outskirts of Peshawar," he said. "They are living with families of the *Azad Hind* Freedom fighters."

"Dad, I want to go to Peshawar," Khin May pleaded. "I want to see Neil."

"I don't think we should do that, daughter," Devi Lal answered gently. "The police must be watching us and will follow us. Besides, the British are supposed to free India soon. If Neil stays in hiding, I'm sure no action will be taken against any of the Freedom fighters after the country gains independence."

The newspapers reported that civil unrest was intensifying throughout India. Some elements of the Indian military had allegedly begun to go on strikes. In some areas, Indian soldiers and sailors were said to have revolted against their English commanders. International pressure was mounting on Britain to grant India its freedom. The government in London finally sent an official mission to India to work out the details of handing over power to the Indians. The leader of the Muslim League Party, Mohammed Ali Jinnah, however, continued his insistence that independence must be accompanied by partition of the country on religious grounds.

"Britain *must* create an Islamic nation of Pakistan," he demanded.

Gandhi was deeply bothered by the thought of dividing the motherland. He offered Jinnah the prime ministership of independent India. Instead, Jinnah called on all Muslims to demand a separate country. Jinnah's inflammatory message fueled centuries of religious antagonism and strife. The results were tragic. Communal riots broke out between Hindus and Muslims in Calcutta.

Sikh taxi drivers there went on a bloody spree. Their religion was founded in the 16th Century to protect Hindus from the atrocities of invading Moguls who were forcing them to convert to Islam. The Sikhs now went about in a frenzy, killing Muslims, looting and burning their homes. During the summer of 1946, over five thousand Hindus and Muslims hacked each other to death in Calcutta and another thirty thousand were injured.

Gandhi and the other leaders were aghast at the bloodshed in a city gone insane. Hindus and Sikhs blamed Muslim fanaticism for causing the riots. Muslims accused Sikhs and Hindus of centuries of discrimination against them. Whatever the reason, Hindus and Sikhs on one side and Muslims on the other, went on senseless rampages, looting, burning and killing their neighbours.

"*Naana*, why do people kill each other in the name of religion?" Sophia asked her grandfather while reading the newspaper to him.

"It often just takes a misunderstanding or one misguided individual to light the spark, and violence results," he answered.

"I hope something like this never happens here in Rawalpindi. Nusreen is a Muslim. She and her parents have been so nice to us."

"Yes. Let's pray that such madness does not erupt elsewhere in India."

Their prayers, however, went unheeded. Communal riots spread to several cities as armed mobs sought reprisals for the reports of atrocities committed against their brethren in Calcutta.

Early in September, riots broke out in Bombay. Scores were killed, and thousands injured. Then, in October, the districts of Noakhali and Tippera in the province of East Bengal exploded. The predominantly Muslim population of the area attacked Hindus mercilessly. Homes were looted and burnt, men were butchered and women carried away.

Gandhi went to Noakhali and, accompanied by a small group of followers, walked from village to village, preaching his message of love. They stayed in the homes of Muslims and implored them to protect their "Hindu brothers."

Shortly thereafter, rioting broke out in the province of Bihar. The large Hindu population there, incensed at reports of atrocities committed by Muslims against Hindus in East Bengal, went on an orgy of revenge. The Indian leader, Jawaharlal Nehru, rushed to Bihar. Like Gandhi in Noakhali, Nehru traveled extensively throughout the province. In Noakhali, the mostly Muslim police stood by as riots occurred around them. In Bihar, the police opened fire on rampaging mobs, killing many of the rioters. After a week, during which thousands lost their lives, the rioting abated.

One evening, Sophia was reading the newspaper to her grandfather when she stopped with a sharp intake of her breath.

"What is it, Sophia?" he asked.

"*Naana*, Neil's been arrested!"

Devi Lal sat up. "Read to me, child! What does it say?"

Sophia read the small item under the headline, *Terrorists Suspected of Train Derailment Arrested Near Peshawar.*

The paragraph which followed said that three young terrorists had been arrested on the outskirts of Peshawar. They were prime suspects in the derailment of a troop train outside Rawalpindi earlier this year. The article gave Neil's name, along with those of his two fellow students. It said that the terrorists had been taken to Peshawar jail.

Devi Lal left for Peshawar the next day. Distraught, Khin May wanted to rush to see her son, but agreed to wait until her father found out what was going to happen. While Devi Lal was gone, Jeet stayed with Khin May and Sophia. She also accompanied them to the temple to offer prayers for Neil.

Devi Lal went to Peshawar Jail but was not permitted to see his grandson. He went to the law courts and appealed to one office after another. Then he met the lawyer provided by the *Azad Hind* organization to defend the three young Freedom fighters. His name was Ram Bhagat and he had been allowed to see Neil in prison.

"Doctor Ji, your grandson is well and asked that you not worry about him," Bhagat said. He was an imposing looking man of about fifty, and spoke in a deep strong voice.

"What's going to happen, Mr. Bhagat?" Devi Lal asked.

"I'm filing all the necessary paper work to defend the three young men, Doctor Ji. The courts are loaded with cases and it's going to be awhile before they'll even set a trial date."

"Can I do something in the meantime? Can I provide some money to pay my grandson's legal costs?"

"No, don't worry about it. Azad Hind is taking care of everything."

"My daughter is very anxious to see her son. Will the authorities permit us to visit him?"

"Oh, perhaps I didn't mention, but Neil has been charged with treason. He's being held in solitary confinement in an isolated wing of the prison and, other than one lawyer who is allowed only two brief visits a month, no one else is permitted to see the prisoners."

Devi Lal returned to Rawalpindi and gave Khin May and Sophia the barest of details about Neil's incarceration, and dwelt more on the thorough preparations by Azad Hind to defend him.

That evening, Karam Singh came to see Devi Lal to inquire about Neil.

"If there is anything at all that I can do, Doctor Ji, please call upon me. I'm here to help you."

"Thank you, Karam Singh," Devi Lal answered. "Thank you very much."

"I'm also worried about the situation here, Doctor Ji," the burly Sikh confided. "We are surrounded on three sides by Muslim neighbourhoods and there may be trouble as news of riots elsewhere reaches here. Perhaps we should make plans to defend ourselves."

Devi Lal was surprised at the landlord's concern. "I don't think there'll be trouble here, Karam Singh. Hindu and Muslim Punjabis have much more in common than the Hindus and Muslims in other parts of India."

"The same is true in East Bengal, Doctor Ji, but there the Muslim majority started killing Hindus. When news of these incidents came out, Hindus in Bihar killed ten thousand Muslims."

Unknown to them, Khin May and Sophia were listening to their conversation. Sophia clung to her mother's arm and stared at her, wide-eyed.

"When the milkman made his delivery today," Karam Singh continued, "he told me that his cousin had gone to an adjacent Muslim village. There he heard the people discuss the massacres of Muslims in Bihar. There was talk about reprisals."

"What precautions can we take other than hope and pray that the killings don't spread to Punjab?"

Karam Singh lowered his voice. "Several of us shopkeepers held a meeting. We are quietly purchasing guns and swords. I would advise you to do the same, Doctor Ji. Purchase a firearm."

"I don't believe in violence, Karam Singh. My job is to save lives — not to kill."

Karam Singh shook his head. "But you must protect yourself and your family, Doctor Ji. I'm planning to replace the wooden door at the bottom of the stairs with one made of iron bars. I would advise you to keep this door to your terrace bolted at all times."

That night Sophia had trouble falling asleep. When she did, her dreams of homes burning and people dying recurred. She woke up with a start. "Dear God, please don't let it happen here." she moaned.

Later that week, Devi Lal received a letter from his son. Hari asked his father's approval to get engaged to Stephanie Brown. Devi Lal replied at once, sending his blessings. Their concern for Neil overshadowed the joy of Hari's engagement.

On 20th February, 1947, Britain announced that self-rule would be granted to the Indian people shortly. India's Viceroy, Sir Wavell, was called back and replaced by Viscount Louis Mountbatten, cousin to

King George VI. Mountbatten had served as Supreme Allied Commander of Southeast Asia during World War II and was trusted by the Indian leaders. He met with them upon his arrival and started to work out details of the transfer of power. Jinnah refused to accept anything short of a separate Islamic nation of Pakistan.

"If not," he threatened, "there'll be civil war and a bloodbath of the magnitude the country has not seen before."

Nusreen's parents had invited Sophia, Khin May and Devi Lal for lunch on a Sunday. Mr. and Mrs. Ali Bhutt sat in the drawing room talking with Khin May and Devi Lal. Sophia was with Nusreen upstairs in her bedroom.

"It's deplorable that we Indians can't get along with each other and live in peace," Ali Bhutt said. "I'm afraid there's going to be trouble here in Punjab too, Doctor *Sahib*."

"Unfortunately, I think you are right," Devi Lal agreed. "Let's hope the British are able to maintain law and order. When the country is granted its freedom, the people may come to their senses."

"Doctor *Sahib*, I am planning to send Nusreen and her mother to Karachi where they will stay with my brother-in-law. I don't think it'll be safe for them to remain in Punjab."

"I don't want to go, but my husband is adamant," Mrs. Bhutt added.

"What about Nusreen's Senior Cambridge examinations?" Khin May inquired.

"I met with Sister Margaret Rose, the school principal," Mrs. Bhutt answered. "She informed me that they intend to have the tenth standard girls take Punjab University's matric examinations in March. With the threat of riots occurring in Punjab, St. Brigid's School does not want the students to miss the opportunity of taking at least the matric exams. Then, if the Senior Cambridge exams are given in December, those who wish can still take them."

"I've spoken to my brother-in-law," Ali Bhutt added. "Nusreen will be able to take the matric examinations in Karachi."

Turning to Devi Lal, he continued, "Doctor *Sahib*, It might be a good idea for you to send Sophia and Khin May away too — perhaps to New Delhi."

"I'm sure we'll be quite safe here in Rawalpindi," Khin May spoke quickly. "We don't know anyone in New Delhi. Besides, as long as my son is in prison in Peshawar, I don't want to go any further away from him."

Sophia and Nusreen had been sitting quietly for some time. "When are you leaving for Karachi?" Sophia asked.

"We leave next week. My father is very stubborn about it. He has already made train reservations."

"I'll miss you, Nusreen."

Nusreen came to her friend and embraced her. "I'll miss you, too, my sister. But I'll write once a week. I'll pray to God that we are able to see each other again soon."

Hatred, violence, and bloodshed spread like wild fires from one end of Punjab to the other. It had started in Lahore on 4th March. A group of Hindu and Sikh students held a meeting in front of the Government College to protest the murders of two Hindus at the hands of the Muslims. The police arrived and fired at the protesters. Several students were killed. Rioting broke out, and Hindu and Sikh shops were looted and burned. Many people were stabbed in the narrow lanes of the bazaars.

Elsewhere, minor confrontations exploded into violent, bloody encounters. City after city in the province became engulfed by riots, and any semblance to law and order soon disappeared. The British authorities were stunned by the fury with which the bloody riots started spreading and seemed unable to cope with the chaos, or not to care.

Sophia missed her dearest friend who had been gone almost two weeks. She was also very worried about her brother. The matric examinations were approaching but there were fears that, if the riots spread, the examinations might not be held. The image of Neil in prison came to her mind. How's he managing, she wondered. She read that prisoners were locked up in small cells. Her heart went out to her brother.

Sophia could not understand why there had to be so much hatred. Earlier, she read about a young American woman who had joined Mahatma Gandhi and accompanied the 77-year-old Indian leader as he went from village to village preaching love, harmony and understanding. She had taken an Indian name and wore a sari. She lived the simple, austere life of the followers of Gandhi, often staying in *harijan* villages.

I wish I could do the same, Sophia thought. After dinner, she spoke to her mother about it.

"You need to finish your examinations first, Sophia," her mother answered. "You're only sixteen. Later, we can talk about it."

Khin May did not want her daughter to go. She had already lost Tim. With Hari gone to America and her son in prison, she couldn't even think about her daughter going away.

They had just gone to bed when the night's quiet was suddenly broken by a distant cry.

"*Allah O Akbar,*" a man's voice called out. Sophia listened intently. Other voices joined in, loudly chanting, "*Allah O Akbar.*" She knew the words meant "Allah is Great," and are usually said by Muslims at prayer and she always loved hearing the chant. But this somehow sounded different. She sat up in her bed. Then she heard shouts of "Kill! kill!" followed by screams and pleas of "Oh, God, save us!"

Devi Lal and Khin May were also up and they all rushed to their windows. The night was sultry but Sophia felt a cold shiver run through her body. The pathetic screams and pleas for help continued.

"*Naana*, what's happening?" she cried out.

"I'm afraid the madness has spread to Rawalpindi," Devi Lal answered with a sigh. "Innocent blood is being shed in the name of religion."

Khin May put her arms around her daughter.

"What will happen to us, *Naana*? Are we safe in our flat?"

"We should be all right here, Sophia," her grandfather tried to sound reassuring. "The new iron door to the steps is strong. Hopefully the inhabitants of Mandir Gallie will act responsibly."

The sound of gunfire erupted. An orange glow lit the sky in the distance and soon flames became visible. They stood at their windows for a long time, watching, horrified. Dense black smoke rose, silhouetted against the starlit sky. Their hearts heavy, they returned to their beds but sleep was impossible. Their minds kept imagining what must be going on around the burning homes.

With the break of dawn, the neighbourhood quieted down.

"*Naana*, you must not go for your walk, today," Sophia pleaded.

"Yes, child, I won't. But we should buy vegetables and other food items we'll need for the next few days. I'll go down when the shops open."

Around ten o'clock, Devi Lal went down to the gallie and joined the group of men standing in front of Karam Singh's shop. One of them was telling the rest about last night.

"A mob of Muslim peasants attacked several homes of Sikhs and Hindus and set fire to them. Two women and three children in one home died. The Sikhs had guns and fired on the mob. The fighting lasted for hours. Several Hindu and Sikh men as well as five or six Muslim attackers were also killed."

"Where were the police?" another man asked. "They're supposed to protect us. Didn't they show up?"

"We can't rely on the police to help us," the first man angrily responded. "Most of them are Muslims."

"There'll be retaliation — wait and see," Karam Singh said calmly. "It'll be their turn tonight. They'll suffer and die."

Then, turning to Devi Lal, he continued. "Doctor Ji, you should close your clinic early today. I'll send some men to fetch you."

"I don't think you need to do that, I should be all right."

"No, Doctor Ji, you have to walk through a Muslim neighbourhood — it'll not be wise to take any chances," Karam Singh insisted. "We'll also accompany Sophia to school in the morning and walk back with her after school. It's not going to be safe even in the daytime."

"Thank you Karam Singh," Devi Lal answered gratefully. "That will be very nice."

Kassim came to Murree Road the next day and waited near the Convent School. He kept looking down the road, trying to spot the girl. Periodically, he glanced at the man sitting in the *tonga* across the road and nodded at him. After months of planning, he had worked out his scheme and was finally going to fulfill his obsession.

Kassim had obtained the help of a friend who lived in a village near Rawalpindi and owned a *tonga*. His plan was to grab the girl and carry her off to his friend's house. Once there, he would have the *mullah* from the village mosque pronounce them man and wife. He would stay with his young bride in his friend's house for a few days and then take her to his village near Peshawar.

Kassim heard about the riots of the previous night. This morning he had ridden in the *tonga* past several burned homes. He wasn't interested in killing Hindus or Sikhs for, after all, a considerable portion of his money-lending business was with them. Now, waiting, he was getting impatient. Then he saw the girl with the long golden hair walk toward him with her mother. To his annoyance, three men carrying *lathis* accompanied them.

Kassim's face turned red. He had not expected any trouble. Why could the stupid Muslim peasants not have waited another day before attacking the homes of the Hindus and Sikhs? Now he wasn't sure if he could succeed in carrying away the young girl. He quickly slipped into a doorway and stood watching as the girl walked toward him.

Kassim had not seen Sophia for many months and was pleased that the girl of his obsession had blossomed into a stunning young woman. He yearned to possess her even more but restrained himself from rushing and snatching this jewel. One of the men with the *lathis* was a burly Sikh, and wore a *kirpan* around his waist. Even though Kassim was prepared to fight for what he wanted, he considered it unwise to take on the three armed men.

The girl walked past him. Can I grab her and get away? Oh, if I could only possess her, he thought. It was too late and he knew that he couldn't succeed. He crossed the road, seething with anger and, pushing a beggar out of the way, climbed into his friend's *tonga*.

Devi Lal returned from the clinic at five o'clock, accompanied by three men from his neighbourhood. All the shops on Mandir Gallie closed their doors early and Karam Singh locked the iron gate to the steps. No sooner had darkness set in when the night air was filled with slogans of hatred from crazed mobs, followed by the pathetic cries of their victims.

This time, it was Hindus and Sikhs who were out seeking revenge. Beating drums and screaming religious slogans, they converged on Muslim homes. The Sikhs shouted, *"Jo Bole Soh Nehal, Sat Siri Akal!"* and the Hindus yelled, *"Shiri Ram Bhagwan Ji Ki Jai!"* Pitched battles were fought in several parts of the city between well-armed Hindus and Sikhs on one side, and Muslims on the other. Neighbours turned against neighbours, and blood tainted the streets of Rawalpindi. Yet there were isolated acts of compassion. In some instances, Hindus and Sikhs protected their Muslim friends. In other areas, Muslims stood guard in front of the homes of their Hindu and Sikh neighbours.

The residents of Mandir Gallie had met earlier and decided there wasn't going to be any bloodshed on their street. Hindus, Sikhs and Muslims pledged they would, together, safeguard their neighbourhood. Yet Sophia found studying for the examinations to be very difficult. Armed men from her neighbourhood walked her to school each day and, even in school, there was now tension between some Hindu and Muslim girls. The city seemed to have settled into a pattern of relative calm during the day but the nights were filled with senseless brutality and orgies of killing.

If things were bad in the cities, they were worse in the countryside. Inflamed by exaggerated news of atrocities committed in other parts of Punjab, Muslim mobs went rampaging. They slaughtered, raped, looted and burned Hindu and Sikh villages. Bands of roving Hindus and Sikhs did the same to Muslims. Places of worship were desecrated and destroyed by both sides. The green fields of wheat, for which Punjab was famous, were now tainted red from the blood of thousands of innocent victims.

The matric examinations were ten days away but no one was sure if they would be held. Sophia had prepared as best as she could. The rioting and killings were now taking place even in broad daylight and all schools were closed. Sophia heard Karam Singh talking to her grandfather in the evening, as once again gunfire was heard and the night sky glowed with burning homes.

"The situation for us Hindus and Sikhs looks very bleak in Rawalpindi, Doctor Ji. But I'm afraid escaping south to Amritsar will also not be easy. It appears that trains are not running. Our people trying to escape by roads are being attacked on the way by Muslims."

"We should be safe here on Mandir Gallie as long as Hindus, Sikhs and Muslims continue to protect each other. Don't you think so?" Devi Lal asked.

"The few Muslim neighbours we have may not be able to protect us very long, Doctor Ji. I have heard that, in several towns, Muslims have attacked the homes of other Muslims who harboured Hindus and Sikhs. I'm told tribal Muslims by the thousands are coming from the Northwest Frontier Province to kill us and loot our homes."

After Karam Singh left, Devi Lal sat with his shoulders hunched over and his head resting on his hands. He felt dejected and tired and was wondering what he could do.

"Don't worry, Dad," Khin May said to him gently. "I'm sure the British will not allow the riots to continue indefinitely." Devi Lal looked at her.

"Now I regret having brought you and the children to Punjab," he answered with a sigh. "I had thought that, after Burma, this would be a safe place."

"We did the right thing by leaving Burma, Dad," Khin May responded quickly. "No one had any inkling of what was going to happen here. God willing, India will get its independence soon and, once Neil is released, we can all go back to Mandalay."

For some inexplicable reason, relative calm returned to Rawalpindi towards the latter part of March and the killings stopped. Armed British soldiers guarded the D.A.V. High School building where the matric examinations were to be conducted. Sophia was escorted each day by Karam Singh and three other men from Mandir Gallie. The second day of the examinations, riots broke out close to the school and the soldiers rushed out to separate the warring factions. Sophia's mind was in a daze as she worked through the examinations, trying to write answers to the questions.

When on the last day the examinations were over, Sophia quickly walked to the school gate and started searching for Karam Singh among the people waiting outside. He wasn't there and her mouth went dry thinking what would happen if no one came to fetch her. Most of the students had already left and by now Sophia was in tears. Then she saw Karam Singh and four men from Mandir Gallie come running toward the school gate. One of the men had removed his white turban and held it pressed against his shoulder. The turban showed a large red stain.

"Come, daughter, come quickly," Karam Singh beckoned, "We need to hurry." He grabbed Sophia's hand and they started running. They sped through several side streets, and at one point, went past a home that was still burning.

Sophia felt her heart pounding. After dashing through the narrow streets, they approached Murree Road and Karam Singh poked his head out from behind a building. Signaling the others, he again grabbed Sophia's hand and they ran across Murree Road toward Mandir Gallie.

From a distance, someone yelled, "There they are! Let's get them!"

It was the same group of Muslims who had chased Karam Singh and his companions earlier, and had slashed one of them with a sword. Although the mob came running, they were too far away and Sophia and her protectors were able to reach the safety of Mandir Gallie. Karam Singh quickly opened the lock securing the iron door and they ran up the steps.

"Thank God you're safe," Khin May exclaimed, opening the door to the terrace. "We were worried sick about you."

"I'm all right, Mama," Sophia answered breathlessly, "but this man who came to fetch me is injured."

Devi Lal made the man lie down on a *charpai* and, with his daughter's help, cleaned and sutured the wound.

"Thank you so much for bringing my granddaughter home safely," Devi Lal said as he bandaged the man's shoulder. "I'm most grateful!"

The British continued their negotiations with the Indian leaders, and now seemed eager to hand over power to the Indians and get out of this mess. Finding no other solution, Mountbatten acquiesced to Jinnah's demands that India be divided. A Boundary Commission, headed by an Englishman, was established, and after brief deliberations, proposed the division of Punjab. The western half would go to Pakistan, along with several other provinces in Northwest India. The eastern part of Punjab was to remain with India. Similarly, the province of Bengal was to be divided between the two countries.

On 6th June, the British announced the final plans for the partition of India under which the cities of Lahore and Rawalpindi and surrounding villages were to be a part of Pakistan. Hindus and Sikhs living there panicked. Amritsar and other neighbouring cities and towns were to go to India and Muslims living there started fleeing. Soon trains and roads were choked full in both directions with terrified people carrying their pitiful belongings. The carnage intensified and Punjab turned into a living hell. The masses fleeing on foot and by trains were attacked by bloodthirsty mobs who committed unimaginable atrocities against the helpless, pathetic refugees.

There had been no news about Neil other than a short note from Mr. Bhagat. *The British authorities are reluctant to set a trial date*, he wrote. *I think they believe that, with granting of independence, the prisoners will become the Indian Government's problem. That will be good for your grandson.*

Another two weeks went by and, although several Hindu homes in adjacent neighbourhoods had been looted and burned, Mandir Gallie, so far, had been spared. But the residents continued to live in fear.

Karam Singh came to see Devi Lal once again. "Doctor Ji, I will not allow my wife and daughter to fall into the hands of the Muslims," he said softly. "Could you please tell me the quickest, least painful way for them to kill themselves should the need occur?"

Aghast, Devi Lal could not answer for a few moments. "Dear God, I never dreamt it would come to this!"

"Hindu and Sikh history is replete with acts of such brave sacrifices by our women," Karam Singh commented. "They killed themselves rather than be taken captive by Muslims. They leapt from the ramparts of forts and drowned themselves in rivers. Some courageous women also sought the purest form of self-immolation — by setting themselves on fire. We must be prepared for the worst."

Devi Lal's shoulders sagged and he sighed deeply.

"I don't have any medicine, Karam Singh, that will bring about instantaneous death. Other than a gunshot directly into the brain or the heart, or a deep dagger wound into the heart, I don't know of any other way."

Karam Singh's eyes narrowed. "By the grace of the Gurus, it will then have to be the *kirpan* of the Sikhs that our women will have to resort to," he resolved.

The night was dark and Mandir Gallie was quiet. Devi Lal was trying to sleep but his thoughts kept wandering. He was thinking about their life in Burma. How far away all of that seemed. His home in Mandalay, the long journey — surviving it. And now this!

Suddenly the night's stillness was pierced by a distant cry, "*Allah O Akbar! Allah O Akbar!*"

A chill ran down his spine and he started praying that the dreaded words wouldn't be repeated. But the feared call became louder, and he got up and went to the window. A mob was entering Mandir Gallie wielding swords, axes and scythes.

"Death to the Hindus and Sikhs! Kill them! Kill them!" the Muslims screamed.

Sophia and Khin May had also rushed to their window and stood with their arms around each other.

The mob started breaking down the doors to the shops. The wooden door of a shop shattered under the blows of several axes and the attackers dragged the helpless Hindu shopkeeper to the middle of the street. The man let out a pathetic scream as an axe split open his skull.

"Oh, how horrible," Sophia moaned, turning her face away. She started sobbing and Khin May drew her away from the window.

Suddenly a shower of bricks rained down onto the street from windows and rooftops. Some of the bricks smashed onto the heads of the frenzied mob. A man with a large hammer started pounding on the iron door of Karam Singh's building.

A thunderous explosion reverberated through the gallie. Karam Singh had fired his double-barreled gun. The man swinging the hammer at the iron door now lay crumpled on the ground. As more bricks came down on them, the mob retreated to Murree Road, dragging some of the injured with them. They stood at the entrance to Mandir Gallie, screaming threats. "We won't stop until the last Hindu and Sikh in the city has been killed!" they yelled.

Sophia and Khin May sat on a bed, their eyes reflecting the terror they felt in their hearts. Devi Lal stood leaning against a wall, unable to speak. Death and destruction had arrived at their door step and they were trapped.

The mob gradually disappeared, promising to return the next night to finish what they had started. Sleep eluded the terrified residents for the rest of the night. As dawn broke, Devi Lal went to his window. The street below was littered with bricks and blood and the remains of the gutted shop were strewn all over. Lying in the middle of the debris was the battered body of the shopkeeper. Two other bodies lay along the side of the street. The pool of blood next to their heads indicated the men were probably killed by the bricks thrown from above. The man Karam Singh shot had tried to crawl away, and lay dead near the entrance to the Gallie.

As the sun rose, Karam Singh came down to the street and gradually the other shopkeepers and residents also came out. Standing in small groups, they spoke in low voices. The shopkeeper who had been killed lived alone and none of the other residents were aware of his having a family.

"What should we do, Karam Singh?" one man asked.

"We must take all of the bricks back to our terraces," the Sikh answered. "The next time, toss them where more of the attackers are crowded together."

"What should we do with the dead bodies?" another man asked.

"Leave them be. Let the British come and remove them," Karam Singh replied. "If they aren't taken away by the afternoon, we'll drag them to the end of the gallie."

"I hope the police or the army comes to rescue us," a man spoke angrily.

"They won't come to our aid," another answered bitterly. "They are busy protecting their own homes and those of the foreigners."

"I have plenty of milk in my shop," Karam Singh told the others. "If you need some, come and get it."

"I have vegetables for anyone who needs them," another shopkeeper offered.

Most of them gratefully accepted the offers and all of them carried the bricks back into their homes. They then bolted their doors behind them.

Around ten o'clock, a municipal refuse truck and an army jeep stopped at the entrance to Mandir Gallie. Several soldiers got out and walked through the debris with their guns on the ready. One of them then signalled to the men in the refuse truck and four municipal sweepers carried the corpses and tossed them into the truck. The soldiers returned to their jeep and, followed by the truck, drove away.

Sophia and Khin May talked in quiet tones and Devi Lal did not say much. They all looked tired and pale. They were about to sit down to a sparse lunch when the sounds of a screaming mob erupted again, this time from the street behind their house.

"Oh God," Sophia cried. "The people behind our building are being killed!"

The noise of the mob intensified as the armed men indulged in their orgy of killing and looting. The pathetic cries of the victims sent shivers of fear through the residents of Mandir Gallie. They sat in their homes, wondering if later in the day — or that night, or the next day — it would be their turn.

From the terrace, Devi Lal saw smoke rising from the building directly behind theirs. Dear God, if the fires spread, will they have to run out on the street? He hoped those living across the street would give them shelter.

The afternoon wore on and the noise of the mob gradually subsided. The wretched weeping of the few survivors was all that could be heard. Flames were visible, rising from the burning building. Devi Lal was frantic, wondering what they should do, when he was startled by someone banging on the iron door downstairs.

"Open the door!" a man yelled.

Devi Lal rushed to the window and was surprised to see a group of police constables standing on the street. Could this be a ruse by the Muslims? he wondered.

"It is I, Doctor *Sahib* — open the door. You must come with me!" It was Ali Bhutt.

Devi Lal sighed with relief, thanking God that in their hour of despair Nusreen's father had come to help them. As he rushed down the stairs to open the gate, he saw Karam Singh standing in his doorway at the first-floor landing.

"It's all right, Karam Singh. A Muslim friend has come to rescue us."

Devi Lal opened the gate. "Doctor *Sahib*, this is my friend, Inspector Neeaz Khan," Ali Bhutt spoke quickly. "He has consented to help me take you, Khin May and Sophia to my house. There is not a moment to waste. We must leave right away."

"Thank you, Ali Bhutt, thank you very much," Devi Lal answered. Then, pointing up the steps at Karam Singh, he added. "There's another family in this building. Can they come with us?"

The police inspector cut in. "No, no, we don't have time to take anybody else. If you're coming, do so now. If not, my constables and I have to leave."

"Doctor Ji, don't worry about us," Karam Singh called down to Devi Lal. "By the grace of God, we will be all right. Take your family and leave."

He then disappeared behind his door. Devi Lal ran up the steps and immediately returned with Khin May and Sophia. Karam Singh locked the iron gate behind them. They were surrounded by the constables and quickly herded to the police truck waiting at the entrance to Mandir Gallie. The truck raced down Murree Road. Shops on both sides of the road had been looted and some buildings were burning. Dead bodies were visible lying on the pavements along the road. Sophia sat in the truck, ashen-faced, and started trembling. Khin May put her arms around her daughter and drew her close.

Thank you, dear God, for saving us, Devi Lal prayed in his mind, wondering what Ali Bhutt had to do to get the police to help.

The truck screeched to a halt and Ali Bhutt quickly led them past two armed watchmen at the gate of his house. The police truck sped away. As they entered the drawing room, Devi Lal turned to Ali Bhutt. "I'm deeply grateful to you," he said.

"No, no. Please don't mention it," Ali Bhutt answered, raising his hands. "Things are going to get worse. Thousands of tribal Muslims have come into the city and, unfortunately, no Hindu or Sikh is going to be safe in Rawalpindi. You'll stay in my house until you can be evacuated to the Indian side of Punjab."

Raju was petrified. He didn't want to die. Let the Muslims slaughter others, but he somehow had to get away. Then, fortunately for him, he ran into Kassim and pleaded with the money-lender to help him escape the wrath of the Muslims. Kassim was enjoying seeing Raju squirm as he hadn't forgotten the thief's refusal to help him kidnap the convent school girl. Raju was now on his knees.

"Please, Khan *Sahib*, please help me! I'll do anything you ask."

Kassim's eyes lit up. "All right, you dog. If you help me get the girl from Mandir Gallie, I'll help save your worthless hide."

"Yes, Khan *Sahib*," Raju quickly answered. "I can tell you where she is. The girl was taken to the home of a Muslim family behind the convent school. It's the home of Ali Bhutt, the wealthy contractor."

Kassim felt pleased. All was not lost. He took Raju to his friend's home and gave him a Pathan vest and turban. "Wear these over your *salwar kameez* and walk slow, but with long strides and a swagger," Kassim laughed, "and you may pass for a Pathan."

Raju now felt safe as he walked along Murree Road and the burned and looted neighborhoods. I must somehow get to the safety of the Indian half of Punjab before the Muslims find out who I am, he kept repeating to himself. Walking, deep in thought, he did not notice where he was and suddenly found himself surrounded by several men.

"Look at this tribal Muslim. He's walked into our midst," a young Sikh sneered. "Let's see how brave he is when we slowly slice him up."

Raju stopped abruptly. "No, no, you are mistaken!" he pleaded, raising his hands. "I'm a Hindu."

The men around him laughed. "What a brave Pathan," one of them teased. "He's afraid of receiving his own medicine."

Raju started backing away. "No, no, please, I *am* a Hindu!" he begged. "Let me show you — look, I'm not even circumcised," he cried, trying to quickly lower his *salwar*. Laughing loudly and calling out Hindu and Sikh slogans, the men pounced upon him.

That evening, Mandir Gallie again drew a frenzied Muslim mob. They came bolstered by hundreds of armed tribesmen. Bricks came showering down upon them, but they were too many. Karam Singh fought off attacks on his building, firing his rifle from the window of his flat until he ran out of ammunition. The iron gate finally gave way and, sword in hand, he fought the men trying to climb up the steps. Injured and exhausted, Karam Singh knew he could no longer hold off his assailants.

"Salutations to the Gurus!" he yelled at the top of his lungs. Hearing the pre-arranged signal, Jeet and Kiran unsheathed the *kirpans* in their hands. Placing the pointed ends over their hearts, mother and daughter plunged the steel blades deep into their bodies.

By dawn, no Hindu or Sikh man, woman or child was left alive along the entire length of Mandir Gallie. The flames from the house behind had spread to Karam Singh's building. The Sikh's dying wish, therefore, came true. His enemies were not able to violate his women nor possess his home.

Khin May and Sophia were in Nusreen's bedroom on the second story and Devi Lal was in an adjacent guest bedroom. The windows were closed and the curtains drawn. It feels strange, being in my friend's room without her, Sophia thought, remembering the many happy hours they had spent there together.

"What's going to happen to us, Mama? Will we be able to go back to our home?"

Khin May patted her daughter's hand. "Let's hope and pray that we can, Sophia."

Just then there was a knock at the door and Ali Bhutt entered, carrying a tray with some food. "It's best that you eat here in your room, Khin May," he said. "Not all of my servants are trustworthy. I'll ask Doctor *Sahib* to join you."

With darkness came the sounds of gunfire. Hindu and Sikh homes were being attacked in the next block. A noisy mob came running along the street in front of Ali Bhutt's house.

"Muslims, beware! Do not harbour Hindus and Sikhs in your homes!" they called out.

Several men armed with swords and spears stopped at Ali Bhutt's gate. "We know you are harbouring Hindus!" they yelled. "Bring them out to us."

The two watchmen held their guns at ready. Undaunted, the men continued their frenzied screaming.

"Give us the Hindus or we'll burn your house," they demanded.

Ali Bhutt came out of his home, holding a gun. "There are no Hindus here!" he yelled at the mob. "Go away! Go back to your homes!"

The men stayed at the gate, angrily continuing their demands. Then someone hurled a rock, shattering the glass in the drawing-room window. The noise of the breaking glass reverberated through the house and Sophia's face turned pale. She sat on the edge of the bed with her hands tucked under her knees. Devi Lal wondered how long Ali Bhutt would be able to hold off the mob. He felt terrible that helping them could result in their friend's home, and perhaps even his life, being placed in jeopardy. Yet, he wondered what would have happened to them had he not come to their rescue.

More rocks were thrown by the men on the street. Ali Bhutt reappeared at his door and this time, pointing the gun over the heads of the crowd, he fired. "If one more stone is thrown at my house, I swear to Allah, my guards and I will shoot straight at you," he yelled.

The mob slowly retreated. "We'll be back," they yelled. "We'll bring guns with us!"

Ali Bhutt returned to his drawing room and fell into a chair. He was perspiring, his heart racing. What could he do? The mob was going to be back, of that, he was sure. If they brought guns, he and the two watchmen would not be able to fight them off. He had to get his friends to a safer place quickly, but where could they go? Then it occurred to him — he would take them to the church. They would be safe there. The mob would most likely loot his home, or worse still, burn it, but at least they would not be able to harm his friends.

Ali Bhutt raced up the stairs. "Doctor *Sahib*, I don't think we can hold off the mob if they return with guns."

"I'm sorry, my friend, that we've brought this upon you," Devi Lal answered, placing his hand on Ali Bhutt's shoulder.

"No, no — don't think about it. Right now we must worry about getting you to safety before they return. It's almost dawn. I think we can smuggle you out the back gate and take you to St. Brigid's Church. You should be safe there. I don't think they'll dare attack the church. I'll then go and seek help from the police."

Khin May took Sophia's hand and followed her father out of the room.

Ali Bhutt, gun in hand, led the way down the steps. Leaving the house through a back door, he summoned one of the armed watchmen. It was still dark as they quickly walked by the kitchen and the servants quarters. They exited the compound through a small gate. An alley ran between the rows of homes. Ali Bhutt walked fast, signaling Devi Lal, Khin May, Sophia and the watchman to follow him.

Coming to the end of the alley, he raised his hand and stopped. He peered cautiously around a wall. The street on both sides appeared deserted. Again, he quickly led the way, praying that they would reach the church without being spotted.

Suddenly Ali Bhutt stopped. They could hear voices from straight ahead. Signaling to the rest to follow, he quickly got them into a side street, where they stood in a doorway. The voices grew louder. In the first light of dawn, Devi Lal saw dozens of men carrying boxes, radio sets, sewing machines, metal trunks, and even articles of furniture on their heads. One man boasted of raping two women before slitting their throats. Devi Lal's eyes misted as he saw blood dripping from a sword held by one of the men.

As the voices of the looters faded in the distance toward the fields,

Ali Bhutt whispered, "Let's go. Hurry!"

Once again they walked briskly toward the church. Coming to the junction with Murree Road, they again stopped. The road was deserted. Now they started running. Sophia's heart was pounding and she kept looking at her mother and grandfather.

They reached the large iron gate of the church. Ali Bhutt tried to push it open and saw, to his dismay, that the gate was secured by a thick metal chain and a lock. He angrily rattled the chain, but to no avail.

"I just remembered," Devi Lal spoke, quickly. "The caretaker's hut is along the side wall of the church." They ran around the wall to the side. Reaching a window, Devi Lal nodded and Ali Bhutt rapped on the small, dirty glass pane.

"Who is it?" a man's voice sleepily asked from the inside.

"I'm Ali Bhutt. I want you to open the church gate."

"Go away! The gate is not to be opened today."

Devi Lal held up his hand at Ali Bhutt. "Feroze Khan, it is I, Doctor Devi Lal. I have my daughter and granddaughter with me. We need to take shelter in the church. I'll be grateful if you would open the gate for us."

"Oh, yes, Doctor *Sahib*," Feroze Khan answered quickly. "Please come to the gate. I'll open it at once."

As they returned to Murree Road and the church gate, they heard the roar of a mob in the distance. Feroze Khan came running and unlocked the gate.

"Please stay inside the church and do not leave," Ali Bhutt said, as Devi Lal, Khin May and Sophia went through the gate. "I'll get Inspector Neeaz Khan to come and help us."

Khin May put her hands through the iron gate and grasped Ali Bhutt's arm. "You've been an angel of mercy! Thank you so much for risking your life to save us."

"Our people have gone insane, daughter," Ali Bhutt said. "God knows where this will all end. Please don't thank me. I need to go now and contact the police."

Feroze Khan locked the gate and ushered Devi Lal, Khin May and Sophia to the church.

The interior of the church was dark and cool and they quietly walked toward the altar. Halfway there, Sophia pointed to the right.

"Let's go into the chapel of the Virgin Mary," she whispered. Entering the chapel, Khin May started sobbing. For the sake of her father and daughter, she had maintained her composure through the night's ordeal. Now she couldn't hold back any longer. Devi Lal put his arms around his daughter.

"We'll be all right, child," he said gently.

Sophia looked at the angelic, white marble statue of the Virgin Mary. She put her hands together and prayed.

Devi Lal led his daughter to a bench. They sat down, exhausted. How long would they have to wait here? Would the Muslim police come to their rescue again?

Devi Lal dozed off. He was awakened by the cries of "Kill all of them!" He stood up. Khin May and Sophia looked at him, their eyes wide with fear.

The unmistakable sound of a hammer striking metal came echoing into the church. Devi Lal shuddered as he realized what was happening. The mob had seen them enter the church compound and had now begun breaking down the gate. The chain was strong and the lock would not give, but the men kept swinging the hammer. The clanging sound echoed through the church and Khin May and Sophia trembled with each blow. The hammering suddenly stopped. There was a moment of silence and then loud shouts.

"Kill the Hindus! Kill the Hindus!"

Feroze Khan stood on the church steps, stunned, not knowing what to do to. I must protect Doctor *Sahib* from harm, he kept thinking.

The men entering the church compound were too many, and armed. He had nothing but his bare hands. He had to find Ali Bhutt. They must get the police. He ran through the compound as fast as he could. He took the small, side gate leading into St. Brigid's Convent. He would seek help from the man who had brought Devi Lal to the church.

The mob poured into the church compound and noticed a man running out of the side gate. Someone yelled, "There they go! Catch them!"

The mob ran after Feroze Khan. Two men went towards the church door. The slim, tall figure of Father Finnegan appeared, blocking the door. The priest raised his hand.

"This is a Christian House of God. You cannot enter here to commit murder. Go away! Do not break the sanctity of this shrine!"

One of the men knocked the priest out of the way, sending him stumbling down onto the concrete steps.

Devi Lal pushed Khin May and Sophia toward the back of the statue of the Virgin Mary. "Get back there. Hide behind the statue," he urged them.

"No, Dad, I'm staying with you," Khin May answered calmly, holding her father's arm.

The church door burst open and the two men holding swords rushed inside. They stood in the middle of the church and looked around. One of them sighted Devi Lal and Khin May. Letting out a bloodcurdling scream, he ran into the chapel of the Virgin Mary. Devi Lal felt no fear as he stood, shielding his daughter. He looked at the man rushing at him with a sword. Devi Lal tried to raise his right hand as the man lunged and thrust his sword.

"Oh, my God!" Devi Lal moaned, and slowly fell to the ground. Khin May screamed. Falling to her knees, she cradled her father's head in her arms. Her body shook convulsively and she sobbed.

The man pushed Devi Lal out of Khin May's arms. Throwing his bloodied sword down, he grabbed Khin May and lifted her to her feet. She struggled, clawing at his face. The man wrestled her to the ground and started tearing off her *kurta*. The second man stood over them.

"You can enjoy her," he said, laughing. "I'm going after the other who got away."

Khin May continued struggling, kicking with her knees. She pushed hard and the man rolled away. Pulling a knife out of his pocket, he flicked it open. With one swift move, he thrust it's eight-inch blade into Khin May's chest.

Hearing her mother's scream, Sophia ran out from behind the statue of the Virgin Mary. She saw her grandfather on the floor, a pool of blood spreading around him. Her mother lay on her side with one arm stretched out. Blood gushed out of a small hole in her chest. Sophia gasped and a glazed look came over her eyes. She froze, unable to utter any sound or to move.

The assailant turned to the young woman and his eyes lit up. Grabbing her in his arms, he fell to the ground. He tore her *kameez* open. Sophia lay under him, her eyes staring at the face of the Virgin Mary.

The lust in the man's eyes turned to annoyance when he felt someone tapping him on the shoulder. Angrily, he turned around. A big tall Pathan with a large mustache was smiling down at him. Kassim was relieved. He had arrived in time, before the girl of his dreams could be possessed by another.

"Go away," the man said angrily. "This one is mine!"

Kassim flipped open the knife in his hand. Still smiling, he thrust it in the man's back, sinking the long blade to the hilt. He wiped the knife clean with the man's shirt and pushed him away with his foot. Reaching down, he lifted Sophia in his arms and walked out of the chapel.

Ali Bhutt had not found Inspector Neeaz Khan but instead saw an army jeep with Gurkha soldiers in it coming towards him. He flagged them down and pleaded with them to save his Hindu friends.

"They've taken shelter in that church there. I beg of you, hurry. Save them!"

The sun had now risen and the heat was already intense. The soldiers sped to the church and looked around the yard. But there was no one there. The young corporal waved at his companions and they started walking back towards the gate. Then, from the corner of his eye, the corporal detected a movement next to the church, and turned to look. What a strange sight, he thought.

Standing there in the haze of the bright sun was an old man frantically gesturing towards the church door. He wore a faded gold tunic and an ancient-looking crown. His hair was long and matted. He had a scraggly flowing beard. That's odd, the corporal thought. A moment ago the compound was empty. The image of the old man faded and then reappeared. Is it a mirage, the corporal wondered.

He hailed one of his companions and the two turned around towards the church door. The baffled corporal blinked his eyes. The old man had disappeared. The soldiers affixed bayonets to their rifles and entered the church.

Kassim walked through the church and turned towards the door. Two Gurkha soldiers suddenly appeared before him. Kassim stopped and, lowering Sophia gently, laid her down on the floor. Then, taking out his knife, he flipped it open. He advanced slowly toward the first soldier. When he got near, he lunged with the knife. The Gurkha deftly sidestepped and thrust his rifle forward.

Kassim did not see the bayonet that went in and out of his chest in a fraction of a second. He stood with his mouth open and his eyes staring. The knife dropped from his hand and he slowly crumbled to the ground.

Ali Bhutt came running into the church. He saw the Gurkha soldiers and the body of the Pathan but could not see anyone else. He walked further in and then his eyes witnessed a sight that would haunt him for the rest of his life.

Sitting on the ground in front of the statue of the Virgin Mary was the pathetic figure of Sophia. She was cradling the head of her grandfather with one arm, and gently rocking back and forth. Her other hand was slowly stroking her mother's face lying on the ground next to her. Her eyes were glazed and vacant.

Tears streamed down Ali Bhutt's face. His body shook with sobs and he went down on his knees. "*Yah Allah*, what havoc have you brought upon these people?" he cried.

Feroze Khan and Father Finnegan now arrived, and each looked at the scene in stunned silence. Father Finnegan made the sign of the cross.

"Oh, my God — what brutality! And that, too, in the name of religion."

Ali Bhutt turned to the priest. "This child will have to be looked after," he said between his sobs. "There's no one left from her family."

"I'll go and get the nuns from St. Brigid's Convent," Father Finnegan answered.

Wiping his tears, Ali Bhutt reached out to Sophia. "Come, daughter, let me take you out into the open."

Sophia did not show any sign of having heard or seen him and sat expressionless, rocking her grandfather and stroking her mother's head.

Father Finnegan soon returned, accompanied by two nuns. Sister Anna Marie's hand shot up to her throat. Uttering a faint cry, she ran and knelt down next to Sophia. Tears filled her eyes. She pried Devi Lal's head from Sophia's arms and gently laid him on the floor. Then she took Sophia's hands in hers. "Come with me, Sophia," she said softly and led her out of the chapel.

Feroze Khan knelt down next to Devi Lal's body. "*Hazoor*, they were such good people," he said to Ali Bhutt. "Why did something like this have to happen to them?" he sobbed.

"Those butchers murdered a saint," Ali Bhutt whispered, his voice unsteady. Raising his hands, he said, "Let us pray to Allah that the soul of this noble man and his daughter go to heaven in peace."

The two Muslims knelt down in a Christian house of worship and prayed to Allah for the soul of a Hindu and his daughter.

"Can't we do something different for them, Ali Bhutt *Sahib*?" Feroze Khan asked. "It will be a terrible shame for their bodies to be tossed into the refuse trucks and taken away for common disposal."

"Yes, you're right," Ali Bhutt answered, wiping his tears. "The least we can do is to provide them with the last rites of their faith. I will talk to the Gurkha soldiers and seek their help. We will take the bodies to the cremation grounds of the Hindus."

Later, as the funeral pyres consumed the remains of Devi Lal and Khin May, the only mourners present were the two Muslims whose lives had been touched by Devi Lal.

A short distance away, in the village of the *harijans*, a little girl played in the dirt. "Joyti, come now, come into the house," her mother called from inside her hut. The child did not know that the man whose body was being cremated had also helped her parents.

Late the next day Feroze Khan took two brass urns and collected the ashes from the cremation grounds. By the time he returned to the church it was nightfall. He placed the urns side by side in a storage room of the church. Coming out of the shrine, he turned in the direction of Mecca and knelt down to pray. When he stood up, he looked up at the heavens just as two shooting stars silently streaked across the sky.

Sister Anna Marie opened the door and peered into the room. Sophia lay on the bed, curled up, her eyes wide open. She had not spoken a word nor shed any tears. The nun knelt down by the bed.

"Sophia, this is Sister Anna Marie, your friend," she said gently.

Sophia's face remained expressionless. Her eyes looked straight ahead, unblinking. Sister Anna Marie came out, closing the door behind her.

"How's the child doing?" Sister Margaret Rose, the Principal of St. Brigid's Convent asked.

"I don't know, Sister. She hasn't said a word, nor has she cried," the young nun answered. "She has stayed curled up on the bed since we brought her in. I'm very worried about her."

"Stay with her, Sister," said Sister Margaret Rose. "I'll bring some food. Try to see that she eats at least some thing."

Sophia resisted attempts to feed her and remained in bed in the same position throughout the night. Sister Anna Marie had also stayed awake, praying all night, asking God's help for her unfortunate young friend.

Sister Catherine watched Sophia during the day. Toward evening, Sophia allowed Sister Anna Marie to lead her out into the courtyard of the convent. Later that night, Sister Catherine forced Sophia to drink a little milk. She stayed up while Sophia dozed fitfully, waking up now and then, moaning.

Three days had gone by since Sophia had been brought into the convent. Sister Anna Marie was in the principal's office.

"I'm extremely worried about Sophia, Sister. She hasn't eaten much and shows no emotion whatsoever."

"The child must be in a state of deep shock. It's not surprising. It must have destroyed her mind to see her grandfather and mother killed before her eyes. I'll speak to Father Finnegan to see if a doctor from the General Hospital can come to see her."

August 15th dawned: India received its independence and the nation of Pakistan was born. The Indian National flag was hoisted atop the Red Fort in Delhi, accompanied by joyous celebrations. In Karachi, the flag of Pakistan was raised by Mohammed Ali Jinnah and Pakistanis celebrated the creation of their Islamic State.

But there was no celebration in Punjab, as all hell had broken loose! If the earlier killings were horrifying, what happened now was unimaginable. The opposing factions went at each other with barbaric, wanton savagery. The air was filled with the smoke of burning villages, towns and cities, and the cries of the victims. The Army tried to intervene, but the orgies of killings, rapes and looting continued.

Then a massive exodus began. Hindus and Sikhs fled Pakistan, carrying pitifully meager belongings with them. Many Muslims from India started their trek towards Pakistan. The largest exodus in the history of mankind took place. By the time it would be over, fifteen million people, uprooted from their homes, would flee, seeking safety.

Hindu and Sikh men, women and children left, in columns sometimes ten miles long. Some rode bullock carts, *tongas* and bicycles, but most walked. They had no protection from the searing heat of the summer, nor from Muslims who attacked them at will. As the elderly and the frail fell, they were left to die on the roadside. Muslims from East Punjab were fleeing in the opposite direction, headed toward Pakistan. They, in turn, were attacked mercilessly by Hindus and Sikhs. The roads leading from both directions to the newly created border were littered with the dead, rotting in the hot sun. The helpless refugees slept on the roads at night, pushing corpses to one side. There was no shelter and they dared not stray from the roads. Hundreds of thousands would die miserably in the brief period of a few months.

Sister Margaret Rose was in her office and, since early morning, had been working on plans for the closure of St. Brigid's Convent. Her Superiors in the Mother House in Dublin had left the decision on the future of the convent with her. Most of the students at the school were

Hindus. With the formation of the Islamic State of Pakistan, she doubted if Muslim girls would be allowed to return to a Christian school.

The thought of closing the convent saddened her. She had been a part of the school for many years and had served as its principal for the past six. She was also concerned about the safety of the nuns. So far, they had not been bothered. However, there had been rumors about a convent in Kashmir being attacked by a group of tribal men. Several nuns had been raped and the convent looted.

There was a gentle knock on the door.

"Come in," Sister Margaret Rose called out.

One of the nuns poked her head in. "Inspector Neeaz Khan is here to see you, Sister."

"Oh, yes. Please send him in," Sister Margaret Rose answered, getting up.

"Good afternoon, Inspector. I'm pleased to see you. What brings you to the convent?"

"*Assalamu Alaikum*, Sister," the Inspector said, raising the cane in his hand towards his head. "My friend, Ali Bhutt, asked me to deliver this package to you. It contains some items of clothing belonging to his daughter Nusreen which he thought the Hindu girl could use."

"That was very thoughtful of Mr. Bhutt. How is he?"

"Actually, he took my advice and left for Karachi. Our people are very angry with him for harbouring Hindus in his house. I told him that he should stay away from Punjab until the situation here stabilizes. He asked me to provide you with assistance in getting the girl out of Pakistan."

"I'm pleased to hear that, Inspector Khan. In fact, we could use some help right now. Sophia is not well and I would like to have her seen by a doctor from the hospital."

"I'm afraid that will not be possible," the inspector answered, shaking his head. "The riots are continuing and most of the doctors have fled the hospital."

The nun's face showed her disappointment.

"I'm planning to send the rest of the nuns back to our home in Ireland," she said. "We're going to close the school. I intend to stay back to somehow dispose of the school property. Are there trains running to Delhi, Inspector, and will it be safe for the nuns to travel?"

"Yes, trains have started running again, but they are packed with refugees. Not only are the insides of the compartments completely full, but every square inch of their roofs is occupied. It's crazy."

"How can the nuns get to Delhi, Inspector?"

"How many nuns do you have?"

"There will be fourteen of them and of course Sophia will accompany them."

"Well, they will have to go to the railway station and take their chances," the inspector answered, shrugging his shoulders.

"Can we count on your assistance to get them safely to the station?"

The inspector smiled. "Yes, of course, Sister. The Pakistani police will be only too pleased to help you. When do you wish for them to go?"

"They can leave as early as tomorrow."

"Good. Have them ready by eight o'clock. I shall escort them to the station personally."

The riots continued all day and well into the evening as jubilant Muslim crowds attacked Hindu and Sikh homes with impunity. As night fell, the savagery intensified and entire blocks went up in flames.

After their evening prayers, Sister Margaret Rose asked the nuns to assemble in the dining room.

"You shall be leaving for Dublin tomorrow morning," she told them. "Police Inspector Khan and his constables will be here at eight o'clock and will take you in their truck to the railway station. You will have to try and board one of the refugee trains going south to India."

"What about you, Sister?" one of the nuns inquired. "Won't you accompany us?"

"No, I must stay back and try to sell the Convent properties. I shall follow you as quickly as I can. Sister Catherine will be in charge during the journey and you will, of course, take Sophia with you."

Sister Anna Marie packed her small suitcase. Her mind felt numb. She should be excited about going home, but this convent had been her home for so many years and she was going to miss it. She also placed in her suitcase the clothes Nusreen's father had sent for Sophia. She had tried to get Sophia to talk, but to no avail. She stayed with her all the time.

The next morning the police truck entered the convent compound close to nine o'clock. The nuns had been waiting for over an hour, their suitcases packed and ready.

"*Assalamu Alaikum*, Sister," Inspector Neeaz Khan said. "I see your nuns are ready."

"Good morning, Inspector," Sister Margaret Rose answered. "We are all pleased to see you. Thank you for coming to help us."

The inspector barked an order and several constables jumped out of the truck and started loading the suitcases. Sister Anna Marie came out, holding Sophia by her hand. The moment Sophia saw the constables, she stopped. Her body stiffened and her face appeared agitated.

"It's all right, Sophia," Sister Anna Marie spoke softly. "We're just going for a ride. Come, we'll be fine."

Sister Catherine turned to Sister Margaret Rose.

"You look after yourself now, Sister. Leave as soon as you can."

She was about to say more but Sister Margaret Rose raised her hand. "There's no time to be wasted on goodbyes, Sister. Get into the truck and let the good inspector take you to the station."

The constables helped the nuns climb into the truck, but when it came to Sophia's turn, Sister Anna Marie helped her and moved her deep into the truck. The constables climbed in. The Inspector nodded at Sister Margaret Rose and got into the seat next to the driver. The truck exited the compound and drove along Murree Road toward the station.

The nuns sat quietly. Some looked out of the back of the truck. The Muslim constables stared at the nuns.

"Is she a Hindu?" one of them asked Sister Anna Marie.

Sister Anna Marie glared back. "Her father was an Irishman."

"Well, then she is an Anglo-Indian," said the constable with disdain.

Sister Anna Marie turned away to look out the back of the truck.

Murree Road was crowded with a stream of refugees headed for the railway station. Old men and women, walking with difficulty, mothers carrying infants, men with bundles on their heads trudged along. There was pain and suffering on their faces and terror in their eyes. They had lost everything, and this was not their country anymore. However, they were the lucky ones — or so they thought.

The streets around the station were packed with humanity. Refugees from the towns and villages in the vicinity had come to Rawalpindi in hopes of getting onto a train. Many wore fresh scars of the savagery they had endured. Approaching the station, the truck had to slow down. The driver blew the horn and the sea of refugees parted to allow their new masters to go through.

A tall young man dodged out of the truck's way. He was wearing a *salwar, kameez* and turban and his face was hidden under a beard. He had just gotten off a train coming from Peshawar and started walking quickly towards Mandir Gallie.

God, please let me find Mama, Sophia and *Naana* safe, he prayed silently.

The police truck stopped at the station entrance and the constables helped the nuns with their luggage. Military troops stood guarding the station.

The August heat was intense and the platform jam-packed. Inspector Neeaz Khan led the nuns through the crowd, waving his cane authoritatively. Arriving at the middle of the platform, he stopped.

"You should wait here. Try to board the train when it arrives." Then, with a flourish of his hand, he continued. "I hope you will return to Pakistan sometime soon."

Getting no response, the Inspector turned around and marched out of the station.

The nuns stood huddled together. Sister Anna Marie held Sophia's hand firmly. The heat was stifling and the smell from the people crowded together, nauseating.

The sound of an approaching engine made the crowd surge forward. The nuns were carried along, desperately trying to stay together. Before the train had even come to a stop, every compartment was packed with refugees and many started climbing on to the roofs. Others grabbed whatever handhold they could find on the side of the train and, within minutes, nothing of the compartments themselves was visible. Without warning, the train lurched and started moving, knocking several people from the roof.

Two more trains had come and gone. The nuns had been at the station without food or even water for over six hours. Sister Catherine was frustrated and getting very angry. Her responsibility was to get the nuns back to Ireland, and she intended to do so. She looked around desperately, hoping to find someone who would help them. Two young Sikh men noticed the panic in her eyes.

"Do not worry, Sister," one of them said. "We will help you get onto the next train."

Sister Catherine attempted to smile. "Thank you very much. It will be very kind of you."

Darkness set in and the few lights on the platform provided scant illumination. Sister Catherine was deep in prayer when she heard an approaching train. Brakes squealing, it came to a stop. To the amazement of the waiting refugees, most of the compartments were only partially filled. Sister Catherine looked up, and there before her was an open compartment door.

The two young Sikhs yelled, "Sisters, let's go! Hurry!"

Quickly they boarded the train, helped by the two men. They rushed deep into the compartment and sat crowded together. People poured in from both sides and soon the compartment was packed. Men, women and children stood in the aisles, jammed together. The air became stifling. The light from the single small electric bulb was blocked by those standing. The refugees waited. Several infants were crying. Then the train started moving.

Sister Anna Marie sat with her back to a window and twisted her head periodically to catch the warm breeze blowing in. As the train traveled slowly through the city, she could see several buildings burning. Occasional bursts of gunfire could be heard. The train was going over a bridge across a road. Sister Anna Marie looked down and gasped. The road beneath was littered with dead bodies. In the glow of the street lights, she saw a decapitated head of a man lying next to the body of a young child.

One of the victims who was still alive was crawling on all fours through the mess of limbs and bodies. There was blood all over and the stench of death was heavy. Sister Anna Marie turned away, nauseated. Covering her face with her hands, she started sobbing. Sophia sat next to her, staring into the darkness of the compartment.

The train picked up speed and left the lights of the city behind. Its first stop was Mandra Junction and the train started slowing down. As it approached the station, it did not stop, but instead, picked up speed, rolling past the platform and out of the station. Those on the train who were able to peer onto the platform knew the reason. None of the passengers waiting at the station were going to be able to board. They lay there by the hundreds, massacred. Not a single man, woman or child was alive.

The train continued rolling through the night. Many of the refugees inside had fallen asleep. The ones standing slept leaning against each other. Those on the roof and the many hanging onto the sides of the compartments dared not sleep. Some of the stations where the train stopped were empty. Others showed signs of the carnage that had taken place earlier.

As dawn broke, the train rolled into Lahore. This large city was experiencing bloody riots and massacres, matched in savagery, perhaps, only by those taking place in Amritsar, the holy city of the Sikhs. The station was packed with Hindu and Sikh refugees and many vainly tried to board the train. For some inexplicable reason, the train remained at Lahore Station for almost two hours, but the passengers were afraid to get off even for a few moments.

The engine blew its whistle and the train rolled out of Lahore Station. The passengers felt relieved.

"The Indian border is not far from here," one of the young Sikhs told the nuns. "We shall soon be safe."

Leaving the city behind, the train rolled through a sea of wheat fields. Then it slowed down and came to a halt.

"What's going on? Why did we stop?" Sister Catherine asked. "Are we at the border?"

"I don't know why the train has stopped," the Sikh answered. "This is not India."

They heard a distant buzzing sound. Suddenly the people sitting on the roof started screaming. An armed mob was running toward the train from both sides. Cries of "Kill the Hindus and Sikhs!" spread terror throughout the train. Those in the compartments raised the wooden window shutters and bolted the doors. The two young Sikhs drew their long *kirpans*. Sister Catherine turned to one of them.

"What's going to happen?"

"Well, it is time for us to die, but with the grace of the Gurus, we will take some of the enemy with us."

The mob of thousands, holding swords, spears, scythes and guns, descended upon the train. Gunfire erupted. Women and children screamed. Dragged from the train, they were slaughtered mercilessly. Some men on the train fought back with whatever arms they had. A few clawed at their enemies with their hands, only to be cut down. The nuns prayed. The carnage continued. Agonizing screams of the victims were drowned by the frenzied yell of the mob.

The slaughter went on. The compartment where the nuns rode was now being attacked. The two young Sikhs fought with the sword-wielding attackers. They slashed and stabbed, downing several of them. But they were outnumbered as more and more of the mob boarded the compartment. The young Sikhs went down among the bodies of other victims.

The attackers left to continue their gruesome massacre in the next compartment. One fierce-looking, bearded man holding a bloodied sword turned back at the door and came toward the nuns. Sister Catherine stood up, defiant. She quickly bent down and grabbed the *kirpan* out of the dead Sikh's hand.

"We are Christian nuns from Ireland. Don't come near us!" she said in a loud voice.

The Muslim stopped. Pointing his sword at Sophia, he asked, "Is she a Hindu? Give her to me and the rest of you can go safely."

"She's not one of you!" Sister Catherine shouted back angrily. "Her father is Irish and she's going with us."

"Let me look at her," the man said, advancing.

Raising the *kirpan* high above her head, Sister Catherine screamed, "You'll have to fight me first, and then the rest of the nuns."

The man laughed and advanced, sword held high. Then he stopped abruptly and stared wide-eyed at one corner of the compartment. He could not believe what he was seeing. A strange old man in a faded gold tunic and an odd crown had suddenly appeared. He was standing among the mangled bodies on the floor and was staring at him angrily. His hair was long and matted and he had a scraggly flowing beard. He was now gesturing wildly towards the compartment door. The Muslim was perplexed. This was unreal, bizarre. What was happening? He lowered his sword.

"All right, all right!" he said to the nun, backing away. "Keep her. We've taken enough young girls already."

Turning around, he stepped on some of the dead lying near the door and hastened out. Sister Catherine slumped down onto a seat, trembling like a leaf. The *kirpan* dropped from her hand.

The train started moving again. The nuns sat in their seats. Some of them were sobbing, others prayed. Sophia had not moved but continued to stare ahead with a vacant look on her face.

A baby's cry came from the mangled bodies on the floor. Sister Catherine leapt to her feet.

"Come, sisters, there's work to be done! We must see if any of these poor people are still alive."

Stepping over the bodies on the floor, and trying to avoid the pools of blood, Sister Catherine went to where the baby's cries were coming from. She lifted the infant into her arms and carried it to their end of the compartment.

Some of the nuns went from one body to another trying to see if there was life remaining in any of the pathetic figures. One of the Sikh youths moaned and Sister Anna Marie rushed to his side. She knelt down and gently raised his head, placing it in her lap. The young man had a deep stab wound in his stomach, and a gash on his right shoulder. He was bleeding profusely. Slowly opening his eyes, he looked up into the nun's face.

"I took care of three of them before they got me," he said slowly.

"Yes, you did," Sister Anna Marie said softly. "You were so brave."

The young man smiled. His eyelids slowly closed and his head drooped.

The nun made the sign of the cross and prayed, tears streaming down her face. The young man's blood stained her tunic. The train kept moving.

Sister Anna Marie had lost all sense of time. It felt as if it had been ages since they boarded the train in Rawalpindi. How long had they been riding? Why were these poor people slaughtered? When was this nightmare going to end?

The train started slowing down. The wooden shutters were still closed and the heat and stench in the compartment were unbearable. Sister Catherine was not sure where they were and wondered if another mob was waiting to attack the train. Will we be spared this time or will they kill us all?

The train entered a station. The grim-faced railway employees, police and army personnel standing on the platform did not have to be told what the contents of this train were going to be. From a distance, they had seen that not a single person was sitting on the compartment roofs or hanging from its sides. On a refugee train coming from Pakistan, it meant only one thing. These people in the Indian city of Amritsar had already dealt with two such trainloads of corpses earlier in the day. As the red carriages rolled by, they saw the freshly painted message on the side of a compartment.

"A gift from Pakistan to India," it read.

Hindus and Sikhs had also taken revenge and for every such train, they sent back one full of massacred Muslim refugees. The message painted on the outside read,

"A gift from India to Pakistan."

When the train stopped, Sister Catherine was surprised at the eerie silence outside. All she could hear was the distant hissing of the steam engine. The door to the compartment was flung open. The nuns tensed. Sister Anna Marie pushed Sophia behind her. Then several Sikh soldiers entered. Noticing the nuns crowded in the corner, one of them called out, "Do not worry — you are safe. This is Amritsar. You are in India."

"Thank you, Lord Jesus!" Sister Catherine prayed. "Thank you Mary, Mother of God. Thank you for sparing our lives!"

They were helped off the train and taken into a waiting room. The nuns washed the blood off their hands and their tunics as best they could, and were served hot tea and food. Sister Catherine handed the baby to one of the officials. Ambulances had taken away the few who were still alive. The gruesome task of removing the dead continued.

An Indian Army officer came to the waiting room. "Arrangements can be made for you to stay in Amritsar for a few days," he said. "Or, if you wish, you can be placed on a train leaving for Delhi."

"If possible, we would like to go to Delhi," Sister Catherine replied. "We plan to return to Ireland."

"All right. Please wait here. I'll see if seats can be secured for you on one of the trains."

The nuns were given seats on an evening train. Before they boarded, volunteers again provided them with a meal. The train was crowded. The fourteen nuns, along with Sophia, were in a small, second-class compartment. Sophia sat in a corner, leaning against the wooden wall, her feet tucked underneath her. Sister Anna Marie had helped her change into a fresh *salwar* and *kameez* and also forced her to eat a little.

Sister Anna Marie sat swaying with the movement of the train. The rhythmic clatter of the wheels almost lulled her to sleep. Her thoughts went back to the time when she had first arrived in India six years ago and had traveled by train from Bombay to Rawalpindi. She was young, and eager to get started with her assignment as a teacher at St. Brigid's Convent School. She had fallen in love with India and its people and relished her work.

How can one person endure such pain, Sister Anna Marie thought, looking at Sophia. She wondered how long it would be before her young friend would recover. Perhaps it's a blessing she's blocked out the memories of the gruesome tragedy. She was relieved they were taking Sophia to Ireland with them. The change might be helpful in eventually healing her wounds. Then her thoughts went to Dublin. Sophia will like the Motherhouse. She would take her friend to meet her parents and show her the city.

Sister Anna Marie dozed off. The compartment swayed violently, and the wheels clattered noisily as the train moved from one track to another. Sophia moaned. She appeared agitated. Sister Anna Marie placed her hand on the girl's shoulder and gently shook her.

As the sun came up, the train slowed, approaching Delhi station. The refugees coming from Pakistan were helped by officials and volunteers. Large numbers of Muslims sat huddled on the platform, terror showing on their faces. They waited for trains to take them to their new homeland. Armed soldiers and policemen were everywhere.

While in Delhi, the nuns were to stay at the Convent of Jesus and Mary on Baird Road. An Indian official arranged for the nuns to be taken there in an army lorry. Muslim neighborhoods surrounding the railway station had been looted and burned, and some buildings were still smoldering. The lorry drove to the convent and entered its gate.

"The Lord has brought us out of Punjab safely," Sister Catherine said to her fellow nuns. "We shall rest and make plans for our return home. We must pray for Sister Margaret Rose and for the victims of this colossal tragedy consuming the country."

The tragedy indeed was colossal. By the time the madness would be over, fifteen million people would be witness to the senseless, unimaginable brutality that was consuming their land and would become a part of the greatest human migration in history. The exact death toll would perhaps never be known, but estimates would place it around 600,000.

Yet the perpetrators went unpunished. They celebrated the freedom of their countries — Hindus and Sikhs in India, Muslims in Pakistan. They sang, danced and feasted. They continued to go to their temples, their *gurudawaras* and their mosques.

Did any seek forgiveness for the heinous crimes they had committed? Perhaps not. But most assuredly, when their turn came and it was their day of reckoning, their karmas would catch up with them and dispense the justice that history may not.

The Lonesome Journey

$\mathcal{W}$iping his glasses with a white handkerchief, the young Indian doctor sighed, "I'm sorry, I can't tell you how long she'll remain in this state. She may recover within days. Conversely, it might take years before she can finally overcome the shock."

Sister Catherine was sitting across from the specialist in his small office. He looks awfully young, she thought. But there were at least half a dozen framed diplomas on the wall behind him. With that many degrees, the man must be qualified, she mused.

"Totally blocking one's memory is nature's way of protecting the individual who has been exposed to extreme shock. The person continues to function but has no recollection of past events."

"What will happen when she does remember, Doctor?"

"Medical science knows very little about this condition, Sister. Of course there will be a period of intense grief. But, since the realization will take place some time after the event, the person may recover sooner."

The appointment with the physician at Irwin Hospital in New Delhi had been arranged by the principal of the Convent of Jesus and Mary.

"You have been most kind, doctor," Sister Catherine said, standing up.

"I'll be pleased to see the patient again — perhaps next month."

"I'm afraid that won't be possible, Doctor," she answered, shaking the physician's hand. "We're hoping to leave for Ireland as quickly as we can. But I'm most grateful to you for offering to help." Sister Anna

Marie was with Sophia in the examination room. Sister Catherine joined them.

"Come, we can go now," she said. "We can return to the Convent."

Travel documents were needed for Sophia, and Sister Catherine found out that the British government had set up a repatriation office on Parliament Street. British subjects, under special circumstances, were being issued permits to travel to the United Kingdom. Sister Catherine, accompanied by one of the nuns from the Convent of Jesus and Mary, went to the office.

A long line of people were waiting to see the officer in charge. Many of them were Anglo-Indians who were now unsure of their future in an independent India. Although most had not seen England, some of them were now anxious to get there.

When their turn came, the two nuns entered the office. The officer was sympathetic. "You have to realize, Sister, there must be thousands of such young girls in India who have been orphaned and are destitute. We can't allow all of them to go to England."

Sister Catherine glared at the man over her eyeglasses. "Sir, we're not talking about taking her to England. She will be taken to the Republic of Ireland. We intend to be in London only as long as it takes us to find our way to Dublin."

The officer was still adamant. "His Majesty's Government cannot be responsible for allowing every orphan to visit London."

Sister Catherine persisted. "Perhaps I haven't told you, this girl's father was an Irish soldier who was good enough to serve in the British Army. He ultimately gave his life fighting for "your" Majesty's Government. And now his orphaned daughter is being refused permission to go home?"

The man relented. Sophia was brought to the office the following day and the necessary travel documents were issued promptly.

During their stay in Delhi, Sophia had not spoken a word. She did whatever Sister Anna Marie asked, but her face remained expressionless. She ate sparingly and slept fitfully. It took two weeks for the nuns to finalize all of the formalities and obtain seats on a flight to London.

The airplane took off from Delhi airport and climbed slowly, banking and turning to the west. Sister Anna Marie sat next to the window, looking at the lights of the city below. It was past midnight and, from the air, Delhi looked enchanting. Street lights extended for miles in straight rows. The symmetrical design of the twinkling lights, however, was harshly interrupted in several places by fires. Looting, arson and mayhem had continued in several parts of the capital. In the soft glow of the reading lamps, Sophia's face appeared untroubled. Yet, Sister Anna Marie knew the turbulent storms that must be raging in her mind. I'm going to look after you, Sophia, I promise, Sister Anna said to herself, looking at her young friend.

The airplane circled over the city of Karachi where it was to make a brief stop. That's where Sophia's friend Nusreen had moved to, Sister Anna Marie remembered. How strange. She might be in one of those homes down there, she thought. They took off from Karachi and the tiring journey continued. After stops in Cairo, Istanbul, Rome and Paris, the plane finally approached the English Channel.

Sister Catherine felt numb from fatigue and lack of sleep. She thought about the arrangements she would have to make at London airport for their trip to Ireland. She hoped to get seats for all of them on an airplane to Dublin. Or else they would have to take the long and tedious bus and ferry trip. Luckily, seats were available on a plane leaving later that evening.

The flight to Dublin was brief. As they waited for their luggage, Sister Catherine spoke to the nuns.

"We've arrived home safely, Sisters" she said. "Let us pray and thank the Lord for protecting us through our journeys of the past month. Let's ask that His mercy be upon those who are suffering in India. Let us pray for the safety and speedy return home of Sister Margaret Rose."

They hired taxis to take them to the Motherhouse. There was a chill in the air and a steady rain was falling. Sophia sat in the taxi between Sister Catherine and Sister Anna Marie. She had not slept on the plane, and appeared tired. Sister Anna Marie looked out of the window at the late evening traffic. Her thoughts went to her parents and she hoped they were well. She had written to them before leaving Rawalpindi, but wasn't sure if the letter would reach them.

Driving south through the city, the taxis crossed O'Connell Bridge over the River Liffey. They drove past Trinity College and around St. Stephens Green. They entered Donnybrook and stopped at the Motherhouse on Morehampton Road.

Sister Catherine paid the taxicab drivers and the nuns picked up their suitcases. Opening an iron gate, they entered the Motherhouse grounds. One of the nuns pulled on the doorbell. The doors opened almost immediately. The loud, booming voice of Sister Eileen Maher welcomed them. A telegram sent from New Delhi by Sister Catherine arrived only the day before. It had said that fourteen nuns, accompanied by a young orphan, would be arriving shortly. Brushing the raindrops from their habits, the nuns entered the front hallway. Sophia hesitated at the doorstep, but Sister Anna Marie gently led her inside.

"Your rooms have been prepared for you on the second and third floors, Sisters", Sister Eileen announced cheerfully. "And, for our young guest we have a bedroom ready in the guest quarters here on the ground floor," she added.

Sister Anna Marie led Sophia into her room. She helped her change into a nightgown and made her get into bed. Sister Catherine spoke to Sister Eileen and explained Sophia's condition. "The poor child is not to be left alone. One of us will need to be with her at all times. Sister Anna Marie knows her best and will need to sleep in an adjacent bedroom in the guest quarters."

"That shouldn't be a problem at all," Sister Eileen answered. "I'll prepare a second bedroom down here right away."

Sister Anna Marie brought some food on a tray, but Sophia was already asleep. Not wanting to disturb her, she placed some fruit on a bedside table and left quietly. The nuns gathered in the large chapel on the ground floor to say their evening prayers. Sister Anna Marie peeped into Sophia's room several times throughout the night and each time found her asleep.

After their morning prayers and breakfast, the nuns assembled in the library on the first floor and were welcomed by the Mother Superior. She was a tall woman in her early sixties, with a kind round face and a soft gentle voice.

"I understand you witnessed some very horrifying scenes just before leaving India," the Mother Superior said. "Sister Catherine has given me a brief account of your miraculous escape. Welcome back home. Let us pray and thank our Lord for all his mercies."

Sophia slept throughout the day. By evening, Sister Anna Marie became concerned and asked Sister Catherine if Sophia should be awakened.

"No, I think we should let her sleep as long as she wants," Sister Catherine answered. "The poor child must be exhausted."

The following morning, Sister Anna Marie quietly opened Sophia's door and, to her surprise, found her standing by the window, looking out at the garden. Sister Anna Marie tried to sound cheerful. "Good morning," she called out.

Startled, Sophia turned around quickly and raised a hand to her throat. She then moved back and stood against the wall.

"Don't be afraid. It's I, your friend, Sister Anna Marie," the nun said gently.

Sophia slowly lowered her hand to her side and without answering, sat down on the edge of the bed.

"Did you sleep well, Sophia?"

Hesitatingly, she answered softly, "Yes, I think I slept for a very long time." Then, with a puzzled look on her face she asked, "Is that my name?"

"Yes, and it's such a pretty name."

Afraid that Sophia might ask questions about her past, Sister Anna Marie quickly changed the subject. "You must be hungry. Would you like some breakfast? We can go to the dining room and you can have whatever you want."

Sophia fidgeted with her hands and, without looking up, said, "I don't wish to go anywhere."

Pointing at a door on the side of the room, Sister Anna Marie said, "All right. Why don't you go ahead and wash up. I'll bring you some breakfast." She left, closing the door behind her.

"You did the right thing by bringing the poor child with you to Dublin." Sister Catherine and Sister Anna Marie were sitting in the

Mother Superior's office. They had just given her more details of the riots in Punjab and the tragic loss Sophia had suffered.

"We must do everything we can to help the unfortunate girl," the Mother Superior continued. "We'll have her examined by the doctors at St. Vincent's Hospital. Now, you told me that her brother was in prison in India. Did you also say that her only other relative is an uncle who has gone to the United States?"

"Yes, Mother Superior. Those are the only two relatives that we know about," answered Sister Catherine.

"She'll stay with us as long as necessary, and we'll try to locate her uncle through some of our sisters in the United States. You said he's in the Chicago area? We have many Irish living in Chicago. It shouldn't be difficult for them to find this Indian doctor."

Turning to Sister Anna Marie, Mother Superior continued. "You, Sister, will be primarily responsible for the girl's care. I shall send word to the director of St. Vincent's Hospital and ask him to make arrangements for Sophia to be seen by a doctor."

"Mother Superior, I just remembered," Sister Anna Marie said. "Sophia told me of her father's aunt who had raised him. I believe she said this Aunt Colleen lived on a farm near Ventry in County Kerry."

"Do you not know the woman's last name?"

"Well, if it's the same as Sophia's father's, then it's O'Shea."

"Good. We can also try to locate her. As to her brother, I don't know what we can do from here, especially now that those countries have their own governments. I can have someone check with our Foreign Office here in Dublin. But first, we'll get the lass to St. Vincent's. She should start receiving treatment right away."

Neil had run all the way from the railway station and not slowed down until he reached the entrance to Mandir Gallie. His turban had come off and he held it against his chest.

"Oh my God," he moaned, stopping in the middle of the gallie. He turned slowly and, gasping for breath, stared at the burnt hulls of the buildings on each side. "Where's my family?" he cried out softly. "Where are you, *Naana* and Mama! Answer me, Sophia," he moaned, falling to his knees. He buried his face in his turban and his shoulders started shaking. After a few moments, he raised his head and looked around. The street was deserted but the smell of fire and death was overpowering. He slowly stood up and began walking deeper into the gallie. He quickened his pace and started running towards Moti Bazaar. He came upon several Muslims looting some shops.

"Don't go in there!" one of them yelled at him. "There are still some Hindus in the bazaar." He's mistaken me for a Muslim, Neil realized.

The iron door to Bir Singh's shop was shut tight. Neil banged on it with his fists but no one came to open it. He started walking out of the bazaar and again walked past the pile of rubble that was once their building on Mandir Gallie. Then he saw the iron gate, burnt and twisted, hanging by one hinge. He put his hand out and touched the gate. "Where are you, *Naana*, Mama and you, Sophia?" he sobbed.

Nusreen's parents — maybe they'll know, he suddenly thought, and walking out of Mandir Gallie, he started running towards their home. The armed watchman at their gate told him that no one was home. "They have all gone to live in Karachi," he said.

Maybe *Naana*, Mama and Sophia escaped, he thought. I hope to God they did, he prayed. He must look for them, but where could they have gone? They may have fled to Amritsar or Delhi. Neil started walking towards the railway station. He had not eaten since the day before and his prison *salwar* and *kameez* were soiled. The Hindu and Sikh refugees headed in the same direction looked at him suspiciously. I've got to get rid of this beard, he thought. He had a few coins in his pocket. Near the station, he squatted down on the pavement in front of a Muslim barber and had his face shaved clean.

There were no more trains leaving for India that day. With his last two *annas* he bought a *naan* and ate it. He found a little space on the crowded platform and went to sleep among a sea of refugees.

He was suddenly awakened by a lot of commotion around him. It was still dark and for a moment he didn't realize where he was. Then he saw the train standing at the platform with refugees fighting to board it. Neil got up and started pushing his way towards the train. The compartments were already full, but he spotted a tiny space on the footboard of a compartment, and climbed on to it. He grabbed the handrail and stood wedged in the middle of several men. The train suddenly lurched and started moving. A man next to Neil lost his balance and fell off. Neil hung on, his arms wrapped around the handrail.

The train picked up speed and was soon traveling fast, leaving the city behind. The refugees were relieved to be headed towards safety and prayed they would make it across the border. Most of them had not seen the flatbed carriage immediately behind the engine, with a contingent of heavily armed Indian Army soldiers on it. Other than the discomforts of the journey, these refugees were to be spared the tragic fate of the thousands who had preceded them.

The train kept moving all day with only a few brief stops to allow more coal and water to be taken on for the steam engine. Neil and the men standing on the footboards did not dare get off in fear of losing their space to refugees waiting at these stations. Some of the stations still showed evidence of the carnage of the previous days. Neil felt nauseated and quickly averted his face. His arms and legs were sore, but he somehow found the strength to hang on and endure the pain. He had not eaten anything since the previous evening, nor had he drunk any water.

The train started slowing down. It was approaching a small station and began passing another train full of Muslim refugees coming from the opposite direction. The people in the two trains looked at each other, not with hatred but more with a sense of sympathy, for after all, theirs was but a common fate. Neil suddenly got a fleeting glance of a bearded man seated at the window of the other train and a flash of memory brought a moment of joy to his heart. "Sher Khan," he screamed, reaching out with one hand. But his voice was drowned by the ear-shattering clatter of the wheels as the two trains picked up speed and sped away in opposite directions.

Arriving at Lahore, the train was for some reason held up at the station for almost two hours. The refugees were perplexed and did not know what was happening. There seemed to be a lot of activity on the platform with Pakistani military personnel talking to some Indian Army officers.

Then the train left and, sometime during the night, it crossed the border. When it came to a stop at Amritsar station, Neil got off the footboard and almost stumbled. The refugees rushed out of the compartments, their faces showing the strain of the past months. Many wept with relief: some knelt and kissed the ground. Neil pushed his way through the crowd and accepted a cup of hot tea from a volunteer. "Where can I inquire about my family?" he asked.

"There is a registration desk in the outer station hall. You may check there," he was told.

Neil stood in line for an hour, but when he reached the desk, he was disappointed. There were no entries for any from his family.

"I'm very sorry, but your family may have gone on to Delhi," he was told by the harried but sympathetic man at the desk. Neil found his way to the food kitchen just outside the station, and ate. He then slept through the night curled up on the floor of the station platform.

Early the next morning he boarded a train for Delhi. Arriving there, he searched through the entire station and then, asking directions, went from one refugee camp to another. He ate in the camp kitchens and slept in a tent on the camp grounds. Lonely and miserable, he didn't know what to do. He went looking for a job, and after a week, finally was able to get one as a waiter in a restaurant.

The images of his family constantly stayed in his mind. He felt frustrated and angered. He had to do something about it — he had to find them. Could they have gone back to Mandalay? He bought a train ticket with the money he received for the four weeks he had worked and traveled to Calcutta. He had hoped that somehow he would be able to travel on to Burma. He hung around the docks for several days, trying to find work on one of the passenger ships or freighters sailing for Rangoon. What if they hadn't gone to Burma, what would he do then? In the meantime, he had to feed himself and found work at a construction site unloading bricks from trucks. Standing next to other labourers, he had to toss the bricks, one by one, up to a man standing on a bamboo scaffolding about fifteen feet above him. At night he slept with the other laborers on the pavement in front of the fancy shops on the Esplanade.

One day, a fellow worker told him that freighters sailing for England often took on able-bodied men for round trips, especially if they could speak English. "The food is great and the pay is four times what we get here tossing bricks," the man said.

"Why haven't you gone?" Neil asked.

"I don't speak English and they also told me I was too old," the man complained.

Neil went back to the docks the next day and gave his name to a freight agent. He inquired several times, and then a couple of weeks later, was given a job on a freighter. "You are to help the cooks in the galley, wait tables and wash dishes," he was instructed.

The cabin he shared with three other seamen was smaller than his prison cell in Peshawar Jail, but the food was good and he didn't mind the work. They sailed around the island of Ceylon and headed towards the Suez Canal. But the seas in the Indian Ocean were very rough, and Neil remained violently sick most of the time. Once through the Canal and the Mediterranean Sea, they ran into rough weather again. Neil felt immensely relieved when the ship docked at a pier on the Thames River near London. The freighter was to remain in port for about a week before returning to Calcutta.

"Oh, I can't go through being seasick for another four weeks," he moaned to Rashid, one of his cabin mates. "It'll kill me."

"I have a friend in the city," the man confided. "I can take you to meet him. Perhaps he can help you stay on here."

"You mean 'jump ship'?" Neil asked, surprised.

"Yes," Rashid answered. "Many Indian sailors have done that. I would myself, but I have a wife and children back home."

"What if I get caught? Is your friend trustworthy, and will he help me?"

"Oh yes, I know Abdul Rehman very well. He's from my village near Dacca. He works as an assistant foreman in a factory in the East End of London. You won't get caught if you stay out of trouble with the police. If you want, I'll take you to my friend's place."

Torn between his yearning for his family and the dread of another long sea voyage, he eventually decided to jump ship. Perhaps he could return to India after a few months.

The next morning, Neil followed Rashid out of the docks area. They had been paid the previous day and, other than the clothes he was wearing, he left his meager belongings on the ship. They came out onto a busy street. Two police constables were standing on a corner.

"Let's go back," Neil whispered. "They'll see us."

"Relax," Rashid answered, tugging Neil's sleeve. "Keep walking. You're drawing needless attention to us."

They took a tube train and got off at Aldgate East where Rashid's friend lived not far from the station.

Abdul Rehman welcomed them to his tiny flat. "Don't worry, there'll be no problems," he said, smiling at Neil. "You will be okay." He was a short dark-complexioned wiry man in his forties, and spoke fairly good English, although with a heavy Indian accent. "Come, we'll have an ale in the pub on White Chapel Road. Then I'll take you to a restaurant for some good Bengali food."

True to his word, Rehman proved to be most helpful. He was a congenial kindly person and invited Neil to stay with him as long as he needed to. Neil slept on an old sofa in the small living room of the flat and, within a few days, was able to find a job on the second shift in the same factory where Rehman worked.

Weeks passed and Neil gradually got over his fear of being an "illegal". He bought himself some clothes and had even started venturing out of the East End, taking the tube to different parts of London. Through Rehman, he met a few other Indians, some of whom were also "illegals". He started sharing the cost of the flat with Rehman, bought groceries and cooked breakfast for both of them in the morning. He ate a late lunch at a small restaurant on White Chapel Road before starting work at four o'clock. On Sundays, he was off and would join Rehman and his friends for a couple of beers at the pub they frequented. He found the East Enders of London to be friendly but minimized his contacts with them for fear of being found out.

One day at the restaurant, a new waitress came to take his order. She was tall and skinny, and her blonde hair was tied into a tight knot behind her head. She spoke in a soft gentle voice and quietly served him his meal. "Is your roast all right? Would you like some more tea?" she asked.

"Yes, it's great. I would like another cup, thanks," Neil answered, looking at her. She does have an attractive face, he thought, especially when she smiles. Over the next few days, he started noticing her more and came in a little earlier to be able to stay longer. He found out that her name was Jenny Smith and she lived in the neighborhood. She had recently moved to London with her parents from York where she had also worked as a waitress. She liked to go to the cinema on Sundays and had never eaten Indian food before.

After about a month, Neil had picked up enough courage to ask her if she would like to go to the cinema with him. Jenny had agreed and Neil took her out. After the movie, they stopped at an Indian restaurant on Tottenham Court Road. Neil told her about his past and his family.

"Oh, you poor boy," Jenny said gently. "You must miss them something terrible."

He asked about her family and she told him about them and about growing up in York. They seemed to enjoy each other's company and continued to go to the cinema every Sunday, and then to dinner. They had become good friends and Jenny had opened up quite a bit, telling him about one day wanting to go to college. "I don't know what I want to be, but I always enjoyed my studies."

"Bring your lady friend to meet me," Rehman had teased after Neil told him about Jenny.

"All right, I'll do that. I'll bring her to the pub next Sunday."

They had gone there, and Rehman appeared very pleased to meet her. "A pint for me and my friend and a sherry for the lady," he called out to the pub owner.

"Hey, keep your bloody voice low," a man sitting by the bar yelled in a thick cockney accent. "Who the bloody'ell you think you are, you damned darkie?"

Rehman flinched. "I'm sorry, there's no need to be rude in front of the lady," he said, turning away.

"Look at the bloody airs the darkie is putting on. You'd think he's a bloody maharaja or something," the man continued, his voice getting louder.

"That's all right, mister," Rehman said, looking over his shoulder. "Just stay calm."

"Who the bloody hell are you to tell me what to do," the man yelled angrily and staggered over to their table. He grabbed Rehman by his collar and dragged him out of his chair. Neil stood up and tried to free Rehman.

"You're drunk, mister," Neil said, pushing his way between them. "Leave him alone. He's done you no harm."

"And who the hell are you?" the man asked, swaying a little on his feet. "Another darkie, or a half-breed?"

"Look, we don't want any trouble with you," Neil said, trying to keep his temper under control, "but watch what you're saying."

"You bloody nigger," the man yelled and, raising a fist, lunged forward. He hit Neil on the side of the jaw, sending him reeling. He then pounced on Rehman and started pummeling him.

"Don't fight, Neil, don't get involved," Rehman pleaded, covering his face.

The man now had his large hands around Rehman's neck and was choking him. Neil tried to pull him away but could not. In desperation, he picked up a chair and brought it smashing down on the man's head and shoulders.

Jenny had sat, petrified, staring wide-eyed. "Are you all right, Neil?" she asked, going to him.

"Yes, I'm okay," he answered, staring at the man lying sprawled on the floor. Just then two constables walked into the pub. An ambulance was sent for and questions asked. Neil was to be taken to the police station. "What's going to happen to him? What — what are you going to do?" Jenny asked.

"Well, a report will have to be filed and he'll have to spend the night in a cell," one of the constables answered. "We'll see how the other bloke does by tomorrow morning."

Things had not gone well at the police station, especially when it was discovered that Neil was in England illegally. Besides the charge of getting into a pub brawl and severely beating up a man, Neil was going to be charged with entering the United Kingdom without a visa and being gainfully employed without an appropriate work permit. The report from the hospital the next morning was not encouraging. The man had suffered a concussion and had not regained full consciousness. Neil was formally charged, arrested and imprisoned to await trial.

In Chicago, Hari had been worried sick over the safety of his loved ones in Rawalpindi. Radio broadcasts and the newspapers in Chicago gave extensive detailed accounts of the riots and massacres in Punjab. Hari had sent two telegrams but had not heard from them. Oh God, I hope they're safe. I hope they were able to escape, he prayed.

Stephanie was most solicitous and tried to reassure him. "Don't worry, honey," she said gently. "They must be fine. With all that's going on, there's probably no way for them to reach us. We'll continue to pray for them each day."

"Thanks, Steph," Hari answered. "Thank you for your support." She was so caring and he loved her dearly. His thoughts went back to the time they had first met. He was in the hospital canteen in Imphal having coffee and she had asked if she could join him. She was a gregarious person and laughed easily. Right from the beginning Hari felt relaxed and at ease with her.

Stephanie was an attractive young woman with more freckles than Hari had ever seen on anyone. At five feet nine, she was almost as tall as him, and carried herself with agile grace. Her blond hair was cut short and her pug nose and easy grin gave her a slightly impish look. Hari was dazzled by her smile.

"It's all due to my dentist and the braces he put on my teeth," she said, laughing. "You should've seen the buck teeth I had as a child!"

Stephanie had taken an instant liking to this shy good-looking physician, and took the initiative in the progression of their courtship. They went together for almost a year and gradually fell in love. Hari came to the United States in October of 1945 and started his surgery training at the University of Chicago Hospital. Stephanie had met him at O'Hare Airport and had helped him find a one-bedroom furnished apartment on Woodlawn Street, not far from the hospital which was on South Maryland Avenue. Soon after that, they talked about getting engaged.

Stephanie was not surprised when Hari told her that he was writing to his father to seek his approval. She had already told her parents about him. The first weekend after Hari received his father's blessings, Stephanie took him to Racine, Wisconsin to meet her parents.

Mildred and Russ Brown received Hari warmly. Their home on the shore of Lake Michigan was large and elegant. They all spent a pleasant afternoon sailing in the family's large sailboat. Russ Brown was an oral surgeon and talked to Hari at length about health care and medicine. Russ had received his dental degree from Marquette University in nearby Milwaukee. He was on the staff of several hospitals and had been granted fellowship in the prestigious American College of Dentists in recognition of his services to his profession and community. Stephanie's mother, Mildred, was a nurse and had also attended Marquette. She worked as a volunteer at a senior citizen care center. The Browns were delighted when their daughter told them that she was getting engaged. Russ opened a bottle of champagne and they celebrated.

The following summer, Hari and Stephanie were married in a simple ceremony held on the lawn of the Browns' home overlooking Lake Michigan. They had driven north for their honeymoon to the village of Bayfield, on the shores of Lake Superior.

Now, a year later, Hari was desperately awaiting news from his family.

"Honey, wouldn't it be better if you went to India and looked for them?" Stephanie asked.

"Yes, I've been thinking about it, Steph. They may be in a refugee camp in Delhi, or worse, still stuck in Rawalpindi."

"You should get an American passport, dearest, in case you have to travel to Pakistan," Stephanie suggested.

It took almost four weeks before Hari was sworn in as a United

States citizen and issued a passport, and that too, only after Russ Brown contacted Joseph R. McCarthy, the Republican Senator from Wisconsin, in Washington, D.C.

Delhi towards late 1947 when Hari returned, was overflowing with refugees. The camps established by the government were no longer able to handle the hordes that came from the north and parade grounds, playing fields, and even pavements along most roads were occupied by refugees living in tents and makeshift shelters.

Hari checked into the Marina Hotel in Connaught Place, and went searching from one camp to another but found no trace of his family. Deep down in his heart, he knew that had they gotten out, they would have contacted him. He felt dejected. Could they still be stuck in Rawalpindi? He stopped at several government offices and inquired. "Are there any refugees still left in Pakistan?"

Finally, at one office, he received the answer he wanted to hear. "Yes," he was told, "Indian Army convoys travel to Lahore and Rawalpindi once a week and bring back small groups of refugees."

His spirits soared. He had to go to Rawalpindi, but how? Could he fly there with a U.S. passport? The answer was no, there was no air service between the two countries as yet. "Besides, you are a Hindu. It'll be too dangerous for you," he was told. He sought permission to go with the next convoy but was turned down.

Coming out of the government office, he ran into Major Mahadeva, an Indian Army friend of his with whom he had served in Imphal. They greeted each other warmly and talked. As luck would have it, Mahadeva was to lead an army convoy in three days, into Pakistan.

"Can you help me, Kedar?" Hari pleaded. "I must locate my family. I've got to go to Rawalpindi."

"You mean you want to accompany me? It'll be tough, Hari. I can't take civilians with me."

"I don't care. Maybe I can go dressed as a soldier," Hari answered. "You can borrow a uniform for me, can't you?"

"Yes, I guess I can," Kedar Mahadeva answered reluctantly, wondering what he was getting himself into.

Dressed in the uniform of an Indian soldier, Hari sat with Kedar

Mahadeva in a jeep leading a convoy of ten military trucks. They left early in the morning and drove to Amritsar. They crossed the border where four Pakistan Army jeeps joined them as escort. They spent the night in the Army Barracks in Lahore Cantonment. Their people were killing each other, but these officers had been comrades until being separated into two armies. They were cordial to each other and sat drinking whiskey and sodas late into the evening, talking about the good old days. The next morning the Indian Army convoy and their Pakistan Army escort drove to Rawalpindi.

Hari searched vainly among the refugees waiting to be evacuated. He asked his hosts to take him to Mandir Gallie. The devastation of the building in which his family had lived brought tears to his eyes. "Oh God, they've got to be safe," he prayed. Who would have information about them? The only friend of his family that he had met was Ali Bhutt. He went to his home.

"I'm sorry, Son, I'm very very sorry," Ali Bhutt said, opening the door and recognizing Hari.

Hari broke down. "Tell me what happened," he asked.

Ali Bhutt talked softly, tears streaming down his face. "They received a proper cremation, Hari. Their ashes are stored in the church."

"What about Neil? What happened to him?" Hari asked, wiping his tears.

"I don't know, Son, I don't know where he is. I tried to reach him but all political prisoners were released the moment the British relinquished power. But Sophia was taken to Ireland by the nuns. Hari, you must go to her."

A devastated Hari collected the urns containing the ashes of his father and sister from Feroze Khan. He rejoined the military convoy which picked up the remaining refugees who had miraculously survived the massacres and returned to India.

Hari's deep sorrow was tinged with a sense of guilt. He shouldn't have left his family and gone off to the States. Maybe if he had stayed, he would have forced them to leave in time and they would have been all right. I've caused their death, he cried in his heart. What could he do now? He must go to Sophia and also search for Neil. What about his father's and sister's ashes? If only he could return them to the city they loved. Yes, why not. That's what he would do. That's what he must do.

Air service was now available between New Delhi and Rangoon. Hari flew to Burma, taking the ashes with him. He took the overnight train to Mandalay, memories torturing his mind. No, he didn't have the heart to go to Sein Pun, but went instead to the shores of the Irrawaddy and boarded the Mingun ferry. The home for the elderly that his father had built was still there. Daw Mu, he learnt, had died two years earlier of natural causes.

Hari carried the ashes to the little white pagoda by the river's edge where they used to picnic. His eyes took in the familiar panorama around him and he prayed. Did he hear the voices of Neil and Sophia playing in the shallow waters by the shore? Was that Khin May admonishing them to be careful? His body began shaking with silent sobs. Then it was time to catch the last ferry back to Mandalay.

The pagoda studded Sagaing hills were bathed in the afternoon sun, and it was so peaceful on the river. Very slowly, Hari gave up his sister's and father's ashes to the Irrawaddy. "Welcome home, dearest Sis. Welcome home, Dad," he said softly, his voice choking. "May your souls rest in eternal peace."

Doctor Michael Lynch, the medical director of St. Vincent's Hospital in Dublin was a general practitioner. Over the years, he had received considerable experience in practically every field of medicine. Serving as a young army doctor during the latter part of World War I, he had pulled many shell-shocked soldiers out of the trenches in Europe. More recently, during World War II, he had again served in the army and treated not only the physical wounds of the soldiers, but helped them cope with the psychological after-effects of war.

Looking at the quiet young woman sitting in front of him, and based on the history the nuns had given him, Dr. Lynch recognized he was dealing with an acute post traumatic emotional stress disorder. He examined Sophia very gently. He checked her reflexes, looked for any signs of paralysis or muscle weakness of either side of the body. He then examined her eyes and ears.

Later, he spoke to Sister Catherine in his private office. "I didn't find any physical disease that is afflicting the young lass," he said. "I believe her condition is a result of the severe shock she experienced. I'll order a skull x-ray to rule out any organic lesion."

"How long will she remain in this state, Doctor?" the nun asked.

"Her memory may come back in bits and pieces — as flashbacks. It may be triggered by something familiar, but she mustn't be forced to remember the past. We must let nature take its course. She has disassociated herself from what happened, thus sparing her mind from pain." Dr. Lynch picked up a pipe from an ash tray on his desk. "May I?" he asked.

"Yes, please go ahead," Sister Catherine answered. "What else can we do to help the child?" she asked.

"She needs to be kept in pleasant surroundings and avoid any excitement. It may help her to get involved in some creative hobby where she can see positive results. Gardening would be a good diversion. A pastime, such as needlework or knitting, would also be good to keep her mind occupied. I would like to see her again in about a month. But of course, if there's any change in her condition, please let me know and I'll see her right away."

Sophia gradually settled into a daily routine established for her by Sister Anna Marie. She spoke little, and did not ask questions. Each morning when it was not raining, she worked in the garden, attending to the vegetable and flower beds. During the afternoons, she sat in the library, quietly reading books given to her by Sister Anna Marie. She was learning needlework from Sister Eileen and seemed to enjoy working with the bright-coloured threads. When asked a question, she responded politely but only with the fewest of words.

Of the fourteen nuns who had arrived from India, only Sister Catherine and Sister Anna Marie remained at the Motherhouse. The others had been given fresh assignments. Some were sent to provincial houses of the Order in London and other cities of England and Ireland. Others went to serve at hospitals and schools in Africa. Sister

Catherine was given an assignment at St. Vincent's Hospital. In addition to looking after Sophia, Sister Anna Marie was to help with the chores at the Motherhouse.

The Motherhouse was quite large, but its furnishings were austere. The ground floor consisted of an entrance hallway with a reception desk. Then, along one side were a visitor's waiting room and the Mother Superior's office. A large Chapel of Christ the King, with stained glass windows, occupied almost half of the ground floor. On the other side were the guest quarters consisting of three bedrooms. Additionally, there was a storage room and the stairs leading to the first floor.

The first floor had the smaller Queen of Peace Chapel, a library and the recreation room. A large kitchen was located between the nuns' dining room and a smaller guest dining room. There was also a tapestry room and a storage area. Sleeping rooms for the nuns were on the second and third floors.

The spacious grounds were surrounded by a high brick wall and consisted of well-tended lawns, flower beds and a vegetable garden. An outdoor chapel was located on the left rear corner of the grounds and vegetables and flowers were also grown in a greenhouse in the right rear corner.

The day after Sophia had been examined by Dr. Lynch, Sister Anna Marie was showing her the ground and first floor of the house. When they entered the Queen of Peace Chapel, Sophia appeared startled by the statue of the Virgin Mary. She raised her hands to her throat and became agitated. Then she moaned softly and ran out of the chapel.

Sister Anna Marie followed her, and took her across the hall into the library. She made her sit down on a bench next to a window. Sophia's hands were trembling. Sister Anna Marie put her arms around her shoulders.

"It's all right, Sophia," she said gently. "I'm with you. It's all right."

The next morning the sun rose in a clear blue sky. Birds were chirping and the gardens were radiant with flowers. The late September air felt fresh and warm.

"You might take Sophia for a walk this afternoon," Sister Catherine suggested. "It's such a lovely day."

"Yes, I think I'll do that, Sister. Perhaps I'll take her to Herbert Park," replied Sister Anna Marie.

Later, when they walked out of the building, Sophia seemed reluctant to leave the grounds of the motherhouse. Sister Anna Marie took her hand.

"It'll be all right, Sophia," she said encouragingly. "We're just going to the park, and if you wish, we'll return home soon."

They went across Morehampton Road and walked the short distance to Herbert Park. They walked along the River Dodder which formed the southern edge of the park. Children played all around them and people sat on park benches. Others walked through the gardens. Several boys in their teens came running, chasing each other, screaming loudly. They wove their way in between the children and the people walking. Sophia became alarmed and, had it not been for the firm grip with which Sister Anna Marie held her, she might have fled.

"It's all right Sophia. Come, we'll return home now," Sister Anna Marie spoke softly, leading her out of the park.

Sophia remained restless throughout the evening. In the middle of the night, Sister Anna Marie was awakened by moaning sounds coming from Sophia's bedroom and quickly went in. Sophia was asleep but was tossing around, her hands flailing in front of her. Sister Anna Marie gently shook Sophia's shoulders. The young girl sighed deeply, and quieted down. She turned onto her side, and continued sleeping.

Colleen O'Shea had been visited by her parish priest and told of the arrival of her nephew Tim's daughter in Dublin. A week later, she went to see Sophia. The old woman walked with difficulty and the bus and train ride from Ventry had been tiring. She peered through tired eyes at the pretty young girl in front of her. They were standing in the visitors' waiting room of the Motherhouse.

"Sophia, this is your Aunt Colleen," Mother Superior said with a smile. "She's come from Ventry to see you."

"*Fáilte go h'Éireann, tír breithe d'athair*," the old woman mumbled, placing her hands on the young girl's shoulders.

Sophia looked puzzled. "She greeted you in Gaelic," Mother Superior explained.

"What did she say," Sophia asked softly.

"She said, 'Welcome to Ireland, land of the birth of your father.'"

The meeting was awkward. "Is Tim's lad also here?" Colleen O'Shea asked the nuns.

"No, we don't know where he is," Sister Anna Marie answered. "He's probably still somewhere in India."

After a short stay, Colleen O'Shea left to return home.

"Who was my father?" Sophia asked later that evening.

"His name was Tim O'Shea," Sister Anna Marie answered gently. "He was a soldier in the British Army." She felt relieved when Sophia didn't ask more.

A month later, the Mother Superior received a letter from the parish priest in Ventry. Upon her return from Dublin, Colleen O'Shea had signed a paper on which she had asked the priest to write out her wishes. At her death, her sole possession, the cottage in which she had been born and lived all of her life, was to go to Neil and Sophia, her only known living relatives. The priest added that Colleen O'Shea had died peacefully in her sleep two days earlier.

Time went by and Sophia appeared less tense. She had been seen by Dr. Lynch once each month, and the skull x-ray turned out to be normal. She had not as yet spoken about her past, nor had she asked any more questions. She busied herself studying in the library or working in the greenhouse and the tapestry room. She seemed to look forward to her Sunday afternoon outings with Sister Anna Marie. They gradually ventured further away from the Motherhouse. They took a bus and rode it along Morehampton Road and Leeson Street all the way to St. Stephens Green.

One afternoon, they took the bus to Trinity College and walked to the River Liffey. The Sunday before Christmas, they rode on the top deck of a double-decker electric tram, and looked at the decorations in the shops.

Another month passed by and there seemed to be little additional change in Sophia's condition. Sister Anna Marie didn't know what else could be done to help her young friend. Would it be better for her to forever block out the past from her mind and continue to live as she was?

Or should she confront her grief and then go on with the rest of her life?

She spoke to the Mother Superior again.

"I'm not sure, but I think it would perhaps be better for the child to recall her past. She'll grieve, but time and prayers will help heal her wounds. At least after that she can start living a normal life," the Mother Superior said.

"Should we ask Dr. Lynch about it?"

"That's a good idea, Sister. I'll accompany you and Sophia to the hospital."

Dr. Lynch examined Sophia at length. "Apparently, so far, she hasn't encountered anything significant to trigger her memory of the past," he said. "Yet, it could happen at any time. Trying to force her to recall past events may be dangerous." After thinking for a moment, he continued. "If it can be arranged for her to be taken to London, I would like to have a colleague of mine, a prominent physician on Harley Street, examine her. She seems to handle her outings well, doesn't she? Perhaps the change of scene will also be good for her."

"That can be arranged, Dr. Lynch," Mother Superior answered. "We have a provincial house in London, in Brompton. I can have Sister Anna Marie take her there."

"Good. I'll contact my friend and request an appointment."

"What about his fees, Doctor? We may not be able to afford them," Sister Anna Marie inquired.

"Don't worry about it. I know Jonathan Campbell very well. I'm quite sure he will oblige me by not charging a fee."

Three weeks later, early in March, Sister Anna Marie and Sophia journeyed to London. They took a bus to Dun Loaghaire where they were to board a ferry for Holyhead on the northwest tip of Wales. From there, they were to travel to London by bus.

At Dun Loagharie, Sophia looked curiously at the ferry they were to take. "Can we go see the paddle wheel?" she asked.

The nun masked her surprise. "This ferry doesn't have a paddle wheel, Sophia," she said gently. "Come, let's find some seats."

The bus ride from Holyhead to London was long and tiring. Arriving in London late in the evening, they took a taxi to Brompton Place.

The Provincial House consisted of three floors, somewhat similar to the Motherhouse in Dublin, but much smaller. Sophia and Sister Anna Marie were welcomed by the Mother Provincial and shown to their bedrooms on the second floor.

Sophia's appointment with Dr. Jonathan Campbell was for eleven the next morning and after breakfast, the Mother Provincial brought out a map of the underground trains.

"You'll need to catch the tube at Knightsbridge, a couple of blocks from here," she said, pointing at the map. "Get off at Piccadilly Circus and take the Bakerloo Line to Regents Park. Harley Street is only a short walk from there. After seeing the doctor, if you wish, you could take the lass to Regents Park. It's a beautiful day and she might enjoy seeing the gardens."

Sophia sat across from the gray-haired, tall dignified man. He seemed kind, and had asked her a few questions. She felt comfortable talking with him. He gave her a book on London to look at before he left the room.

"That's a very sweet young girl you have there, Sister. I spoke to her briefly today, and would like to see her again next week. How long do you plan to stay in London?"

"We can stay as long as is necessary, Doctor. We have a Provincial House here in Brompton."

"That's good," Doctor Campbell nodded. "My friend, Michael Lynch, has sent me her medical records. He's given you very sound advice on how to care for Sophia. I suggest you continue following his directions. Keep her occupied with pleasant activities. When the weather is good, have her spend as much time outdoors as possible. You may want to give her simple responsibilities she is capable of handling. However, you need to be careful, and watch her. She should not feel overwhelmed at any time."

They came out of Doctor Campbell's office. "There's a nice park near the tube station, Sophia," Sister Anna Marie said. "Would you like to see it?"

"Yes, that would be nice," Sophia answered.

They walked to Regents Park and stayed there for more than an hour. Sophia's delicate face, charmingly framed by her long, shimmering golden-brown hair, appeared calm.

"Are there any jasmine bushes in this park?" she asked.

The nun was getting used to Sophia's occasional questions that hinted at her remembering events and things from her past. "No, there aren't any," she said quickly, looking at Sophia's face, then added, "Perhaps we should be going back now. We're late for lunch."

The next couple of days were cold and damp. The skies were overcast and a steady drizzle kept falling. Sister Anna Marie and Sophia did not venture out. The change in the weather seemed to affect Sophia and she sat quietly most of the day, reading her book or doing her needlework. Then the clouds broke, and the sun came out. After the morning chores were over, Sister Anna Marie decided to take Sophia on an outing.

It was Saturday and the streets were packed with shoppers. They crossed Brompton Road. Taking Montpelier Street and then Trevor Place, they walked along Kensington Road towards Hyde Park. The park was crowded. People sat on benches and on the grass, soaking up the sun's warmth. Children ran and played. Young couples held hands and strolled along the Serpentine, a body of water that snaked through the length of the park. Sister Anna Marie and Sophia sat down on a bench at the edge of the pond. Several ducks were noisily scurrying over the water, gobbling up pieces of bread thrown by people on the shore. A large black dog ran along the pond, barking at the ducks.

The air was filled with the fragrance of spring. Sophia inhaled deeply, and sighed. Sister Anna Marie turned toward her quickly. Sophia looked on serenely at several little ducklings paddling furiously to keep up with their mother. Sister Anna Marie thought she even saw the beginnings of a smile on Sophia's face.

On Tuesday morning, they went to Harley Street again and Dr. Campbell asked Sophia questions about her daily routine. At first, her answers were brief, but she gradually opened up and told him about her stay in Dublin and the trip to London. She seemed to like and trust this gray-haired man. He was kind and gentle and made her feel at ease.

Returning from Harley Street, Sister Anna Marie stopped just before entering the Provincial House. "Oh, I forgot," she said. "We should have gone to the corner shop to buy some milk. Well, I'll get it after lunch."

"I can get it for you now," Sophia volunteered.

The nun hesitated. But then she remembered Dr. Campbell's advice to give her more responsibilities.

"Thank you, Sophia, that's very nice of you," she said smiling. "Here, let me give you some money."

She stood in the doorway and anxiously watched as Sophia walked back and entered the shop. A few minutes later, much to her relief, Sophia came out and started walking toward the house.

A week passed quickly during which Sophia made several trips to the corner shop. On Saturday they went to Hyde Park again and walked along the entire length of the Serpentine. Doctor Campbell was pleased with the progress Sophia was making and encouraged Sister Anna Marie to let her be a little bit more independent.

The next day, the morning chores finished, they came out of the kitchen. "I have some letters to write today, Sophia. Could you go to the park alone?"

"Sure. I know the way there and back," she answered. You needn't come with me. I'll be back by twelve noon."

Sister Anna Marie waited and worried and kept glancing at the wall clock. She managed to write only a few lines of a letter to her father in the hour Sophia was gone.

A few minutes before noon, she was relieved to hear the front door open. Sophia walked in, her face flushed. This time, there was a distinct smile on her face.

Nearly five weeks had gone by since they arrived in London and now, whenever the weather was good, Sophia went to the park alone. She was almost finished with the needlework floral design she had started. Sister Anna Marie had obtained more books for her to read from the neighbourhood library.

Yet at night, Sophia seemed restless. She frequently moaned in her sleep and acted as if she were having nightmares. One night, Sister

Anna Marie was suddenly awakened by the sounds of crying. She went quickly to Sophia's room and found her sitting in her bed, holding onto a pillow, sobbing.

"Hush, Sophia," she said softly, taking her in her arms. "Everything's all right. Don't cry."

In the morning, neither said anything about what had happened during the night. The nun wondered if she should let Sophia go to the park by herself. Sophia, however, appeared calm. The skies were overcast but it was not raining and Sister Anna Marie decided to let her go.

The big black dog was there again, running up and down along the pond, barking at the ducks. Sophia sat down on a bench, wishing the dog would go away. She closed her eyes but, instead, envisioned the dog grabbing a duck and shaking it. Blood spurted out and the little duck lay dead. Sophia got up and quickly walked away, covering her ears to drown out the dog's incessant barking. She felt bothered, her mind deeply agitated.

Billowing dark clouds filled the sky and threatened to burst open at any moment. The wind was now blowing in strong gusts and it had turned quite chilly. Sophia drew her sweater closer around her neck and started back towards home, her mind filled with strange thoughts.

She left the park at the southern end of the Serpentine, but instead of walking along Kensington Road, she inadvertently crossed it and started walking down busy Brompton Road. The pavement was crowded with pedestrians and the noise of the heavy traffic added to the confusion in her mind.

Arriving at an intersection, she started to cross the road. She reached the pedestrian island in the middle, and the busy traffic started rushing by again. She stood there, waiting. It had turned very dark and the street lights had come on. Loud thunder echoed over the roar of the traffic speeding by.

Sophia's attention was suddenly drawn to a brightly lit, large display window of a store across the road. She stared intently. Her heart missed a beat. Her eyes became riveted unblinkingly on the scene in the window. Confusing thoughts exploded in her mind. A tall, slim, elderly man in a dark flannel suit was sitting on a bench next to a pretty, young woman. A little girl in a bright yellow dress was in front of the bench, bending down to pick up a white bunny rabbit. A golden-haired cocker spaniel was crouched, looking at the rabbit.

A ray of recognition flashed through Sophia's head and jumbled thoughts and clouded memories flooded her mind. She struggled as bits and pieces of her memory floated by. A bolt of lightning flashed. Before the last echoes of the thunder had reverberated between the tall buildings, it suddenly all came back — and the floodgates opened. Reaching out with one hand towards the panorama in the window, she moaned, "Oh, where've you been, Mamma and *Naana*? I've missed you so much! You, too, Sweetpea and Mr. Fluffy."

Her pent-up, grief-stricken mind burst with an outpouring of heart-rending sobs and profusion of tears. Trucks, buses and cars noisily rushed by. Unmindful of the heavy traffic, Sophia stepped off the island. A double-decker bus was coming down the road. The expression on the face of the driver suddenly turned to horror.

"Cor blimey, what's this bloody lass doing?" He slammed on the brakes, knowing very well that the big bus was not going to stop in time. "Jeez's," he groaned, "she's gonna be crushed to death."

Are There Truly Rainbows?
Is There a Tomorrow?

Aaron Schwartz came out of Hyde Park and paused by the Edinburgh Gate near Kensington Road. He was slim and almost six feet tall. His features were delicate and his hair dark brown. He took off his gold-rimmed glasses and started cleaning them with his handkerchief. Just as he was about to cross the road, a young woman came rushing out of the park and almost collided with him.

He turned sharply to look at her. What an exquisitely beautiful face she had, he noticed. But her large greenish-blue eyes appeared troubled. She brushed by him, holding the lapels of her sweater close to her long graceful neck. He was left with the soft fragrance of her windblown golden-brown hair cascading down to her waist.

Aaron stepped off the pavement and followed the girl as she started crossing Brompton Road. She reached the pedestrian island in the middle and stopped. The traffic on the other side had started moving. Aaron ran over and stood next to her. The heavy traffic was now speeding around them in both directions. A flash of lightning brightened the darkened skies and the roar of thunder reverberated down to the road. Aaron heard the girl say something unintelligible.

Then, to his surprise, she stepped off the island. A double-decker bus was speeding directly towards her and she was going to be run over. Instinctively, he leapt forward and, grabbing her by the waist, quickly pulled her back with him onto the island. The bus hurtled by, its brakes squealing and tires screeching.

"Hey, are you crazy?" he said, holding her. "You almost killed yourself." He felt her body tremble and she started sobbing.

The traffic slowed and he helped her across the road. She broke loose from him and ran to a display window. She placed her hands against the glass pane, as if trying to reach in. A clap of thunder drowned the sounds of her sobbing. He followed her and stood next to her, wondering what he should do.

Sophia's body convulsed and she shook her head slowly from side to side. The floodgates were opening. Her mind struggled to remember. She saw bombs falling and Mandalay burning. She remembered not being able to save her rabbit, and the anguish of parting with loved ones. She remembered the trek, and the news of her father's death. She saw men with bloodied swords and she started falling. Aaron grabbed her and held her up. Tears streamed down her face.

"Please tell me," she asked between sobs. "What happened to my mother and to my *Naana*? Where's my brother? Where's Uncle Hari?"

Then she started to remember — the Chapel of the Virgin Mary in Rawalpindi, the flashing sword, her grandfather in her arms, and her mother bleeding. She went down on her knees before the window.

"Did my Mama and *Naana* get taken to the hospital?" she moaned. "Where are they? Oh, God, they can't be dead!"

Aaron stood, shielding the young girl from the passersby on the crowded pavement. Gradually her body stopped shaking and she tried to stand up. Aaron helped her to her feet.

"I'm sorry," Sophia cried, wiping her tears. "I'm sorry I bothered you."

"It was no bother at all," he answered. "Don't hold back. Let your grief out."

"I'll be all right now. Thank you very much for your help."

Aaron handed her his handkerchief. "Where do you live? Let me take you home."

Sophia raised her hand toward Brompton Place. Aaron gently guided her forward. Her tears kept flowing.

They arrived at the Provincial House, but Sophia could not find her key. Aaron knocked on the door and a few moments later, Sister Anna Marie opened it.

"Dear Lord, what's wrong, Sophia? Are you all right?"

"I know!" Sophia sobbed. "Sister, I know what happened to my mother and to my grandfather."

"Oh, you poor dear child. Come in. You're cold. Come, let's go up to the kitchen."

"Please tell me all that happened, Sister. I need to know everything."

The front door slid closed behind them. They climbed the stairs and sat down in the kitchen. Sister Anna Marie spoke softly. Sophia listened quietly, tears streaming down her face.

"What about my brother?" she cried.

"Mister Ali Bhutt promised to contact Neil as soon as he was released from prison. Mother Superior is trying to locate your uncle in Chicago. I'm sure it won't be long before he comes to see you."

Suddenly Sophia remembered, "Oh, I forgot to thank the man who helped me," she said, holding up the handkerchief in her hand. They went down the stairs and to the front door. Sister Anna Marie came out and looked up and down Brompton Place. It was now raining heavily.

"He left without my thanking him," Sophia spoke softly. "I feel terrible! He was so kind."

"I'm sorry, but it's my fault," Sister Anna Marie apologized, closing the door. "I was so relieved to see you I didn't even ask his name. Come, let's go back to the kitchen. I'll warm some milk for you."

"No, Sister, I'd like to go to the Chapel."

Sister Anna Marie took Sophia's hand and started leading her to the main chapel.

"No," Sophia stopped her, "I want to go upstairs to the Chapel of the Virgin Mary."

Sister Anna Marie was taken aback. She remembered how agitated Sophia had been when she was shown the Chapel of the Virgin Mary in the Motherhouse in Dublin.

"If you want to. Come, we'll go there," she said, and led her up the stairs. They knelt side-by-side, and Sophia looked up at the statue of the Virgin Mary. Memories came flooding back and she started sobbing again. Sister Anna Marie began praying aloud, "In the Name of the Father, and of the Son, and of the Holy Spirit. Amen. Our father, Who art in heaven, hallowed be Thy Name; Thy Kingdom come; Thy will be done on earth as it is in heaven. Give us this day our daily bread, and forgive us our trespasses as we forgive those who trespass against us, and lead us not into temptation, but deliver us from evil. Amen.

Hail Mary, full of grace, the Lord is with thee; blessed are thou among women, and blessed is the fruit of thy womb, Jesus.

Holy Mary, Mother of God, pray for us sinners, now and at the hour of our death. Amen. "

Sophia's sobs gradually subsided and she bowed her head in prayer. Sister Anna Marie continued.

"Glory be to the Father, and to the Son, and to the Holy Spirit;

As it was in the beginning, is now, and ever shall be, world without end. Amen."

Early the next morning, Sister Anna Marie called Dr. Campbell's office. He asked that Sophia be brought in right away.

"It must have been very painful for you, my dear child," he said.

Sophia talked and Dr. Campbell listened, only occasionally asking a question. Later, he spoke to Sister Anna Marie.

"She seems to be handling her grief but it's too early to tell. I'd like to see her again on Thursday. But please call me at once should there be any problem."

Two days later, in the afternoon, the doorbell rang. Sister Anna Marie went to see who it was.

"Yes, may I help you?" she asked the young man standing outside.

"Good afternoon. I'm sorry to bother you. I just wanted to find out how the young girl is. She seemed to have been very upset."

"Oh, yes, you're the person who helped Sophia the other day," Sister Anna Marie said, smiling. "I'm so glad you came. Sophia felt badly that she was not able to thank you."

"She must be all right. I'm sorry to have bothered you." He was about to turn and walk away.

"No, please wait. Please come in. I'll call Sophia. I know she'll want to thank you personally."

Aaron entered the visitors' waiting room and stood awkwardly in one corner. He heard the door open and turned. There, standing before him was the girl, shyly looking at him.

"I'm sorry to have disturbed you. I just wanted to see if you were all right."

"I'm glad you came," Sophia said softly. "I'd like to thank you for helping me the other day. I must have been a great deal of trouble to you."

"No. You weren't any trouble at all."

"My name is Sophia. Sophia O'Shea."

"I'm Aaron Schwartz." Then, awkwardly, he turned towards the door. "I should leave. You must be busy."

"Oh, I still have your handkerchief. But I'd like to wash it before returning it."

"Perhaps if you happen to come to the park again, this Saturday, you could give it to me."

"Yes. All right. I'll bring it Saturday morning."

Dr. Campbell saw Sophia again on Thursday and was relieved to find her a little more composed. Yet he was concerned and asked Sister Anna Marie to bring her in twice a week until he was satisfied that she had recovered fully.

Sophia spent most of her time praying and helping in the kitchen. When Saturday came, she went to the park and met Aaron Schwartz. They talked, walking along the Serpentine. She found out that he was born in Vienna and was studying to become a lawyer. They sat on a bench by the pond's edge and she told him about her life in Burma and the burning of Mandalay. Tears had come to her eyes but she quickly wiped them away.

"No, you mustn't hold back. Grieve. Get it out. That'll give you strength," he said.

Sophia spoke about their escape from Burma and her life in Rawalpindi. When she got to the riots, she broke down again and could not continue.

"You don't have to tell me any more now," Aaron said gently. "But let your tears flow."

When she had calmed down, they got up and started walking out of the park.

"May I see you again?" he asked.

"Yes, I'd like that," she answered, looking at him. Crossing the road, he held her elbow and helped her through the traffic.

"Aaron and I are seeing each other again on Tuesday," Sophia told Sister Anna Marie as they tidied the kitchen after dinner. "Is that all right?"

"Sure, Sophia, it's good for you to make friends," Sister Anna Marie replied. "You should see him."

They met in the park on Tuesday and sat down on the grass. He urged her and she started to tell him about the riots, and losing her mother and grandfather. She wept while she spoke and Aaron held her hands. When she finished speaking, he gently wiped her tears.

"Come, let's walk to the rose garden. The blooms are particularly beautiful this time of the year," he said.

They met again on Saturday. "What about you," Sophia asked. "You haven't told me much about yourself."

It was a pleasant sunny day. Aaron had taken off his coat and had rolled up his shirt sleeves.

"There's not a lot to tell," he answered, smiling.

He looks quite handsome when he smiles, she thought. "Why do you have those numbers on your arm?" she asked.

"Oh, that's nothing," he answered, quickly rolling down his sleeves. "Just something that happened some time back."

The muscles of his jaw had tightened, and a hard look came over his eyes.

"Won't you tell me about your childhood? About growing up in Vienna?"

"Someday, perhaps, I will tell you. Come. Let's walk back. It's time for you to get home."

Sister Anna Marie couldn't help notice that Sophia seemed less morose whenever she talked about Aaron.

"He's been very understanding," Sophia told her. "He makes me talk about the past and said it was all right to cry."

"That's good, Sophia," she said. "It helps to get your grief out into the open." She did decide that she would mention Sophia's friendship with Aaron to Dr. Campbell.

On Sunday, Aaron came to the Provincial House. Sophia had been waiting and they walked together to Hyde Park. They sat down on a bench and watched children playing. A large alsatian and a small dachshund were chasing each other. The dachshund with its short stubby legs was having trouble keeping up with the alsatian. In desperation, it grabbed the large dog's tail in its mouth and allowed itself to be dragged along. Sophia and Aaron both laughed out loud.

"You know, you look even prettier when you laugh."

Sophia blushed and lowered her eyes. A serious look returned to her face.

"I'll never get over my grief," she sighed. "Life doesn't have the same meaning any more."

"That's how it feels now, Sophia. But life has to go on. There's an old Yiddish adage, '*Lebedika tsoras koompt men uber*', which means that as long as we are alive, we shall overcome. You must look to the future with hope. You may not think so, but there will be glorious tomorrows. There will be beautiful rainbows that your loved ones have wished for you."

They stood up and started walking to the rose garden. Aaron reached out and took her hand in his.

They met twice during the following week. "Today, young lady, we'll go sightseeing," Aaron announced cheerfully. "I'll serve as your guide and show you some of the wonders of London."

It was warm and the dark clouds that earlier had covered the sky were breaking up. They took a double-decker bus to Buckingham Palace and spent an hour walking around it. They then walked into St. James Park. The flowers were in full bloom and London was pretty as only it can be on a sunny summer's day.

Walking deep into the park, they found a secluded spot and sat down on the grass in the shade of a tree. It was quiet and peaceful. Other than the chirping of the birds in the trees and occasional distant screams of children at play, nothing else disturbed the tranquility of their little corner. Sophia lay back on the grass. Aaron removed his coat and folded it.

"Here, let me place this under your head."

Sophia looked at Aaron and smiled. Through half-closed eyes, she studied his face. He is handsome, she thought, and so gentle. Yet at times there was a hardness in his eyes and in the way the muscles of his jaw tightened. She wondered why.

"Why are you looking at me so intently," Aaron asked.

"I'm trying to learn more about you."

"Well, what is it you want to know?" he added, smiling. "I've already told you, I was born in Vienna twenty-one years ago. I live alone in a one-room flat in Russell Square. I work as a clerk in a solicitor's office and I am studying part-time, hoping to become a lawyer."

"Where do your parents live, Aaron? Do you have any brothers and sisters?"

Aaron's face turned serious. "They are no longer living," he said, his voice turning edgy.

"I'm sorry," Sophia said, sitting up. "I didn't know. What happened?"

"They were killed by Nazis in a concentration camp," he said through clenched teeth, turning his face away.

"Oh my God," Sophia moaned. "Why did that happen?"

"It happened because some demented men decided to annihilate an entire race. They wanted to get rid of every Jew on the face of this earth, along with others they considered unfit. They tortured and killed six million human beings."

"You don't have to talk about it, Aaron," Sophia said gently, touching his face. "It must be so very painful."

"You're the first person I've said anything to, Sophia. I've held my past bottled in me all this time. It's been hell, but I believe that we can't look at the future without first facing our past. We must confront the realities of what happened to us and to our loved ones so we may learn to live with hope and expectations."

"You said you were born in Vienna. Tell me about your family."

"My father was a lawyer and my mother a concert pianist," Aaron said, looking into the distance. "She was the most beautiful woman I'd ever seen. I also had a younger sister, Sylvia. She was an angel. We had a nice apartment on a beautiful street and life was good. But it all changed suddenly."

"What happened?" Sophia asked softly.

"The Nazis came and took all of us away. It was in November of 1939. They confiscated all of our properties and herded us into trucks. We were locked up in a camp called Mauthausen. We were humiliated and beaten. They put the men to work carrying large stones from a quarry, up a steep climb, which came to be known as the steps of death. Any man who stumbled was shot at the spot. We boys were put in another room and also had to work cleaning the camp, as well as removing the ashes from some ovens they had in a lower room. We had to throw the ashes over the edge into the quarry. Some of the older boys warned us not to stay too close to the edge as Nazi guards enjoyed picking up boys and throwing them over the edge. After one year, my mother, sister and I were moved and we never saw my father again."

"Oh, how terrible, Aaron," Sophia said, taking his hands into hers. "Were you freed after that?"

"No, we were taken in cattle trains, traveling many days in the cold, with no food, to another camp. Hundreds died on the train even before reaching this camp."

"What sort of camp was it?"

"It was a death camp. It was called Auschwitz."

"Did you get to stay with your mother and sister?"

Aaron got up and stood with his back towards Sophia. "No, the very first day we got there, my mother and sister were sent to the gas chambers and killed."

She couldn't see his face but knew that tears had to be filling his eyes. "Oh, dear Aaron," she said, gently. "You've suffered so much, and here I've been burdening you with my problems."

"We have to share our grief, Sophia," he answered. "Only then can we give each other strength."

She stood up and went to him. "Is that where they put the number on your arm?"

"Yes, that's where they stripped us of our identities as well as any dignity that we had left. We were starved and beaten and had to toil all day. Thousands were shot for no reason whatsoever. They carried out medical experiments on women and children. I don't know how I survived, but survive I did. It was as if there was some supernatural power protecting me."

She took his hands and made him sit on the grass next to her. "What type of work did they make you do?"

"We had to constantly dig ditches and graves outside the camp, in the cold, for the people who were either shot or those who died of hunger and disease. We had to remove the ashes from the ovens where they burned many of the bodies. They would shave the heads of the victims before sending them to the gas chambers and also make them take off their clothes and shoes. We had to pack the hair in bundles and sort out the shoes and clothes. One day, I cried so much because I found a pair of little red shoes that looked like the ones Sylvia wore."

Sophia took him in her arms. "Dear God, that must have been so painful. Where did you sleep, Aaron? What did you eat?"

"We slept in barracks on bare wooden bunks or on the floor. There was no heat in the winter. We were given a bowl of watery soup in the morning and once again in the evening. All of us looked like skeletons and didn't have any strength left."

"Did any try to escape?"

"Yes, but the Nazis usually caught them and executed them in front of the entire camp. One day, seven prisoners had escaped from a work detail. By evening they were rounded up and shot to death in front of all of us. We were made to stand in rows in the cold to witness the execution. And then, to punish us further, the Nazi guards went down each row and shot every seventh man in the side of the head. A guard was coming down the row in which I was. From the corner of my eye, I counted, and to my horror, realized that I was going to be shot next. But then something very strange happened. The guard went past me, and instead, shot the person standing next to me, the eighth man. I don't know what saved my life, but I almost felt as if there were someone standing in front of me, protecting me."

"God protected you, and I'm so very glad, Aaron. How long were you in Auschwitz?"

"I was in this living hell for four years before we were freed."

"What happened? Did the British come and rescue you?"

"We started noticing a change in the attitude of our Nazi guards towards the end of 1944. They appeared sullen and had stopped laughing. We all felt that the war must not be going well for them. Then one day, the guards started destroying the gas chambers and ovens. They burned piles of paper and ordered all of us to start marching out of the gate. Those who were not able to walk were shot. It was snowing and the cold was bitter. They marched us all day. At night we had to just lie down in the snow. Two other boys and I escaped and hid in some trees. The next day we saw some American soldiers and they took us to a Red Cross camp. We were given food, clothing and shoes and flown to England."

She gently lowered his head into her lap. "Rest now, Aaron, these memories must hurt so much."

"It's helped to tell you about them, Sophia," he said, closing his eyes and letting her fingers gently soothe the ache in his temples.

After a while Aaron stirred. "Come, let me walk you towards the Thames. You're supposed to be sightseeing this afternoon."

They stood up and started slowly walking hand-in-hand. They left the park and walked along Downing Street. "This is Number 10, the house of the Prime Minister," Aaron said, pointing at a doorway in front of which a constable was standing. They crossed Whitehall and walked towards the Victoria Embankment. They sat down on a bench and watched excursion boats taking groups of sightseers on the river. Bright flags on the boats fluttered in the wind and children waved at Sophia and Aaron.

The sun had started setting. "I should get you back home," Aaron said, taking her hand in his. They took the train to Knightsbridge. They rode silently, with his arm around her and her head resting on his shoulder. They walked to Brompton Place and stopped at the door of the Provincial House. Aaron leaned over and gently kissed her on the lips.

"Will I see you tomorrow?"

"Yes," Sophia answered. "Yes, I'd like that very much." As she stood leaning against the closed door behind her, Sophia felt strange emotions racing through her heart. She touched her lips with her fingertips. Never before had she been kissed by a man: a strange tingling ran through her body.

"Hello, Sophia. I'm glad to see you. Did you have a nice day?"

"Oh, yes, Sister," Sophia quickly answered, startled out of her dreams. "I had a very nice time. Aaron took me to see Buckingham Palace. After that we walked through St. James Park and sat by the River Thames."

"Come, let's go up to the kitchen. You must be hungry." While Sophia ate, she and Sister Anna Marie chatted.

"You've a good friend in Aaron. He seems like a very nice person."

"Yes, he is, Sister. I like seeing him. Is that all right?"

"Of course it is. He appears to be a very decent person."

"Yes, he really is. His parents and younger sister were killed during the war. They were in a concentration camp and suffered a lot. He told me about it."

"My God, he's a survivor of the holocaust."

"Do you know about it, Sister?"

"Yes, it was the most terrible thing that could have happened."

"Somehow, talking with him is helping me."

"That's good, Sophia. Share your grief with him. You'll each give the other strength."

"You've been so very kind to me, Sister. I owe you so much. I've been thinking. I'd like to find some work so that I can support myself. I'm also anxious to pay back the money that you spent on me."

"You've been no trouble at all, Sophia," Sister Anna Marie said with a smile, busying herself at the sink. "And besides, I didn't spend any money on you. Your ticket to Ireland was bought from the St. Brigid's Convent account."

"I've been wondering what I should do with my life, Sister. I do want to find my brother and uncle. I'd like to go back to school, and then perhaps to college. Earlier, I'd even thought that, like you, I could become a nun."

Sister Anna Marie was surprised. "That's indeed a noble idea, Sophia. It would be a significant commitment. You need to give it a lot of thought. There's no hurry. I've written to Mother Superior. We'll most likely stay in London, at least for the time being."

Sophia slept well that night although she did dream again about the war and Mandalay burning. The next day she went to the library and browsed through the section on entrance requirements for colleges. She borrowed a book about British medical schools and brought it back with her.

At two o'clock in the afternoon, Aaron came to fetch her. He had promised to take her to see the Kew Royal Botanic Gardens. They hugged each other, and holding hands, walked to Knightsbridge tube station. They chatted and Sophia told him about the book she had borrowed from the library.

"Do you want to become a doctor?"

"I'd like to, though I know it's not going to be easy. My grandfather was a physician. Ever since I can remember, I've always wanted to be like him."

"You must have loved him very much."

Sophia's eyes softened. "Yes I did! He was very special."

"Tell me about him," Aaron asked.

Sophia looked at him.

"It's all right," he continued. "We need to tell each other about those we cared for most."

They entered the gardens and mingled with the large Sunday afternoon crowds. Sophia told Aaron all about her grandfather, about his work, his courage and his deep love for his family. "He gave us so much," she said softly. "There was so much good in him. He cared a great deal for the poor and those suffering. I wish I could be like him and help the needy."

"You could," he answered, taking her hands into his. "If you make up your mind, you will. Your grandfather has left you such a rich legacy and there's nothing better you can do to honour his memory than to follow in his footsteps."

"I'm glad you feel that way, Aaron. I would like to become a physician. I'd like to one day go back to India and work there."

They walked to the food stands and Aaron bought ice cream for both of them. They held hands and strolled along the flower beds, and they smiled.

Sister Anna Marie continued to take Sophia to see Doctor Campbell twice each week. At the last visit, Dr. Campbell again talked to Sophia at length.

"Well, young lady," he finally said, "as much as I'm going to miss you, there's really no need for you to come to see me anymore."

"Thank you very much, Doctor Campbell. You've been so kind to me."

"Now remember, if ever you feel the need, I'm always available."

Sophia shyly hugged him before leaving. On their way back from Harley Street, they passed the shop on the corner of Brompton Place. Sophia slowed down. "I'd like to see if they'll give me a job," she told Sister Anna Marie. "There's always a queue of shoppers in the morning, and again in the afternoon. Perhaps I could work behind the counter."

"Why don't you go in and inquire?" Sister Anna Marie suggested.

Sophia went in and the owner of the shop offered her part-time work. She could start the next morning. Sophia was elated.

"Sister, I'll continue with the chores at the house. I won't let the work at the shop interfere with it."

"Well, you mustn't overdo it," Sister Anna Marie said smiling. "Don't worry about the work at the house."

Sophia's days were now busy. Each evening she saw Aaron briefly, but on weekends they spent more time together. She also managed to read a lot. She frequently bought the daily newspaper and read it from front to back. She borrowed books from the library and read them hungrily.

Time went by and then one day Sister Anna Marie received a letter from the Mother Superior. "She's asked us to return to Dublin," she told Sophia.

"How long have we been away?"

"It's almost seven months now."

"Has it been that long? How soon do we have to leave?"

Sister Anna Marie knew what was going through Sophia's mind. "Well, why don't we stay another week. We'll return next Monday. That'll give you time to let the owner of the shop know and he can find someone to replace you."

"That's a good idea, Sister," Sophia said, relieved.

That evening Aaron met her after she finished working at the shop. I'll be leaving for Dublin next Monday, Aaron," she said.

"Oh, are you? I'm going to miss you terribly, Sophia."

"I'll write to you often," she promised. "Then, as soon as I can, I'll come back to London."

Aaron took her in his arms. "I don't want to let you go," he whispered. "Why can't you just stay on in London?"

"I'd like to, Aaron. But so much has happened in the time I've been here. I've a lot of thinking to do. I need to decide what to do with my life."

"Will you promise to write often?"

"I'll write to you each day," she answered softly. "I promise."

They kissed tenderly.

"Don't forget. There'll be many wonderful tomorrows. There *will* be rainbows," he whispered.

Sister Anna Marie and Sophia returned to Dublin.

"You seem to be deep in thought, child."

Sophia was startled. She was sitting on a bench in the garden by the outdoor chapel of the Motherhouse. "I was thinking and praying, Mother Superior," she answered, standing up.

"You look concerned, child. Are you worried about something?"

"I've been thinking about my future, Mother Superior, and what I should do with my life."

"What is it that you would like to do? "

Sophia hesitated a moment. "I'd like to go to college. Then, if I'm accepted, I'd like to go to medical school and see if I can become a physician. Someday I'd like to go back to India and work with the untouchables and the lepers."

"Yes, Sister Anna Marie told me of your conversations with her.

What about the young man, Aaron? Sister Anna Marie said that you and he have become good friends."

"Yes, Mother Superior. He's a wonderful person. He's helped me a great deal!"

"You need to sort things out very carefully in your mind, Sophia. Keep praying. You'll see that prayers often provide answers to perplexing questions."

Several weeks went by. Sophia and Aaron wrote to one another almost every day. They professed their love for each other and now Aaron had written, pleading with Sophia to come back to London.

"We should meet and discuss our future plans," he wrote.

Sophia talked to Sister Anna Marie.

"You should go, Sophia. If you and Aaron love each other, you two must talk and decide what to do. If you wish, I'll speak to Mother Superior in the morning."

"If you think it's all right, Sister, please do so. I'd very much like to see him again."

Sophia journeyed back to London, this time traveling alone. Aaron met her upon her arrival and held her in his arms for a long time. He took her to the Provincial House where she was to stay.

The next morning they went to Hyde Park and once again walked along the Serpentine.

"You can't imagine how much I've missed you, Sophia," Aaron said, tenderly kissing her hand. "I can't see life without you."

"You've come to mean so much to me also, Aaron," she answered, looking up into his eyes. "I love you so very dearly."

They stopped and he took both of her hands into his. "Will you marry me, Sophia?" he asked softly.

Tears came to her eyes and her heart ached for her to cry out yes. But there were so many questions about her future in her mind.

"You hesitate, Sophia," he said tenderly. "Are you not sure of your love for me?"

"No, no Aaron," she answered. "I've never been more sure of anything else in my whole life."

"Then what is it, dearest?" he asked brushing her hair back.

She hesitated. "It's just that I don't know what the future holds for us, and if we were to get married what kind of a wife would I be to you. I so want to honour my *Naana's* memory by somehow continuing his work. It's going to be so difficult."

"I'll help you, Sophia," he spoke softly. "I'll be by your side all the time. We'll work together. We'll make our lives worthwhile."

"But how will we manage, Aaron? I'm just eighteen and I have no one."

"We'll manage, Sophia. We have each other. We'll help each other. That's all we need."

"Are you sure, Aaron?"

"Yes, I too am more sure than I have ever been about anything else in my entire life."

"Oh Aaron, I love you so much," Sophia whispered, putting her arms around his neck.

Happily and excitedly they walked back through the park. Hand in hand they entered a jeweler's shop on Brompton Road. Together, they picked an engagement ring. Crossing over to the pedestrian island on which they had first spoken, Aaron turned to face Sophia. The sun was shining brightly and the few clouds in the sky were white and fluffy. The busy traffic flowed on both sides of them.

"Will you, Sophia O'Shea, accept this ring as a token of my undying love and devotion for you?" Aaron spoke tenderly.

"Yes, I will. Oh yes, I do," Sophia answered softly.

He slipped the ring on her finger and, standing in the middle of busy Brompton Road, they kissed.

Aaron excitedly started making plans for their wedding. Sophia laughed.

"First, I need to go back to Dublin and tell Sister Anna Marie and Mother Superior." She hesitated and then added, "I'd like us to wait a little while before we get married."

"Of course. I understand," he answered, noticing the look in her eyes. "We'll first find your brother and uncle. God willing, they'll be at our wedding."

Aaron took Sophia to his place of work and to Russell Square where he lived and proudly introduced her to his colleagues and friends.

"Can you come to Dublin with me, Aaron? We can give Sister Anna Marie the good news together, and you'll also get to meet Sister Catherine."

"I'd like to go with you, Sophia."

Sister Anna Marie met them at the door of the Motherhouse. "I'm so happy for both of you," she said, hugging Sophia. "I also have great news for you, Sophia. The Mother Superior heard from the Bishop in Chicago. Guess what? They've located your uncle at the University of Chicago Hospital where he's working as a surgeon!"

"Oh, God! Is that true?"

"Yes, yes, it's true! He'll be coming to see you soon."

"Are you sure, Sister, that it is my Uncle Hari?"

"Yes, I am absolutely positive."

Sophia's eyes filled with tears and her shoulders shook with silent sobs.

"I'm so glad! Thank you, dear God! Aaron, did you hear? My uncle has been located."

"We have another piece of good news. Sister Margaret Rose has returned home from Rawalpindi."

"Oh, good. How's she?"

"She's fine. She asked about you and is anxious to see you." Sister Anna Marie couldn't help notice the hint of sadness suddenly appear in Sophia's eyes.

"Come. Come in," she said quickly. "You must see Mother Superior and give her the great news of your engagement."

Aaron stayed in Dublin for three nights in a small hotel on Leeson Street.

"You showed me London," Sophia said to him the next morning. "Now it's my turn to take you sightseeing and I'm going to show you all of Dublin!"

They rode a bus past St. Stephen's Green to Trinity College. They walked through the college's square and then visited Dublin Castle. They crossed the River Liffey strolling on to O'Connell Bridge. Sophia showed Aaron the Four Courts and the Custom House. All the while they talked, making plans. They agreed their wedding should take place in London.

"What type of a ceremony would you like, Sophia?" Aaron asked.

"I don't know, Aaron. I would like a religious ceremony. Wouldn't it be great if we could have wedding rites from all of the religions we both have been exposed to?"

"That's a wonderful idea, Sophia. Let's try and do just that. It'll be so appropriate," Aaron said, enthusiastically. After thinking for a moment, he added.

"And when we have children, we'll raise them respecting all religions."

Sophia smiled shyly. The next day, she took him to St. Stephen's Green. They walked through the gardens and along the ponds. They looked at the fancy hotels and shops on the streets adjacent to the Green. On their way back, they went looking for an old synagogue that Aaron's friends in London had told him about. They found it on Adelaide Road and were invited in by a man standing in the doorway.

"Will it be all right for me to go in?" Sophia whispered.

"Of course it'll be all right. Come. Let's go in." They climbed the steps and entered the temple.

"It's absolutely beautiful," she said softly, and they each prayed silently.

When they returned to the Motherhouse, Sister Anna Marie excitedly handed Sophia a telegram that had arrived earlier.

"Aaron, my Uncle Hari is coming to Dublin! He'll be here in three days."

They decided Sophia should stay back in Dublin until after her Uncle's visit. The next morning, therefore, Aaron returned to London alone.

The day of Hari's arrival, Sophia waited on pins and needles. She met him at the door and leapt into his arms. They hugged and cried.

"Oh, it's so nice to see you, Uncle Hari. I've missed you terribly!"

"You've also been constantly in my thoughts and prayers, Sophia. You can't imagine how delighted I was when I received the phone call telling me you were safe and here in Ireland."

They held hands and walked on the grounds of the Motherhouse. Hari told Sophia about his trip to Rawalpindi and his taking the ashes of his sister and father to Mandalay. Sophia started sobbing.

"That's what *Naana* and Mama would have wanted," she said, wiping her tears.

"What about Neil, Uncle Hari? Can we find him?"

"I'm sure we will, Sophia. Don't worry. I've asked the American Embassy in New Delhi for help. I'm sure that we'll be united with him soon."

"How's Aunt Stephanie? I'm sorry, I didn't even inquire about her."

"She's fine," Hari answered. Then, reaching into his pocket, he continued. "You have a cousin, Sophia. Stephanie and I have a son. He's three months old."

"Oh, that's wonderful, Uncle Hari!" she said, hugging him. Hari showed her a photograph. "He's very handsome, just like you. What have you named him?"

"It's Davy Russell Lal. We call him Davy, which is pronounced the same way as my father's name. Russell is Stephanie's dad's name."

"That's very nice for him to have the names of both his grandfathers."

"Now tell me about this young man you're planning to marry. He must be very special."

"Yes he is. He not only saved my life but also helped me put my life back together." Sophia then briefly told Hari how she and Aaron met.

"When are you planning to get married?"

"We've set the wedding date for April 16th. You must come, Uncle, and if you can't at that time, we'll change the date."

"I'll be there. Don't you worry about it. In fact, I'll come a week or so earlier. Then I can help with any last minute arrangements."

"You must bring Aunt Stephanie and Davy, also."

"I don't see why not. Davy will be about nine months old. We should be able to bring him."

"How long will you stay now in Dublin?"

"Well, I've taken a week's leave from the hospital. I was planning to spend a couple of days in London. A very close friend of mine from my days at the Medical College in Rangoon, now practices in London.

Ram and Leela Mohan will be very cross if I don't stay with them. What are your plans, Sophia? Why don't you come with me to London? I'm anxious to meet this young man with whom I'm going to have to share your affection."

Sophia put her hand on Hari's arm. "I'll always love you, Uncle Hari. And, yes, I want you to meet Aaron. I'm sure you two will get along very well. I was planning to go back to London after you left. It'll be great to go with you. I stay at the Provincial House near Knightsbridge. I have a job in a shop nearby."

"Why don't you stay with me at my friends' house while I am in London? Ram and Leela will insist on it anyhow."

Before leaving for London, Sophia went to see Mother Superior. "I'll be leaving with my uncle, Mother Superior. I don't know how to thank you for all that you and the sisters have done for me."

"You don't have to thank anyone, dear child. May God bless you. I know you'll have a wonderful wedding. I shall pray for your happiness."

Sophia then went to see Sister Catherine. "You must come to my wedding, Sister. I'll be very disappointed if you aren't there."

"I'll be there, Sophia. Don't you worry," Sister Catherine answered, peering over her glasses. "You're going to make a radiant bride and I'm not going to miss seeing you on such an important day of your life."

Sister Anna Marie walked Sophia to the gate where Hari was waiting in a taxi.

"I shall miss you, Sister. You must come well before the day of the wedding."

"Yes, I will," Sister Anna Marie answered, hugging Sophia. "You look after yourself, now, you hear? And don't work too hard."

Sister Anna Marie waved goodbye as the taxi turned around and headed towards the airport.

Ram and Leela Mohan lived in a spacious and comfortable home on Upper Phillimore Gardens near Holland Park. Dr. Mohan's medical practice was on Kensington High Street. Their greeting and welcome of Hari and Sophia was warm and enthusiastic. Sophia called Aaron at his work, and he came over that evening. She met him at the door and they embraced and kissed. She then brought him into the drawing room and introduced him to Hari and to the Mohans.

"So you're the young man who has stolen my niece's heart," Hari greeted Aaron, shaking his hand.

"No, it was I who was smitten by Sophia and pleaded with her to marry me," Aaron answered, a broad smile on his face.

"How exciting. A wedding!" Leela beamed, welcoming Aaron.

"Yes. Let us know what needs to be done, Sophia, and we'll help you," Ram added.

"No, no, Ram! This is a woman's job," Leela said quickly. "You men will only cause problems."

Turning to Sophia, she said with a smile, "Sophia, you and I will take care of all the arrangements, once the two of you decide the type of wedding you want."

Sophia laughed. "Thank you very much. That's very kind of you. Actually, Aaron and I have talked about it. We've decided the ceremony should include a little bit from several religions."

"What a wonderful idea!" Leela answered.

"We both would like to have parts of Hindu, Jewish, Buddhist and Christian ceremonies included in our wedding."

"Do you want proper priests to perform the ceremonies?" Leela asked. "It may be difficult to find Hindu and Buddhist priests."

"It doesn't matter who performs them," Sophia answered. "Aaron has already asked a friend of his from Austria to help with the Jewish ceremony. I intend to ask two of the nuns from Dublin to recite Christian prayers."

"Then the rest will be easy," Leela added. "We have close friends here from both Burma and India. We'll select one from each country and ask them for help."

"Sophia and I are trying to find a suitable place where the wedding can be held," Aaron said. "We both feel that the ceremony should be simple, and followed by a brief reception."

"I have the perfect solution!" Ram Mohan said excitedly. His wife looked at him suspiciously. "You'll have your wedding right here in our house!"

Leela showed her surprise. "Why, Ram, you've come up with a splendid idea!" Turning to Sophia and Aaron, she pleaded, "Please say 'yes'. It will be such fun. As you can see, we have all this space."

Sophia and Aaron looked at each other. "But that would be too much trouble. We don't wish to impose upon you," Aaron said.

"Great," Leela declared, clapping her hands with pleasure. "Then it's all settled."

"Yes, that's wonderful," Ram added. "But let me warn you. Nothing Leela runs is simple. Believe me, with her planning, the reception will be anything but brief!" Everyone laughed.

"Oh, all right. So it won't be simple," Leela complained. "Weddings are supposed to be fun! Now let's go and have dinner and then, Sophia, you and I will start planning seriously."

Sophia greatly enjoyed Hari's stay in London. The day he was leaving, Hari took her aside and gave her two hundred pounds. She tried to refuse but he insisted.

"I'm doing well at the hospital in Chicago. I want you to spend this money on yourself. I'll send more for the wedding later."

Sophia's shattered life was mending. She was grateful for all the help and love she was receiving from those around her. She worried about her brother and prayed for his safety. Her days were busy, but during the night her nightmares returned and she would dream of bombs falling, Mandalay burning and people dying.

Time passed quickly and Sophia and Aaron had their wedding invitations printed. They went to the Registrar's Office in St. Catherine's House on Kings Way and applied for a marriage license. Leela arranged for a seamstress to sew Sophia's wedding dress.

Aaron and Sophia had dinner with the Mohans several times. Leela showed them the covered back veranda and the large, adjacent enclosed garden where the wedding and the reception would be held.

"It's only three weeks away," Leela cooed. "I'm so excited! It's going to be a wonderful wedding, Sophia. We'll have balloons and coloured lights and lots and lots of food."

Hari wrote that he, Stephanie and Davy planned to arrive in London ten days before the wedding.

Two days before they were to fly to London, Hari returned home from the hospital very excited. "Steph, where are you?" he called, rushing in. "I've got great news!"

"What is it, Hari?" Stephanie came out of Davy's room laughing. "What's happened?"

"A letter, Steph. Neil is alive! I just got this from him," he said, waving a sheet of paper in his hand.

Stephanie took it and started reading. "My God, he's in prison!" she said, looking up.

"Doesn't matter. He's alive. We'll get him out."

"Oh, that's wonderful. How did he get your address?"

"Well, here, read his letter. He says that he remembered I was going to join the University of Chicago Hospital and that's what he wrote on the envelope!"

"Sophia will be so happy. Oh, Hari, we must get him released before the wedding. Contact an attorney as soon as we get to London."

The prisoner in Wormwood Scrubs prison, block C, cell number 256, was surprised to hear his name called. He glared at the guard through the iron bars of his cell.

"Come on, move," the guard yelled. "There's someone out here to see you."

Neil got out of his bunk slowly and shuffled out of the iron door the guard had opened. He had not shaved since being incarcerated and a short thick beard covered his face. Who could have come to see him on a Monday, he wondered disinterestedly. Jenny came only on Saturdays and Abdul Rehman on Sundays. His eyes softened thinking about Jenny. After all these years of hating the English, he found it ironic that he was falling for her. And good old kind Abdul. Neil remembered the first time they had met. Rehman had bought him a beer. "I'm not a very good Muslim," he had said. "I shouldn't be drinking alcohol." And here he was, in trouble with the law for having gone to the aid of his Muslim friend.

Neil followed the guard into the visitors hall and walked towards the chair the man pointed at. He ran his fingers through his hair and looked through the glass partition. He couldn't believe his eyes and stood there, awestruck. Oh God, is it true or am I dreaming? There, sitting before him, was Uncle Hari. Neil placed his hands on the table in front of him and leaned towards the glass.

At first, Hari seemed not to recognize the person staring at him. The face was fuller and the shoulders broader. Then he quickly pushed his chair back and stood up. The two looked at each other for a few moments.

"Oh, it's so good to see you, Uncle Hari," Neil said softly.

"It's great to see you, Neil," Hari answered smiling.

"Where are Mama, Sophia and *Naana*? I looked for them all over but couldn't find them."

Hari hesitated. Neil searched his face for answers.

"Sophia is all right, Neil. She's right here in London," Hari said.

"That's great. What about my mother and grandfather? Where are they?" Neil quickly asked.

"I'm sorry, son," Hari answered gently, shaking his head. "I'm very, very sorry."

"What happened to them?" Neil asked, his voice trembling. "Were they killed in Rawalpindi?"

Hari did not answer. Neil slumped down into the chair behind him. Hari's eyes filled with tears. Briefly, he told Neil what had happened.

"Oh my God, how terrible," Neil moaned, tears flowing down his face.

"They're at peace, Neil. Remember what the *Bhagavad Gita* says, 'For the soul there is neither birth nor death.' Only their bodies have perished. Your mother and grandfather have moved on and are fine."

"Oh, I wish I had been there to help them," Neil cried, his face showing the anguish he felt in his heart.

"You can't blame yourself, Son. Your mother and grandfather wouldn't want you to do that. I'm arranging for your bail. It shouldn't take us long. Sophia will be anxious to see you!"

"How is she doing, Uncle Hari?"

"She's had a very difficult time, Neil, but is getting over it. In fact, she is getting married in a week. Nothing will give her more pleasure than to have you be at her wedding."

"I want to see her, also. But not here, Uncle Hari. Not in prison. Please don't tell her about me as yet. At least not until I'm free."

"I've got a good attorney for you, Neil. You'll be out of here in a couple of days."

"Thank you, Uncle Hari. Oh, it's so good to see you!"

Sophia had taken an instant liking to Stephanie and, as for Davy, she fell in love with him right away. Sophia had moved to Ram and Leela's house where Hari, Stephanie and Davy were staying.

Hari met with the attorney again. The bail had been posted and Neil was to be released the next morning. That evening, Hari decided he could tell Sophia.

"Oh, thank God!" she cried excitedly. "Where is he? When can I see him? How's he doing?"

"Neil is fine. He's right here in London," Hari answered with a smile.

"Well, let's go and see him now, Uncle Hari!" she said, tugging his arm.

Slowly, Hari told Sophia about Neil. "I'm sure once the trial is held, he will be set free. The attorney believes there was enough provocation for Neil to have attacked the man. The attorney said that the judge may consider the time Neil has already been in prison to be sufficient punishment."

"Oh, I hope so, Uncle Hari. I hope so."

Sophia again had trouble sleeping at night, but this time she was worrying about Neil. When she did fall asleep, her dreams came back. Her brother was handcuffed, Mandalay was burning and people were dying. She woke up in the morning with a headache.

Hari had already left for Wormwood Scrubs prison. Neil insisted on first going back to Abdul Rehman's flat.

"I must change my clothes and get rid of this beard," he said.

Sophia was beside herself, worrying. What if something goes wrong and they don't let him out. Finally Hari returned accompanied by Neil.

The meeting of the brother and sister was most poignant. They did not say much but wept and held each other in a tight embrace for a long time.

"You've grown so tall, Neil."

"And you, so much prettier."

"I'm so happy you're here in time for my wedding!"

"Where's this man you are marrying? I'd like to meet him."

"Aaron is making some last minute arrangements. But he'll be here this evening. I want him to meet you, also."

They talked off and on all day, but avoided mentioning their mother or grandfather. They both knew in their hearts how painful it must be for the other. There would be time later to talk about the past and to share each other's grief.

"I'd like to invite a friend to your wedding," Neil asked.

"Of course. You can invite anyone you wish. Is it someone special?"

Neil smiled. "Yes, I think so. Her name is Jenny. I've only known her a few months, but she's a very nice person."

Aaron arrived at five that evening and Sophia introduced him to her brother. Sister Catherine and Sister Anna Marie also came, as well as the others Leela and Ram had invited for the rehearsal dinner.

The Jewish ceremony was to be performed by Aaron's friend, Harry Blumenfeld. For the Buddhist ceremony, Ram Mohan had asked Doctor Khin Maung, a Burmese friend from Hammersmith Hospital. The Hindu ceremony was to be conducted by another of Ram's friends, Raj Mehta.

"I am an engineer by profession," Mr. Mehta told Hari. "I have never performed a wedding before. My grandfather, however, was a priest of the Mohyals and officiated at weddings in the Mohyal community in Punjab, the Northwest Frontier and Baluchistan."

Sister Anna Marie and Sister Catherine were also to participate in the wedding ceremony by offering prayers and blessings.

Dinner was an enjoyable event and the guests chatted happily. Later, Sophia sat in a chair with Davy in her lap, surrounded by Neil, Aaron and Hari. Stephanie stood next to the chair, with her hand on Sophia's shoulder. Neil had said something which made Sophia and the rest laugh. Sister Anna Marie looked at them from across the room.

God knows, you deserve some happiness now, Sophia, she thought. May the Lord bless you and your loved ones.

The covered veranda and the enclosed garden were decorated with balloons and streamers. White wooden chairs had been rented, and strings of coloured lights hung, to be turned on later during the reception. Food had been ordered and was ready in the kitchen to be served after the wedding. Drinks had been placed on tables at each corner of the veranda, and in the back garden.

All of the guests were seated before two o'clock. Besides those helping with the ceremony, they included several friends of Aaron from his office and also from Austria whom he had met in London. Sophia had invited the owner of the shop where she worked, as well as Doctor and Mrs. Jonathan Campbell. Ram and Leela had invited several physician friends of theirs from Burma, and some of their neighbours.

Soft music was provided by four musicians seated in one corner of the veranda. It was a pleasant, sunny day and the garden was ablaze with flowers.

Aaron, dressed in a black suit, looked very handsome but seemed a little anxious. One of his friends stood next to him, and they were talking in quiet undertones. Exactly at two o'clock, Sophia appeared at the door from the drawing room. She looked exquisite in her wedding gown. Her long hair shone brilliantly and a bouquet of flowers in her hand matched the colour of her flushed face. Neil and Hari walked on each side of her. The music played softly as Sophia came to stand next to Aaron. Hari and Neil moved away and sat down.

Doctor Khin Maung came and stood next to Sophia and Aaron.

"We shall perform a Buddhist ceremony of tying of the hands," he said. "The bride's left hand is tied to the right hand of the bridegroom with a silk scarf. This is carried out by an honoured couple especially chosen by the bride and groom. Sophia and Aaron have asked Doctor and Mrs. Mohan to perform the ceremony."

Ram and Leela came forward. Placing Sophia's left hand into the right hand of Aaron, they tied the two hands together with a pale pink silk scarf. Aaron gently squeezed Sophia's hand and she glanced at him and smiled. A large silver bowl was held below the tied hands. Then, taking another silver bowl, Ram and Leela poured scented water over Sophia and Hari's hands.

"According to Buddhist custom," Doctor Khin Maung added, "this solemnizes their union."

For the next ceremony Mr. Raj Mehta came forward. Leela placed a round tray with several lit candles onto a small low table.

"The bride and groom will perform the Seven Steps ceremony," Raj Mehta explained. "This is an important element of Hindu marriage rites going back over three thousand years. Sophia and Aaron will now take the first seven steps of their lives together, holding hands as husband and wife."

At each step, he helped them recite prayers.

"With God as our guide, we take these our first seven steps together. With this first step, we pray for unity and everlasting love between us.

Taking our second step together, we ask God for strength of our relationship and good health.

With our third step we pray for a joyous and prosperous life together.

The fourth step we take with prayers for each other's true happiness.

With our fifth step we pray for progeny.

Taking our sixth step together as husband and wife, we pray that the seasons all prove to be favorable towards us.

And with the seventh step, we vow to fulfill our duties to our families and pray for true and everlasting companionship between us."

Sophia and Aaron were then directed by Raj Mehta to stand in front of the candles.

"These candles represent our sacred fire," Mehta explained, "essential to a Hindu wedding. The bride and groom will walk around the fire four times, symbolizing the sacredness of their union."

Holding hands, Sophia and Aaron walked together around the candles and, with Raj Mehta's help, recited the following prayer.

"God, the Supreme Being, who existed before the creation of this universe, and will exist after it, may we pray together to this Supreme Being for a hundred autumns, and may we enjoy the blessings of a happy and healthy married life together for a hundred autumns."

Tears threatened to flood Sophia's eyes. If only Mama and *Naana* were here. She sensed a soft gentle breeze caress her face and she held back her tears. "I love you, too, Mama and *Naana,*" she whispered.

Sister Anna Marie and Sister Catherine came and stood on each side of Sophia and Aaron. They made the sign of the Cross and Sister Anna Marie started, in a soft voice, reading from the New Testament:

"Love is patient and kind; love is not jealous or boastful. Love does not insist on its own way; it is not irritable or resentful. It does not rejoice at wrong, but rejoices in the right. Love bears all things, believes all things, hopes all things, endures all things."

She then offered the wedding prayer.

"Eternal God, our creator and redeemer, as you gladdened the wedding at Cana in Galilee by the presence of your Son, so by his presence now bring your joy to this wedding.

"Look in favor upon Aaron and Sophia and grant that they, rejoicing in all your gifts, may at length celebrate with Christ the marriage feast which has no end."

Sister Catherine spoke next. "In celebration of your Irish heritage, Sophia, I'd like to give you and Aaron three Irish blessings.

May good Saint Patrick bless you,
And keep you in his care,
And may Our Lord be with you
To answer every prayer."

"This next is a Gaelic blessing;" Sister Catherine said, adjusting her glasses.

"May the road rise to meet you. May the wind be always at your back. May the sun shine warm upon your face, the rain fall soft upon your fields. And until we meet again, may God hold you in the palm of his hand."

She paused for a moment and then continued:

"Now the third blessing goes like this.

In the name of dear Saint Patrick
This brings a loving prayer
May you forever be within

God's tender love and care
May your heart be filled with happiness
Your home be filled with laughter
And may the Holy Trinity
Bless your life forever after. "

Mr. Harry Blumenfeld began the Jewish ceremony and instructed Aaron's friend, who was serving as the best man, to hand the ring to Aaron. He then helped Aaron recite an ancient wedding vow while placing the ring on his bride's finger. Mr. Blumenfeld explained,

"Giving the ring to his bride, Aaron said, 'Behold, thou art consecrated unto me with this ring, according to the law of Moses and of Israel.'"

Sophia and Aaron were then handed a glass of wine to share. While they sipped the wine, seven wedding blessings were given by Aaron's friends. Mr. Blumenfeld then placed a paper bag near Aaron's foot.

"The last rite of a Jewish wedding requires the groom to break a glass with his right foot. This ceremony is to tell us that, even as we rejoice and celebrate, we must remember the serious side of life and its fragile nature." Aaron turned to Sophia and smiled. Then, lifting his foot, he stomped on the paper bag. The glass shattered with a loud noise and the guests applauded.

"Mazal Tov, Mazal Tov," they called out.

Smiles and laughter were all around. Many of the women were teary-eyed. Congratulations were offered the bride and groom. Hari, Neil and Stephanie hugged them.

"May God bless both of you with a very happy and healthy married life." Leela beamed, "And may you have lots and lots of children!"

The musicians started playing a lively tune. Someone suggested that the bride and groom have the first dance. The musicians switched to a slow waltz. Aaron took Sophia in his arms and they danced. Soon others joined in.

Toasts were offered by Hari, Neil and the best man. Dinner was served. Dusk was setting in, the coloured lights added their enchantment to the garden. The music was lively and everyone was laughing and enjoying themselves.

Leela was delighted. The wedding had gone off so well. The guests had eaten heartily and were having a great time. Ram and Hari were standing in one corner, conversing. Neil had just introduced Jenny to Sister Anna Marie. The guests held hands and joined in a Jewish circle dance. Sophia and Aaron were made to sit in chairs and were carried aloft by the dancers.

Leela went to the garden to see if there were enough drinks on the table. She was about to return when she sensed someone standing in a far corner of the garden. She turned to look and was startled to find an old man with long, matted hair and a scraggly beard standing staring at the people. He had on a faded gold-coloured costume and wore an odd-shaped crown. In the dim light, he appeared almost as a shadowy ghost. Leela had certainly not seen him at the wedding, of that she was sure. How did he get into the enclosed garden, she wondered.

Then the old man spoke. "I have come to see the Mandalay *thu*," he said in a strange scratchy voice.

Leela became very nervous. "Who did you want to see?" she asked.

The man smiled and raised his hand. Pointing a bent, sinewy finger at the dancers, he said, "There she is, the blessed one — Mandalay's Child. I see her."

Leela felt helpless. She wished Ram or Hari would see her and come to her rescue.

The old man continued talking. "She is protected by the *Nats*. The Lord *Min Mahagiri*: the Spirit of the Great Mountain, the Exalted *Nat Bodaw*, Lord Grandfather of Mandalay and *Aungpinle*: the Lord Master and keeper of the White Elephants, they all favour her. She crossed swift rivers and dangerous mountains. She walked through infernos and came out unscathed. The *Nats* chose the young man to be her consort and brought him through his journey safely. The thirty-seven Lord *Nats* of Burma all send their blessings." The old man grinned happily.

Leela looked pale. She quickly turned to see who the man was pointing to. She saw Sophia high in the chair, holding onto its arms, laughing. Leela turned around again towards the old man but he had disappeared. There was no one there! She felt a cold blast of air hit her face and a chill ran through her bones. She moved a step forward and looked closely. All she could see was some brownish-red dust on the ground where she thought the old man had stood. There was a stale musty odor in the air.

Did I imagine the whole thing? she wondered. Shuddering, she turned and quickly walked back towards the dancers.

"What? What did you say?" Aaron called loudly as he was whisked past on the chair, carried by his friends. "I can't hear you!" The music was fast and lively. The dancers in the circle sang and twirled around.

Sophia, leaned closer. "I didn't have it last night," she yelled again, smiling.

Aaron laughed. "What didn't you have last night?"

The music softened and slowed down. The chairs were brought together. "I didn't have my horrible dream," Sophia said shyly.

The dancers lowered the chairs. Aaron and Sophia stood up and held hands. "That's wonderful, Sophia," Aaron spoke gently. "You know, we are now one. Our nightmares are over. God Almighty has heard our prayers. There is a tomorrow. There will be rainbows, I promise you — many, many glorious rainbows that our ancestors have wished for us!"

Sophia closed her eyes. "Thank you, God," she prayed softly. "Thank you so very much!"

The music lifted their hearts.

The Spirits smiled, and Mandalay burned no more.